KEVIN J. ANDERSON

PLAY

HEX WORLD BOOK 2

aethonbooks.com

PLAY (HEXWORLD BOOK 2)
© 2021, 1989 WordFire, Inc.

This book is protected under the copyright laws of the United States of America. No part of this publication may be reproduced, stored in a retrieval system, or transmitted, in any form or by any means, without the prior permission in writing of the publisher, nor be otherwise circulated in any form of binding or cover other than that in which it is published and without a similar condition including this condition being imposed on the subsequent purchaser. Any reproduction or unauthorized use of the material or artwork contained herein is prohibited without the express written permission of the authors.

Aethon Books supports the right to free expression and the value of copyright. The purpose of copyright is to encourage writers and artists to produce the creative works that enrich our culture.

The scanning, uploading, and distribution of this book without permission is a theft of the author's intellectual property. If you would like to use material from the book (other than for review purposes), please contact editor@aethonbooks.com. Thank you for your support of the author's rights.

Aethon Books
www.aethonbooks.com

Print and eBook formatting by Steve Beaulieu. Artwork provided by Fernando Granea

Published by Aethon Books LLC.

Aethon Books is not responsible for websites (or their content) that are not owned by the publisher.

Originally published in slightly different form as Gameplay, 1989

This book is a work of fiction. Names, characters, places, and incidents are the product of the author's imagination or are used fictitiously. Any resemblance to actual events, locales, or persons, living or dead is coincidental.

All rights reserved.

*A previous version of this book was published under the title Gameplay, but it has been revised and re-edited for this release.

ALSO IN SERIES

HEXWORLD

1: ROLL

2: PLAY

3: END

THE BOOK OF RULES

"Always remember this: every character on Hexworld was created by the Outsiders. We exist solely for the amusement of those who Play our world. Our ambitions, our concerns mean nothing—everything is determined by the roll of the dice."

—*The Book of Rules*

PROLOGUE

Melanie blew warm breath against the map of Hexworld, trying to make the paint dry faster. She didn't want the other players to see what she had changed. David would probably call it cheating—but their game would keep playing itself, no matter what they did.

Melanie wanted to win.

A shoebox of acrylic paints lay on the card table in the study. Some of the colors had dried up, with lids cemented by hardened paint. But the bottle of deep forest green had some sluggish drops left at the bottom.

The map's hexagons of terrain were bright and vivid colors, like some lost Arabian mosaic. They represented mountains, forests, seas, deserts. Melanie pulled a strand of long brown hair behind her left ear and blew again on the wet paint. She looked at where the mysterious "Rulewoman" supposedly lived on the map, in one of the forest-terrain hexes deep in the south. The complexity, the patterns of the map were dizzying.

Hexworld—they had created it as a fantasy world setting for a role-playing game, she and Tyrone, Scott, and David. The four of them played there, embarking on imaginary adventures into imaginary lands every Sunday night for the past two years.

Melanie had painted the map herself, acrylics on a smooth sheet of wood, using rulers and protractors to lay down the precise grid of hex-lines between sections of terrain. No store-bought map kit would do for *their* world—it had to be something personal, something she created herself. Hexworld needed to be different from all the other worlds available in simple boxed adventures.

Melanie and the others put a great deal of themselves into Hexworld. Perhaps too much.

But times changed, and the Game went on and on. One entire race of characters, the Sorcerers, departed from the world in a magical Transition that turned all of them into six powerful Spirits: three white Earthspirits and three black Deathspirits.

David wanted to end the Game there. He said it wasn't fun anymore. But Melanie and the others outvoted David, and so they kept playing. David could not leave them. The Game had too much of a hold on all of them. Instead, he made an attempt to destroy the world, but he had been thwarted.

Now, though, David had finally made up his mind—if the others would not let him quit, then he would create a new monster, Scartaris, to devastate the entire map and suck every spark of life dry.

That would end the Game once and for all.

But Melanie planned on stopping him. They both had to play by the rules—but rules could be advantageous, especially if you bent them a little ...

Melanie carried the altered map out of her father's study. She could hardly tell where she had repainted the one hexagon. They would not notice, since she had not changed the terrain type, in which case she could argue—as Scott would—that she hadn't changed anything relevant anyway. But she had *placed something there*, under the paint, into the world of Hexworld.

She didn't know if it would work, if her world could ever have any true connection with the characters *inside* Hexworld. But this had to be the way, if anything. It had to be.

Somehow during their last gaming session, she managed to communicate to her characters about the growing threat of Scartaris in David's designated section of the map. Her three characters, Delrael the fighter, his scholarly cousin Vailret, and the half-Sorcerer Bryl, had tried to protect their land from Scartaris by creating a giant barrier river that severed the eastern half of the map from the rest.

But now she knew, as did her characters, that the Barrier River would not stop David's creature. It would only trap half the inhabitants of Hexworld on the wrong side—with the growing threat of Scartaris.

She stared at the blue line of hexagons that indicated the river slicing down the map. It still gave her shivers to think about it. Hexworld showed its own power the previous week, during their last gaming session.

This had become much more than a game to all of them.

In their imaginary adventure, the new river came surging through a channel from the Northern Sea to pour across the plains—and as the four players watched, Melanie's painted map reflected the change all by itself. Hexagons of forest, grassland, and swamp terrain turned *blue*, right in front of their eyes. Scott, the "rational" one, had been amazed and terrified, unable to hint at an explanation.

But Melanie knew the explanation. It was so simple. After being steeped in the gaming fantasy as dictated by the rules, Hexworld had developed its own magic.

And Hexworld was not going to accept its destruction without a fight.

If she could do anything to help, even if it meant stretching the rules a bit behind the other players' backs, then Melanie felt obligated to do so. After all, not many people ever had the opportunity to save a world, not even an imaginary one.

Satisfied that the new paint had dried, Melanie carried the map board out to the kitchen and started to prepare herself for the Game. The future of her world would be in the roll of the dice.

CHAPTER 1
ENROD'S CROSSING

Something is terribly wrong here. My own city of Tairé has succumbed. People I have known for years act strangely. At times, even I do not know what I have done or where I have been. And the untainted lands to the west have cut themselves off from us with a great river. We are trapped and alone. We have been sacrificed. They didn't even give us a chance.
—Enrod, *Annals of Tairé*, final entry

The Sentinel Enrod stood on the eastern shore of the Barrier River. The black hex-line that separated the water from overhanging willows and reeds extended razor sharp as far as he could see, north and south.

Off in the distance, across the impassable expanse of water, he could see the green rolling line of forest terrain, lush and healthy. Farther north, Enrod could see the broad expanse of a hexagon of grassland. All green, all growing, safe and protected from the evil to the east.

Enrod gritted his teeth. His hand squeezed the eight-sided ruby, the Fire Stone, he had carried all the way from Tairé. The corners of the gem dug into the skin of his palm. Enrod paid no attention to the pain. He was the last remaining full-blooded Sorcerer male on Hexworld, now that Sardun was gone. Enrod had used his reserves of magic to keep himself healthy and relatively young-looking. But now the haunted weight of too many years shone out from his eyes.

He looked at the green forest terrain across the River. His eyes widened and turned bright. The terrain would not stay green for long. Alien tendrils crept up within him, sliding along his spine, inside his skull, like some invading leech. Visions of fire and sorcerous destruction marched across his imagination.

Enrod's dark hair had been tangled in the long journey across the map, but he paid no attention to it. Whenever he thought of something else, any other distraction, he felt sharp pain in his head. It would all be better once he brought destruction to the other side of the River, once he showed *them* what it was like in his city of Tairé.

Threads of Sorcerer blood whipped through his veins like snakes, whispering to him constantly: *Use the power! Show the Stronghold that they cannot cut themselves off and leave the rest of Hexworld doomed.*

They thought they were so safe, so protected. A human fighter character named Delrael had created the River to keep Enrod out. To keep all the Tairans out. To keep every living thing in the east away from the sanctuary of the untouched forests, the protected lands.

Enrod felt trapped and compelled. It was appalling what they had done. The memory made his thoughts become dark, uncontrolled. He had to destroy the Stronghold. Destroy them. Wash the land in flames. Explosions. Devastation.

He shook his head. The buzzing returned, making it hard for him to concentrate. His feet were blistered and bloodied from the long journey. But he couldn't quite remember traveling to get there. Days and days seemed like a blur of hex-lines, changing terrain, vast distances.

He kept losing track of time. It used to bother him, but it happened so often now. He would blink and find himself someplace, or realize he had been doing something that he just didn't recall. A warm, pulsing blackness filled the empty spots in his memory.

Something was wrong in his city of Tairé too. He thought of his home, the streets, the buildings, the other people, all they had worked for. *Something was wrong!*

Something ... from the east. Dark and full of power, growing, devouring. Something deadly from Outside. Ages ago, the same thing had happened, a growing force planted by one of the Outsiders just after the Transition—Hexworld would have ended then, except for the miraculous appearance of the Stranger Unlooked-For who had saved them all.

Now they needed another miracle.

The buzzing in Enrod's head convinced him that everything could be fixed if he would just devastate the land around the Stronghold. The human characters Delrael and Vailret, and the traitorous half-Sorcerer Bryl, had caused all the problems on Hexworld by creating the Barrier River.

Enrod could not question that thought or the pain and confusion would start again.

Tairé had suffered enough in its history. They built the city in terrain that had endured the worst battles of the Sorcerer wars. The land itself was desolated, hexagon after hexagon turned into wasteland, desert.

The Wars had ended long ago. The two warring factions of Sorcerers made their peace and then embarked on the Transition, turning themselves into six ethereal Spirits who then ignored all the wreckage they had caused.

But young Enrod had not joined the rest of his race in the Transition. An idealist then, he stayed behind because the Sorcerers had done too much damage to Hexworld. They could not simply go away without making amends, without trying to help the other characters survive the aftermath. *Enrod* vowed to make amends. *He lived in Tairé, in the middle of the worst devastation. He* wanted to heal the land, to bring it back to what it had been.

The six Spirits held the power to make everything right again with little more than a gesture, if they cared....but they too disappointed him. After the Transition, the Spirits vanished completely, gone on to whatever interested them without a thought for everything they left behind. They had not shown themselves in the two centuries since.

Enrod despised them for it. The Spirits had abandoned Hexworld, when they could have been so much help. Perhaps they could even stand against the whims of the Outsiders.

Enrod spent his life in Tairé helping the human characters to build their city, to heal the land. First came small garden plots, nurturing the soil, growing outward, expanding to cover the hills with grass again. Plants sprouted on their own. Stands of trees grew on some of the hills. Living things took another foothold in the desolation. Enrod saw his life's work coming to fruition.

Though he had the Fire Stone—one of the four most powerful magical items in the Game—Enrod needed it little. He used the power of his own sweat and effort. Characters working together made their own kind of magic....

Then it all changed. The plants withered and died. Enrod began to have nightmares, sensing something terrible growing in the mountains near the eastern edge of the map.

The new-planted forests became skeletal black sticks on the hills. The ground cracked, and the windswept dust scoured the nearby hexagons clean. The characters in Tairé became listless. Their life seemed to drain away from them along with their free will, their hopes. The city fell silent in the midst of its desolation.

Desolation.

As the land across the River would be.

Enrod stepped back away from the edge of the water into the forest. Despite his sense of urgency and the need to unleash his anger, he forced himself to work with care. He selected appropriate trees, all about the same size and thickness.

Holding on to the thin, straight trunk of an oak, he looked at the Fire Stone. Each facet of the ruby showed a number from one through eight. Enrod concentrated, then tossed the Fire Stone on the scattered dead leaves at his feet.

The ruby came to rest against a moss-covered rock. The number "7" faced up. If Enrod had rolled a "1," his spell would have failed —but instead, he summoned nearly as much magic as the eight-sided Stone could command. He hated to waste so much power on such an insignificant task.

Glowing red spangles filled his hand. The power awakened in him, eager, dancing at his fingertips.

He gestured and sent the sorcerous fire into the earth, incinerating the roots of a tree and severing it neatly from the ground. Smoke and powdered dirt spurted into the air. The smell of burning sap and green wood stung his nostrils.

Enrod contained the fire in his fist and braced himself, pressing the bark against his shoulder. He let the trunk slide down against a larger tree until it thumped against other bushes and came to rest.

Enrod directed the burning spell at the fallen trunk, stripping the side branches away. The curls of flame peeled off the bark, leaving a steaming naked log on the forest floor, blanketed on each side by damp leaves. The spicy scent of charred wood reminded him of more peaceful days in Tairé, as characters gathered around bonfires in the harvested fields....

The birds in the forest fell silent. He could hear the motion of the Barrier River as it poured along its course, bounded by the sharp hex-line.

For a moment, Enrod hesitated. What was he doing here? He

couldn't remember. He blinked his eyes and turned to look behind him into the forest terrain.

But then the throbbing power of the Fire Stone in his hand distracted him, and the black buzzing came roaring back into his head, like a storm through his thoughts. The buzzing left only one idea untouched. Destruction. Devastation. Get across the River and make things *right*. Burn them clean. Start everything new and fresh, after a white-hot cleansing fire....

He wrapped his fingers around the corners of the Fire Stone and directed the hot power at another tree, and another, until he had a line of neat logs scattered in the forest, seared clean of bark and branches. Steam and gray smoke made his eyes water. His vision grew blurry.

Night fell.

Dawn came.

Enrod swam up out of a dream sea of hypnotic blackness and chaotic thoughts to see that he was standing barefoot in the rough mud of the riverbank. His hands were raw and bleeding, studded with splinters from the logs, from the vines he had used to lash the logs together to form a raft. He had woven thin green tendrils into strong ropes, then coated them with oozing sap to seal them. After lashing the logs together, he had coated the ropes, the knots, with a thicker layer of pitch and baked it into a glassy varnish with the Fire Stone.

Enrod didn't remember doing any of it.

He wondered if it had really been only a day. Smears of mud and ash stood out on his tattered white robe. Far from the powerful Sentinel of Tairé, he looked like a man who had been crumpled, badly used, and poked back to life again.

His back cried out with pain as he hauled the heavy raft to the water. Enrod stepped over the black hex-line and sank up to his knees in the cold river. The mud soothed his torn and blistered feet. The hem of his robe soaked up the water.

He rocked the logs of the raft, pulling, dragging. It slid partway over the hex-line and became easier to move. Enrod climbed back onto the shore and used a thin pole to lever the raft over the edge. He hopped onto the smooth logs, picked up the pole again, and gave a push that strained his ribs, shoving the raft over the hex-line and into the grip of the river.

Enrod sat down on the raft, smelling the water and letting it carry him downstream. Before long, he stood up again and pushed the pole into the riverbed, gaining leverage and inching the raft across the current.

He had an appointment to keep. He had to destroy the other half of the world.

Fallen trees thrust up from the surface like the fingers of drowning men. The water itself roiled brown and muddy, still cutting its channel and bearing debris from its journey. Beneath the current, Enrod imagined forests, houses, the skeletons of travelers, wandering monsters, all who had been caught in the flood. According to the map of Hexworld, the new course of the Barrier River had swallowed up an entire village.

The current brushing against the sides of his raft seemed to whisper to him, all the dead voices gurgling up from the river bottom begging Enrod for revenge. How could any character dare to do this? What right did they have?

He would lay waste to the land, turn hexagon after hexagon to flames and ash. He would destroy it all, level it.

The raft lurched, as if it struck an unseen bump in the River. Enrod swayed and regained his balance. The brown, silty water flattened out like glass in front of him. A streak of light, yellow and searing, shot back and forth beneath the surface. The smell of ozone, like the air after a thunderstorm, drifted up to him.

Everything grew quiet, deathly quiet, but the air seemed charged with crackling power. Enrod tensed, confused.

Deep beneath the water, foam bubbled up, disturbing the smooth surface. The churning increased until spray gushed to the sky. Mist appeared from nowhere, swathing the horizon and leaving him isolated in the middle of the River.

Enrod pulled up his wooden staff, holding it in his hands like a weapon. He let the raft drift, but it remained in place, anchored invisibly from below.

The bubbles gushed higher, then opened up like a gigantic mouth, a trap door letting something *emerge.*

A triple shadow lifted itself from the depths of the water, rising ... and kept rising, filling Enrod with awe. Three forms, hooded and spectral, clad in black tattered cloaks, pouring upward into the sky. His bones vibrated with thunder beyond the range of his hearing.

The three figures surged with dark power until they towered over the Sentinel, impossibly high. Their attention focused down on him like sharpened spears.

Enrod could not move.

He had seen them once before, two centuries ago, on the field of the Transition. They had not spoken then, but hung in the air surrounded by fallen empty bodies of the Sorcerers and grass and mountains in the distance. In silence, they had departed with their three white counterparts, the Earthspirits. Enrod thought they would never come back. All the characters on Hexworld had given up on them.

The Deathspirits.

The buzzing dark presence suddenly left Enrod's head, deserting him entirely. Without the driving force, he was disoriented, like a marionette with severed strings. He couldn't remember anything for a moment. He looked at the Fire Stone in his hand and realized what he had been about to do. He couldn't understand what had been possessing him.

The ruby Stone leaped out of his hand, wrenched away with such force that its sharp corners sliced his fingers. He felt blood running down his palm, but he could not take his eyes away from the immense Spirits. The Fire Stone rose in the air, spinning and glittering far out of reach.

All three Deathspirits spoke in unison. The words echoed on the wind with such power that Enrod felt his bones humming, his eardrums straining.

"We created the Fire Stone to *protect* Hexworld and our half-breed children. We cannot allow the Stone to be turned to such destruction."

Enrod collapsed to his knees, squeezing his eyes shut and covering his ears. He felt on fire, under the intensity of a magnifying lens focused on the sun.

"You would have abused your great power, Enrod. Unforgiveable.

"You will *never* cross this River.

"You will *never* go back to your home until the end of the Game.

"You must take this raft back and forth forever, at the mercy of any other character who intends to help the world. Not once to rest, not once to reach shore."

Enrod could not move. He wanted to hide, he wanted to beg forgiveness, he wanted to jump off the raft and drown himself in the River. But his muscles locked him in place.

"Hexworld faces a threat from Outside that could destroy everything. And so we have returned. Our world may not yet be doomed.

"But you have doomed yourself."

With a howl of cold wind, the cloaked figures sank beneath the River. The water gurgled, then became glassy smooth. The Fire Stone vanished with a *pop* into thin air.

Milky mist rose up in front of Enrod, blocking the far shore of the River. He turned, and the opposite shore had also vanished. He stared, wide-eyed in shock and dismay.

I didn't mean it! I don't know what happened!

But the Deathspirits were gone. He could not argue with them. He would never be able to argue again.

Enrod's muscles locked up. His blood turned to ice as the horror struck him, growing from the pit of his stomach until he wanted to crumble and die. All the work he had done for Tairé, for Hexworld —he couldn't understand what had come over him, what possessed him. Even now he was appalled by what he had thought of doing.

Enrod felt himself drawing deeper and deeper into his own mind, filling the emptiness where the black buzzing had once been. From now on, it would be his only refuge.

His body took control of itself. His arms lifted the pole and thrust it into the water, pushing down and seeking the bottom of the River.

Enrod looked straight ahead. His jaws ground together. His eyes widened. He could not move. He could only push his raft along, moving nowhere.

With aching arms, Enrod began his endless journey.

CHAPTER 2

SPIRITS IN THE NIGHT

The six Spirits have gone from Hexworld and they will never return. Why have they abandoned us? Are our lives so trivial to them? How soon they forget everything they once were.
—Sardun's memoirs

Delrael plodded to his bedchambers in the main building of the Stronghold. His head ached, his body felt stiff, and he wanted to explode from inactivity.

Once again, he and the other characters had resolved nothing—another day wasted, and they still had thought of no way to fight Scartaris, the Outsiders' evil creature growing in the east.

He hated all this talking and planning. He wanted to *go* somewhere.

Delrael had returned to the Stronghold two weeks before with Vailret and Bryl, successful in their quest to create a Barrier River and to rescue the Sentinel Sardun's daughter, Tareah. But then they had learned from blind Paenar that the Barrier River would not stop Scartaris after all....

Every day, Vailret insisted that they meet with other characters to discuss the problem, to brainstorm. There had to be a way, Vailret said, there always had to be a way. He usually knew about things like that. To be fair, the Outsiders had to play by their own Rules; they needed to provide some solution to every problem they posed.

"Or maybe not, in this case," Delrael said.

No one could suggest a plan of action, not even Tareah. They knew too little about their enemy.

Delrael found it impossible to sit around and wait. He was a fighter trained to action, not discussion. He needed to meet a problem head on, to fight, to explore, go adventuring, and, as the primary Rule of Hexworld dictated, *have fun*. When all else fails, go on a quest.

Finally, he and Vailret came to the conclusion that they should just head east. Maybe they could do something there if they tried. Perhaps Enrod, the full-blooded Sentinel in Tairé, could help them...

Delrael stood in the doorway of his room. It had once been his parents' master chambers, but that had been many turns before. Fielle, his mother, was dead of a fever, and his father Drodanis had gone away, searching for the mysterious Rulewoman far away in the south.

It was warm for the late summer night, but Vailret's mother Siya had built a roaring fire in the hearth. Light glittered from chests of gems stacked against his wall, plunder from some of Delrael's earlier quests. The room smelled clean and resinous from the burning wood. Siya had tossed herbs into the hearth again.

His bed beckoned to him. His body yearned for a good night's sleep. Worked up and anxious, not knowing what to do, Delrael hadn't been resting well, frustrated by a problem he could not grasp.

Even his younger cousin Vailret, the thinker and scholar, found himself just as much at a loss.

With a sigh, Delrael loosened his oiled leather jerkin and

removed it, stretching his arms. The muscles popped into place. It felt good to relax. While sitting around, he had mended his armor. He needed to work on his archery skills a little more tomorrow.

Someone knocked on the door before he could lie down. Delrael sighed and went to the door.

Siya stood there, small and rigid. "I've drawn another hot bath for Tareah. I don't know how she stands it—I can barely put my hand in the water. But she says it helps her aches. I wonder how much longer this will last."

Delrael nodded. "Depends how long she keeps on growing."

The Sentinel Sardun had held his daughter in the body of a child for three decades, not wanting her to grow up before another full-blooded Sorcerer could be born at random by the Rules of Probability. But when Sardun died, his spell was broken. In only weeks, Tareah grew at a remarkable rate, catching up with lost time. In the balloon ride back from the island of Rokanun, she looked like ten-year-old girl: now she appeared fully grown.

But her bones and muscles ached from the strain. Hot, hot baths helped, she said. Siya and Delrael tried to make her as comfortable as possible.

Tareah had blossomed into a beautiful woman, though she still felt uncomfortable around groups of characters after the isolation in her father's Ice Palace. She was making the effort to learn social skills that Delrael took for granted.

"Why don't you make her some herb tea so she can rest better?" Delrael said. "And if there's anything I can do for her, tell her to be sure and ask." He wrapped his hand around the edge of the door.

"But I need to get to sleep now, Aunt Siya. Sooner or later, we're going to leave on a quest again."

She scowled, but Delrael raised his hand to stop her from saying anything. "We're not doing it just for fun this time. You know that. We're trying to save our world."

But after he closed the door, removed his clothes, and pulled on an airy nightshirt, Delrael closed his eyes in concern. His head kept ringing from too much discussion.

Working together, they had defeated Tryos the dragon and driven away Gairoth the ogre. But if Scartaris was powerful enough to obliterate the map of Hexworld and *literally* destroy every hexagon of terrain, they would need something more potent than magic Stones and hand-held weapons.

Bending down, Delrael picked up the jeweled silver belt his father had given him. The belt was an ancient relic, crafted by the old Sorcerers before they embarked on the Transition. Delrael had earned it for doing well in his battle training. If only the vanished Sorcerers knew what was becoming of their world now…

At the moment, though, he wanted sleep more than anything. Maybe an idea would come in the night. Still staring at the belt in his hands, Delrael dropped backward onto the bed—

A lightning bolt like ice shot through his body. His heart stopped. His vision turned into the blinding white of a snowstorm.

He landed on his back in the dew-spangled grass of a starlit meadow. The cool air around him was like the shock of falling into a mountain stream.

He paused a second to blink in astonishment before his fighter reflexes took over. Delrael leaped to his feet, crouching in a battle stance—but he was barefoot, clad only in his nightshirt, holding only a silver belt in his hand. He felt helpless and naked as he glanced around, trying to find a branch or something to fight with.

Overhead the greenish aurora, Lady Maire's Veil, lit the clearing. Through a break in the trees, Delrael could see Steep Hill, on top of which stood the walled-in Stronghold. He had been somehow transported into one of the neighboring forest-terrain hexes. He hadn't the slightest idea why.

"Who's there?" Delrael said quietly. Then, squaring his shoulders, he spoke in his loudest battle-commander voice. "I said who's there!"

After a moment, he wondered if he should have said anything at all.

The forest sounds vanished. It made Delrael wonder if all the creatures had some sort of rapport with ... with whatever had brought him here. The trees stood completely still, then began to sway on the edges of the meadow. The wind picked up. Spangles of light wove in and out of the air, drawing rough shapes that towered impossibly high and yet might not have been there at all.

Delrael blinked his eyes again and again. The outlines grew sharper, taking form as the breeze turned to a roar. The tree branches clattered and scratched against each other. Delrael's brown hair blew back away from his face.

He squinted into the stinging wind, but the white light grew brighter and *brighter* until it coalesced into three discrete forms, giant hooded shapes. They stood taller than the trees, stretching up toward the glowing aurora.

"We are the Earthspirits. We have come back to save Hexworld. And you must help us."

Delrael didn't know what to say. His jaw dropped. Vailret had told enough stories about the Transition—he knew how powerful the Spirits were. The wind rang in his ears. He thought he was shouting, but his voice felt pitifully small. His words sounded limp and inane even to him. "How can I help? Can you destroy Scartaris?"

The Earthspirits paused at that, then spoke again in unison. "We have been gone too long. We are not aware of what has taken place since we departed.

"We sought a way to escape from the Game, to leave the map behind and seek our own *reality*. We found ways to avoid the Rules, but we cannot break them entirely. We are bound to Hexworld—its Rules are fundamental to our existence.

"The Deathspirits learned this too, but they wish to embrace chaos. They would form their own Rules, make their own maps, Play their own new games.

"They were our enemies in the Wars. We have not communicated with them since the Transition."

Silence hung in the wind for a moment.

"But the Wars are over." Delrael felt giddy at his own brashness for interrupting. "Scartaris is our enemy now, but we don't stand any chance against him. Unless you can help."

Delrael shrugged off his doubts. No character ever won a gamble without first placing a wager.

"Scartaris is ... unknown to us. We do not know if we will win against him." The Earthspirits paused a beat. "But if we are to fight, *you* must take us there."

Delrael stood straight, brushing the damp folds of his nightshirt. "Take you there? What do you mean? Can't you just ... go?"

"We are bound by Rules of travel, as are all characters on Hexworld. But it is much more difficult for us to cross hex-lines. We are not substantial enough.

"Also, Scartaris has the power to destroy the map and end the Game any time he wishes. If he knows we are coming for him, he will not wait."

Delrael felt disappointed and helpless. "Why doesn't he get it over with, then?"

"The Outsider David is a vindictive one. He wants to make all characters watch the destruction of Hexworld first.

"You must deliver us in secret. The Outsiders are not aware of our return to the world. They can know nothing of this quest. We are beyond them now—Hexworld has its own magic they do not realize."

Listening to the Earthspirits speak, Delrael began to feel confident again. As the giant forms loomed over him, he sensed their power, their invincibility.

"We will disguise ourselves. A dim part of us remembers the silver belt you carry, remembers creating it as an ornament so long ago."

Delrael clenched the glittering belt self-consciously, wondering what they would do. Then he cursed his own selfishness.

"Lay it on the ground," the Earthspirits said. "We will meld ourselves to it, take substance in the metal. We can do little to assist you, though we can shield you from the manipulations of Scartaris once you get closer to him.

"Carry this belt across the map. When you reach Scartaris, we will emerge. We will take him by surprise."

Silence settled down on the meadow. The white Spirits waited for Delrael.

With trembling hands, he laid the shining belt down on the grass. The light from the Earthspirits glinted off the gems and the polished hexagonal sections of silver. He backed away, stumbling into a fallen tree. But he could not tear his gaze from the Spirits.

The Earthspirits changed. They moved. Their light glittered and swirled in a funnel, pouring down into the metal of the belt. Dazzles of color floated in front of Delrael's eyes. He shielded them, blinking, as the wind continued to howl, focusing downward. Leaves broke away from branches and swirled around his head.

The Spirits streamed down into the silver links. Delrael tried to imagine how so much power could fit within the belt.

Then the silver swallowed the last glints of white with an audible *pop*. The wind ceased. Torn leaves and broken twigs settled to the ground, and everything fell silent again.

His ears ringing, Delrael crept forward. His feet were wet, along with the hem of his nightshirt. His eyes were wide and childlike when he touched the belt. For a moment, it was blistering hot, then the silver grew bitterly cold before adjusting itself again. Tracings of frost etched across the gems before evaporating into the cool night.

Delrael picked the belt up in his hands. The silver throbbed against his fingers, vibrating with a rhythm that faded toward stillness.

He would have to be careful about what he said to anyone if the Outsiders truly were not aware of this quest. Not even the Rule-woman Melanie could know.

Then Delrael smiled. At last they had their weapon. At last they had a way to win against Scartaris.

He fastened the belt around his damp nightshirt. He didn't feel tired anymore. He wanted to talk to Vailret and Bryl and Tareah immediately. They needed to set off as soon as possible. No more sitting around and talking.

He looked up through the trees to see the silhouette of Steep Hill and the Stronghold. Delrael realized it would be a long walk barefoot back home.

Tareah sat back in the deep wooden tub, drawing her gangly legs up and tucking her knees close to her chin. The legs seemed so long to her, so awkward, as if they belonged to someone else. The rough surface of the wet wood rubbed against the bumps of her spine.

Through half-closed eyes, she saw wisps of steam rising from the bath. The warm water soaked into the throbbing in her joints. Old Siya argued with her that the water was too hot, but Tareah found that only this would help. When she climbed out, dripping, to dry herself, her skin would be angry red, but she would feel better, numbed for a while.

Her muscles relaxed under the coaxing of the bath. She let her mind and her body drift. She felt painfully lonely, lost and unsure of anything. Her stable and predictable world had been thrown into chaos since Tryos the dragon kidnapped her, since her father died in the destruction of his Ice Palace, since she found out the Outsiders were trying to destroy Hexworld. Tareah's new adult body was difficult to control, grown too fast. She seemed like a stranger inside herself.

In the deserted bath chamber, after the others bedded down for the night, Tareah listened to quiet sounds, nightbirds and insects in the cooling air. Autumn would arrive soon. On the equinox, the characters would celebrate Transition Day, the anniversary of when all her forefathers had transformed themselves into the six Spirits. Delrael had promised her they would make a big celebration in the village this year. He said he would do it for her. She smiled at the thought.

The most important anchor in all her turmoil was the friendship of Delrael and Vailret. They poured so much attention upon her that she felt special again, as when her father Sardun cared for her. Delrael reminded her of the monumental heroes in the old legends of the Game, adventurous, sure of himself, brave and strong. Vailret had all the intelligence and background of a respected scholar—he could talk intensely about many subjects, but he was often self-conscious around her. She sighed and forced a smile.

The open fire on the hearth heated another cauldron of water in case Tareah needed her bath warmed again. The hissing and snapping of the flames soothed her, eased her into a doze. She drifted. She let her eyes sink closed as she smelled the water, the damp wood.

A sharp pain snapped inside her head. Tareah became dislocated, floating, with nothing to hold on to. She felt the Sorcerer blood within her—she knew what it could do, but all at once, it didn't seem strong enough. Tareah blinked her eyes again and stared at the fire. The flames throbbed, running together like melted wax. She grew dizzy. She seemed disembodied.

Without knowing what she was doing, Tareah slipped under the water of her bath.

She opened her eyes, but through the bathwater, she saw clear images. She didn't need to breathe, didn't even think of it. She felt no alarm at all. The water she smelled and saw was not from inside her bath....but from the Barrier River. She felt a swaying raft beneath her feet. She saw giant, shadowy shapes, hooded figures, heard booming voices.

A man with wild dark hair and black beard stood on the raft. Like an invisible observer, Tareah felt the anger in his heart, the alien fury that controlled him from far away.

Her Sorcerer blood recognized that this was Enrod, the Sentinel from Tairé.

She heard the Deathspirits pronounce judgment on Enrod, she learned what he had been about to do to the land. In horror, she stared at him, but she could feel no sympathy when the Deathspirits stripped him of the Fire Stone.

In her head, she heard the words ringing out, spoken to *her*:

"The Fire Stone was meant to assist the characters of the Game. As the last full Sorcerer character, you must now receive the Stone. We trust no one else with the decision. Take it and win the Game. Or lose. We have done our part. We care no longer."

Then the vision left her completely.

As she blinked, Tareah found she was under water, in her own bath, cramped and unable to breathe. She pushed her head up above the surface, sputtering and spraying water from her mouth. She blinked her eyes. Thick brown hair streamed wet down her neck.

Her eyes focused, and she saw something different about the fireplace. The flames curled against the split logs like yellow tatters. Wisps of steam danced up from the surface of the cauldron of heating water. Smoke rose into the chimney, but left the room filled with the smell of burning wood.

Gleaming at the foot of the hearth, among the orange coals, lay the brilliant eight-sided ruby. The Fire Stone, red and pulsing with magic.

~

The musty dampness of the stonecutter's caves filled Delrael's nostrils. The torches and lanterns they carried flickered in the drafts of sluggish air, throwing light against the hewn rock walls. The smoke mixed with the heavy smell of stone dust and earth.

Delrael crossed his arms over his leather jerkin, looking at the dim chamber. He brushed dirt off his pants. Vailret followed him in, found a rock outcropping to sit on, and lounged against the wall. He looked thin and gaunt in the uncertain light, but his eyes were bright and intense.

Bryl the old half-Sorcerer sat by himself, glancing around as if frightened by the shadows, the oppressive weight of rock around them. Tareah waited next to Vailret.

In the silent hours before dawn, no one knew they had gone to the caves. They had much to discuss, in private, away from the villagers and—they hoped—away from the prying eyes of the Outsiders.

Vailret coughed and wiped his mouth on his sleeve. "We've got half a hilltop of rock over our heads to shield us. Maybe the Outsiders won't be able to hear us here."

Bryl cringed at Vailret's mention of the weight of the rock. Delrael looked at the low ceiling and nodded, but he kept his voice quiet anyway. "The Outsiders must not know anything about this. It's something we have to decide."

He didn't know where to begin. He had already told them in a brief whisper about the Earthspirits. At the same time, Tareah had burst out of the bath chamber, wrapped in a blanket but dripping onto the wooden floor. Wide-eyed, she held the glowing ruby Fire Stone in her hand...

"The Earthspirits promised to help us destroy Scartaris," Delrael said. "We might have a good chance now, especially if Tareah has the Fire and Water Stones, and Bryl has the Air Stone."

Bryl fondled the Air Stone, the four-sided diamond that created illusions. Gairoth the ogre had used it to overthrow the Stronghold by making the other characters believe he commanded an indestructible army of other ogres.

Tareah fumbled at her waist to undo the lashings of a small cloth purse. She drew out the sapphire Water Stone, shaped like a cubical six-sided die. For centuries, it had been held by Tareah's father, Sardun the Sentinel. At Vailret's urging, Sardun had used the Water Stone to create the Barrier River; now, after Sardun's death, Tareah took the Water Stone herself. She held it next to her new Fire Stone, blue fire in one hand, red fire in the other.

Delrael smiled. "Scartaris is still there, and the Outsider David still wants to destroy us—but we can fight back now. This is our Game too!"

Vailret rubbed a finger along his lower lip. "We've got to be careful about this, though."

Delrael grimaced—he hated to hear his cousin say that.

"Scartaris must know we're trying to stop him. It's rather hard to hide something like the Barrier River, you know. And when we confronted the Outsiders in that deserted Slac fortress, we learned all about each other's intentions."

Bryl and Tareah muttered, and Delrael fidgeted in impatience. But Vailret looked at them. "We should assume that the Outsider David is already sending something to kill us, a monster or two. If he wants to end the Game so much, he won't take any chances. He'll come to get us directly—and the longer we sit here, the easier a target we make."

"Not unless he thinks it might liven up the Game," Delrael said. "Remember what we're here for. Rule #1—always have fun."

Vailret snorted. Bryl squirmed, nervous and trying to avoid the issue. Tareah put her hands on her hips in an awkward, unsure gesture. "Well, what are we going to do?" she said.

"First and most important, we have to make sure the Outsiders don't learn about the Earthspirits and their involvement," Delrael said immediately. "That could be our loaded dice." He touched his silver belt, but he felt nothing unusual. "I have to carry them to Scartaris—but we need to make it look like we're just going on a quest to find out more about our enemy."

"*We?*" Bryl said. "Who all is going on this quest? We just got back from one!"

Delrael frowned at him. "We're supposed to enjoy going on quests, Bryl. That's what we were all created for. It's just a game."

"This just might take the Outsiders by surprise." Vailret smiled. "That'll teach them to leave loopholes in the Rules!"

"So are the four of us going on this quest?" Tareah asked. Her voice carried an impatience for banter. She had been brought up studying the famous historical quests of the Game. Delrael knew she considered it to be very serious stuff, nothing to be made light of.

"I have to go," Delrael said, running his fingers along the silver belt, "since I'm carrying the Earthspirits. And, Vailret, because you can think fast, and you *know* things we wouldn't even consider. That might help. I'd like you to come too, Bryl, so we can use your Sorcerer magic."

Delrael lowered his voice. "I want you to stay here." He touched her shoulders, then slid his palms down to hold her arms, hooking his thumbs on the insides of her elbows.

She bristled. "Stay here? But I owe it to Hexworld to fight as much as you! Now that Enrod's gone, I'm the last full-blooded Sorcerer on the map. I have to come with you!"

Delrael held up one hand to stop her. "Tareah, you've been at the Ice Palace all your life—you never gained any experience. Questing isn't something you learn offhand. It would be too dangerous to you, *and to us*, to have an inexperienced character in the party. You know the Rules, you know the probabilities."

Tareah was angry with him. He'd thought about this so much,

but when he explained it to her, it seemed a weak and simple excuse. He wasn't good at explaining things. But when Tryos the dragon had kidnapped her, Tareah sat around waiting to be rescued because that was what she *thought* she was supposed to do. He didn't want to count on someone who would play according to what she remembered of distorted legends and cut-and-dried interpretations of the Rules.

He sighed and softened his voice. "Look, I'm not just being over-protective. I need someone powerful to stay and guard the Stronghold while we're gone. Vailret just said it—there's no telling what Scartaris might send here. I want somebody at the Stronghold who can fight back. You have the Water Stone and the Fire Stone— you might need them. The characters in the village might need you."

Tareah still said nothing to Delrael.

"I'm going to speak to Tarne too—he's a fighter, an old veteran from the days when my father ran the Stronghold. He kept the characters safe when Gairoth took over. I think the two of you can stand against anything Scartaris has."

Tareah seemed to be considering what Delrael said; finally, she nodded. "You're right. That goes along with the other adventures I've studied. I'll stay here."

Tareah clicked the two gems together in the palm of her hand. "But it doesn't seem practical for me to have *two* Stones, if I'm just sitting behind a wall all day long."

She held out the eight-sided ruby to Bryl. The ruby glowed like a blazing coal. "Take the Fire Stone with you. The Deathspirits told me I should do with it as I see fit. The Water Stone was my father's. The Fire Stone ... I don't feel comfortable with it, not after I know what Enrod was going to do. Not after the anger I felt in his mind."

Bryl reached out his hands in amazement and took the gem. He stared with twinkling eyes and awe written on his face. "I don't really want to go on another quest," he said, "but now I feel a lot safer."

"None of us is going to be safe," Vailret said. "Not until this is all over."

INTERLUDE: OUTSIDE

Melanie arrived at Tyrone's house for the Sunday gaming session. Standing on the doorstep, she watched a trail of her breath rise into the damp air. She tucked the heavy map of Hexworld wrapped in an old blanket under her arm. It had begun to drizzle outside, and she did not want the wood or the paint to get wet.

Melanie was surprised to find herself the last one to show up. Normally, David came late just to annoy them, but this time, he appeared anxious, as if he knew exactly what he wanted to do. That worried her.

David's eyes were bloodshot and he looked tired—Melanie wondered if he had been sleeping well, or if he had been plagued by nightmares.

She greeted everyone as Tyrone returned from the refrigerator carrying a round of sourdough bread. The bread's center had been hollowed out and filled with a white and green coagulated mass.

"Leek, spinach, and feta cheese dip," Tyrone said.

Scott frowned at the loaf and straightened his glasses. "I thought you were kidding when you told us that."

Tyrone set down a plate of bread chunks he had cut from the middle of the loaf. "It's good—try it. Have I ever let you down?"

"Yes," Melanie and Scott said in unison.

"Oh, just try it."

David sounded gloomy when he spoke. "Are you *sure* we want to keep playing?" Melanie caught an undercurrent of hesitation in his voice. She didn't even feel like speaking to him. He made her frightened and angry at the same time.

She uncovered the map, draping the damp blanket on a chair. The blue line of the Barrier River stood out like a scar, reminding them what had happened the week before.

"What's going to happen this week?" he asked. "Are you sure you're not afraid?"

"I'm not afraid," Melanie said.

Scott could barely keep his eyes off the blue line that had appeared by itself the week before. "I'm not afraid really either." He frowned. "But I'm very curious to see if anything else happens."

"We pretty much finished up Mel's adventure last week, with the dragon being killed and all," Tyrone said. "What are we going to start with?"

"There's more to the adventure than that," David said.

"A lot more." Melanie realized she had snapped at him.

"Come on, guys. Make nice." Scott kept his voice down then caught himself.

"I'm going to send my characters on a quest to the east," Melanie said. "Delrael, Vailret, and Bryl—the usual bunch."

"For what? What are they going to do?" David asked.

"They have to find out about that Scartaris monster you sent against them. No better way than to go there themselves."

"I'll squash them. I've got so much to put in their way."

Melanie stiffened. "Yes, but you can't know they're coming unless one of *your* characters encounters them. By the rules. Just because you know what's going on yourself, David, doesn't mean your characters will know."

She tapped her fingers together. "And speaking of that, I

want to introduce a new character tonight. It's a golem." She looked at the map, but in the bright light over the kitchen table, she could not tell which hexagon she had repainted. "I'm going to have him encounter my characters in Tyrone's section."

"You can't just do that!" David stood up.

"Why not? She hasn't introduced anybody new in a long time." Tyrone took a sip of his soda. "And we've never played a golem character before."

"I rolled all the details already. Here's a printout of his statistics." Melanie passed around a sheet of paper with numbers jotted down in columns. "His name is going to be Journeyman."

"You should do that when we're around." David frowned at the paper, the numbers.

Melanie made a disgusted sound. "Come on, David. I'm just saving us time. You think I'm trying to cheat or something? Look at the scores."

"I think a golem would be neat," Tyrone said.

Apparently seeing he wouldn't win any arguments on the subject, David shrugged. "Doesn't matter, you know. Not against Scartaris."

"It might," Melanie said with a slight smile and looked at the map in the light, tracing the line of the Barrier River, the sections of terrain between her characters and David's ruined portion of Hexworld. She hoped her plan would work.

She distributed new printouts of the log sheets. She kept track of every week's game in her father's computer. Over the years, she had compiled a three-ring binder, a book-length journal of all their games and adventures.

They glanced at the new pages and shuffled them aside, except Scott stopped, picked up his copy, and stared down at it. "Hey, when did that happen, Mel?"

"What?"

David blinked at his printout and turned pale. He pressed his jaws together.

Tyrone looked at Melanie's copy as he reached for his dip. "This says that Bryl's got the Fire Stone. And what's this? 'Enrod came to destroy the land with the Fire Stone. He tried to cross the Barrier River on a raft and was stopped by the return of the Deathspirits, who cursed him to journey back and forth across the River forever. They presented his Fire Stone to Tareah, who gave it to Bryl in his quest.' Interesting, Mel, but ... well, shouldn't we have *played* it?"

Everyone looked at Melanie. She blinked her eyes, baffled. "But ... this isn't something I wrote up at all."

Scott made his mouth a straight line. "Nobody else has access to your yad's computer, Melanie."

David sighed and put both elbows on the table. He looked pale and afraid. "Of course it happened that way! You know it's right." He stared at them then shook his head. "Didn't you guys *dream* it? It was so vivid, I woke up sweating. "I could see Enrod. I could hear what he was thinking about blasting all the trees around the Stronghold, and building his raft and crossing the River." Sweat appeared on his forehead; he brushed it away in impatience. "And those big black-hooded things coming up and yelling doom and gloom at him and taking away the Fire Stone. You had to dream the same thing."

"I don't remember my dreams," Scott said.

Tyrone scratched his cheek below his ear. "You know, now that you mention it, I do remember something like that. And it was weird because it wasn't *me* in the dream. Yeah, I remember it now."

Melanie recalled the dream too, like a vivid slap in the face. "There's more going on here than I thought." She felt a perplexed hope, but she didn't know what to do with it. "If the Deathspirits came back, what about the Earthspirits?"

Scott pursed his lips. Melanie watched him; he became very uncomfortable when he didn't know how to explain things. "Wait a minute—I thought we decided not to play the Spirits. They were gone for good because they were too much for us to handle."

"The game is starting to play itself," David insisted. "It's coming alive. It's out of control. *This* is reality—" He slapped a palm on the tabletop. Their glasses of soda and the dice jingled on the table.

"We have to stop it!" The urgency in his voice was frightening. "Let's all agree, all right?" David's eyes pleaded with them. "We can try a trivia game or something if you still want to keep meeting on Sunday nights. Let's just stop *this* game."

Melanie swallowed hard and drew herself up. In annoyance, she flicked her hair behind her ear.

"If it's truly coming alive, David, then it's a wonderful, magical thing. Something here is greater than we ever dreamed of. We have no right to kill it."

She snatched the dice on the table. "Let's get started."

CHAPTER 3

ACROSS THE BARRIER RIVER

When embarking on a quest, characters travel primarily on foot, according to the guidelines set forth in Rule #5 and the accompanying tables. However, characters shall be free to use any other available transportation to speed them on their way.
—The Book of Rules

Though important quests usually started at dawn, Vailret, Delrael, and Bryl set out from the gates of the Stronghold in the dark hours before morning. The near-autumn air carried a cold snap, and the stars shone bright and sharp.

On the crest of Steep Hill, the Stronghold overlooked the terrain all around, the hexagonal fields, the rapid stream that rushed along the hex-line. A double-walled stockade surrounded the main buildings, defenses that had withstood many attacks and fell only once, to Gairoth the ogre.

Vailret stretched his arms back and felt the warmth of his jerkin and the woolen sweater wrapped around them. He had not gotten much sleep, and his muscles ached—but it felt good. Vailret ran his fingers through straw-colored hair, tangled from tossing and turning all night.

Delrael moved about with energy and excitement, obviously eager to be off again. He was a character of action who hated to ponder things until all spontaneity was gone. Of course, he often got himself into trouble because he never thought about what he was doing. He bore a sturdy sword from the weapons storehouse and left the bow and arrows behind this time.

Tareah waited with Vailret's mother Siya at the main gates to see them off. Beside them stood the old bald veteran Tarne, awake and alert with bright eyes.

When Sardun's daughter waved good-bye, Vailret felt amazed at how she changed in the month he had known her. They spent a lot of time together, exchanging legends and stories they unearthed, clarifying historical details that Tareah had learned from her father.

But Vailret could see the stars in Delrael's eyes when he looked at her, and he cared for his cousin too much to risk a potentially difficult situation. And fighter characters spent much more time impressing women than nearsighted scholars did anyway.

Tareah still looked disappointed that she would not be accompanying them, but she drew herself up, proud to have the responsibility of guarding the Stronghold.

Beside her, the big veteran Tarne appeared grim and ready. He had kept the villagers protected in the forests during the months when they needed to hide from Gairoth and his ogres. Now Tarne crossed his arms over his chest and nodded farewell to them.

Siya, though, looked devastated and afraid for them. Her husband Cayon had been killed in a senseless quest. He had been the typical Hexworld fighter character: cocky, talented, living for the moment and adventuring for the fun of it. But Cayon was slain by an ogre on one of his "fun" adventures. It had destroyed Siya.

She was a new type of character on Hexworld. She wanted an end to all of the tedious questing. It was time to settle down and establish their lives, support themselves, grow their crops, take care of the villagers and the other characters. But while she ran the domestic affairs of the Stronghold, she still felt left out, not treated with respect. She was overprotective of Vailret. She tried to do the same to Delrael, but he ignored her.

Vailret knew everything she was thinking—he could see the emotions ripple like changing waves on her face. But Siya held her tongue because she realized how much was at stake this time. Vailret greatly respected her for that.

As they departed, Siya said only, "Luck." Vailret smiled. The three of them started down the path into the darkness.

The lights in the village below had been doused for the night. Only a dull glow came from the blacksmith's workshop, where Derow always kept the fires banked. Before dawn seeped into the eastern sky, the questers left the village behind and crossed the first line of hexagonal fields bounding the forest terrain.

Bryl mumbled, "If characters have stopped questing so much, why do I always find myself walking back and forth across the map?"

Vailret's hands were numb from the chill; he crossed his arms and kept his fingertips under them. He turned to look at Delrael. His cousin's face was grim, concentrating on the journey.

Delrael's lost father Drodanis had sent them a spectral message from the Rulewoman Melanie, describing the threat of Scartaris and commanding them to find some way to stop the end of the Game. The three of them had created the Barrier River to protect them for a time.

But Drodanis had sent no other message, provided them with no further suggestions. Together, they were aware of the Earthspirits trapped in Delrael's silver belt, but they couldn't speak a word of that out loud. Characters could never know when the Outsiders might be listening.

The quiet between them seemed uncomfortable, strained. Vailret cleared his throat and spoke in a bemused tone. "I wonder if we really grasp what we're doing. Think about the implications beyond our adventuring to defeat Scartaris."

He raised his eyebrows. Delrael shook his head, as if tired of thinking.

"Do we really want to save Hexworld if it means rekindling the Wars all over again?"

Bryl wiped his hands on his sky-blue cloak, trying to get rid of some pitch on his palms.

"What are you talking about?" He scowled at the pines around him.

"Well, isn't that what we're trying to do, get the Outsiders interested again by stirring up as much trouble as we can? Our normal, peaceful existence is so boring to them, they want to quit the Game. Maybe the only way we can keep their interest is to start all those endless battles and constant slaughter again."

Vailret sighed. His half-formed thoughts began to frighten him. "Starting the old Sorcerer Wars was a pretty trivial thing in the first place. We shouldn't have too much trouble if we want to do it again."

Delrael adjusted the sword at his side. The silver belt around his waist looked gaudy in contrast with his scuffed and mended leather armor. "I thought nobody knew how the Wars started. It was so many turns ago."

Vailret shook his head. "Tareah knew the story. It's sad in one way and stupid in another. Would you believe a wedding party, an athletic contest?"

He shrugged. "Of course, legends make things too simplistic. They ignore all the sociological factors of the characters, how the Sorcerers divided into two camps just waiting for a spark to set them at each other's throats.

"Our two athletes, one from each faction, were Sesteb and Turik. The Sorcerer Lord Armund had married his Lady Maire. The couple hosted a gala wedding feast at Armund's lakeside palace, then they began an afternoon of games. Games—" Vailret shook his head. "Fun and games—think of all the trouble they've caused us."

"Think of all the fun we had," Delrael countered.

"Games were simpler then. The main sport was to see who could throw a stone farthest out onto Lord Armund's lake, Sesteb or Turik. Turik was muscular, but Sesteb was clever and wiry.

"Lord Armund arranged to have a line of boats strung out on the hexagonal lake, so characters could float a marker where each stone landed. Turik flung his stone first and reached the ring of boats. Nobody believed Sesteb could ever match it.

"But Sesteb picked a small flat stone. He stepped up to the edge of the water and cast it at an angle, skipping it across the surface of the lake. On its last bounce, the stone jumped past the ring of boats."

Delrael laughed. "Good strategy."

"Well, you can imagine what happened. The other characters had placed high wagers on the game, so of course Turik's supporters said that Sesteb had cheated, while the others argued that Sesteb's stone went the farthest and nothing else mattered. Both sides refused to pay their wagers, which led to open hostility before long. It didn't help that everybody had too much wine at the wedding feast either.

"Lord Armund demanded that the two groups make peace so they didn't ruin his wedding celebration. He went to Sesteb's supporters and asked them to begin the competition all over again—but they killed Armund in their drunken anger and tossed him out of their tent."

Bryl made a rude noise. "I thought old Sorcerer lords were a little more dignified than that."

Vailret agreed. "So you might think. When the Lady Maire witnessed the murder of her new husband, she used her sorcery to spawn an ugly, vengeful monster—the first ogre, which then slaughtered the characters that had killed Lord Armund. Turik's supporters created their own monsters to continue the fight, then Sesteb's friends made even more powerful ones to defend themselves."

Delrael and Bryl looked at him as they continued to walk. The path ahead of them zigzagged clearly through the trees.

Vailret continued. "Sure, some characters called for peace, but the others enjoyed the war games even more."

"I'll bet the Outsiders had a hand in that," Delrael said.

"The saddest part is that Turik and Sesteb were themselves the best of friends and refused to take part in the fighting. But the other characters forced them to engage in a duel to the death. More games. Being a lot stronger, Turik killed Sesteb and then carried his friend's broken body with him to the lakeshore. Turik walked out until the waves closed over his head."

"How dramatic," Bryl said.

Delrael shook his head. "Shows what happens when you play a game without having the rules set down beforehand."

The trees ahead of them parted, and Vailret caught his first close glimpse of the Barrier River. Grayish brown, the River roiled in its pondering progress from the top of the map to the bottom. The water hauled buried debris from what had once been normal terrain.

The bank was a sharp black line where the forest ended and the water began. A transition zone of sticky mud bordered the hex-line, glistening wet. Vailret could hear the water moving, pushing against hidden obstacles. The river carried with it a smell of decay from the rotting remains of woodlands and quiet meadows drowned in the flood. A few birds flew out over the water, hunting for insects.

"And *that* isn't going to stop Scartaris?" Delrael shook his head. "I don't understand what we're up against."

Vailret stared across the water. "The River might buy us time if Scartaris sends an attacking army—but we need to prepare for a different type of enemy. Scartaris might have been what turned Enrod against us."

"Sure looks like an effective barrier to me," Bryl said. "It's a full hex wide—how are *we* going to get across?"

"You're going to swim, of course. Bring a rope with you," Delrael answered with a straight face. He probably had not even considered the problem before now.

The half-Sorcerer glared back, but Delrael's expression showed no humor. Bryl looked away, scowling. He took out the Fire and Air Stones, but the gems could not help them.

Vailret spoke, but he knew they weren't going to like it. "Tareah said Enrod could carry us. On his raft."

Delrael and Bryl did a double take. Vailret kept himself from smiling, though he enjoyed the astonishment on their faces.

"She told me that when the Deathspirits cursed Enrod to take his raft back and forth, they said he had to assist anyone trying to save the world. Or something like that. We of course have spotlessly pure intentions—" The corner of his mouth turned upward.

Delrael frowned. "Since Enrod tried to destroy us all, maybe Bryl shouldn't flaunt the Fire Stone too much."

Bryl stuffed the ruby gem up the sleeve of his blue cloak. "I sure don't want him angry with me. He's a full-blooded Sorcerer."

"We have to figure out how to summon him first." Vailret squinted at the distance. His eyesight was never terribly good, but he thought he saw a smudge across the water.

"We might not have to worry about that," Delrael said. "There's a bank of mist coming—straight toward us."

The air felt cold and clammy around them as the fog rolled in. They could hear waves lapping against an object in the water, then the silhouette became clear. A raft.

A tormented-looking man used a long pole to haul the raft close to shore, but he remained carefully away from the hex-line. Enrod the Sentinel looked disheveled, once massively built, but now wiry. His black hair and beard showed streaks of gray spreading out around his cheeks and temples. A wild glaze covered his eyes, directing his sight deep inside, where he was trapped with his own thoughts. The Deathspirits had cursed him only a short while ago.

Enrod did not look at the travelers, did not speak a word. He merely worked his pole, turning the raft toward the opposite shore. He paused a moment, then dug the pole into the river mud and pushed. Slow to gain momentum, the raft moved a few more feet away from the shore.

"Wait!" Vailret hurried to jump onto the raft. The lashed logs swayed as he gained his balance. Delrael leaped over to join him. Bryl hesitated at the edge of the River then jumped across.

Enrod's raft moved with greater speed, rocking as the Sentinel worked his pole. They drew away from the shore, then mist closed around them in a damp cocoon.

The mist muffled even the noise from the River, and all other sounds fell away. The line of trees on the shore faded into murky skeletal shapes then vanished altogether.

The hush around them made Vailret afraid to talk, but Bryl finally whispered, "I can't see where we're going. How do we know we're making any progress at all?"

Enrod gave no sign that he even realized the passengers had joined him on the raft. The dirty sleeves of his robe flopped around his wrists as he raised the pole, dripping water and river mud, then pushed down again.

"What if he wants to keep us here?" Bryl whispered again. The half-Sorcerer's eyes were wide, and he hunched down into his cloak, as if trying to hide. "We're the ones who created the River. We're the ones he was coming to blast with the Fire Stone. I don't see the Deathspirits here to protect us—what if their curse isn't strong enough?"

Vailret had no answers for him, but Bryl's fear struck home. After another moment in silence, Delrael said, "Shut up, Bryl. Thanks for pointing that out to him."

Enrod gave no sign that he had heard.

Vailret stared at the cursed Sentinel. Enrod's eyes were red and unfocused, possessed. He had been driven into madness somehow; he had wanted to blast all the hexagons into blackened cinders. Did he know that his imagined enemies stood directly beside him? Did he know that Bryl carried *his* Fire Stone no more than two steps away?

"Enrod? Enrod, can you hear me?" Vailret stood beside him, but the Sentinel did not flinch.

"I've heard many legends about you. I know what you attempted to do for Tairé. You remained behind from the Transition to help rebuild the blasted lands. You wanted to atone for all the damage done in the old Sorcerer Wars."

Enrod fixed his eyes at the blank wall of mist in front of him. He lifted his arms and pushed down on the pole.

"Enrod," Vailret continued, "we know the Outsiders put something in the east, a monster called Scartaris who's going to destroy Hexworld. Can you tell us anything about him?"

The dark-haired Sentinel seemed to be in a world of his own. He moved jerkily. His eyes did not blink.

"Enrod, please help us!"

Enrod lifted his pole out of the water.

"The whole Game is at stake!" Vailret clutched at the Sentinel's tattered white sleeve, trying to yank his attention away from the raft.

In a lightning blur of speed, Enrod snapped backward with his right foot, scooping it behind Vailret's legs. He slashed with the mud-dripping pole and jabbed with his elbow.

Vailret tumbled, sprawling to the deck of the raft. He skidded and grabbed at the pitch-covered logs to keep from falling into the water.

In a fluid motion, Enrod composed himself again, thrust his pole back into the River, and pushed on.

It all happened so fast that Delrael could do little more than bend over to catch his cousin. Bryl blinked in astonishment.

Enrod acted as if nothing had happened at all.

Vailret coughed and tried to catch his breath, opening and closing his mouth. Then he climbed back to his feet, brushing himself off. He said nothing, but continued to watch Enrod out of the corner of his eye...

Before long, shapes appeared in the mist ahead of them, the dark silhouettes of trees from the far shore. Vailret squinted as they approached closer until the fog around the raft broke open, letting him see the hex-line of the shore.

Enrod moved toward the bank, stopped the raft just before touching, then held it in place with the pole. He turned his neck on sluggish muscles to look at the three passengers, but he made absolutely no sign of recognition. He began to turn the raft around again.

Delrael jumped to the shore, clearing the hex-line and landing on the dry forest soil. Bryl scrambled off, splashed in the mud, and joined the fighter.

Vailret turned again to plead with the Sentinel. "I wish you could help us, Enrod."

His back turned to Vailret, Enrod hesitated and then pushed the raft away from the bank. Vailret jumped across the widening gap of water and landed beside his two companions.

Vailret shook his head. "He's so powerful, and the whole map is in such trouble. I wish his magic wasn't wasted like this!"

"Are you forgetting he was going to blast our entire land?" Bryl said. "He wanted to destroy us all. The end result would be the same as Scartaris."

As the raft moved away again, the island of mist curled around Enrod and swallowed him up until Vailret could no longer see him or the raft or, after a few moments, the mist itself.

"We'll never know."

Delrael rubbed his hands together and turned to face the forest terrain stretching away from the river. "Let's get going. We've got plenty of hexes to travel."

A strange voice interrupted them from beside the River. "Hold your horses! Play it again, Sam." The voice was deep and hollow, and did not belong to any of them. A burble of mud from the bank made Vailret look down.

The thick clay opened a hole like a mouth, with lips protruding and moving to form words. But the quality of the voice changed, becoming loud and abrasive. "Listen to me when I'm talking to ya, boy! Now, pay attention!"

Bryl stood to the side, but Delrael leaned over the mouth in the mud. Vailret looked around for a stick, wondering if he should poke at it.

"Where's the beef?" the mouth continued in a different voice again. "Four out of five dentists surveyed recommend sugarless gum for their patients who chew gum."

"This thing isn't making any sense at all," Delrael said, glancing at Vailret. "What is it?"

"What's up, doc?"

A bulge pushed up from the surface of the mud, then became a rounded lump straining harder until it grew into a blockish, clumsily formed head made of clay. It drew a great gulp of air through its mouth, then exhaled with a whistle through the caverns of its nose.

"Ah, how sweet it is!"

The head struggled, then a neck emerged, forming out of the mud as it rose. The shoulders and torso squeezed up as if forced out of a mold from below.

"I want to get out of here," Bryl said.

The clay man emerged from the bank until it stood as tall and as burly as Delrael. It flexed both arms and blinked empty eye sockets.

The clay man bent over the river, splashed some water on its skin and rubbed down a few rough spots with its hands.

"Well, surprise, surprise, surprise!" Then he turned to face the three of them. The clay of his lips formed a wide, misshapen smile, showing soft, sculpted teeth. "You deserve a break today!"

He patted his clay chest so hard that he made an indentation. Perplexed, he smoothed over the mark. Clay eyelids came down over the empty sockets, then blinked up again.

"G'day, mate! My name is Journeyman, your friendly neighborhood golem. I'm from the government—I'm here to help you. I was sent by the Rulewoman Melanie to join your quest to destroy Scartaris. One for all and all for one!"

CHAPTER 4

SLAVE OF THE SERPENT

All character races were created by the Sorcerers to fight in their wars: humans, Slac, khelebar, werem, ogres, ylvans. Do not forget, however, that the Sorcerers also created individual monsters according to their imaginations. Many of these monsters still wander the map with no other purpose than to cause havoc. Questing characters should beware of such monsters, as their methods of fighting will be unfamiliar, and their weaknesses will not be known.
—Preface, *The Book of Rules*

The veteran Tarne woke in the middle of the night with ice in his stomach and a crawly feeling on his skin. He stared at the unfamiliar ceiling, and he knew the aurora in the sky would speak to him again.

With the silent step of a practiced fighter, he slipped out of his borrowed quarters in the Stronghold's main building. He stood on the wide open grounds enclosed by the hexagonal stockade walls.

The greenish light of Lady Maire's Veil swirled and shone down upon him with visions of the future.

Tarne stared upward, heedless of the bunched muscles in his

neck. He was able to see things in the aurora ever since his head injury. It had been his last real fight, part of Drodanis's vengeful ogre hunt after Cayon was killed...

Tarne had been delirious for a while, slow to heal. His scalp felt as if it had been pierced with white-hot needles, visions, ideas of what would come in future turns of the Game. He shaved his head, exposing the network of scars, thin and thick, from the knocks he had taken during other quests. With smooth skin on his head, with nothing to stop the flow of thoughts, everything seemed clearer to him. When he watched the shimmering aurora, sometimes everything fell perfectly into place.

His last vision had shown Gairoth invading the Stronghold with his army of ogres. Tarne foolishly tried to fight against the prediction and led a group of desperate defenders, to no avail. He could never force the visions to come to him—and he could do nothing about what he saw.

Vailret insisted that this kind of magic was fascinating in its own right. Tarne had no Sorcerer blood, and as a pure human character, he should have no magical abilities at all.

But anomalies happened. Hexworld operated on the Rules of Probability, where even unlikely things were statistically possible. Tarne had visions of the future. Bryl's former apprentice Lellyn, also human, could work any imaginable form of sorcery. Even the mighty Earthspirits and Deathspirits, by their very existence, tied the Rules in knots. It seemed that some things were more powerful even than the Outsiders.

Tarne suspected Hexworld had its own kind of magic the Outsiders knew nothing about. And that magic was awakening in these last days of the Game.

The throbbing aurora above confirmed his guess. Then sent him a message.

The green folds of Lady Maire's Veil made him see images in his head. They made no sense to him, but a part of him understood:

Clenching, coiling, preparing to strike. An enemy approaching, evil, death.

The bright white streak of a meteor stitched across the aurora, startling Tarne. Then the shooting star faded and was gone.

Tears ran down the veteran's face. The chill night breeze made him feel cold tracks on his cheeks. He was very afraid.

He had learned one thing from his visions—fighting against them was useless. The visions showed him only things over which he had no control. But at least he knew what he had to do, what role he must play.

The night was silent and cold. The next day would be the autumn equinox, when Sardun's daughter Tareah planned to lead the villagers in a celebration of Transition Day. When he thought of that, the veteran felt a pang inside. He went to the gates of the Stronghold and opened them up.

He would tell no one about this. It was better that way.

He walked across the bridge covering the trench and worked his way down Steep Hill in the dark. Tarne thought of too many things, and he tried to empty his mind of thoughts. His entire body was in turmoil. He had no time for any of this. No time at all.

He walked into the silent and darkened village until he reached his own home. He lit a candle. The inside smelled musty, closed-in. He had covered all the windows now that he spent most of his time guarding the Stronghold.

The light from the candle jumped around the walls. He went to a corner of the room and dug his fingernails into the wood of one of the hexagonal floor tiles. He lifted it, then popped up the adjacent tile to uncover a shallow storage area he had dug out beneath the floor.

Tarne paused, sighed, then forced all the memories away. He reached in to pull out a long bundle wrapped in rags. Peeling away the cloth, he stared down at the notched but well-cared-for blade of an ancient sword. The sword had been used centuries before in the old Sorcerer wars; it had been used in previous years when Tarne himself was a fighter. The orange candlelight made it glow with the blood and fire of past victories.

He reached under the floor once more and pulled out his old suit of leather armor. He had oiled it well before wrapping it up for storage. Everything was still intact, mended of scuffs and cuts, studded with chain links for extra protection. He brushed off dust and powdered dirt. He never thought he would need either the sword or the armor again.

Of all the fighters of his generation, Tarne was left here alone. After his injury, he gave up fighting and questing to become the village shearer and weaver. Some of the designs of fate he saw in the aurora he wove into his personal tapestries; no one but himself could understand them.

Tarne slipped on the leather armor and patted it against him. He listened to the chains jingle in the dimness. The armor seemed to grow on him again, become part of his body.

He held on to the sword, gripping the handle. Yes, it felt right. His reflexes and all the old training awakened. On impulse, he whirled and slashed at the candle on the table. The flame went out.

On her unfamiliar bed, Tareah lay back but couldn't sleep. The lonely darkness did not comfort her. Her bones and joints ached again; she wondered if it would ever get better.

Back in the Ice Palace, when she couldn't sleep, she got up and wandered the cold rainbow halls, or picked through Sardun's collection of ancient artifacts, or stood on the balcony of the high tower and looked out at the checkerboard of mountains and wasteland terrain.

. . .

Tareah climbed out of bed, feeling the cold air on her legs. Many thoughts kept her awake. She missed Delrael and Vailret. It upset her that they hadn't taken her along, but she was also frightened, overwhelmed that they had left her with the duty of watching over the Stronghold.

Tareah dressed, pulling one of Siya's warm shawls over her shoulders, and tugged her boots on, a pair of Vailret's old comfortable castoffs. She had plenty of things to do, especially in preparation for tomorrow, the anniversary of Transition Day.

Her father had pounded into her a respect and a wonder at the Game and the accomplishments of her race. The villagers seemed to know nothing about their own heritage—yet human characters had undertaken many of the greatest quests, the most difficult journeys. She was in awe of them for what they had done.

According to what she had seen, though, the characters were drifting away from that way of life. Instead of treasure hunting and fighting monsters, they had become farmers, villagers, peaceful people. Siya said that they were sick to death of the shallow, adventurous life.

Tareah crept into the courtyard. The door moved silently as she opened it. The night air was cold and fresh, warm compared to the nights far in the frozen north.

Transition Day. She grinned with excitement. She would tell the story to all the villagers. They could rejoice and be happy in their heritage, how Hexworld had come to be. And then they would let off the fireworks.

Tareah smiled as she strode across the courtyard to the weapons storehouse against one wall segment. The storehouse held several small clay containers filled with firepowder. Bryl, Vailret, and Derow the blacksmith concocted a powder that would flash and explode in brilliant colors. She wondered what kind of magic the sealed clay containers held—some fire spell rolled up inside a little package? A hand-length of fuse dangled out from the containers.

During the celebration, they would use an old catapult to fling the containers into the air for the show.

She looked forward to that most of all. Vailret talked about the spectacle, his eyes gleaming. It would be like the meteor shower that came every autumn.

Vailret fascinated her. He knew so many of the same things she did; they could talk for hours. But Delrael kept her in awe. He was so much like the legendary fighter characters she had read about. She adored listening to his adventures and his questing. He was exactly what she expected a fighter character to be.

Bryl, though, she did not know—he was a magic user, yet his attitude was strange to her. She couldn't understand his bitterness or his reluctance to learn.

Leaving the firepowder where it was, Tareah turned away from the door of the storehouse then stopped. Under the light of the aurora, she could see the training equipment in the yard. The wooden sword posts were monuments by themselves in the shadows, the hanging sacks, the archery targets. They looked like scarecrows in the darkness.

The Stronghold gate stood wide open. Tareah stared at it, wondering how that could be. She heard someone coming up the hill path. She didn't know if she should sound the alarm or just watch.

A bulky well-muscled man walked through the gate. He stood in shadow for a moment, then closed and secured the gate. It took her a moment to recognize the veteran Tarne—only now he carried a long sword she had never seen him bear before. And he was clothed in leather armor. Metal chains jingled and glinted in the faint light.

But Tarne would never fight unless he had to. What was going on here? The gate was opened, Tarne was armed—treachery? Something none of them knew about?

Tarne had always seemed completely on their side in the Game.

But all characters were like puppets on a string if the Outsiders decided to manipulate them...

On the verge of saying something, Tareah paused and looked at the fighter from the shadows of her hiding place. He did not know she was there. She would watch and see.

The veteran walked slowly in his armor, as if under a burden. He seemed ... afraid, very tense. But he moved with dignity. He walked to the training area and stood still. He rested the sword tip on the ground in front of him, squared his shoulders, and *waited* for something.

Tracks of sparkling tears ran down his cheeks. Sardun's daughter felt a shiver dance along her spine. Was he betraying them?

The fighter stood motionless in the darkness. Dawn would come soon. But Tareah felt, as she watched, that something else would come sooner...

The night filled with tension, a buzzing—and then in front of Tarne, the air rippled and seemed to tear. The veteran cringed, only for an instant, but he held his ground.

An ear-splitting roar burst from beyond hearing, channeled closer. Tarne remained standing, braced and ready for whatever was coming. He raised his blade, either in salute or defense.

Tareah hid deeper in the shadows by the storehouse.

A hole in space appeared in front of the fighter. The air snapped, and a huge, vague form appeared as a solid shadow, then burst into sharp clarity. A monstrous figure stepped out, hulking forward in long strides.

It was an enormous hairy beast bearing a gigantic snake— Tareah had never seen anything like it, not in all her studies of the fighting monsters from the ancient wars. She wondered why it had come, how Tarne knew it would arrive.

The demon stood fully ten feet tall and three wide, though it walked hunched over, carrying a great burden. A pelt of thick, blackish-brown hair covered its body, but its head and chest plate were reptilian. The head seemed large for its body, almost square, with a gaping mouth out of which lolled a forked tongue.

The monster bore a tremendous serpent entwined around its body, a sickening green with oily rainbow scales and fiery red pupilless eyes. The scarlet glow shone like embers.

From her hiding place, Tareah felt the hairy demon's deep-set eyes strike her with an overwhelming feeling of sadness and pity. She blinked to shake away the emotion. She wanted to shout for help, but the other villagers lived too far away. She didn't have the Water Stone with her, and only Tarne could actually fight the monster.

The serpent reared up upon seeing the armored fighter standing before it. The hairy monster did not move until the serpent coiled and squeezed the demon's massive ribs, urging it forward. The tree-trunk legs stumbled toward Tarne.

"You are called the Slave of the Serpent," Tarne said. His voice sounded strong, empty, different. "I have been waiting for you."

The Serpent hissed, and the scarlet light blazed brighter. "Who are you?"

"Go back to Scartaris. There's nothing for you here." Tarne said the words as if he had memorized them, as if they were expected of him.

"Scartaris must have the Fire Stone back. Must destroy fighter named Delrael and any other character who would quest against Scartaris."

Tarne swallowed. "Then I am Delrael." He held his sword before him, waving the tip back and forth. "I'll take any quests I want if I can save Hexworld."

Tareah wanted to cheer for him—she could write down the legend of his brave fight to defend the Stronghold.

"Give back the Fire Stone!" the Serpent said, bobbing its head up and down.

"Sorry, we need it right now."

By the storehouse, Tareah watched with wide eyes, saying nothing. They were about to battle, just like in the old stories. Tarne was a talented fighter, a veteran of many quests and campaigns. He remained silent as he faced the demon and glared at the Serpent.

She didn't know if she was expected to help fight. But Delrael had called her inexperienced. She would only get in the way, maybe even hurt Tarne's chances.

The Serpent urged the lumbering Slave forward, nipping it. The fangs dripped foul-smelling venom. The monster heaved itself forward, reluctant to move closer to the fighter.

The Slave halted a moment as its pitiful eyes met the bald veteran's. But the moment was shattered as the Serpent savagely sank its fangs into the Slave's neck, making it howl in pain and rage.

Tarne leaped in, moving with a smooth grace that belied his age. The chains on his armor reflected starlight and the greenish aurora. He surprised the demon with his attack, feinting, shifting the Slave's guard, and slashing at its belly. The notched edge of the old blade sliced through the monster's tough chest plate, but the Slave looked more angry than injured.

It swung a clawed fist at Tarne, but the fighter hacked into the massive paw. The beast roared and swung backward with his other arm, catching the fighter with a glancing blow. Tarne spun but recovered his balance as the Slave struck again.

The sword from the old Sorcerers flashed up as the Slave tried to maul him but instead impaled its own forearm on the tip of the blade. The monster howled, jerking its injured arm away from the sword, then swatted at the blade with its other paw.

Tarne saw his chance and thrust in at the chest plate, but the Slave's thick hide protected it from serious harm. It lashed again with a wounded arm, but the monster moved slowly. Tarne dodged and came back in, hacking with two-handed strokes.

He looked up and his eyes met the Serpent's.

The huge snake began weaving back and forth, swaying and hissing like a rhythmic fire with green wood. The Serpent kept the fighter's eyes locked to its own. From her hiding place, Tareah could see the veteran becoming entranced by the hypnotic movement, dropping his guard.

Tareah stood up. They didn't see her. She had to do something, use one of her spells.... She couldn't run and get the Water Stone, and she felt small and defenseless. She could attack with a minor fireball, perhaps, or a bolt of energy—but her aim might not be good enough, since the two opponents stood so close. The bald fighter stared at the swaying Serpent, dazed.

"Tarne!" she finally shouted.

The Slave swung with its deadly claws, using all of its massive muscle power to rake across Tarne's chest. The fighter sprawled on the ground with part of his armor hanging in tatters and broken chains. The snapped links gleamed bright in contrast to the tarnished older metal.

The armor had protected Tarne, though. He climbed to his feet, gasping and trying to suck air back into his lungs. He blinked, but he looked stunned. He turned to stare in amazement at Tareah. The Slave came at him again.

The fighter met the charge head on, whirling the old sword in a random pattern of cuts and slashes. Tufts of fur and drops of thick yellow blood flew from the demon. With a burst of energy, Tarne drove in so forcefully that the weakened Slave stepped back.

Blood oozed from slashes in its thick skin, running to the ground and leaving viscous, yellow pools. The monster wheezed and panted, making weak attempts to defend itself.

Tarne stopped and took a step back, holding the dripping sword in front of him. The Slave appeared dazed and began to topple backward. The veteran watched with an astonished grin on his face. He flashed a glance back at Tareah.

Abruptly, unexpectedly, the huge Serpent flashed downward,

stretching its body longer than seemed possible. Fangs glistened with drops of diamond-like venom. The fighter looked up, and the snake struck. The hollow fangs punctured his armor and sank into his chest, gushing a mouthful of venom into his bloodstream.

Tarne fell.

By the weapons storehouse, Tareah gasped and watched the veteran collapse writhing on the ground. Ready to scream, she stood seething and helpless. She was untrained in using her magic for combat. If her spells failed....

The hairy Slave howled something like anguish into the growing light. But the Serpent was blood-maddened, pushing the massive beast back toward the stricken fighter.

That aroused Tareah's anger enough that she screamed back at it. "Get away from here!"

The demon turned to face her. The Serpent opened its mouth to hiss. More venom dripped smoking onto the ground. The Slave took a step toward her.

Then Tareah remembered the firepowder.

She ducked inside the storehouse and snatched one of the clay casks. The back of her mind nagged at her, that she shouldn't be using *human* weapons, that her simple fire-starting spell was far too trivial to be used in any battle that anyone would remember.

The Serpent coiled around the Slave's neck. The hairy beast spread out its giant arms, splaying its claws and dripping globs of yellow blood down its fur. It roared into the approaching dawn, then strode toward Tareah.

She decided not to worry about fighting tactics. She closed her eyes and summoned up the fire-starting spell. It was a trivial spell, something anyone with a trace of Sorcerer blood could do easily—and Tareah succeeded the first time.

The fuse hissed and sizzled as the spark ate its way down.

The Slave charged at her.

She tossed the cask at the demon. "Catch!"

The firepowder exploded in a brilliant flash of fire and light, spraying the Slave of the Serpent with burning streamers and chunks of clay.

Tareah fell backward against the wall of the storehouse, rubbing her blinded eyes and gasping. Stinging chips of pottery fragments slashed her face.

She saw the smoking demon charge howling around the training yard. It charged into the upright logs of the double wall, sending a shower of the packed dirt trickling down. The monster beat at flames burning on its shoulder, its chest.

On the ground, Tarne still cried out in spasms. Spittle ran down his cheek back to his ear.

The Serpent reared back and glared at her. "Delrael is dead. No more quests! Scartaris will come back for Fire Stone!"

The rip in the air opened up again with a snap, and the howling beast plunged back into it. The Slave of the Serpent was swallowed up by nothing, disappearing.

Panting, Tareah ran to where the veteran lay trembling on the ground. Two blue flames burned from the puncture wounds on his chest, blackening the leather of his armor as the venom coursed through his bloodstream. He grimaced and shuddered, gripping the ancient sword.

He crawled forward, but Tareah stopped him. His eyes were glassy and unseeing. She stroked his cheek, muttering nonsense to him. Her magic could do nothing to stop the burning poison, to bring him back from death's stranglehold.

Tarne said nothing intelligible, which also confused her: all the legends had led her to expect dying characters to make a final dramatic speech before death.

The veteran stared at the glow of sunlight in the eastern sky rising up toward dawn, as the aurora overhead dimmed. His gray eyes did not close. The fires inside him burned out in a burst of dark energy, and he crumpled to ashes within his ancient and damaged vest of armor.

"Let the Game go on forever, and may your score always increase," Tareah whispered for him, the accepted farewell for a trusted companion.

Tareah stood up, blinking her eyes. Old Siya hung by the doorway of the main building, then moved mechanically toward the fallen fighter. An expression of complete horror hung on her face. Tareah wondered how long she had been standing there, attracted by the noise of the fight.

Tareah remembered the tears on the fighter's face, the fear in his eyes; she remembered how he had arrived in armor, waiting. Tarne had *known* ahead of time. He had deceived the demon into thinking it had slain Delrael. He had known this battle would kill him! And yet he had come anyway.

Tareah realized that she was now completely alone. She had no one to help her fight against whatever else Scartaris would send against them.

The dead fighter's ashes left a black stain on the ground.

CHAPTER 5

JOURNEYMAN

Rule #3: Questing characters may join with any other characters they encounter. Note, though, that the alignment of such newfound companions might not be clear. All characters have their own quests, their own preferred outcome to an adventure.
—The Book of Rules

Journeyman clapped his clay hands together and stretched his face in a grin. "Well, are we off to see the Wizard?"

Bryl looked at the perplexed expressions on the faces of Vailret and Delrael, relieved to see their skepticism. It was a nice switch, since they usually trusted everything without a thought of caution. Bryl shook his head and scratched at his thinning gray beard. After seeing some of the things Delrael did on impulse, Bryl was surprised the fighter had lived as long as he had.

"Wizard?" Delrael said. "We're going to find Scartaris, not just some magic user."

"Merely a figure of speech." Journeyman strode off into the forest terrain ahead of Delrael and Vailret. Bryl wrung some water out of his blue cloak, sighed, and followed them. The forest grew denser, but the quest-path marking their way shone plain on the ground. The sounds of the Barrier River faded, leaving them in the forest by themselves.

"Why do you always say such strange things, Journeyman?" Vailret asked.

"I don't know nothin'. I just work here," the golem said.

"Yeah, like that."

"Well, I was created by the Rulewoman Melanie, so I have some ... connection with the Outside. I can see some of the things she sees, know some of the phrases she knows."

Bryl scowled in exasperation at Vailret and Delrael. They acted as if they believed what the golem said, just on the basis of his own word. When Scartaris was out to destroy the world, how could they trust *anything*? How could great questers be so naive? If the Outsiders wanted to eliminate their own world, who could trust any other character? Bryl huffed and came up close behind them, looking sidelong at the golem but speaking to Delrael.

"How do we know he's from the Rulewoman? The Outsider David might have sent him to kill us while we sleep."

Delrael frowned as if the thought had never occurred to him. Vailret scratched his blond hair and nodded. "He's got a point, Del."

Bryl sighed, relieved that they had conceded that much.

Journeyman spread out his hands and splayed his fingers even wider. "Cross my heart and hope to die?" When that didn't appear to be good enough, the golem drew himself up, swelling his chest and stretching the pliable clay to make his shoulders broader.

"The Rulewoman Melanie commanded me to destroy Scartaris. That is my quest and that must take priority. I would rather join forces, offer my services, and accompany you—but if you don't trust me, I'll go alone."

He tilted his head forward on a rubbery neck. "Delrael, I know your father Drodanis. And I've seen Lellyn, Bryl's apprentice. They both reached the Rulewoman and her Pool."

Delrael snapped his head up, blinking. Bryl saw a haunted look in the fighter's brown eyes.

Journeyman nodded. "Your father is well, though he is in a daze most of the time. Drodanis wants to forget. He wants to be without pain, without memories. He wants to stop playing. And on Hexworld, when a character wishes to give up the Game, there is nothing left of him."

Delrael reached out to snap a twig from a branch. His knuckles were white, but he made no comment. Vailret put a hand on the shoulder of his cousin's armor.

"What about Lellyn?" Bryl asked. The boy had been rather likeable, although an affront to his teacher. A pureblooded human who somehow, through the Rules of Probability, was able to work more magic than Bryl himself could. The boy worked spells intuitively, wielded greater power than his teacher, but Bryl had still taught the boy what little he could, before Drodanis took him along on his quest.

"Lellyn is a rulebreaker in many ways," Journeyman continued. "He was nearly destroyed by his own doubts. The Rulewoman froze him in a block of forever-ice, sunk to the bottom of her Pool, for his own protection."

"Why would she do that?" Bryl said.

Journeyman tilted his head up again and moved a branch out of the way as they began to walk again. The branch gouged tracks into the soft clay of his arm. Absently, he smoothed his skin back into place.

"None of us is *real*. We are made-up characters created for the Outsiders' amusement. You know that. We all know that. But the Rulewoman herself is a manifestation of one of the Outsiders. She is so beautiful, with her long brown hair and her big eyes filled with all the colors of mother-of-pearl. She moves with such grace and power…" Journeyman paused, as if daydreaming.

"And when Lellyn saw her, maybe he saw more than he should.

Somehow in his mind, he knew that she was *real* and he was not. That doubt grew and grew until, when he completely disbelieved in his own existence, he would have vanished, winked out, annihilated. *Reality* is a powerful thing, too much for anything on this world to handle.

"In the last instant, the Rulewoman froze him to save him from his own doubts. He is still here, but he is not here."

As Journeyman spoke, Bryl remembered the ruined ship that had carried the Outsiders David and Tyrone into the Spectre Mountains near Sitnalta. That was how the Outsiders had brought Scartaris into the world. He also remembered the Scavenger, Paenar, who had come to the deserted fortress looking for treasure, and found instead the Outsiders. He had taken a brief glimpse of the Outsiders in their *real* forms, and the sight had blasted his eyes from their sockets. Yes, *reality* was a powerful thing.

Grudgingly, Bryl decided not to push the argument. They trudged on, crossing a hex-line into another section of forest terrain by mid-afternoon. Journeyman snapped his fingers and sang something about being "king of the road."

Vailret's eyes gleamed wide with delight. "Journeyman, tell us something about the Outside, since you can see parts of it. What's it like?"

The golem grinned his huge smile again, puckering flexible lips. "More wonders than you can imagine! Good to the last drop and squeezably soft! Refrigerators that make their own ice cubes, fabric softener that goes into the dryer, microwave ovens, trash bags with handle-ties built right in!"

Most of the words made no sense to Bryl—which was to be expected, since the Outside was such an alien place.

"But the *games* they have! No wonder they've grown bored of Hexworld. They have interactive computer games, role-playing simulators, and video games that hook up to your own television set. And Trivial Pursuit—did you know that *King Kong* was Adolph

Hitler's favorite movie?" The golem lowered his voice to an awed whisper. "And they have a great Sorcerer named Rubik, who created a colorful enchanted cube that can either enlighten Players or drive them insane!"

Vailret frowned. "You lost me on most of what you just said. That song you were singing a while ago, was that an Outside song?"

Journeyman clapped his hands again with a wet, soft *splat.* "I'll bet you I can name that tune in … three notes!"

Then he sang a long ballad about a man named Brady with three sons, who met a lovely lady with three daughters, and how they overcame their difficulties and became a single family unit. Journeyman then sang a sea adventure of how five passengers had set sail for a three-hour tour, but a storm shipwrecked them on a deserted shore. Over time, they had formed the kingdom of Gilligan's Island.

Vailret grinned. "When we get back to the Stronghold, please make sure I write those down."

"What you mean 'we,' paleface?" The golem became serious. "I don't expect to return. My quest doesn't leave much room for that."

Before Journeyman could say anything else, a high-pitched whine grew in the air. Delrael stopped and put his hand on his silver belt. His face appeared puzzled, then frightened. The piercing sound drifted louder and stronger until it hurt Bryl's ears. It seemed to be coming from the silver itself, where the Earthspirits had hidden themselves.

Delrael grabbed at the catch of the belt and yanked it from his waist. The belt vibrated and bucked in his hands like an angry snake, still sending out its shrieking noise. Blue and white sparks skittered along the surfaces of the gems. Delrael dropped the belt to the forest floor. The noise suddenly ceased, and the rush of silence struck them like a whip cracking. The silver belt lay still among the twigs and curling leaves, shining in the forest shadows.

Delrael gawked at his belt in utter shock. Sweat stood out on his forehead. Vailret squinted down, but he offered no explanations.

Journeyman seemed unduly confused, astonished. "What was that? Which way did he go?" The clay eyelids in front of his hollow eyes blinked and blinked.

Delrael flicked his gaze at Vailret, then at Bryl. They couldn't even talk about it. They couldn't say anything about the Earthspirits, especially not in front of Journeyman. Delrael could not try to communicate with the Spirits either. The Rulewoman could be watching, and so would the other Outsiders. They had to maintain absolute secrecy about their quest.

But what if something had gone wrong? Was it a signal of some kind, a calling—or did they just hear the death scream of the Earthspirits? Perhaps Scartaris had somehow destroyed the Spirits, and when the companions got to the end of their quest, they might find themselves helpless after all. Bryl tried not to think of such things, but terrible possibilities floated in the back of his mind.

Delrael swallowed and picked up the belt, fastening it with trembling fingers. "Hmmm." He shrugged, feigning a casual attitude. "Well, it's stopped—we shouldn't waste any more time here. We've got lots of hexes to travel."

The day passed, and as darkness fell, they reached the edge of their third hexagon for the day. The Rules forbade them to go farther, so they camped beside the black line. Another hexagon of forest terrain waited for them on the other side.

Vailret and Delrael talked with Journeyman. Bryl wondered and worried, trying not to think of what lay ahead or about the implications of the Earthspirits' scream from the belt.

Journeyman scratched lines on the dirt and taught Delrael and Vailret an Outside game called Tic-Tac-Toe. Bryl always felt left out. Sometimes it made him angry; other times it just depressed him.

He recalled his parents—his father Qonnar, a full-blooded

Sorcerer, and his mother Tristane, a half-breed. They had used their magic to try to save Delrael's ailing great-great grandfather—but he had died anyway of a wasting disease. His widow, Galleri, then married a rough and close-minded human fighter named Brudane. Brudane started rumors that perhaps Bryl's parents had actually poisoned the old man and not tried to help him.

Qonnar and Tristane grieved deeply for the old man's death. They felt they had not done enough to save him, and they did little to fight the accusations, which made the rumors grow. Finally, in their guilt and despair, Bryl's parents underwent the half-Transition on their own, annihilating themselves in sorcerous fire and liberating their spirits to wander the map.

Bryl had been a mere boy then, but he watched in horror. His mother and father did not even say good-bye; they gave him no advice and ignored him. In the last instant before the blinding light consumed her, Tristane met her son's eyes—but Bryl saw no recognition there. He was not even part of their lives. Their misery was all-important to them. They didn't bother to consider what it would be like for Bryl to grow up alone under the shadow of their implied guilt.

At any time, it might have been better for Bryl if he had wandered, gone to a different village where they did not know his past or his confused conscience. But he was afraid to leave. Some of the young villagers around the Stronghold taunted him. All characters around him were human—no one was qualified to train him how to use his Sorcerer abilities, and Galleri and Brudane certainly did not concern themselves with the problem. He knew only a few simple spells his parents had taught him in his early years, and a few others he had learned on his own.

In his mind, Bryl knew that he had grown up with his abilities stunted. Had he been properly trained at the right time, he could have been a powerful magic user. Three-fourths of his blood was from the Sorcerer race that ruled Hexworld so many turns ago. But nearly all the Sorcerers had vanished in the Transition, combining themselves into the Earthspirits and the Deathspirits. Few characters on Hexworld could claim to have Sorcerer blood anymore.

Then the human boy Lellyn had come along, flaunting his abilities, his enthusiasm, and his impossible Sorcerer powers that he should never have had. Bryl wanted all those incredible spells, the power that took years and years of effort and struggle and training. But he didn't have years and years, and he didn't have the patience.

Tareah had the skills, but Bryl didn't seek to learn any forgotten spells. The desire to better himself, the challenge, had backfired on him many years before.

That was why he attached so much importance to the Stones: Air, Water, Fire, and Earth. He had used the Water Stone and linked with the *dayid* of the forest to save the panther people in Ledaygen. He had used the Air Stone to trick Gairoth the ogre into leaving the Stronghold. The Stones gave him his power immediately. That was the best way.

"Tic-tac-toe, I win!" Journeyman said. Delrael grumbled and smoothed the dirt with the flat of his hand before drawing a new grid for another game. "Tomorrow, we're playing with dice instead."

They next morning, they set off into the forest terrain. Journeyman looked around and smiled. Bryl hated the way he grinned all the time.

"In this hexagon, there's supposed to be a village of ylvan, the forest people. Maybe we'll come across it."

Delrael trudged on. He looked flustered from losing so many games to Journeyman at the campsite. "How do you know that? I don't recall anything marked on our master map at the Stronghold."

Vailret looked around in the forest. "An ylvan village is hidden in the trees—you wouldn't know it was there until you were right under it." His eyes gleamed. "They're said to be master woodsmen, like chameleons in the forest."

"But how do *you* know it's there, Journeyman?" Delrael asked.

Journeyman shrugged his shoulders in a ripple of gray-brown clay. "It's marked on the map the Rulewoman Melanie uses."

The forest all around them looked the same as always, with trees and shrubs, vines, moss, and the faint but clear trail leading toward the east. But around midday, the birds and insects fell silent, replaced with the sounds of a struggle and a chilling, familiar bellow.

"Haw! Haw! Haw! BAM!"

Terror jabbed like an icicle down Bryl's spine. He knew that sound—Gairoth. He remembered being captured, drugged, placed inside a giant jellyfish in a stinking cesspool in the swamps. The massive ogre had forced Bryl to teach him how to use the Air Stone...though an ogre should never have been able to use magic.

Delrael stopped and cocked his head. He looked concerned, then a smile drifted onto his face.

Vailret met his cousin's eyes. "Be careful, Del. Gairoth almost got you last time."

Delrael appeared to be intensely aware of everything around him. Bryl had seen him this way before. The fighter motioned the rest of them to silence, then he crept ahead through the underbrush.

Bryl would have been perfectly content to remain where he was, to turn and bypass the ylvan village. But then they heard a thin, angry voice piping out. "Go away and eat rocks, you Loser! Why don't the rest of you help me?"

Vailret moved ahead to join his cousin, and Journeyman nonchalantly shouldered branches aside. Bryl held the Fire Stone in one hand and the Air Stone in the other—even with all that power, he felt frightened of Gairoth.

They looked through a clearing of branches, dry moss, and some leaves blushing with color from an early autumn frost. Massive trees stood straight and high, crowded together, but the undergrowth in one area had been cleared away. Dangling from the lower and intermediate branches of the great trees hung large globes of woven sticks and grass and leaves, meshed together and sealed with hard golden sap. The sap varnish glistened in the light of a small fire on the ground and the green-filtered sunlight above.

The hanging "nests" were the dwellings of the ylvan. Clumsily mounted pelts hung drying, and rotting, on a few branches. On the ground, four of the little people, about chest-high to Bryl, stood by a smoky fire. Beside them, arranged rocks marked a communal gaming area that looked as if it hadn't been used in weeks.

The ylvans' hair was dark reddish-brown, their eyes deep-set but dull, as if a milky film of cataracts had crawled over them. The men wore trimmed and pointed beards; the women's hair had been tied in green ribbons. The ylvans all wore outfits of leather dyed green and crosshatched with blotches and stripes that would make them invisible as they moved among the tree branches.

The fire had died to embers, untended. Too late, one of the ylvans had added a leafy green branch to the fire, which only made pungent smoke curl up to the sky.

"Master woodsmen?" Delrael whispered to Vailret. "Looks pretty sloppy to me."

Vailret appeared concerned. "But the ylvan are supposed to be shadows in the trees, expert ambushers. Something's wrong."

Near the ylvans in the clearing stood Gairoth the ogre, looking befuddled and angry. His muscles knotted like a twisted tree trunk. His one eye glowered at the four listless and dazed ylvans who stood by their fire and refused to shrink away from him in terror, or even to take notice of the ogre at all.

Fear made Bryl cringe even from his hiding place. Gairoth's furs were stained, worn, and falling apart; the spikes on his wicked club were pitted and rusty. Gairoth's eye was bloodshot, underhung with a bag of tired skin. The ogre's skin was grayish and unhealthy-looking, peeling with splotches and rashes. He appeared miserable and furious.

Journeyman had an exaggerated expression of distaste sculpted onto his face. "Gross! Gag me with a spoon!"

Gairoth waved a ham-sized hand of dismissal at the four ylvans by the fire and looked around the rest of the dangling settlement. He strained upward and swung the club to rip out the bottom of one of the low-hanging nest dwellings. Dirt and twigs pattered down onto the ogre's head, and he snorted in annoyance. But then some ylvan possessions tumbled out: small wood carvings, colorful flowers, pots containing gems, and small bits of treasure. Basket-like furniture, a chair perhaps, fell partway through the opening and then caught.

One of the other ylvan picked up a crossbow and turned it around. She paused, as if forgetting what she had been about to do, and then reached for an arrow. The ylvan dropped the arrow, bent over with sleepy slowness, and tried three times before she managed to pick it up. When she finally fitted it into the crossbow, she gestured at the ogre and fired. The arrow missed.

Bryl heard a sound inside the torn nest, a sluggish movement. Gairoth hooked the bottom of the gash with the spikes of his club, then pulled it down until he could reach it with his fingers. The branches above creaked.

The ogre pawed around into the opening until he grabbed something. He tugged, and an old ylvan tumbled out to land roughly on the ground with little more than a grunt of surprise.

Gairoth scowled. "Bah—too old."

The ylvan sat where he was on the dirt. His dark eyes were also covered with a milky dullness. He reached inside his camouflaged tunic, withdrew a knife, and stared at it.

"You leave him alone!" The piping voice came again, and an

arrow whizzed through the air to stick in the ogre's furs. Gairoth roared.

Bryl looked around to see. Finally, he spotted another ylvan blending into the tree shadows. This ylvan was younger than the others, with barely a fuzz of beard along his cheeks and chin. He swung around from where he hung halfway up one of the trunks, then slithered down looped ropes set into the side of the tree. He landed on his feet.

"Come on, you big clod!" The ylvan shot another crossbow arrow that nicked Gairoth's chin, enough to make him roar.

The little man crouched and glanced at the ylvans by the fire, at the old man who had been torn out of his home. Bryl noticed other dull faces peering from openings in the hanging dwellings. Somewhere above, in a long-delayed reaction, a child screamed. No one seemed aware of what was going on. Some moved slowly, half-asleep; others shook their heads, as if to drive away a buzzing that overpowered their thoughts.

Gairoth strode across the clearing. In only three steps, he towered over the young forest man who had defied him. The ylvan stood his ground.

The ogre yanked out a sack tucked into his fur garment, popping another of the seams in the shoulder. As the ylvan nocked another arrow, Gairoth scooped him up and pawed him into the sack.

Two of the ylvans by the fire had taken out their own crossbows. One tried to fire without first nocking an arrow.

The young ylvan continued to struggle, but Gairoth twisted the mouth of the sack shut and tossed the bundle over his back. The little man cried out as he struck the ogre's shoulder blades. The bag squirmed and kicked, venting forth muffled curses, but Gairoth ignored it. He let out a gravelly sigh that sounded like heavy furniture scraped across a stone floor.

Gairoth did not look happy, but resigned. "Fresh meat not good like *aged* stuff."

He glared at the other ylvans, who stared down at their crossbows and knives, as if struggling to remember what to do with them. Above, the child screamed again. Gairoth looked at the broken nest home, at the dazed old ylvan man on the ground who had finally succeeded in picking himself up.

The ogre sneered and, swinging his club in front of him, he stomped off to the other side of the clearing. Bryl could hear him mutter while he crashed along. Occasionally, Gairoth would smash his club against a tree, grumbling "Delroth! BAM! Delroth! BAM!"

Vailret turned to his cousin. "I think he still remembers us. Wasn't Delroth his name for you?"

Delrael pursed his lips and nodded. "Just no pleasing some people."

"Well, ah, we should get on with our journey now." Bryl could not keep his voice firm. He felt obligated to try and make them see sense, to set their priorities. But he *knew* what they were going to do anyway.

"We have to go rescue him. It's part of the Game, you know." Delrael sounded distracted when he answered, already making plans.

"We need to continue our quest and destroy Scartaris." Bryl tried one more time. "Journeyman, you have to get there too. We can't delay."

Journeyman pondered before answering, "Incidental adventures don't happen by accident. There's always something to be gained. Look in *The Book of Rules*."

Vailret raised his eyebrows at him. "I thought you didn't want to go on this quest in the first place, Bryl."

"I don't! But I don't want to face Gairoth again either. You don't know what he did to me!"

"Yes we do," Vailret and Delrael answered together. "You've told us enough times."

"Well, why didn't we fight back right then, when the other ylvans could help?"

"They didn't help him," Delrael said.

Bryl sat down heavily. Branches and leaves cracked beneath him, and he found his seat very uncomfortable. Arguing further would be wasted effort.

He hated questing.

CHAPTER 6

TALLIN AND THE OGRE

The Outsiders do not Play fair. Of all character races, ours is the smallest, the weakest, the fewest. We ylvans have faced more persecution, a greater number of attacks, a higher level of misery. We are the scapegoats of the Game.
—Kellos, ylvan village leader

Delrael led the others along the path, waiting for the ogre to stop so they could put their plan into action. The air around them smelled damp and muddy.

Gairoth found a hollow where puddles of water stood among sunken trees and mashed leaves. Marks showed where a creek gathered during the rains of the spring. He squatted down on the wet earth, crossed his pale and puffy legs, then wiggled his buttocks into a better position. He contemplated the squirming sack in front of him.

Gairoth had tied the end in a knot, but now he couldn't get it undone with his clumsy fingers. The ogre worked at it, trying not to tear the sack. He pursed his thick lips and glared at the bundle.

The scrappy ylvan struggled inside the sack. "Let me out of here, you Loser! Your breath smells like a dung heap!" One of the small arrows poked through the cloth and jabbed Gairoth in the palm. The ogre cried out, then slapped at the sack with enough force to roll it over.

Gairoth rose to his feet. Clods of mud and dried leaves stuck to his backside. "Gairoth squash you flat! Be like pudding! Haw! Too hungry to let you age right!" He raised the spiked club over his head to pound the sack.

Delrael prodded Journeyman's shoulder, but the golem was already in motion, striding through the trees and making no effort to hide himself. He swelled up his clay chest, contorted his facial features into an angry grimace, and cleared his throat. "What's all this, then?"

Gairoth bristled for a moment, stunned. He held the club in front of him.

Journeyman continued with a sigh of impatience. "Are you going to release that young fellow without any trouble, or must we go through the motions of humiliating you with a drawn-out defeat?"

Gairoth hefted the giant club on his shoulder like a baseball bat. "No talk! You trick Gairoth! I kill you!"

Journeyman waved his wide clay hands in a gesture of dismissal. "Go away, boy, you bother me. I'm not trying to trick you. I'm being perfectly up front with what I want. Give us the little man back, that's all."

"Bam!" Gairoth lurched one step forward, snarling.

Journeyman stood his ground. The expression on his face became cold and tough. He intoned in a low, threatening voice, "Go ahead, make my day!"

Gairoth swung the club down with all his might—and squashed Journeyman flat with a wet thud. The golem's head and chest caved in, oozing out to the side. He looked like a giant mud ball someone had stepped on.

Vailret let out a gasp of surprise. Delrael surged to his feet, blinking in shock. So much for the help the Rulewoman Melanie had sent them. He drew his sword and cried out.

"Gairoth!" The fighter charged into the clearing before he could think about what he was doing.

Gairoth stared down at the flattened golem with an expression of disappointment. But when he heard Delrael approach, his jaw dropped, then he grinned with angry glee. "Delroth!"

He pulled his club free of the wet clay with a sucking noise and turned to meet the fighter. "Haw! Haw!"

"Del! What are you doing?" Vailret called.

"Oh no," Bryl said.

But Delrael paid no attention. He landed with both feet spread, holding the sword out. He seemed pitifully small against the ogre. Vailret's father must have looked like this, fighting alone against an ogre—and dying.

"Gairoth be hurt by you!" Drool ran down the ogre's chin. "Cesspools gone, Rognoth gone.

Now I kill you! BAM!"

Delrael became acutely aware that he had worked out no plan for this situation. Maybe Vailret had a point in suggesting that characters think things through prior to taking action.

Before Gairoth could make good his threat and swing the club, Delrael lunged in. He slashed sideways and then up, cutting a gash on the inside of the ogre's thick arm. It was a minor wound, but it must have stung. Delrael skipped back, dodging forest debris.

As expected, Gairoth yowled in pain and swung with all his might, almost overbalancing himself. Delrael jumped out of the way and tried to run behind the ogre for another thrust. Maybe if he could slash Gairoth's other arm and make him drop the club—but the ogre swung his weapon again and Delrael had to block it directly with his sword. A crash rang through the forest.

Delrael's arm went numb from fingertips to shoulder. He couldn't even tell if he still held his sword or not.

Delrael shook his head, stunned. He tripped backward on some of the branches underfoot, rolling as he fell. The sword dropped beside him and he picked it up with his left hand. He didn't know how to fight left-handed.

"Haw! Haw!" Gairoth said.

"Are you guys going to help me or what!" Delrael shouted.

Bryl took out the Air Stone and the Fire Stone and shuffled them from one hand to the other. "Do something!" Vailret said.

Bryl said, "Which one should I use?"

"I don't care!"

Bryl picked up the Fire Stone, looked at it, then closed his eyes. He tossed it on the forest floor, hoping for a high number. He rolled a "1." His spell failed.

"Wouldn't you know it?"

"Gairoth, you big dummy!" Vailret cried out as he ran downhill into the hollow. It was an impulsive act, something Delrael might have done. He pulled out his short sword, though he had no idea what good it would do against the ogre. He slipped in the mud but grabbed branches to keep his balance and plunged on.

The ogre looked up, giving Delrael a moment to roll farther away. The rusty spikes on the club looked sharp, and thicker than Delrael's fingers.

From the sack, the point of an arrow emerged again, opening a gash. Little hands poked through and tore the material, sawing with the arrow tip, until the young ylvan poked his head through. He squirmed with his shoulders until he finally got the sack down about his waist. He didn't try to climb out, but instead grabbed his crossbow, nocked an arrow, and shot it.

The arrow struck the back of Gairoth's wide left leg. The ogre released the club with one hand and slapped at the arrow. In doing so, he let the heavy club fall to his side, banging his own knee.

Delrael climbed to his feet, propped on his sword. With his left hand, he bent the other arm to raise the blade and block another blow. His shoulders were trembling, and he knew he wouldn't be strong enough.

But behind Gairoth, the flattened bulk of Journeyman squirmed. The golem rose back up, reforming himself from the soft clay. Without a sound, he pushed his head and shoulders into shape out of the central mass of mud and drew more moisture from the soft forest floor.

His chest and legs rippled, redistributing the clay, flowing most of it into one forearm and fist that became as massive as the golem's body core itself, one giant hand the size of a heavy boulder.

"Just what the doctor ordered, Gairoth. Have a taste of your own medicine."

Before the ogre could turn in response, Journeyman slammed his huge fist down on Gairoth's head. "BAM! See how you like it."

The ogre's eye rolled up. His jaw dropped slack, and he tumbled like a falling tree, face first into the mud and leaves. His club fell beside him.

Journeyman slapped his palms together in finality. "How do *you* spell relief?"

They left Gairoth stone cold in the hollow as they hurried down the quest-path in the forest terrain.

"Glory hallelujah!" Journeyman babbled about his adventure. He tucked and nudged pieces of clay back into place. "Oh, what a feeling!"

"Yes, it was a good one, wasn't it?" Delrael said. He shook his tingling and sore right arm.

The ylvan man brushed off his camouflaged leather suit and took out a sewn cap that sported a red feather. "I'm not much for formalities, but my name is Tallin. Thanks for rescuing me—you did a good job against the big clod! It's nice not having to fight all by myself for a change."

"Rule number one, always have fun," Delrael said, shrugging his shoulders. They introduced themselves according to gaming protocol and each told his areas of expertise.

"Why were you the only one fighting against Gairoth?" Vailret asked. "Was something wrong with the others?"

Tallin strode ahead as if he knew where they were going. Delrael had trouble keeping pace with him.

"They were trying to fight. You saw them, and how sad it was. I didn't do anything but yell at Gairoth from the trees until he started wrecking things. The old man he pulled out of the nest was Tranor. He tells good stories and he knows more dice games than any character I've ever seen."

Tallin watched the forest floor, and his face bore a bemused expression. He rubbed his fingers together on the tip of his pointed beard.

"Tranor used to tell me stories about the old Sorcerer wars, how the ylvan once were the terrors of the forest, ambushing any enemy that entered our forest terrain. Hah!" Tallin sounded excited. "We could be invisible in the trees, and run up among the branches, shooting down with our arrows. We survived the Scouring, when some of you high-minded human characters decided to wipe out the other races on Hexworld."

Delrael looked for some resentment in the ylvan's eyes, but he saw none. After the Sorcerer race departed on their Transition, the remaining character races were left to fight over the map. Human characters rallied with some of the half-breed Sorcerers to defend against the reptilian Slac. Other human fighters, thinking themselves brave, went to extremes and tried to exterminate all other character races. In their fear and fanaticism, they struck at even the benign ones, like the ylvan or the panther people, the khelebar.

That was many turns ago, though, and Tallin did not seem to carry a grudge.

"I stayed with my people. *Somebody* has to take care of them, since they all seem to have knocked their heads against a tree too many times," Tallin said. "Even though they turned into a bunch of sore Losers even before they went into their daze. They stopped playing games for enjoyment. Kellos, our village leader, turned them sour, made them afraid and suspicious, for all the good it did them. They still succumbed to whatever put them in a daze anyway. They could have been having fun instead of worrying all that time. I've been getting food for them, since they don't seem to have any interest in doing it themselves."

Vailret repeated his original question. "But what's wrong with them? Why are they acting like that?"

Tallin knitted his eyebrows and looked at Vailret. "Do I look like someone who sits around and explains things all day? Normally, they would have fought like hornets, especially with Kellos stirring them up. Now, though, they're just sleepwalking—well, you saw. What's gotten into them? Is it some kind of spell? You tell me. I don't understand these things."

Vailret stared ahead, eyes fixed but unfocused on the little man's green cap. Delrael couldn't imagine any reason, but then Journeyman spoke up.

"Scartaris has the power to manipulate other characters with his mind, as if he is a Player in his own right. He can control actions, even from this great a distance."

Tallin looked at them, puzzled. "What's a Scartaris?" Nobody answered his question.

"Wonderful...." Bryl said. "What's going to stop it from happening to *us*?"

Delrael thought the Earthspirits in his belt might protect them, if the Spirits were even still alive.

"As a matter of fact," Bryl continued, "what protected Tallin? He should have been controlled just like the others."

Journeyman raised his lumpy eyebrows, like two hairless caterpillars arching themselves for battle. "Enquiring minds want to know."

"Maybe *he's* a spy, planted here to join our group and sabotage our quest," Bryl said. He glared at the little man.

"Bryl, you said that about Journeyman too." Delrael frowned at the half-Sorcerer with open skepticism.

"Look, I didn't *ask* you to come rescue me." Tallin flared his nostrils, angry and insulted, but he managed to hold his temper. Delrael admired that. "Are you suggesting I *pretended* to get captured by Gairoth? You've got mud for brains."

But Vailret's face carried a doubtful expression. "If your entire village was corrupted by Scartaris, how did you alone stay untouched?"

"Brilliant question. I probably never would have thought of that one myself!" Tallin looked at the rest of them with a haughty expression, and then turned to Delrael for support. "How should I know? I've told you the truth."

Delrael pursed his lips. "If he was working with Scartaris and the Outsiders, he'd make sure he had a good cover story."

"Good point," Journeyman said.

"Wait a minute." Vailret motioned with his hands for them to calm down. "We all know about some of the rulebreakers. Characters like Lellyn, and like Tarne. Maybe certain characters have a natural immunity, something Scartaris can't touch. It would fit with the Rules of Probability."

"Maybe this is Hexworld fighting back with flukes of its own, twists in the Game," Delrael said.

Vailret's eyes sparkled with the possibility. Delrael could see how intrigued he was by the idea. "And what if the Outsiders don't know anything about it?"

Delrael clapped the ylvan on the back to get them all moving again.

Tallin said, "Can you give me a hint about where we're going? I don't waste much time sitting around and planning things, but I wouldn't mind having the end goal in sight."

"My feelings exactly!" Delrael said, smiling.

"I take it that means you're joining our quest?" Vailret asked.

Tallin blinked. "You don't expect me to go watch the other ylvan stare at trees all day, do you? After they just watched Gairoth carry me off, I don't feel much attachment to home anymore."

The sun was low in the west, shooting its last rays between the tree trunks, when they neared the edge of the last hexagon they could travel in a day. A cool breeze sprang up from the east, rippling the forest leaves.

Just ahead, they could see the sprawling vista of the next hexagon, at last a break from the forest terrain. Flat, unpleasant-looking desolation spread out into the dusk. Delrael took a deep breath of the forest smells and knew that would all change the next morning when they crossed the black line into the rocky desert.

On their long walk, Delrael had warmed up to Tallin, a companion with whom he could discuss strategy, adventuring, and tactics. He explained about the Outsider David trying to end the Game, and of their quest to find a way to stop Scartaris. He said nothing about the Earthspirits hidden in his belt.

At camp, Tallin gathered wood, explaining how to stack it for a better fire. He refused to let Bryl use a spell and started the fire himself with a rough stone and the metal from his belt buckle. Annoyed, Bryl let him have his way.

Upon seeing the pack food his companions intended to eat, the ylvan snorted in disgust. Tallin secured the crossbow on his shoulder and scrambled up the trunk of a tree, finding fingerholds where none appeared visible. He called down from the branches, "This shouldn't take long." His mottled green clothes blended into the forest shadows and he vanished in the leaves.

Delrael lost three more games of Tic-Tac-Toe to Journeyman, tied one, and won one. Vailret played idly with his own set of dice. Tallin dropped down into the clearing, holding two quail. "Quite an improvement over standard pack food, especially stuff that's been replenished by a spell too many times."

Bryl looked miffed, but the prospect of fresh meat seemed to brighten him. He changed his mind, though, when he was assigned the task of plucking feathers. Tallin spitted the meat and left it to cook above the flames of the campfire, bowed over the heat on thin green branches. The smell was deliciously inviting as the quail sizzled in the smoke. They could hear the meat hissing against the burning wood.

"Is it finger-lickin' good?" Journeyman asked, watching them eat. They cleaned every bone on the two carcasses. "I can't believe you ate the *whole* thing!"

After the meal, Tallin piled wood on the campfire so it would burn all night. Journeyman remained on watch as the others brought out blankets, settling down on the leaves and forest grass to sleep. Bryl brushed branches away and moved three times before he found a comfortable spot. Tallin lay by himself in a light sleep.

Delrael propped his head against the smooth bark of a maple tree. He bent his knees, rubbing the pliable *kennok* wood of his left leg, and kept his feet warm by the fire as the autumn air cooled down for the night. The taste of the meal remained in his mouth, and he could smell the smoke from the low campfire. He looked at the young ylvan beside them and felt safe and content as he drifted off into sleep.

~

Gairoth listened to the pounding of drums inside his head. Pain made the bones in his skull vibrate. Leaves and dead grass stuck to his face. He pawed them away, smearing his cheeks and skin with muddy markings.

The ogre looked around the hollow. Delroth was gone. The torn, discarded sack showed him that the little ylvan had also fled—and Gairoth's sack was ruined. He had killed an old traveler for it, though he found little treasure inside. Now he would never find another sack.

Dark, speechless anger bubbled up in him, increasing the pain in his head. He sat up, holding hands against his temples to squeeze the pain back inside.

Rognoth, his pet dragon, was gone, chased far to the north by another dragon brought by Delroth. Bryl the magic user had taken away Gairoth's shiny diamond Air Stone. All the rest of his treasure was gone too, after his Maw had chased him away from the Stronghold.

And when he had tried to go home, Gairoth found a giant river right where his cesspools had been. Right where his *home* had been.

The ogre felt outraged, betrayed, saddened. The ylvan called him a Loser maybe that was true. But it was all Delroth's fault. Gairoth pounded both fists into the soft ground then clenched them in a stranglehold around the end of his club.

The ogre climbed to his feet. He had nothing else to do now.

His teeth hurt. His skin hurt. The inside of his head hurt. All of him hurt. Everything had been so nice before. Before Delroth had come.

Gairoth's mind fixed on the idea. He would take a quest of his own. It sounded right to him, a straightforward solution, something he could concentrate on and never forget. He would follow Delroth and find him, and then smash him with the club. BAM!

He stood up and, his stomach growling with hunger, he tossed aside the torn and empty sack. It had been a good sack. Gairoth found the footprints of the group along one of the clear quest-paths.

The ogre followed them.

∼

Tallin woke the others more than an hour before sunrise. He rubbed his little hands together in the crisp air and blew steam from his mouth. "Come on, let's get going." He nudged Bryl on the ground. "We've got a hex or two of desolation to cover. I've never been out of the forest before."

Bryl rubbed his eyes. "Whose quest is this anyway?"

Vailret held his hands over the still-warm embers of the fire. He flexed fingers that were red with cold.

"He's right." Delrael got up, stretched, then folded his blanket. "The terrain should be easy to follow."

Together, the five of them crossed the abrupt line that severed the hexagon of forest terrain from the desolation ahead. The lush health of the forest disappeared entirely, leaving the ground stricken with blight, dying away into a wasteland. The soil became barren and rocky. Stalks of prairie grass stood in brown patches, dotting the ground.

The coming dawn left a curtain of deep shadow on the flat terrain. The dark Spectre Mountains were visible in the distance as a black jagged silhouette blocking the rising sun. A few stars still prickled the deep blue dome of sky.

As they walked deeper into the hexagon, the dead earth became cluttered with oddly identical boulders, as if something had cut them out of the dirt and scattered them across the plain. The flat ground had a strange, patterned look ahead of them.

In the dim light, and with his poor eyesight, Vailret stumbled upon a series of deep hexagonal wells rimmed by a low mound six feet across. He caught himself, called out to the others, and stared down. The sharply defined hole plunged into the blackness of catacombs beneath the terrain.

"I can't tell what it is," he said.

Delrael picked up a rock and tossed it down. They heard it strike the bottom a moment later. "Not very deep," Delrael said. He tossed another stone at an angle. It pinged against the walls but gave no real hint about the depth of the tunnels.

"Could be just a labyrinth left over from the early days of the Game," Vailret said. "Back when characters did nothing but wander around in dungeons and catacombs, looking for monsters to fight and treasure to steal."

Tallin pointed across the desolation as the daylight grew brighter. "Do you see those other openings? I can make out at least a dozen more holes scattered around."

They moved ahead, and the wells became more and more frequent until they seemed like pores on the surface of the land, connected by an underground network of tunnels. "We've got a whole hexagon of this to cover?" Bryl said.

"Now I don't see why any character would want to leave the forest terrain," Tallin said.

"All this is starting to make me remember something," Vailret said. He slowed his pace, taking time to look around.

"Come on, I want to get out of this place," Bryl said. "Something unpleasant could crawl out of those holes."

"Don't worry. Be happy," Journeyman said.

"We're stuck anyway," Delrael said. "According to the map, there's another hex of desolation after this one, and we can't go any farther than that today."

Vailret nodded. "It's in Rule #5."

Bryl bit his lip and said nothing. He pulled the folds of his blue cloak tight around him. The orange dawn behind the Spectre Mountains looked like fire across the desolation.

Then, between a cluster of the hexagonal wells, they came across a place where the dusty ground was churned and broken. A glossy dark shape lay half buried in the earth.

Journeyman scooped dirt off the polished black form. "Holy ant farms, Batman!" The golem stood back, showing the uncovered carcass to the others.

Bryl gasped. Vailret squinted down, as if trying to remember something he had read. Delrael and Tallin were hard pressed to remain silent.

They gazed upon the dead hulk of an ant ten feet long. Its antennae appeared broken, but the hard exoskeleton retained its shape like a perfect suit of armor.

"Do you remember stories about the Anteds?" Vailret swallowed hard, "We could be in a lot of trouble here."

Tallin kicked at the carcass. "This one's dead enough."

"Yes, but we're standing on a whole *colony* of them." Vailret turned around, but the growing light was not enough for him to make out anything. "We may be better off running back to the last hex of forest terrain and going around the long way. We've got to make up our minds fast."

"I have a bad feeling about this," Journeyman said.

Delrael studied the gleaming black hulk. It wasn't exactly like an ant, but had stockier legs and more powerful joints to accommodate the increased size. He could kill one or two of the giant insects, given a few advantages, good luck, and time to fight.

But he couldn't take on an entire colony, not even with the assistance of his companions.

He looked across the desolation and a chill feeling went up his spine. He could see no end to the colony ahead. Every step they took, every movement they made, sent tell-tale vibrations to other Anteds waiting below.

A loud chirp echoed from one of the holes behind them, inviting an answer closer to their left. Another chirp sounded behind them.

The travelers drew themselves together, looking around. Tallin nocked an arrow in his crossbow. Delrael pulled out his sword, and Bryl removed his two Stones. Journeyman balled his fists into two battering rams.

"It's Howdy Doody time," the golem said.

The Anted chirps grew louder and more frequent, closer to them.

CHAPTER 7
CATACOMBS OF THE ANTEDS

All characters play games: dice games, games of skill, role-playing games. These things are for our amusement. But we also play power games, games for conquest, dominance, and victory—games of life and death.
—Preface, *The Book of Rules*

Delrael knew they would never make it across the colony that filled the open, desolate hexagon. They could sense the Anteds out there, coming nearer through the tunnels beneath them.

He pulled out his sword, bent his knees, and narrowed his eyes. Adrenaline pumped into his bloodstream, and time slowed down. His *kennok*-wood leg felt completely a part of him, ready to perform. He swallowed in a dry throat, prepared for battle. The excitement of the Game filled him.

"Wonderful," Tallin said. "I leave my forest to get eaten by bugs." The ylvan placed a small arrow in his crossbow and stood beside Delrael. His green-splotched forest camouflage made him look conspicuous on the rocky brown ground.

"Bryl, get ready with your Stones," Delrael said, not looking at the old half-Sorcerer. He swung his blade in the air, loosening his arm.

Bryl bit his lip and said nothing. He clacked the four-sided diamond and the eight-sided ruby together in the palm of his hand. His skin turned pale with fear.

Vailret pulled out his own short sword and stared down at the blade. He sighed and imitated Delrael's stance. Delrael knew his younger cousin lacked confidence, and interest, in fighting. Maybe that was why Vailret always wanted to plan things so far ahead of time, to minimize conflicts.

Delrael heard a clattering in the holes near them, a strange inhuman sound. A glistening black head rose up, waving antennae like stiff leather whips. Serrated jaws opened and closed like sabers on well-oiled hinges. The ant head swiveled back and forth, as if scanning them.

"Sufferin' succotash!" Journeyman said.

The Anted used powerful jointed legs to heave itself over the rim of the hexagonal mound. Two more insects climbed out of nearby holes. Orange dawn light flashed on their polished chitin. The insects chirped together with a pounding, grating rhythm. Other Anteds drew nearer.

Acting on his own desperation, Bryl took the Fire Stone, closed his eyes, and rolled it at his feet. "Give me luck this time!"

The eight-sided ruby landed in the soft dirt with the "4" facing up. Bryl clapped his hands and snatched the Fire Stone back, calling up the spell. He surrounded the five of them with a ring of fire that bloomed up from the rocky ground, bright and deadly, sealing them off from the Anteds. The nearest insects chittered and reared back.

"Safe as the Stronghold walls!" Bryl said.

"Would you mind explaining what good it does?" Tallin asked. "The Anteds just have to wait you out."

Bryl avoided the question. "I've got four more spells after this one."

Delrael paced back and forth, holding his sword. Behind the flames, another shape emerged from a tunnel opening, moving among the milling Anted forms. It looked human, or nearly so, and rode on the back of one of the insects. The part-human creature let out a series of guttural noises, poor imitations of the Anted chirps.

"What is that disgusting thing?" Tallin dropped his voice so Delrael could barely hear it over the din of insect chirps and the roar of the flames. "Is it a human character?"

The figure gestured and made more noises, as if barking orders. The bright flames made too many long shadows in the dim morning, masking out details.

Bryl wiped sweat off his forehead. His knuckles whitened as he strained to keep his wall of flames up.

"Looks like we don't have to wait anymore." Delrael shifted his grip on the sword.

An Anted thrust its head and forelimbs through the rippling wall of fire. Its antennae burned, smoking and writhing. The Anted collapsed with a moan like bending metal as its insides cooked within the black armor. Delrael heard popping and sizzling; a sour stench steamed up from cracks in the insect's shell.

Another Anted came forward, sacrificing itself next to the first. It tumbled, legs curled into the air. A third Anted died, completing a bridge across the fire.

Bryl squeezed the Fire Stone, trying to push the fire up through the insect bodies, but his spell faded. Bryl fell to his knees, exhausted, curling his lip to keep the fire burning. The flame died away, leaving only black and smoking rocks. He blinked, disoriented for a second, and hung his head. Other Anteds clambered over their fallen comrades.

Vailret turned around, squinting in the smoke and stench, trying to appear threatening with his short sword. Journeyman punched his fist into the palm of his other hand with a loud smacking sound.

Delrael touched his sword hilt, ready to die fighting. "Luck," he said to all of them.

The part-human character rode on the back of one Anted where he could survey the attack. The rider appeared to have been a human once, but was now stunted and twisted. His hair had fallen out in patches, and his eyes bulged wide and unblinking. His skin was pasty pale, as if he had been isolated from sunlight for years—but it also had an oily gleam when the light struck it at a certain angle. He wore plates of black chitin, broken shells from the Anteds, on his back and sides. The chitin looked as if it had grown in, rather than just tied on.

The part-human figure gestured in the air, showing fingers that had fused together. The nails had become solid and grown down over his knuckles in a hooked claw that resembled those of the Anteds.

"Wait!" Vailret called. "What do you want?"

The part-human creature rode his Anted through the other insects, emerging at the front. He cocked his head to look at them. He sniffed the air. His saucer-like eyes did not blink. The other Anteds pressed close beside him, gaping open their sharp jaws.

"Maybe we'd better not fight," Vailret whispered. He gestured for them to lower their weapons. "Just surrender for now."

Delrael remembered the role-playing game his father and Bryl had put him through on his eleventh birthday, making him imagine he had been taken captive by a tribe of vicious worm-men. Vailret had a similar role-playing adventure about being captured by the cruel reptilian Slac. "Are you sure you want to be taken alive?"

Vailret looked at him, and Delrael knew what he was thinking. Neither of them had survived their imaginary captivity in the vivid role-playing game.

"Looks like we're out of luck otherwise." Tallin rubbed his fingers at the point of his beard. "I wish I was back in the forest terrain. The ylvan were boring, but safe."

"I'd rather stay alive, if it's all the same to you," Bryl said.

Vailret called out again to the part-human creature. "We won't resist." He sheathed his short sword and motioned for Delrael to do the same. Tallin put his crossbow back on his shoulder.

Delrael stood motionless, uneasy. His empty hand fidgeted around the hilt of his sword. He shuffled his feet in the dust. He didn't like this at all.

"Take us to your leader," Journeyman said.

The part-human creature made a chuffing, chirping sound from the bottom of his throat. The circle of Anteds grew tighter until one opened its deadly mandibles around Bryl's waist. The half-Sorcerer fainted, slithering down into the grip of the ebony jaws. The Anted lifted Bryl's limp form into the air, then marched toward one of the tunnel openings.

Four more insects came forward for the rest of them. The Anteds stopped chirping.

Delrael ground his teeth together, so tense that he felt as if his muscles would snap. He wanted to lash out, to fight to the death—but his feet dangled uselessly below him when the Anted picked him up. He felt the insect's sharp mandibles even through his leather armor.

The jaws made gouges in the soft clay of the golem's skin, but Journeyman kept nudging the clay back into place.

The part-human dismounted and looked at the dead Anted hulk buried near where they stood.

With both hands, he lifted up the shell of the insect's head and, with a snap of his arms, he twisted it off the main body. With his hardened knuckles, he rapped on the chitin. The exoskeleton rang hollow, and dried, threadlike debris tumbled to the ground. Satisfied, he tucked the empty head under his arm like a trophy and scrambled back onto his mount.

The other Anteds moved forward and descended into one of the openings.

The tunnels slanted downward, twisting deep beneath the surface. Delrael wondered how far they could go before they struck the bottom of the map. The far walls of the tunnel flooded past into murk before and behind him.

The air held a thick musty odor of dust and claustrophobia. The walls were made of fused, gritty sand.

After his eyes became accustomed, Delrael realized the catacombs were not totally dark. Patches of fungus had been smeared on corners and near the curved ceilings, and these glowed with a faint green, barely enough to see by.

The ants covered a great distance in the tangled tunnels before climbing upward again. Delrael was sore and anxious to know what they would find at the end of the journey. The other companions did not speak.

The part-human creature dismounted and scampered ahead, at home in the tunnels. The insects began chirping to each other in a strange chant. The part-human made a loud imitation of the chirps himself, then used his hooked claw-hands to tear at his sides and under his arms. Lines of dried blood marked previous injuries on the stiff skin.

The Anteds carried them into a large sunlit grotto chiseled out of the cementlike walls. Delrael knew before he could blink the bright light out of his eyes that they had entered the queen's chamber. It was what he expected.

"And now for a word from our sponsor," Journeyman said.

The Anteds released their captives. Delrael staggered on numb legs and tingling feet. He rubbed his pinched sides to restore feeling. Journeyman smoothed the gouge marks from his clay torso.

A huge Anted spoke from an odd dais carved out of polished gray stone. "Consort, what have you brought your queen?" Her reedy voice was clicking and cumbersome.

The Anted queen's body was glossy black, but her head was polished liquid-smooth, completely without the many-faceted eyes of the other insects. Her mandibles were smaller, atrophied. Two thin, cellophane wings curled down beside her in a clear amber cloak.

Delrael scanned the throne room, automatically checking options for escape. Out of the corner of his eye, he watched Tallin do the same. He felt a rapport with the tough little ylvan.

In the streaming light from the wide opening overhead, many tunnels branched off from the other walls. Dust motes gleamed as they fell through the sunlight toward the floor.

The part-human creature set down the empty Anted head he had been carrying and crept forward. His lower jaw jutted out, and his words had a garbled whistling quality. "Ryx, Ryx, Ryx...."

"Are these to be alternative choices for me, Consort?" The queen ant spoke to the part-human creature. "Is that why you brought them?"

"No!" The consort-creature scrabbled forward in fear and awe, but eager. He walked on his hands and legs in a bucking, hunch-backed gait that looked oddly natural for him. Delrael saw wide, lumpy ridges along his ribcage, as if another folded set of limbs had begun to grow there.

Consort cooed and made his weird chirping noise as he crawled up to Ryx's feet. He ran his clawed fingers over her limbs, straightening the bristle hairs on her forelimbs. He nuzzled up, rubbing his hands along her abdomen, stroking her golden wings.

Ryx tilted her eyeless head back. Her small mandibles opened and closed. She emitted a high keening sound.

Consort pushed his face against her chitin plates, leaving a wet streak from his thick, damp tongue. "Ryx ... Ryx ... Ryx ..." he said. His claws scraped on her exoskeleton then reached between her mandibles with loving gentleness. He probed her mouth parts.

"I can't give you much more to eat," the queen said. "You will transform too quickly. I don't want to risk that. You are my consort—I don't want anything to go wrong."

"More, Ryx ... more. Hungry." Consort snuffled and whined.

"Just a sip." She reached out with her forelimbs to stroke the plates implanted in his back and the tattered shreds of hair on his head.

A whitish-gold syrup oozed from a channel in the inside of her mouth. Consort jerked forward, lapping it up. He thrust his head deep into the gap between her mandibles, humming and sighing.

Delrael watched in disgust. Bryl turned his head. The other Anteds stood guard around them, motionless.

"Enough!" Ryx pushed the part-human creature away. Rebuffed, Consort hunkered down in front of her. His clawed hands swayed loosely. "That is your reward. What have you brought me?"

Delrael realized Ryx had her head cocked off to the side, as if seeing through other eyes. Consort stared up at the huge queen ant in admiration, then tilted his head sideways to stare at the travelers with his bulging dry eyes.

"Five characters. Questers. One small, one old, one strong, one medium, and ... " He looked long at Journeyman. "And one made of mud."

Consort stood up as straight as he could, swaying his hooked hands around his kneecaps, then turned to face the motionless queen again. He stiffened, and Ryx's feelers vibrated with intense speed.

Ryx raised her head and continued in her humming voice. "A typical adventuring party. What is your quest?" Her polished head turned toward the wall behind the travelers.

Delrael fumbled in his mind, searching for a viable excuse, but his mind went blank.

Tallin's response was quicker. "We're just mercenaries. When the Game slowed down, this blasted peace put us out of work! We heard stories about a battle brewing in the east, and we're making our way there. Any problems with that?"

Ryx tilted her head toward the ylvan's voice for a long moment. Tallin stood defiant next to Delrael. Journeyman looked flat and emotionless; Vailret bit his lip; Bryl scrambled up from his daze on the floor, looking around in fear. The queen of the Anteds shifted her blank head toward the half-Sorcerer.

"You are no mercenaries. That one's afraid of his own reflection."

Ryx vibrated her antennae again with a thin humming sound. The noise bounced around the walls of the grotto. Delrael felt a strange finger poking at the inside of his mind, ferreting out his private memories. Tallin touched his hands to his forehead.

Ryx squatted back on her polished dais. Delrael didn't know how to read any emotion on her face, but her voice hinted at laughter. "You intend to destroy Scartaris? *Five* of you think you can defeat his armies and defenses?"

Delrael flushed in anger. "I didn't say that!"

"Not only that, but the Earthspirits are hiding in your belt, and you intend to take them secretly to Scartaris, where the Spirits will be unleashed to battle him."

Delrael clamped his mouth shut. Bryl let out a quiet moan of despair. Journeyman gawked in shock at Delrael, the silver belt, then the queen Anted.

"Scartaris will reward me for this," Ryx said, tapping her forelegs together. "Consort, remove the belt."

Delrael drew his sword and crouched, looking from side to side and daring the Anteds to come closer. He stepped away from the consort-creature. The lights grew dim around him as he focused his attention on the sword, on any enemy that might come.

"Try it, Ryx! We'll cause more damage than your Anteds have ever seen."

Following Delrael's lead, Journeyman drew himself up, ready to fight. Vailret and Tallin both pulled out their weapons, and Bryl held the Fire Stone. Nobody looked eager for battle. Three Anteds came forward, clacking their jaws but hesitating. The air around them crackled with tension.

The queen lifted her featureless head. "Stop! Consort, you stay away from those weapons. Take them all down to the fungus chambers and hold them there. I need to decide what to do with them."

Consort scampered forward, clutching at Delrael's arm. The fighter snatched the claw-hand away, sweating and looking at the gathered insects. "Come," Consort said. "Come."

The Anted guards backed away from one of the catacomb openings. "You will not resist," Ryx said in a brittle voice. "You have already stretched my patience to its limits."

Delrael looked at the queen, at the other Anteds, then sheathed his sword. "We don't have any choice, again," he said. "We never get to *do* anything in this adventure."

Journeyman restored his swollen fists to normal size. "He who fights and runs away, lives to fight another day."

Consort snatched up the empty shell of the Anted head he had found and swayed forward, walking like an insect. He turned once to see that the others followed him. One of the giant ants entered the passage behind them, keeping watch.

Consort capered ahead of them, exuding coiled power and nervous energy. The tunnels wound downhill again until they saw only the dim greenish light from patches of fungus on the wall. Occasionally, an Anted poked its massive head out of side tunnels, watching the captives' progress. Delrael could sense other insects following in the darkness of the tunnels behind them. Somehow, in her great hive mind, Ryx watched through all of their eyes.

Delrael kept the directions filed away in his mind. As a questing character, he could recall exactly where he had been and how to retrace his steps. He kept his eyes open for any way they might escape or defeat the Anteds, ready to act on it without thinking if an idea came to mind.

They crossed a hex-line etched into the passage, up the walls, and across the ceiling over their heads, as if the Anteds had directly through the black mark that went to the base of the map. "That's half of the desolation hexes," Tallin said. "Things can start getting better now."

The green light grew brighter ahead. Consort turned the corner, leading them to the glowing opening of a wide chamber. Light streamed from it.

"In," he said. He swung his curved hands, gesturing them with his fused fingers. "In, in, in!"

Dripping growths of fungus covered the chamber walls. Mounds of dead things, mulched and unidentifiable, nourished the phosphorescent fungus, food for the Anteds. A wet, rancid smell made the air thick and difficult to breathe.

"What will Ryx do to us?" Bryl asked.

Consort looked up and bobbed his head, grinning. "Eaten. Fresh. Or added here." He bucked his shoulder to indicate the mounds under the fungus.

Vailret tapped one of the ingrown plates on the part-human's back. "Consort, what is your real name? Do you remember?" he asked.

"Consort," the part-human said. "Consort." He shuffled ahead and did not look back at them.

"No, I mean your name as a human character. Do you remember when you first came to Ryx?"

"Ryx!" Consort lifted his eyes up in a worshipful expression. "Made me Consort. Feeds me."

"She's changing you into ... this," Vailret said, "with what she's feeding you."

"Seems to be wrecking his mind too," Tallin snorted.

"I wandered map. Scavenger," Consort said. "Then found Ryx."

He seemed lost in memory, trying to piece together the scattered dice game of his mind. He raked a curved claw-hand across his scalp, tearing up patchy hair. In the green light, Consort's skin looked black and glistening, inhuman.

"Do you remember back then?" Vailret said. "Did you play any games?" He took out his set of dice. Something registered in Consort's eyes when he stared at the dice.

"Games?" Vailret repeated. "Do the Anteds play games with you? Here, let me show you." He rolled the dice. "You have to guess which number will come up. See?" He rolled again.

"Games..." Consort said. His head drifted from side to side, fixing his saucer eyes on the dice.

"Del, come here," Vailret whispered. The two of them played a dice game. Consort did not join in, but he watched with his full attention.

"Or how about this one?" Using Tallin's dagger, they sketched a grid on the floor. Delrael and Journeyman played Tic-Tac-Toe.

As Consort watched, old thoughts finally seemed to break through. "Ryx never plays games. Not these."

"But you used to like to play games, didn't you?" Vailret said. "All human characters do. Here- -roll the dice yourself. Play with us."

Consort awkwardly held the dice in his cupped claws. As he noticed his fused fingers, another thought seemed to jar loose. He stared down at his hands, as if puzzled at what could have happened to them.

They played a few rounds with the dice. Consort went through the motions, obviously not quite grasping what he was doing, but Vailret and Delrael arranged it so that he won the round. Consort's excitement grew, and he became more and more interested.

If only they could be sure Ryx was not watching through *his* eyes too.

"How'd you like to play another game?" Tallin said, grinning so that his pointed beard jutted out. His forest-patterned clothes had lost all their colors in the green light. He winked at Delrael. "You must have played this one, Consort. It's fun, and you'll probably win because you have the advantage."

"Game?" Consort's bulging eyes never blinked as he cocked his head from side to side. "Game?"

Tallin flashed a toothy grin. "It's called hide and seek."

"Yes." Delrael picked up the conversation, fixing on the ylvan's idea. He liked the way Tallin's mind worked. "It's more fun than dice. You stay here and give us time to hide. We'll go out into the catacombs, then you try to find us! Once you find all of us, then you can hide, and we'll try to find you."

"Rule number one, you know," Vailret said. "Always have fun."

"Hide and seek." Consort stood up and made his eerie chirping noise again. "Games."

"All right, stay here and cover your eyes. Wait a long time now; otherwise, it won't be fair. Then you come find us." Delrael smiled but turned his head to the side. "Go!"

Consort hunched by the glowing fungus. He tapped his claw-hands on the hard floor, buzzing to himself. He couldn't close his saucer eyes, but he stared at the wall.

They ran into the dimness, not knowing where they were going. "Head uphill," Delrael said.

"And be quiet," Tallin added. "If we don't bump into any Anteds, Ryx won't know where we are."

At each intersection of tunnels, they chose the one tending upward. Delrael ran with sword drawn. "We have to kill any Anteds right away, before they can signal to more."

They lost their sense of time. Without seeing daylight above, they had no idea how far they had come or how long they had been down in the catacombs. Delrael's sword felt a part of him. His wooden *kennok* leg did not tire. The companions pushed on. Their eyes were wide, their lips white, their teeth pressed together in determination.

He knew they would encounter an Anted soon, very soon. He hoped they could find their way to the surface first.

The hazy green light increased the shadows around them, offering too little illumination to see anything sharply. The air was dense and warm, stifling. Delrael couldn't seem to get enough breath.

His senses were keyed up to a fever pitch. He picked up motion in a tunnel to their right, something trying to move quietly. And then, in the dim light, he saw the clear outline of an Anted head moving forward, ready to spring—

Delrael swung his sword and thrust forward as he plunged in faster than he could think. He hoped the sharp point of the old Sorcerers' blade would break through the chitin and strike something vital in the Anted. The sword plunged home more easily than he had expected, and he twisted the hilt, driving upward. Something was wrong.

"Found you..." said Consort, then he made a gurgling sound of delayed pain.

His hollow Anted helmet slipped off his head and clattered to the floor of the catacombs.

Delrael withdrew the blade and released his grip on Consort's shoulder. The blade caught on one of the implanted armored plates, peeling it from his skin and exposing soft jelly-like tissue. Consort slumped bleeding to the floor.

"Ryx ..." The breath rattled in his throat, gurgling. He made his inhuman chirping sound again before he died.

Delrael stared down at what he had done. He felt more shaken than he thought he should. His mouth was dry, and it hurt when he tried to swallow.

Tallin reached out to grip Delrael's wrist. "We have to get out of here. One less spy to deal with."

"Ryx might know what's happened," Vailret said.

They ran, taking less care to remain silent now. They turned a dozen more times, lefts and rights, and finally, they came to one passage that sloped sharply upward.

A bright golden-blue light sifted through one of the cross-ventilation holes near the ceiling of the tunnel, just above Delrael's eye level. He stood on his tiptoes and looked. "I can see a way out on the other side of this wall."

"No way we can get there." Vailret scowled up at the light. The hole was less than a foot wide, too small for anyone to worm through. "It doesn't do us any good."

"It's close enough," Delrael said. "I'm not going to wander around here anymore. We can get through this."

He used the hilt of his sword to pound at the edges of the opening. The fused sand chipped away and broke, crumbling loose as he worked. "Journeyman, help me."

He moved to one side, allowing room for the golem. Journeyman grasped the edges of the hole and began ripping away chunks of the cementlike sand.

"It might be wide enough for Tallin to squeeze through," Delrael said.

The ylvan came forward, raising his arms as Delrael lifted him to the hole. "Get away if Ryx comes after us."

Tallin glanced at him, then worked his shoulders into the narrow opening, squirming through. "No, I'll wait for you on the other side." The ylvan pulled himself out. "Just don't dink around —Hurry up!"

His knees and feet disappeared through the hole, and they heard him drop to the floor. Delrael passed the little man's quiver and crossbow through to him.

"The opening to the surface is too high for me here. I can't reach it to climb out. Anybody got a ladder?"

Delrael and Journeyman worked furiously widening the hole. "Your turn, Bryl! You can fit."

The half-Sorcerer stood up, appearing uneasy. He brushed at the sides of his cloak and straightened his white hair and beard. Delrael wondered why he looked so frightened.

"I don't like to be separated. Especially not here."

Delrael urged him to the wall. "We'll be with you in just a few minutes. Don't worry."

With a boost from Journeyman, Bryl crawled through the tunnel, scraping his shoulders and elbows. He fell to the floor on the other side then scrambled to his feet. Tallin crossed his arms over his chest and watched the work on the other side of the wall. Daylight from the opening overhead gleamed down, blinding and bright after their hours in the green dimness.

Journeyman worked in silence, but the chipping of steel against stone rang out along with Delrael's grunts of effort. Another noise suddenly joined it. Delrael paused to listen.

Tallin called up through the wall. "The Anteds are coming on *this* side!"

More sounds echoed from other tunnels, like a melodic battle cry. Twelve deadly black insects emerged from different tunnels in the maze.

"Delrael, hurry up!" Bryl said. "I don't think my spells will be enough."

Delrael did not answer them, grunting as he pounded with the hilt of his sword. Sweat streamed down his forehead, and his arm ached. He gritted his teeth and paid no attention.

Tallin slipped his crossbow off his shoulder and nocked an arrow. He removed a dagger from his belt and, without taking his eyes from the Anteds, thrust it hilt-first at Bryl.

"Take this! If you run out of spells, you'll need something to defend yourself with. I'll be too busy to worry about you."

Bryl slipped the dagger up his flowing sleeve. He withdrew the Fire Stone and rolled it at his feet. A "2."

"It's better than nothing," Bryl said. He grabbed up the ruby and held a roaring fireball in the palm of his hand. He waited for the Anteds to make the first move. "I've only got three spells left."

Tallin's eyes flashed as he crouched. He turned in slow circles, watching the insects.

All twelve Anteds rushed at once. Their claws clicked on the hard floor. Tallin shot at the foremost Anted, sinking his arrow up to the fletching in a faceted eye. The Anted wheezed and collapsed, oozing a green blot of ichor. Bryl hurled the blossoming ball of flames to explode in the face of one of the black creatures. Tallin slipped another arrow into the crossbow and fired, but it struck the hard insect armor at an angle and bounced off.

Bryl managed to summon up a smaller fireball with the remainder of the weak spell, and drove off another Anted.

Tallin flipped a third arrow out of his quiver, trying to fit it into the crossbow. An Anted lunged up behind him and opened its jaws.

"Look out!" Bryl cried.

The ylvan whirled as the mandibles clamped around his waist, lifting him high in the air. "Put me *down!* Bug-Eyes!" Tallin pounded on the armored head, slapping the curved surfaces of the eyes. The jaws tightened like scissors around him.

Alone in the echoing throne room, Ryx stared through the eyes of her Anteds in a choreographed confusion of overlapping images inside her head. She shifted her bulk against the smooth and cold texture of the dais.

The bitter taste of Consort's death was like bile in her mind. Everything was lost. They had killed Consort. They had killed her chance.

She sent out a command to all the Anteds.
Kill.

Tallin squirmed, pulling one of his arrows free. He pointed the tip downward to plunge it into the insect's head.

But then the jagged mandibles closed together, shearing through flesh and bone.

Tallin's eyes bulged as the sharp jaws crushed his abdomen. Blood spurted from his mouth.

"Delrael!" he screamed. His crossbow clattered to the floor. Dark red splashed on the Anted's black armor.

"Tallin! No!" Delrael's muscles locked from the sick ice at the pit of his stomach. He could do nothing. He wanted to scream and pound his fists against the walls. He strained to see among the swarming masses of black hulks on the other side. "*No!*"

The Anted shook Tallin's body back and forth like an alligator would, then it released him. The ylvan hit the curved tunnel wall, sliding down at the head of his own trail of blood.

Another insect sprang up to take Bryl in its jaws.

CHAPTER 8
QUEEN'S FLIGHT

RULE #11. When a character fails in combat, he or she may die. Death is final in the Game—that character can never play again.
—The Book of Rules

Bryl could not reach the Fire Stone. He had rolled his spell, but the ruby lay untouched and gleaming on the ground. The Anted squeezed its jaws and lifted him into the air.

In a blur, Bryl's hand snatched out the dagger Tallin had given him. Without pausing to think, he struck down, pushing the blade deep into the Anted's compound eye.

The insect let out a shrill scream, gaping its mandibles. Bryl dropped to the floor on limp legs, holding both elbows against his ribs where blood from torn skin seeped into his blue cloak. A wet stink came from the Anted's gushing wound. Bryl stumbled backward and grabbed the Fire Stone from the floor.

With more power than he realized he possessed, he blasted the wounded Anted into shards of chitinous armor and dripping tissue. The noise and flash of heat rippled through the tunnels, making him wince and back away.

"Delrael!" he called, but he was so frightened that it made his voice only a hoarse whisper. The other Anteds closed in. He wrung as much out of the spell as he could, roasting another two insects. Burning chitin popped and sputtered.

But Bryl's spell faded away, leaving him defenseless again. He pressed his back against the curved catacomb wall.

Beside him, Tallin lay in a pool of blood.

"Tallin!" Delrael's scream was hoarse, but he expected no answer. And received none. He heard only the scuffle of clawed feet, the sounds of Bryl's fire. The stench of burning Anteds came through the wall opening.

Delrael's shock gave way to rage. Sweat ran into his eyes from his dust-clumped brown hair.

"Journeyman can reshape himself and squeeze through!" Vailret said. "He can help Bryl."

"Go!" Delrael shouted.

In a quick gesture, the golem clapped a supportive hand on Delrael's shoulder. "Here's looking at you, kid." Then he elongated himself, stretching the clay into the opening. His feet slithered through and he reshaped himself on the other side, bulging and eager for battle. He balled his clay fists and scrambled into the fray.

Delrael chipped at the wall and listened to the sounds of the fight. Tallin lay dying on the other side.

He smashed the hilt down against the cement-sand, and a thin fracture line appeared. Smaller pieces of the wall flaked off. He could smell his sweat and the dust; his fingers began to sting and bleed. He and Vailret both grasped the rim of the hole and pulled, bumping into each other to get a better grip. A crumbling chunk broke off, falling with the loose sand to the tunnel floor.

"Come on!" Delrael crawled up through the hole. He scraped his elbows against the rough cement-sand, but he pushed his sword in front of him. He hooked his arms over the other side, then heaved himself through, banging his hip and scuffing his leather armor. He dropped beside Bryl with the grace of an acrobat.

He saw Tallin's twisted body on the floor. The ylvan's blood looked thick and dark in the harsh light angling through the opening overhead. He should have thought ahead, planned better.

"Tallin," Delrael said once more, then set his jaw. Holding the sword like a club in front of him, he strode forward at the Anteds. Delrael's ears pounded with a rushing of blood. He chopped with his sword. Vaguely, he became aware of the golem next to him hammering with his fists.

An Anted lunged at Journeyman, and the golem met it with a tightly clenched fist, splintering the chitin of its head in a rayed pattern like a spiderweb.

"It takes a licking and keeps on ticking!" The Anted flowed to the floor as all six legs went limp. "Hmmm, I guess not."

Delrael noticed the periphery of the battle with only enough awareness to avoid any unexpected threats. Bryl squeezed his eyes shut and rolled the eight-sided ruby again. Vailret had elbowed his own way through the hole and jumped toward one Anted, stretching his short sword out to lop off the insect's antennae. Reeling and disoriented, the Anted did not know how to defend itself, leaving it open to Vailret's stab to the brain.

An Anted lunged at Journeyman, jaws gaping wide like a steel trap. The golem braced himself, catching the pincers with his hands, and he spread the viselike jaws. The insect struggled to back away, but still Journeyman applied his strength. After a loud snapping sound, the golem released his hold to watch the ant fall among the others on the floor.

Delrael searched for another insect as the first ant head tumbled to the floor. The decapitated body struggled awkwardly before crumpling. His mind saw only the red of Tallin's blood.

Three more fell. Another exploded in flames as Bryl succeeded with his fourth spell for the day.

One insect circled around behind Delrael, opening its jaws. But Journeyman was there, leaping up and straddling the Anted's back. "Oh, a wise guy, eh? Nyuk, nyuk, nyuk!" He grasped the ebony mandibles and pulled backward. His clay muscles rippled, stretching the Anted's neck grotesquely out of its socket until the pale connecting fibers popped apart.

The last of the chirping noises fell silent. Motionless hulks of the dead insects littered the floor, making it slippery with spattered ooze. No other Anteds appeared.

Delrael pushed his way past the fallen insect bodies.

Tallin.

Bryl was already bent over the ylvan. Delrael kneeled, staring, then he reached forward to brush blood away from Tallin's mouth. Delrael was shaking. He dropped his sword with a clang on the hard floor.

The ylvan's eyes trembled, then flickered open. The pupils were dilated, unfocused. Blood welled up inside them from ruptured capillaries, but still they held a glimmer of life. Tallin's cheeks twitched.

Vailret's voice came over Delrael's shoulder, quiet and compassionate, but also practical.

"We need to get out of here, Del, before Ryx sends more Anteds."

Delrael rose to his feet and turned on his cousin with such a terrible expression on his face that Vailret stepped backward, stumbling on the slippery floor. He caught himself against the wall.

Delrael slumped forward, shaking his chest as he contained his words, everything he wanted to say. He'd had many adventures, but he had never faced the death of a companion. Questing had been too much fun to worry about things like that. Rule number one—always have fun! It seemed like such a ridiculous thing now.

His father Drodanis had watched an ogre murder his brother Cayon. Vailret was beside Paenar when the blind Scavenger sacrificed himself at the volcano. But Delrael had never looked at death face to face before, never watched as the Outsiders removed a character from the Game permanently.

Delrael swung his fist in the air at some intangible foe. The Outsiders had to be watching. "What sort of Game are you playing with us! Why? Are you having fun?" His shoulders trembled. "Tallin…"

The ylvan's bloody lips parted, forming words like the last wind from a dying storm. Delrael bent his ear close to Tallin's mouth.

"Take my crossbow and … use it."

Delrael squeezed Tallin's shoulder, trying to impart some energy back to the ylvan. He had been near death once himself, when the Cyclops attacked him near Ledaygen, but Thilane Healer of the khelebar had replaced his mangled leg with one made of *kennok* wood.

But they had no healers here now, nothing to help Tallin.

"Delrael … I'm glad I knew … you."

Something like a sigh escaped Tallin's lips, and Delrael stared intensely into the ylvan's black eyes. He held on to the camouflaged leather of his jerkin. The cap with the single scarlet feather had fallen off, lying on its side against the wall.

Tallin's gaze lifted, filled with tears of pain, and his eyes met Delrael's once before the ylvan departed.

Delrael froze as ice worked its way up from his gut into his veins and muscles. He stared into the ylvan's lifeless eyes before he lifted his hand to brush Tallin's cheek. A smear of blood dried on the back of his hand.

Silence rang in his ears. No one said anything to him. Delrael drew a deep breath, trying to calm himself, but it didn't work. He stood up, brandishing the old Sorcerer sword at anything that could hear him.

"Damn you, Ryx!" He hung his head. "You and all the Outsiders too."

His words bounced off the sides of the silent tunnel, vanishing into the distance. Bryl had recovered the Fire Stone and cowered beside Journeyman. The golem stood motionless among the destroyed Anteds, waiting to see what would happen next.

Keeping his eyes lowered to hide his fury from the others, Delrael snatched up Tallin's fallen crossbow and fumbled in the torn quiver. He found one unbroken arrow.

Delrael withdrew it and held it in his trembling hands, watching as two drops of Tallin's blood fell to the floor. Sheathing his sword, he tightened his hand around the arrow and took the crossbow with him. "This is all I'll need to kill Ryx."

Delrael went back to the hole in the wall from which they had come. Without another word, he pulled himself up.

"What are you doing?" Bryl said. He scrambled to his feet. Vailret looked as if he wanted to grab Delrael and pull him back.

"I'll have to retrace our steps so I can get back to the throne room." He vanished into the hole and dropped to the other side. "You can come along or not. I don't care."

Delrael fixed his gaze straight ahead, not even glancing at any of the side tunnels. His mouth felt dry and raw, but he used that to increase his anger. The others followed without doubting his skill—Delrael had been on enough gaming campaigns that he knew instinctively which tunnels they had taken.

Behind him, he heard the harsh whispers of his companions. Bryl complained about going to certain death, Vailret vowed not to let Delrael face it alone, Journeyman wanted to continue his own quest to Scartaris, but he also knew the way Hexworld adventures were done. "Ask not what your country can do for you, but what you can do for your country."

Delrael retraced their convoluted flight through the catacombs. He did not care about escaping. He only wanted Ryx. His revenge had a clear target. Ryx had been the cause of Tallin's death.

Ryx.

Delrael did not pause when they passed Consort's stiffening body at the intersection of cross tunnels. Things were different now —he remembered Tallin touching him on the elbow, telling him not to feel guilty about striking down the part-human creature. He listened to his sharp footsteps, steady and determined.

The tunnels sloped upward again, and Delrael strode toward the throne room. His anger had not begun to fade. Tallin's death sent jabs of pain through his chest. The wound would have to be cauterized—by the death of the queen.

They crossed back over the underground hex-line, but still they encountered no Anteds. It was too easy. Bryl moaned that it was a trap. Delrael knew he was probably right.

When they finally reached the throne room, he did not slow. The others waited where the tunnels opened into the vaulted grotto, but Delrael strode ahead without stopping to think. He didn't want to think right now. His eyes burned.

He made no attempt to hide himself or to approach quietly. His boots made loud noises on the hardened floor. He curled his lips as he saw the queen Anted alone on her granite dais.

"I've come to kill you, Ryx." Delrael's voice dripped ice. "For murdering Tallin."

The queen turned quickly, pivoting her massive eyeless head toward him. She made a thin, warbling noise that Delrael could not interpret.

"After you killed my Consort and sixteen of my Anteds, how can *you* want revenge?" Her head bobbed in a convulsive motion and her short feelers waved in the air like whips underwater. "You could have escaped hours ago."

Delrael didn't flinch. "Without you to control them, Ryx, these Anteds would not have attacked."

Ryx drew herself up on the throne, leaning forward and extending two claw-tipped legs. "Without me to control them, they would not be able to move! They are all parts of *me*, controlled by me."

Ryx turned sharply, quivering her antennae. Sunlight from the opening above dappled her bullet-smooth head. "What? Another intruder? I thought no one went on quests anymore."

She pulled the bristly hair from her forelimbs through the inner parts of her mouth, cleaning and combing them. She turned her attention back toward Delrael. Ryx hesitated, as if lost in memories and blanketed in her blindness.

"By killing Consort, you destroyed my chances to form another colony. A character race that could have surged across the map and risen to dominance even against Scartaris's armies. Stronger than human characters, stronger even than the Slac."

She rocked up from the stone dais. Her golden wings straightened to keep her balance. Ryx's mandibles opened and emitted a thin hiss. "He was to be my Consort! I was developing him—he could never have changed entirely, but I would have borne him on a mating flight.

"Our colony of children would have had the strength and armor class of the Anteds, but also the intelligence, independence, and agility of humans! Hexworld could have been ours—but you destroyed him!"

The queen tapped her two forelegs together. A group of Anteds emerged in silence from other branching tunnels. As they approached, Ryx relaxed and seemed more aware—she could see now through their eyes. Delrael held Tallin's crossbow but did not take his gaze from the winged queen.

"Faster than a speeding bullet!" Journeyman shouted as he charged, swinging his battering-ram fists. He picked up one Anted and threw it at the others, knocking them back. "How do you like them apples?"

But more Anteds came. Journeyman smashed a head, whirling in time to kill another insect. The golem stood within the flood of monsters, flailing both arms, smashing and killing, as the Anteds drove in from all sides.

Vailret ran at those on the edges, slashing away their antennae and leaving them disoriented and blinded.

The insects squealed as a wall of flame erupted within their ranks, exploding their polished black bodies from within. Bryl grasped the Fire Stone, red in the face and sweating with his last spell for the day. But for a moment, the Anteds were knocked back out of the queen's chambers.

Ryx appeared stunned, driven against her chair. She leaned forward and drummed her amber wings. Springing up with her powerful hind legs, the queen launched herself into the air. Her eyeless head turned from side to side, but with no other Anteds in the chamber, she could not see around her.

Her wings thrummed as Ryx rose toward the exit hole in the ceiling. "I thought I would keep one of you as my new Consort, but it would not be the same. He is dead. You killed him."

No other Anteds had pushed their way into the chamber yet. Delrael felt a calmness inside, a confidence in the approaching victory.

Ryx veered away and winged upward to escape. She could not defend herself, she could not see. Disoriented and relying on her memory, the queen Anted misjudged the exit hole above. Powerful wings brought her crashing into the jagged ceiling of the grotto. Stunned, Ryx reeled downward.

In the tunnels outside the throne chamber, other approaching Anteds froze in their tracks with no guiding force. They swayed on their feet while Ryx tried to overcome her dizziness. Delrael saw his chance.

Ryx flopped her wings to keep aloft. A thin crack showed in the polished black head. Ryx ascended again, laboring with her wings to circle around the throne room in an uncertain spiral, hoping to stumble upon the way out.

Delrael fitted his blood-tipped arrow into the crossbow.

Disregarding the approaching Anteds, ignoring everything else except for the memory of Tallin and the sight of the ylvan's death, he lifted the crossbow and pulled at the small trigger. "This is for you, Tallin."

In her circling flight, Ryx turned to face the fighter without knowing it. She did not see him, or his arrow.

Delrael shot the crossbow.

Gairoth covered his ears against the insane chirping and roared in annoyance. Spittle sprayed from his thick lips. He swung his club, breaking one of the attacking Anteds into pieces. Others crawled out of their hexagonal openings and swarmed toward him.

"Go away!" The ogre smashed another, then tripped on one that lay dead at his feet. "Stupid bugs!"

He had followed Delroth's easy trail across the barren soil, but then the tracks disappeared near one of the holes. Gairoth searched for hours, muttering in frustration. He couldn't follow the mixed-up insect tracks, and he couldn't see anything down in the dark holes. He didn't want to climb down there. He sat down in the dirt and imagined the things he could do to Delroth.

And then the Anteds came.

Gairoth's club dripped clotting ooze. He pursed his lips and dared the insects to come closer.

The Anteds were unimpressed and took the dare. Gairoth roared his best battle cry and smashed black chitin. Gairoth wished his dragon Rognoth were there to help.

The ogre's arm began to tire, and he could not knock the Anteds away as quickly as they rushed at him. They swarmed over piles of twitching bodies, pulling him down.

"Stupid bugs!" Gairoth battered at hard chitin with his clumsy hands, but he could not throw the giant creatures off him, could not break the grip of the jaws that wrapped themselves around his thick neck, legs, and arms, like scissors ready to cut him to pieces.

Delrael watched his arrow as it passed through the air in a perfect arc. Ryx's mandibles spread wide as if to receive a gift.

The arrow plunged through her mouth, deep into the soft membranes and delicate tissues. The tip embedded itself in the most vital organ, the brain controlling the Anted colony. The small point of the arrow protruded through the chitin at the back of Ryx's head.

Green blood squirted out of her mouth, mixed with the queen's whitish-gold jelly. The brittle armor of her body shattered on the rock floor.

The Anteds in the tunnels collapsed in their tracks.

Bryl panted then slumped down to sit on the floor. He held the Fire Stone in pale, trembling hands. Journeyman stood in front of the ranks of dead Anteds, nudging and smoothing the gouges in his clay skin. Vailret brushed off his tunic, then leaned against a curved wall, propping the blade of his short sword against his leg. He blinked again and again, but his eyes remained wide, unable to believe how he had fought.

Delrael stared at the dead hulk of Ryx lying on the floor like a broken toy, but his eyes saw nothing. "For you, Tallin," he whispered. Delrael rolled his tongue around his mouth, trying to discover some pleasure in the slaughter. Somehow, this hadn't held the thrill and fun that adventures were supposed to have. Was he breaking the primary Rule now? Wasn't this supposed to be fun?

The Game had changed all at once, like a slap in the face. Delrael had always assumed that he would survive, that the Game would go on forever, and the characters would keep playing. He had lived through difficult adventures—against the dragon Tryos, against Gairoth and his illusion army, even against the forest fire and the Cyclops that had destroyed Delrael's leg.

But Tallin had not survived.

He raised his eyes to the ceiling of the grotto and lifted the empty crossbow in salute. His mouth was a grim line, making the muscles of his neck stand out. Turning, he spat at the queen Anted's broken body.

Delrael stood with a stiff back and rigid limbs beside Tallin's body. He molded his emotions into a flat mask. Slaughtered Anteds lay as they had fallen, but Delrael paid no attention. A thick, wet smell of death hung in the air.

The others stayed by the wall, watching Delrael. He looked into the ylvan's motionless, pale face. Blood and Anted grease caked his own clothes and hands. The heavy air made him sick to his stomach.

Delrael drew his sword, scribing a rectangle on the floor. He began chipping away at the fused sand, scooping hunks away into a pile. The sand underneath was a brighter, fresher color than the packed floor.

Vailret came forward. "Can we help?"

Lost in his thoughts, Delrael jumped and stared at him, disoriented, before answering, "No. This is for me to do."

He went to Tallin's body, removing the small quiver from the ylvan's back, and set it with Tallin's crossbow next to the newly cut grave. He picked up the body, trembling as he touched the cold skin. He laid Tallin in the shallow hole, then straightened his arms and legs.

"He would rather have been buried in a forest somewhere, I think." Delrael fought back anger and despair once more. He stared a long moment, thinking. He placed the crossbow across Tallin's chest, then reached for the quiver, removing the two longest arrow fragments.

Tears brimmed on his eyelids, but Delrael had already been through enough sorrow to last him for the rest of the Game. They had a mission to accomplish, a quest to finish.

He turned away without looking at the ylvan again and scooped dirt back into the grave. When he had finished, he patted the hard mound with his hands. He sat still, exhausted and aching both inside and out, before he made himself stand again. He pushed the two broken arrows into the head of the mound, where the arrowheads pointed up at the Hexworld sky.

Delrael turned his back on the mound. The light from the opening above had slanted, showing the approach of sunset. He motioned the others to follow him. "Let's get the hell out of here."

Together, they managed to climb through the hexagonal opening. Delrael stood on the lip, reaching down to help the others.

"Beam me up, Scotty!" Journeyman jumped up and stood on the rocky ground, flexing his gray-brown arms. The sky had an orange cast of sunset.

They had been underground an entire day.

The sun set behind Gairoth, and his shadow stretched out across the flat terrain, pointing which way he should go. He plodded along, stomping dust with his ponderous bare feet.

The Anteds had stopped attacking him and dropped dead.

Gairoth decided he must have frightened the Anteds into surrender. They had all fallen motionless together, leaving him unharmed but buried under them. By the time he crawled out from under the tangle of black bodies and jointed legs, he could find no trace of Delroth.

The ogre began to believe he might have been outsmarted again. His fingers gripped his club so tightly that the ridges from the wood made marks on his calloused hand.

The ogre looked at the sprawling terrain ahead, then he grinned as far as his thick lips could stretch. Four figures emerged from one of the distant holes and set off toward the next hexagon. They were far from his sight, but at least they were visible. He had the trail again.

"I'll bash your head in, Delroth! BAM!"

Gairoth charged across the desolation before night could take his quarry from him.

INTERLUDE: OUTSIDE

Melanie turned her head to blink her eyes furiously. The tears stung. She walked into Tyrone's kitchen before anyone could see the wet tracks on her cheeks. She clinked the ice cubes in her glass to emphasize that she was really just going to get more soda.

The others remained quiet, exhausted from the game. No one else seemed to get so close to their characters. David sat, flushed from his victory.

Melanie could still feel where the sharp corners of the dice had bitten into her palms. *Damn!* she kept thinking. All that rolling for combat, engagement after engagement. She had saved four of them.

But Tallin had died.

"Sorry, Mel," Scott said. She turned around to look at him, reacting a little too quickly. Behind Scott's glasses, she could see concern in his eyes. He alone had not taken part in the Anted battle, preferring to set up the details for his own turn.

"Wow, wasn't that a great combat!" Tyrone grinned from ear to ear, excited Then he noticed the wounded look on Melanie's face. "What's the matter? Don't be pissed off just because one of your characters got killed."

Melanie glared at him with such intensity that Tyrone shrugged and lowered his voice. "Well, we could always change the rules if you want. Plenty of game systems let you bring characters back after they've been killed once—"

"No!" David snapped. He remained at the table, studying the map and his notes, as if he didn't want to take a break between turns. "We decided against that a long time ago. We're not going to change the rules just because she wants to pout. Besides, Tallin was the second character Melanie introduced tonight. It was fair combat, and I won."

"*We* won," Tyrone said. "I played too."

"David is right," Melanie said. Her voice was so quiet, she couldn't believe she was agreeing with him. "I don't want complete power over life and death. We played by the rules. My character lost his combat rolls." She swallowed but found her hands shaking as she filled the glass.

Just because one of your characters got killed, Tyrone had said.

Melanie kept her lips pressed together. That was all it was to them—disposable characters, names and scores they rolled. Puppets to fight and find treasure and get killed. No wonder David found it boring. He had no emotional stake. He didn't care about anything but ending the game. Melanie cared about the rest of it.

The death of Tallin was a sharp ache in her.

"At least I learned what Melanie's trying to do with her characters and her secret quest," David said. He smiled and leaned back in the chair. "But hiding the Earthspirits in a belt? Don't know where you came up with that idea, Mel, but it isn't going to work. I'm not sure we should even allow it." He took off his black denim jacket and draped it over the arm rest, then reached forward to scoop up more of Tyrone's dip.

"If it won't work anyway, then why bother complaining about it?" Scott said with a half smile. "You're the one who keeps wishing the game would get more interesting—let Mel take a few more risks."

"Sounds like fun to me," Tyrone said. David scowled, trapped by his own complaints.

Melanie stopped herself from saying that she had nothing to do with the Earthspirits in Delrael's belt—any more than she had conjured up the Deathspirits to stop Enrod.

It was the game playing itself again.

That sent a thrill up her spine, pushing aside some of her sadness at Tallin's death. She knew something strange was happening with Hexworld. They all knew it. The characters were doing things with their lives outside of the Sunday gaming sessions.

Melanie made a smile of her own, hard and businesslike. She sat back down at the table. "Your *characters* don't know about the Earthspirits, David, so you can't do anything about it. Ryx is the only one who knew, and she's dead."

"Good point." Scott joined them, slouching down in his chair.

"In fact, David, you can't even prepare for my characters, because you officially don't know about their quest. Because of Tarne, Scartaris thinks Delrael is dead and the Fire Stone is still hidden somewhere at the Stronghold."

David drummed his fingers on the table. "I have so many armies camped around Scartaris that nothing could ever get through. I've gathered all the Slac, I've teamed up all the wandering monsters, stirred up some old antagonisms. There's a larger pool of monster fighters here—" he tapped the painted map over the mountains of Scartaris, "—than we ever brought together for the old Sorcerer wars."

He cracked his knuckles. "Your characters will never get through, Mel. I have no doubt of that."

Melanie glared at him, but to her surprise, Scott was the one who made a comment. "Well, David, we'll just have to wait and see.

We've got other characters in this game, you know, not just the ones Melanie's playing."

He picked up the dice and pointed at one of the hexagonal map sections near the city of Sitnalta. "I'm starting there. It's my turn."

CHAPTER 9
THE OUTSIDERS' SHIP

We must continue to learn, continue to study. As Sitnaltans, our quest is to understand everything about the Rules and how they affect our lives. With such an intimate knowledge, perhaps we can defeat the Outsiders and free ourselves from this Game.
—Professor Verne, speech to the Sitnaltan
Council of Patent Givers

Mountain air whistled around the empty turrets of the ancient Slac fortress. The sky above the excavation site was clear and cold and painfully blue.

Professor Verne rubbed his hands together and pushed them deep into his pockets as he walked back and forth outside the fortress. The other Sitnaltan engineers worked meticulously on the Outsiders' ship. When Verne blew steam from his mouth, clumps of frost made his full beard spiky.

Overhead, the wide, blind wall of the citadel was dotted with black spikes and narrow windows from which the Slac could fire down on visitors. Moss crept up the walls, brown and green. A pool of stagnant water half filled a pitted cistern.

The bulk of the Outsiders' vessel lay half buried in the dirt of the courtyard. Boulders and fallen stone blocks from the abandoned fortress had dropped around it.

Vailret and blind Paenar had told Verne and his colleague Professor Frankenstein about the ruined ship. Apparently, the Outsiders David and Tyrone had used it to travel to Hexworld, bringing with them a destructive monster to plant in the east. In exchange for this information, Verne and Frankenstein had constructed new mechanical eyes for Paenar.

"Did you find anything else?" Verne shouted down. He sucked on his lips, making his gray beard protrude. The tip of his nose felt numb in the cold mountain air.

"We don't know," Frankenstein called back from below. He cocked his head up at the other professor. "We haven't figured out what most of this is yet."

Frankenstein had a flushed face and close-cropped dark hair. His eyes bore a fiery, obsessive look, part of his impatient temperament. But Verne found Frankenstein's ideas exciting, and the two professors collaborated well together.

The two of them held more patents than any other inventors in Sitnalta's history. Verne himself didn't even know the total number anymore—nor did he care. The main point was inventing things, creating things, bettering life for the characters in Sitnalta. Some said the two professors were inspired directly by the Outsider Scott, who watched over the technological city.

In the barren courtyard, the Outsiders' ship had crumbled after many turns of disuse. Twisted ribs of metal and cross girders outlined the great size of the fallen hulk. The controls and engines were hidden and difficult to decipher, buried deep beneath the ground. Verne urged the other Sitnaltan workers not to experiment with any devices they found around the ship. He didn't want someone opening up an uncontrolled vortex to *reality*, where they would all be annihilated in an instant.

Professor Verne brushed off his knees and walked down the path into the wreckage of the ship. Around him, remnants of the hull looked as fragile as an eggshell, but patches of the metal gleamed pure and uncorroded, with rainbow colors that Verne had not seen in any alloy produced in Sitnalta. He stood beside the other professor.

"Some of our analytical machines still won't work," Frankenstein snorted. "The electrical ones are the worst."

"We are standing on the technological fringe, Victor. What else can we expect?" Verne bent over to inspect the place where tiny perfect rivets joined two metal sections together. "I am surprised even the mechanical instruments function as well as they do."

Verne drummed his fingers on his chest. In Sitnalta, the characters had developed science and technology enough to overthrow the Rules of magic that held sway for the rest of Hexworld. As the Sitnaltans used their technology more and more, they expanded the radius in which it worked out to a point where science and magic held each other uneasily at bay. Verne called this point the "technological fringe."

The Outsiders' ship lay squarely on the boundary.

A team of three Sitnaltan women in work clothes and lab coats sat concentrating on their sketch pads, measuring and recording detailed portions of the ship. Two other Sitnaltan workers used fine brushes to remove dust and debris from the wreckage.

One burly man, sweating and exhausted, was put to work moving rocks and some of the fallen girders. His face was flushed in the cold air, and he looked put upon because of his strength. Verne smiled encouragement at him.

"Can't we rig up some pulleys and a winch over here to help this man?" Frankenstein called.

"Come on, you're supposed to be engineers!" Two of the technicians hurried to implement the scheme.

Just the presence of the ship itself awed Verne. So alien, so unlike anything else he had seen before. He always had a sense of wonder at how things worked. But this ship was tangible evidence of a visit from the Outsiders. What they would learn just from the shapes of things, the construction, the way the metal was held together—it would give the characters of Sitnalta many turns of intense study.

If they had many turns left in the Game.

Vailret and his companions had brought news of how the Outsiders planned to end the Game. Most of the other Sitnaltans scoffed at the idea. But Frankenstein and Verne had picked up the energy readings of something powerful, something malignant, growing in the eastern section of the map. Only Vailret had been able to explain this anomaly to the professors' satisfaction.

Hexworld would be doomed if they did not find some way to destroy this monster from the Outside. The ship was the key, Verne felt. Perhaps with what they learned from it, the Sitnaltans could find some solution, or some escape. Maybe they could develop a weapon with which to fight back, or maybe, if they could discover how the vehicle worked, they could all escape to a different world.

It had always been a Sitnaltan dream to find a way for human characters to make a Transition of their own, as the old Sorcerer race had done with magic. Human characters should be able to do the same thing—with science. Verne had never heard of a spell yet that could not be imitated by properly developed technology.

"Professors! Come here, we've found something," a woman's voice called. Verne squinted into the shadows of the wreckage and recognized Mayer, the daughter of the Sitnaltan inventor-cum-bureaucrat Dirac. The tone in her voice suggested something important, and Verne and Frankenstein hurried.

They passed through a broken doorway down a tilted metal staircase into a chamber that had been buried in the dirt. Over the past three days, Mayer's team had excavated the room. Dust and dirt still caked the controls and equipment, but a team of men and women used gloves, trowels, and heavy brushes to clean the area. An older woman technician scrambled past the professors, carrying a bucket filled with debris up the groaning stairs to dump it in the courtyard.

Mayer stood there, her short dark hair mussed. Dirty handprints covered her lab coat, but she indicated a polished bulkhead with gleaming panels of buttons and dials. She crossed her arms over her chest and watched the reactions of the two professors, allowing the discovery to speak for itself for a moment. Then she could restrain herself no longer.

"These are the *controls*," she said. Her bright eyes gleamed with awe. "My hypothesis is that this system connects directly to the power source. If you touch the bulkhead, it is still warm after all this time. And there's another sealed compartment directly underneath."

Verne opened his eyes wide and went forward. Frankenstein also looked amazed. "This could be it," he said.

Verne let his imagination wander. He had his best ideas that way. Possibilities sprang into his head, ideas and applications with such an intensity that he wondered if he was indeed inspired by the Outsider Scott.

This ship had an awesome power source, even if it was just imaginary to the Outsiders David and Tyrone, even if they had only created this artificial ship as a prop to act out their games—regardless, it existed here on Hexworld. And it had to do what the Players imagined it would do.

Verne thought of what incredible energies could power such a ship, of the danger and the potential those energies would have if applied in a constructive—or destructive—manner.

"You must be very *very* careful with it," Verne said. "Treat it as if it were the most hazardous laboratory substance we have ever investigated."

"And indeed it is," Frankenstein added. His dark eyes shone with an unfathomable excitement.

Verne turned to Frankenstein and lowered his voice. "It will take some testing, but this could be the key to the most awesome weapon ever introduced on Hexworld."

He took a deep breath. "We could stop Scartaris."

Frankenstein allowed his thin lips to curl up in a smile. "This could be a way for us to prove the superiority of Sitnaltan technology once and for all."

He and Professor Verne shook hands.

CHAPTER 10

THE SPECTRE MOUNTAINS

RULE #4: "Evil" and "Good" are not absolute concepts in the Game. Characters act in their own self-interest. For example, companions on a quest may have the same purpose but for opposing reasons.
—*The Book of Rules*

Vailret watched Delrael deal with Tallin's death, not knowing how he could help. He remembered how blind Paenar had died, but Delrael wasn't there when Paenar rode the dragon down into the boiling volcano. This type of grief was new to Delrael. It seemed to be a rude awakening for him.

The fighter pushed on across the next hex-line just after midnight, when the Rules allowed them to continue for another day. "I want to get away from this place," he said under his breath. His footprints were barely visible in the starlight ahead of them. In the cool air, Vailret sweated to keep up.

They entered a sweeping hexagon of grassland. The grass hissed around their legs as they walked, but they picked out the quest-path even in the darkness. A few small animals rustled along the ground; night birds swooped around the sky, dropping low as they hunted.

Journeyman remained silent, making none of his inane Outsider comments or observations on *reality*. The aurora began to fade into the pinkish-yellow of dawn, and the golem finally turned his head and spoke. He talked as if he had been pondering his words for a long time.

"You didn't tell me about your quest. Or the Earthspirits in the silver belt."

Vailret didn't know what to say. Delrael ignored the conversation entirely.

Journeyman stared ahead and puckered his clay face in an expression of consternation. "You accepted me as a true companion. I told you my quest—that the Rulewoman Melanie planted a secret weapon in me, so that when we reach Scartaris, I will destroy him. But you told me you were just going to find information. You kept secrets from me."

The clay frown deepened. "We were supposed to be one for all and all for one, you know? That's what this questing business is all about. The Three Musketeers, Batman and Robin, Cisco and Pancho, Kirk and Spock, Laurel and Hardy. We're all a team. At least I thought so."

Vailret swallowed and took a deep breath to explain. Delrael strode on, keeping himself isolated. Bryl didn't look as if he wanted to join in the conversation either.

"We swore not to tell *any* other characters, especially not someone from the Rulewoman, even if she is on our side. The Outsiders knew nothing about our real quest. We didn't want Scartaris to prepare for us coming."

Journeyman's clay eyebrows twitched on his forehead. "Scartaris has already gathered armies of wandering monsters; he already contains enough energy to wipe out Hexworld if he feels threatened. He needs only to go through a rapid metamorphosis, and that will be the end of our world. How much more can he prepare?"

Vailret kept his gaze on the dim path as he continued behind Delrael. "Scartaris must not consider us a big enough threat—yet."

The golem stretched his flexible lips in an exaggerated pout. "You still should have told me." Then he shrugged. "I don't care what kind of weapon you have, or what the Earthspirits can do. It's my quest to take care of Scartaris, and I intend to do it. By myself if I have to. Hi ho, Silver!"

Vailret patted Journeyman on the shoulder, trying to reassure him. The clay felt soft and sticky. "Doesn't matter how it gets done—I just don't want Scartaris to wipe the map clean. I won't even ask about your weapon."

"You better not, because I'm not going to tell."

Vailret rolled his eyes and let the golem go ahead of him.

They continued as the Spectre Mountains in the distance became backlit in orange, then sharply silhouetted with dawn. By morning, they crossed into an identical hexagon of grassland.

Delrael remained withdrawn, saying little. In the early afternoon, when they crossed into a lush hex of forest terrain, he appeared even more gloomy. The dense trees seemed to remind him of Tallin...

It took them until early afternoon of the following day to get through the next hexagon of rugged forested-hill terrain. The trees, valleys, and green undergrowth made Vailret think of the khelebar forest of Ledaygen before the fire. They climbed the hills, looking down the steep slopes covered with trees and rock outcroppings. The quest-path guided them back and forth to the top of a ridge.

They trudged on at a steady pace, then stopped early to rest. Vailret and Journeyman played Tic-Tac-Toe on the ground. Delrael watched for a few games, but when they asked him to join in, he declined and went off by himself to sleep.

The quest-path wound ahead of them across the next hex-line

into the steep Spectre Mountains. Though the air was cool, Vailret found himself sweating and itching under his jerkin. His legs were tired, but he had settled into a pace that allowed him to keep going. Delrael gained ground ahead of them, then waited, fidgeting, for the others to catch up.

Vailret thought the sheer mountains ahead were like a wall to cut Delrael off from memories of the Anteds. Perhaps by replacing the anger and sorrow with a quest, Delrael would be able to heal his wound. Maybe climbing the rocky slopes would somehow purge him.

Around them, stones protruded along the path. Tufts of grass and sturdy scrub brush grew in sheltered crannies. Rock walls lurched upward like battlements, wind-carved and rain-washed into stark peaks and deep gullies. The quest-path was smooth and chalky, like hardened plaster washed down from the cliffs.

The sun spilled over the peaks in late morning. They came to a flat promontory jutting westward from the mountainside. Vailret stumbled to the edge for a rest. His lungs burned as he tried to catch his breath in the chilly air. The wind blew around them, ruffling Vailret's hair. Bryl joined him, pulling his blue hood over his face like a cowl.

Delrael squatted down to look back across the vast panorama of the Game board. Perfect hexagons of terrain lay immediately below, forested-hill, forest, grassland; in the distance, they could see the desolation dotted with tiny pock marks of Anted holes. Other sections of terrain swept in a beautiful mosaic to flat dimness at the far edge of the map.

Vailret squinted, trying to determine what he was seeing. Bryl pointed and stretched his gnarled hand out of the billowing sleeve. "Look at that!"

At the first hex of desolation terrain moved a dense gathering of black static the size of a thunderhead. It moved and slithered forward, scattered and fluttering in a formless clump. Vailret's eyesight was not sharp enough to catch any details, but he could tell that the others had no idea what they saw either. Where the dark gathering touched the desert, clouds of dust swirled behind it as if a great army, indistinct and enshrouded in black mist, marched across the hexagon.

"What is it?" Vailret asked.

"Something sent by Scartaris maybe?" Bryl said.

"Still too far away." Delrael stood up, hurling a stone over the edge, and strode off without watching it fall. "We'll get rid of Scartaris before we need to worry about that thing."

For someone with no coordination whatsoever, Gairoth had incredible luck climbing the narrow quest-path into the Spectre Mountains. His big feet found purchase on the tiny outcrops, and he hauled himself up the steep and crumbling trail. His only thought was to catch Delroth.

He saw a ledge, a shortcut to eliminate one of the tedious switchbacks, and climbed up, sprawling on the rough stone. After a second's rest, he reached up to grab another handhold and heaved himself to the next ledge. He lay panting. Sweat ran through his ropy hair, leaving a dirty track on his face. He wanted something to eat.

Then he noticed fresh footprints on the quest-path. Delroth's boots. The ogre pressed his potato-sized nose down to the ground, inhaling deeply in the dirt to see if he could pick up any scent. He grinned. "Haw!"

Huffing and grumbling, Gairoth lurched up the steep path, swinging his club back and forth.

By midday, the four travelers reached the snow line. Sharp cliffs towered overhead, blocking the sunlight and leaving patches of ice on the ground. The quest-path remained clear, but clumps of snow hung over outcrops of rock.

The main wall leaned over them, sloping backward and pregnant with a heavy load of snow on the cliff edge. A glistening sheet of clean snow stretched toward the tops of the mountains, dotted with stark rock outcroppings.

Delrael led them through a series of tight switchbacks as the quest-path threaded its way eastward. On the other side of the path and the rock outcroppings, the mountain slope was steep and broken with terraced ledges.

He walked along, stomping his boots in the snow. The others followed. Only the ruffle of wind brushing snow along the rocks disturbed the silence.

Gairoth pulled himself up another ledge to reach a flat area that intersected the quest-path. He took the straight way up the slope again, but his arms ached from the effort. His nose was red and cold. His ears hurt from the whistling wind. He ate some snow, bit down on a rock, and spat it out.

The ogre stomped up the steep path around disorienting outcrops of stone. Snow turned brown as it melted on his dirty furs. Then he reached a patch where snow had slid down the cliff and drifted across the path. He saw a line of trampled slush, fresh tracks on the quest-path. Very fresh.

"Delroth!" His bellow echoed among the cliffs, causing a tiny patter of dislodged snow from above. Brandishing his club, Gairoth bounded forward.

Delrael heard the ogre's yell and stopped in mid-stride with a disgusted expression on his face. Bryl made a strangled sound of shock. Vailret blinked his eyes to cover his surprise.

"Not tonight, I've got a headache," Journeyman groaned.

Gairoth hurtled around the corner, overbalanced and stumbling on an ice patch. He caught his footing before he could plummet over the edge of the slope. Raising the spiked club, he turned to the fighter.

Delrael pulled his sword free and stood firm on the path, returning the ogre's glare. "I'm getting sick and tired of you, Gairoth."

Gairoth lumbered forward, a grin of triumph on his thick lips. "Haw!"

He leaped ahead and swung his club at Delrael's head, but the fighter skittered backward, slashing sideways with the edge of his sword. Delrael stumbled on the slippery path in mid-swing, and his stroke went wide.

The ogre's spiked club smashed like a cannonball against the rock wall. The whole mountain seemed to shake. The cramped area on the narrow path did not allow the others room to help. Journeyman flexed his arms, waiting for an opportunity.

Gairoth saw his victim still standing and brought up the club for another blow. Delrael stood motionless, his head cocked and listening to a deep rumble above him. The ogre looked up to see pebbles and white mist pouring down like the whitecap on a tidal wave of roaring snow dislodged from the mountainside.

A firm clay arm encircled Delrael's waist and jerked him backward. "Heads up!" Journeyman said, bounding away from the avalanche. With elongated hands, Journeyman held Delrael, Bryl, and Vailret under the overhang of rock.

Gairoth gaped at the white wall of snow coming at him like a stampede. He swung his club to knock the avalanche away.

The wave of ice and snow slammed into the trail, blasting

upward and knocking the ogre off the ledge like so much flotsam. The white cascade swept him bouncing and jostling down the jagged slope.

"Have a nice day!" Journeyman called after him.

Chunks of snow sprayed the four companions, and an aftermath of cold mist hovered in the air. The rumble faded into the patter of settling snow. The only sound breaking the new silence was a far-off roar as the remnants of the snow made its way to the bottom of the canyon. An impassable white barrier of slumped ice and snow blocked quest-path behind them.

"Good thing we wanted to go forward anyway," Vailret said.

The tip of a spiked club broke the surface of the settling snow. A thick arm thrust forward, thrashing around. When Gairoth's shaggy, ice-encrusted head emerged, he sputtered and flung snow from his eye. He squirmed back and forth in the piled drift and caught his footing.

The ogre knocked the snow away from himself, freeing his arms. He grumbled and stamped his cold feet, looking at the steep slope. It would be a long climb back up. But Delroth was up there.

CHAPTER 11
ARKEN'S GATE

I stand by my decision not to accompany you on the Transition. I will not abandon our descendants. If other characters need me on Hexworld, then I must remain and help determine the course of the Game.
—Arken, final address to the Sorcerer council

The quest-path wound along the side of a tall, unfurrowed granite face, with sheer rock to their left and a frightening drop on their right. Wind whistled around the rocks, polishing away any snow that clung to tiny cracks.

The companions came around a curve to where the rock wall jutted sideways, as if a great hand had split the cliff and pushed it over to the right, channeling the quest-path through a narrow cut in the mountain.

But a locked gate blocked their way.

Vailret stopped and blinked. The black gate seemed so incongruous in the rocky wilderness. It towered three times their height, protected on the sides by the smooth rock walls. The bars were wrought iron, gilded with curlicues and sharp spikes, forbidding and unscalable. No other signs of life or civilization showed on the barren terrain.

"Verrry interesting," Journeyman said, curling his voice in a strange accent.

Vailret considered the problem, trying to think of who would place such an obstruction and why. He wondered if it might be a relic left over from the old Sorcerer days, but then some notation should have been made on the master maps at the Stronghold. The locked gate had not been there long.

Delrael made an angry noise and went forward. He looked for a latch, then grabbed the bars, rattling the gate on its hinges. It didn't budge. Without saying anything, he let the look on his face express his anger and impatience.

"Let me try." Journeyman wrapped his arms around the bars, looping into the gate. He pulled with enough force that the iron shivered and hummed with the strain. A few bits of rock flaked off the side of the mountain. But the gate held firm.

The golem surrendered and withdrew his arms. He smoothed the indentations on his limbs and stood looking ruffled. "I could reshape myself and squeeze through."

"That won't help us," Bryl said.

Journeyman shrugged. "I'll go myself if we can't find any other way. My own quest takes priority, you know."

"We're not ready for that yet." Delrael struck his fist ineffectually against the cliff face. He looked around with narrowed eyes. Vailret could see the emotions struggling in him—until now, Delrael had been using the forced march to cover up his other feelings. Now he had to face them and do something. But he didn't know what to do.

One of the lumps of rock shifted on the cliff face above. Delrael jumped back out of the way, ready to defend himself against a trap. Vailret looked up, and his neck hurt in the cold air.

The boulder sprouted arms as they watched. A portion of the

rock raised itself to form a head. The flat gray stone flowed like hot wax. Joints stretched out as a blocky creature uncurled from its camouflage. Jagged stone wings lifted upward, revealing an ugly sculpted figure, human in shape but molded with a lumpy gray texture. Small ridges ran down its back, and demonic horns sprouted from the center of its forehead.

Delrael looked at it with contempt, ready to fight. But Vailret put a hand on his cousin's shoulder and squinted up at the cliff face to make sure of what he saw. "A gargoyle?" He took a step forward and addressed the stone figure. "Is that what you are?"

"You are very perceptive," the creature said.

Vailret had heard references to these creatures in his studies of Hexworld legends. Many of the old Sentinels had destroyed themselves in a final unleashing of sorcerous power, a half-Transition that liberated their spirits into independent wandering entities. Some of these spirits gathered together to form a collective presence, called a *dayid*. But others, the stronger individual spirits, wandered by themselves and formed crude and temporary bodies of stone.

The gargoyle straightened up and directed his hollow gaze at them. He sighed. "You cannot pass this gate. It's not my choice, but I have to stop you."

Journeyman mashed his face into a scowl. "Frankly, my dear, I don't give a damn."

"We need to get to Tairé," Delrael said. He placed his hands on his hips and tried a deliberate lie. "My brother is dying. You can't stop me from seeing him one last time."

"I'm afraid you wouldn't care for Tairé anymore. Much has changed since Scartaris." The gargoyle turned his grotesque stone face up to the sky. "I remember when Enrod wanted to rebuild the lands around the city. Such a shame—all that work, wasted now."

"Who are you, gargoyle?" Vailret asked.

"That's a long story. I've lived for many turns of the Game, first as a Sorcerer lord and then as one of the Sentinels trying to help human characters. By now, the memories are dim. A stone head isn't made to hold too many thoughts, you know." He rapped on his forehead with a granite fist. "My name was, *is* Arken. I wasn't always so weak—now I'm required to guard this gate so that no characters may pass."

"Arken?" Vailret said. He blinked his eyes and took two steps forward, lowering his voice. "*Arken?* That's incredible! Do you know how much I—"

"Who is controlling you, gargoyle?" Delrael interrupted, silencing his cousin. He stared at the gate as if he could will it to vanish.

Vailret frowned at Delrael, still in shock. In all his readings, Arken had been one of the greatest Sorcerers. Only Arken had spoken out against the Transition, arguing that the surviving Sorcerers should help rebuild Hexworld after their endless wars had laid waste to so much of it. Most of them refused to listen, but some had remained behind as Sentinels to help human characters against the other monsters.

The stone gargoyle turned his head toward Delrael. "Scartaris controls me. He grows more powerful every day. The Outsiders want him to win, I think."

Vailret mumbled another question. "But you're *Arken*—we remember you as the first Sentinel, the greatest defender of Hexworld. How can you possibly be in league with Scartaris?" Vailret let his hands fall to his sides. "Don't you know what he's doing? He's going to end the Game for all of us!"

The gargoyle leaned over the mountain face and walked down, perpendicular to the cliff at an impossible angle. He righted himself on the path and came to stare at them.

The gargoyle shook his demonic stone head. "I am bound by the Rules. Scartaris defeated me, and I have to defend this gate to the best of my ability. It doesn't matter if I despise what he is trying to do."

Suddenly, Arken's manner seemed filled with new excitement. He focused his attention at them. "You travelers know who Scartaris is? And you're on a quest eastward?" He held up a blocky stone hand. "No, don't tell me anything—Scartaris will hear! I can guess for myself. Let me keep my hopes up. But I still can't help you."

"You're talking to us, though," Vailret said. "You're answering our questions."

"Certainly. And I'll do everything I can to get around my restrictions."

"Why can't you just let us pass and not tell Scartaris?" Bryl asked.

The gargoyle looked at him, annoyed. "I can't disregard my task for the sake of a whim. The Rules are the Rules, regardless of my feelings." He hunkered down and put his chin in his blocky stone fist. "Perhaps we can think of a different way I might help you."

Delrael kicked at a stone on the path. His lips were pressed together into a thin, white line. "Is there another pass we could go through?" he said. "We need to get moving."

"I doubt it," Arken said. "Scartaris will have guardians on all the quest-paths over the Spectre Mountains anyway. The other gate-keepers might not be so understanding."

"How do we know you're telling the truth, not trying to trick us?" Bryl put his hands on his hips haughtily.

Vailret thought he looked silly. "That's *Arken*, Bryl—don't be ridiculous."

The gargoyle seemed puzzled by Vailret's comment. "Well, you don't know whether I'm telling the truth or not—although I can promise that if I were trying to trick you, I would attempt to be ... a little more devious."

"All right, then, here's a straightforward question." Delrael stepped forward. "*How* can we pass? How can we defeat you?"

The stone gargoyle shrugged. "I don't know. Maybe we can figure out something."

"Could we play a game of dice, Arken? It's simple but effective. High roll wins?" Vailret withdrew his own set of dice. "If we win, you let us pass?"

The gargoyle placed his stone chin on his fist. "Remember that I have more than my share of luck." Arken knelt down to the ground. The cold path and the bleak mountains seemed to have no effect on him. "But if this doesn't work, we can still try something else."

He raised his head to look at all of them. "We'll only be able to use this challenge once, though. It wouldn't be fair if you kept rolling until you beat me one time."

"Fair enough." Vailret held his hand out and raised his eyebrows. "Del, why don't you roll for us?"

The fighter took the dice and looked at them. "My luck seems to have turned sour lately."

"Then it's time to change it. Go ahead and roll."

Delrael rubbed the two twenty-sided dice between his palms and, without interest, let them fall to the ground. A "10" and a "14."

"Not bad," Vailret said.

"Not good," Delrael countered.

Arken brushed the dice into his palm, using one flat stone hand because the blocky fingers were not dexterous enough to grasp the small objects. He tossed them into the air. One die landed flat on the quest-path; the other struck a rock and bounced sideways, coming to rest a few feet away. A "12" and an "18."

"I'm sorry," Arken said. "I told you I had too much luck."

With a scowl on his pinched face, Bryl took out the Air Stone and Fire Stone. They glinted in the bright mountain sunlight. "I have these. They're powerful enough. Can I command you with them? Will they work?"

The stone creature straightened and took a step backward in shock. He reached a crudely formed hand toward the diamond and the ruby, but Bryl snatched them away. The gargoyle rocked back on his clublike stone feet. "Are those what I think they are?"

Vailret nodded. "If you're really Arken, you must remember them."

The gargoyle drew a deep breath. "You make me feel strange about my past. When I saw that so few Sorcerers would refuse the Transition and remain to help their own half-breed children, I begged them to create the Stones. Do you know where the other two are? It's been so long. As I recall, one was lost in the Scouring…"

Vailret glanced at Delrael, then decided to answer anyway. "Yes, we know where they are, though the Earth Stone is not readily accessible."

Bryl had sensed the twenty-sided emerald Stone somewhere in the treasure grotto of Tryos the dragon, but they had no time to search before rescuing Tareah. Vailret wondered how Tareah was faring back at the Stronghold…

"Never bring all four Stones together unless you are prepared for what will happen," Arken said, pointing a stone finger at them. "It's like magical synergy. More power resides in the combined Stones than even the six Spirits possess. A character gathering all four Stones could unleash a new Transition for himself. One character should not have such power."

Arken cocked his grotesque head toward the open sky between the peaks, and his voice took on a wistful tone. The wind whistled around the bars of the gate. "The Transition was an awesome enough thing to do once in the Game."

Vailret cleared his throat, hoarse with awe at a conversation with one of the greatest Sentinels of legend. "I read your description of the Transition. I found it in Sardun's Ice Palace." His voice trembled.

The blocky stone gargoyle turned his head. A long sigh rumbled out of his stone chest. "I remember writing that, but I was too amazed to describe it well. Imagine the Sorcerer race gathered in a shallow valley, waiting. All the characters who were going on the Transition, and some who only wanted to watch."

"We've been to that valley too." Vailret watched the crude face and tried to picture what Arken must have looked like as a great Sorcerer spokesman. "It seemed haunted."

"I don't doubt it," Arken answered. "Five of our leaders were inside a council tent. Even Stilvess Peacemaker was there, the one who had ended the wars. He was so old, he could barely move.

"It was about this time of year, the autumn equinox. The air was cold, and the wind kept flapping the white tent. The other characters waited outside on the plain, ready, in case something should happen. None of them knew what was going on inside. But I did. I was there, their official observer."

"Well?" Vailret asked. His eyes sparkled and his breath quickened. "How did you manage to break the Rules and succeed in the Transition?"

Arken held up one stone hand. "We broke no Rules! It was difficult what we did, yes—but we broke no Rules. Actions on Hexworld are determined by the roll of the dice. Nothing is impossible if you wait long enough and try enough times."

"So what were they doing inside the tent?" Vailret repeated. Delrael shuffled his feet; Vailret wondered if he was curious or just impatient.

"The five of them were rolling dice. Twenty-sided dice, made from pure crystal, perfectly balanced, the finest dice ever seen on Hexworld.

"The five Sorcerers rolled their dice, over and over and over. They did not stop, day or night. They were weary. I watched their eyes turn red. All of them looked haggard. Old Stilvess seemed as if he was about to collapse."

"But what were they trying to do?" Vailret asked.

Arken seemed to ignore Vailret's question. He spread his stone wings with a grinding sound. "At last, all five of them rolled a twenty on the same roll. A nearly impossible roll—*nearly* impossible. A perfect, perfect dice roll, unheard of on Hexworld.

"And when they rolled five twenties, five of the greatest living Sorcerers on Hexworld, they unleashed enough power to initiate the Transition." The stone gargoyle hung his head. "That was when I ran out of the tent."

Delrael sighed and sounded angry. He rattled the gate again with his hand. "That doesn't concern us." He leaned against one of the cold walls of rock. "We have to get past here."

Arken hunched his shoulders and swiveled the crudely formed blockish head to look at the fighter.

"Can we fight you?" Delrael unsheathed his sword, but it looked ineffective against the blocky stone body of the gargoyle.

Arken shook his head from side to side. "I wouldn't advise it. Your sword wouldn't harm me, but I could cause plenty of damage to you."

"What if you had a better opponent?" Journeyman said. "When the going gets tough, the tough get going! A gargoyle and a golem —we should have an equivalent strength class."

Journeyman turned to the other travelers. "He can't really damage me, any more than I can damage him. We could wrestle. If I win, the gate opens and we pass."

Arken clapped his stone hands with a sharp crack. "It sounds acceptable to me. I must warn you, though, that I am bound to *try* my utmost to defeat you. I can't just let you win. It has to be fair."

Journeyman drew himself up, flexing his soft arms. "Go for all the gusto while you can."

Arken worked his jaw, as if finding words difficult. "If the golem does win, I wish you the best of luck on your quest. I want to see Scartaris stopped too."

He faced Journeyman. "Don't worry about causing damage to me. My spirit isn't bound to this stone body. As long as Scartaris holds me here, he controls me. But if you … break me, then I will be free. For a time, at least."

Journeyman made the features of his face run flat as he flowed more clay into his shoulders and arms, concentrating his strength. "It's not just a job, it's an adventure."

Delrael, Vailret, and Bryl stood by the locked gate and watched Arken. The massive stone creature stepped to the narrow part of the path and faced Journeyman.

"Luck, Journeyman," Vailret said.

"Luck," Bryl and Delrael echoed.

Arken planted his stone feet squarely on the quest-path and opened his arms, ready to grapple with the golem. He surprised them all by wishing Journeyman luck as well.

"You can surrender any time," Journeyman said.

The grotesque gargoyle straightened his back. "I'll remember that. Ready?"

"Yes, ready."

With a slap of clay on stone, Journeyman and Arken grabbed each other around the shoulders. Journeyman's hands flattened as he pushed against the stone gargoyle's arms. Arken spread his feet, which seemed to fuse to the rock of the trail.

Neither of the combatants made a sound. They kept their faces neutral. Since they were not human, they did not grunt with the strain, or pant, or show any sign of the exertion they made. The breeze died down, and the cold air retained its claustrophobic silence.

"Irresistible force and immovable object," Journeyman said. "Did you ever hear about that one, Arken? It's a riddle from Outside."

Arken strained and pushed, but his voice sounded curiously neutral. "What is the solution?"

Journeyman's body seemed distorted and stretched with the effort to maintain himself against the gargoyle. "I don't believe it has a solution. The Outsiders can be very strange at times."

The gargoyle lifted one of his blocky stone feet and pivoted, forcing Journeyman to bend and turn his back to the sheer precipice.

"Come on, Journeyman!" Bryl shouted.

Arken's hunched back bent as he took a small step forward, forcing Journeyman closer to the edge. But the clay golem did not move his feet, stretching his legs instead. He slid his arms to get a better grip on Arken's smooth shoulders.

"More powerful than a locomotive," Journeyman said again, but his voice was fainter this time.

Vailret found himself wincing and pressing his fingers into his fists, straining his arm muscles as if that could assist the golem.

Arken's blocky hands left deep indentations in Journeyman's body. The stone gargoyle pushed harder and harder.

"Able to leap tall buildings in a single—"

Finally something snapped.

"—bound!" Journeyman let out a strange cry like the release of a too-tight bowstring, and his clay flowed like liquid. He flung himself backward, bending over upon himself in an impossible angle, out of the way.

Arken, thrusting forward with all his might, suddenly had no purchase and nothing to push against.

He went plummeting over Journeyman, off into space.

Vailret and Delrael ran forward as Journeyman straightened himself up, pulled his body back together and rearranged his clay. He stood tall. They all heard a distant *thock!* as Arken's stone body crashed into the rocks far below.

Vailret didn't want to go to the path edge and look.

Journeyman did not appear flustered. His clay mouth twisted in a beaming expression. "That was the big difference between us, you know, a golem and a gargoyle," he said. "Clay bends, stone doesn't."

The black iron bars of Arken's gate tinkled into nothingness on the rock. A chill wind whistled along the quest-path, motioning the travelers ahead to where the trail was wide and easy.

The shadows of sunset followed them as they passed through

the vanished gateway. Just on the other side of the cut waited the black hex-line where they had to stop for the day. The next hexagon of mountain terrain descended gradually, sloping down out of the Spectres, as if saying that any character who passed Arken's gate deserved easy traveling.

Ahead, the land of Scartaris waited for them.

CHAPTER 12
DOWNFALL OF THE STRONGHOLD

We must keep the legends alive, the stories of brave quests, the memories of past characters who have become heroes. Though the Outsiders wish only to amuse themselves turn after turn, this is still our history.
—The Sentinel Sardun, part of the "Lost Records" buried under the Ice Palace ruins

The villagers gathered in the Stronghold courtyard at sunset to hold a formal ceremony in memory of Tarne. Jagged shadows from the pointed wall crept across the courtyard. The veteran's ashes had been gathered up and buried in a special area near the Stronghold wall, an honored place where Vailret's father Cayon was interred, as well as Delrael's mother Fielle.

Young Tareah rubbed her elbows and knees in the chill air. Her joints still ached, but she listened with rapt attention as the villagers did quest-tellings of Tarne's greatest adventures.

Jorte, the keeper of the gaming hall, spoke of when Tarne had been one of the companions of Drodanis and Cayon, a great fighter and quester. Others told how Tarne was one of the fighters led by Drodanis against the ogres in revenge for the murder of Cayon ...

how Tarne was wounded in that fight and had since seen visions of future turns of the Game. The young farmer Romm described Tarne's warning to the other villagers that Gairoth would take over the Stronghold, and how he led a brave defense against the attack; when that failed, Tarne had led them into exile in the deep forest terrain until Delrael returned and vanquished Gairoth.

Tareah herself picked up the hexagonal tile bearing the veteran's name and placed it on the grave. She remembered the quiet, bald man who seemed to hold so much inside him. A weaver, who wanted no further part in fighting and battles. She stared at the wall, not at the gathered villagers, as she described Tarne's brave fight, alone in the middle of the night to defend them all against the Slave of the Serpent.

Darkness fell, and young Romm lit several torches in the courtyard. The villagers stood around, not certain what to do after the ceremony. They seemed leaderless and disoriented without the bald veteran. Tareah did not blame them—she was new, she had no experience with quests or adventuring. Why should they trust her to lead them?

She had spent her entire life isolated in the Ice Palace with her father, and when the dragon had kidnapped her, she merely waited for some adventurer to come rescue her. Regardless of her Water Stone or how much magic she could use, Tareah still had much to learn.

Vailret's mother Siya stood beside her, looking tired and withdrawn. She wore clean but drab clothes highlighted by a flashing emerald brooch. Siya told Tareah that Cayon had given it to her, stolen from a Slac treasure pit he once raided. Now Siya's face seemed old, and she tied her hair back in a severe bun. Since her son and Delrael had gone on their quest to Scartaris, Siya acted angry and lonely, with nothing more to hold on to.

The stars came out. Night birds made sounds in the forest. Tareah looked up to see the green smear of Lady Maire's Veil across the sky. That made her think of how Tarne must have seen his own death there—yet, even knowing that, he still went to face the Slave of the Serpent.

The outbuildings stood shadowy and empty now, with Delrael, Vailret, and Bryl gone, and Tarne dead. The main hall of the Stronghold echoed with silence. They had no students at the Stronghold for battle exercises or role-playing games. The place was deserted, big and frightening. It reminded Tareah of the Ice Palace and the empty vaults full of relics, now buried under crumbled ice and snow.

She took her eyes away from the sky and saw Mostem the baker coming toward her. Tareah still had difficulty identifying all the villagers in her mind, but she remembered that Mostem had three daughters. According to Siya, Mostem hoped that either Vailret or Delrael would be interested in pairing with one of them. Tareah had never met the daughters, nor had she tried. She was not sure if she should feel jealous—she had trouble pinpointing her feelings, either about Vailret or Delrael.

Mostem's eyes moved from Tareah to Siya, then to the ground. From the way the other villagers watched him, Tareah realized that they had all discussed this beforehand. She let a slight frown cross her face.

Mostem looked as if he didn't know how to begin, and finally, he said, "You're all alone up here now. Are you sure the Stronghold is safe? Do you think you should stay here?"

He didn't wait long enough for her to say anything. "We were talking, uh, I mean, I was thinking that maybe you could come stay with us? Or one of the other villagers. We're not sure that staying at the Stronghold is a good idea anymore."

Tareah was surprised at the suggestion and tried to decide how to react to it, what Delrael would want her to do. But Siya drew herself up, indignant. "What, and just abandon the Stronghold? It's been here intact for generations, and this is *my home!* I don't take that lightly." She crossed her thin arms over her chest. "I will stay here."

Mostem took a step backward and continued to speak to the ground. "We just thought it might be best if—"

Tareah cut him off. "I promised that I would remain here and do my best to defend the Stronghold." She stood beside Vailret's mother. "You know the Rules. I made a vow—I can't break that. I'm not one of those characters who takes such things lightly."

She and Delrael had gotten into arguments on that point before. But this time, she didn't think he would object.

"Besides, look around you." She indicated the double walls topped by sharp points, the weapons storehouse, the heavy gates and the trench around the Stronghold, the Steep Hill path. "This is the most defensible place, the safest spot for hexagons around! And don't forget I have the Water Stone too. If we're not safe here, we certainly won't be safe anywhere in the village."

She raised her voice so the others would hear her clearly. "If you're concerned for our safety, any of you is welcome to stay here and help guard us against attack."

Mostem cleared his throat and looked to the others to see their reaction. The death of Tarne and the threat of Scartaris was too close on their minds.

But Romm the farmer straightened. His blond hair was mussed, and his skin looked dry from spending too many hours outside in all weather. "That's a good idea. We should arrange our schedules so some of us can be up here. We were willing to fight against Gairoth, with Tarne—we shouldn't do any less than that now."

His words heartened Tareah. She nodded to them all. "We do need a stronger defense, now that Tarne isn't here to assist me."

"We can discuss this tomorrow," Siya said. Her stiff movements showed how much Mostem's suggestion had upset her. "We'll roll dice to see who stays up here with us. You *all* could brush up on your training a little."

Apparently relieved, the villagers left, going down the hill into the night and back to their homes. Tareah could hear muffled voices as the villagers went along the path.

Siya and Tareah worked together to swing the heavy gate shut. They fastened the solid wooden crossbolts in place. The shadowy empty buildings inside the walls looked spooky enough that Tareah decided to leave the torches burning in the courtyard.

Before going to bed, Siya and Tareah began the ritual of closing up the Stronghold for the night. With the others to help, they always finished quickly before, but it took them longer and longer each night as the evenings grew colder, now that they were the only two to do everything.

They made sure all the windows were shuttered, the cracks stuffed with rags to keep the cold out. They stoked the main fireplaces with enough wood to keep burning all night long, since it was such a tedious task to rebuild the fires the next day. Tareah saw no point in keeping the entire main building heated and tended, but she didn't countermand Siya's wishes. Siya seemed to attach a far greater importance on maintaining her routine than actually thinking about it.

Tareah was exhausted by the time she reached her own quarters and heaped wood on the fire. Her joints would ache if she did not keep her room warm, which seemed odd to her since she had spent so many years in the bright coldness of the Ice Palace. Over the weeks, she felt as if the pain had faded somewhat, but her body would take a long time to adjust to the dramatic stretchings and twistings her accelerated growth put it through.

She stripped off the formal dress she had worn for Tarne's ceremony and pulled on a comfortable shift, then climbed under the blankets. She lay back in the bed and thought of Delrael and Vailret on their quest, all the stories they were adding to the history of the Game. She wished her father Sardun could be here to discuss them.

Tareah kept the Water Stone with her, even in bed. She ran her fingers over the cool blue facets. They reminded her of the ice in the rainbow halls and crystal towers. She dozed with that thought.

And woke up some time later. The fire still burned bright, so she couldn't have been asleep too long. It was just past midnight, she guessed. She blinked her eyes in the dancing firelight. Her nose was cold, but she could smell the aromatic wood.

Tareah heard scratching, scrabbling sounds. The wood in the fireplace settled with a slump and a small shower of sparks. The noises stopped for a moment and began again with renewed intensity. The scrabblings sounded like rats in the walls, clawing their way out.

Tareah rubbed her eyes on the blanket and tried to see in the wavering orange light. Sharp shadows lay in the corners. Then her eyes came to focus on the dark and churning wall beside her bed.

The wood was crawling with small figures, each about the size of her hand. Emerging from cracks in the wood, pushing themselves out between splinters and scrabbling over each other, along the walls, along the floor.

Tareah sat up, flinging tangled hair out of her eyes, and bit back an outcry. Her blankets were covered with the little creatures as well, tiny ratlike animals, but vaguely human in form. They had ear tufts and pointed faces with sharp fangs. On two hind legs, they walked upright, and they bore two sets of humanlike arms, one sprouting from their shoulders and another set along their abdomen, giving each creature four hands full of sharp claws.

She snapped her blanket, spraying the creatures off her bed and onto the floor. She grabbed for the Water Stone under her pillow, but some instinct warned her not to show it, not to use it just yet.

The ratlike creatures swarmed over the room as they searched for something. They scurried down the mantel of the fireplace, disassembling the wood splinter by splinter with their sharp claws. Now that Tareah had awakened, they chittered among themselves, making no effort to keep quiet.

She kicked her blankets away and rolled to the edge of her bed. Her voice hitched as she tried to call out—but there was no one to help her. She would have to fight by herself. One of the bedposts groaned and broke free from its joint, torn apart by the creatures. The bedframe cracked and dropped to the floor with a *thump*.

More rat-creatures scurried to the storage chests and peeled the locks and hinges from the base wood, splintered the sides, and spilled the treasure from Delrael's past adventurings onto the floor. They searched through the plunder, using four hands to paw and toss away diamonds and gold and silver links as if they were worthless.

"Stop!" Tareah shouted. They hesitated, glaring at her with pupilless red sparks for eyes—empty, as if something had erased the minds behind them. She felt very afraid to look at the hundreds and hundreds of tiny pointed teeth and sharp claws. Then the creatures fell to ransacking again.

The shelves on the wall crumbled, and Tareah's possessions crashed to the ground, breaking and clinking on the floor. Every splinter of wood spawned another of the small creatures as they

pushed out and added to the army. Above the chittering, rustling din, she heard noises from the other rooms.

Tareah jumped out of bed, stepping on squirming furry bodies and trying to kick them away from her. "What do you want?" she shouted. She drew herself up to look menacing.

The rat-creatures fixed their blank gazes on her. Many of them cleared an empty spot on the floor, and others moved into formation with some kind of intent. Dozens of them aligned themselves to form letters with their own bodies.

On the floor, they spelled out "FIRE STONE."

Scartaris knew the Deathspirits had stripped the ruby Stone from Enrod and delivered it to the Stronghold. He had sent the rat-creatures to tear everything apart until they found it.

Scartaris knew nothing about Delrael's quest to bring the Earthspirits across the map—because of Tarne's ruse, Scartaris thought the Slave of the Serpent had killed Delrael. Perhaps Scartaris knew nothing of her Water Stone either. She clutched the six-sided sapphire in her hand.

"No!" Tareah stamped her foot on the ground, squashing one of the rat-creatures and making the others scurry out of the way. "You can't have it." She waited to feel sharp claws and teeth on her bare legs.

One section of the wall slumped down in a shower of broken wood. Flames from the fireplace caught on the kindling. The creatures ran around, dismantling the room.

A few of the rat-creatures on the floor of the room spelled out "WE WILL FIND IT," forming and dissolving one word after another.

From her own room, Siya screamed—but it was a scream of anger and disgust, not pain. The ceiling groaned above Tareah, and she looked up to see the planks buckling.

In her bare feet, trying not to look where she stepped, Tareah ran to the door and struck it with her shoulder to push it open. She ran down the main hall.

Everywhere she looked, the scrambling creatures emerged from the splintered wall and set about ransacking everything in sight. The structure of the main building groaned and creaked above the insane chittering.

Tareah ran out the broken doorway into the cold night. Two of the courtyard torches had burned out, but the other three flickered in the sharp wind. Small, furious sounds came from all buildings within the Stronghold walls.

"Siya!" she called.

Tareah saw the creatures piled on top of each other in the roof structure, throwing pieces of wood in the air and over the edge in glee, digging and searching. Others tunneled in the courtyard, uprooting sword posts. The weapons storehouse crashed and toppled to the ground. Other walls in the outbuildings split and collapsed.

Tareah felt outraged but didn't know how she could fight against the infestation.

Siya burst out the front door, frantic. She had a broom in her hands, and she flicked it right and left to knock away the creatures in front of her. "Get away!" She whacked them off the walls. "Leave that alone! Stop!"

Her gray hair hung down below her shoulders in broad tresses. Several of the creatures grabbed on and yanked, climbing the strands like ropes. Siya tossed her head and flung them off, then chased after them with a vengeance.

"Get away from the door, Siya!"

Siya ran into the courtyard. Chittering, some of the rat-creatures followed her, but most swarmed over the door jamb, peeling away the wood. Two of the shutters cracked and fell off their hinges. New rat-creatures burst up from the fresh wood, flexing their forearms and bouncing down to the ground.

With scrabbling hands in a blur of motion, they fell upon the wooden walls and kept tearing them apart in chunks. Dust and smoke filled the air from collapsed mantels and the burning fires in the hearths. The main building was on fire.

Tareah took out the Water Stone. "I've got to do something." She rolled it on the ground. The six-sided sapphire landed with a "4" up. She grabbed it again and cast her spell at the main building.

The wind whipped up. The already-cool air dropped below freezing. Biting snow blasted down and, with a snap of cold, ice encrusted the Stronghold, freezing the wood solid. The cold itself shattered some of the shutters; the support beams groaned inside from the weight of snow. She heard a loud pop from somewhere inside.

When the wave of cold struck the rat-creatures, they withered and disappeared. Siya chased others with her broom and left blots of fur and blood on the ground.

The assault seemed to have stopped for a moment, leaving a stillness like a held breath. "Did it work?" Tareah asked.

With squeals of angry chittering and a shower of pale splinters, more creatures burst out of the logs in the double wall surrounding the Stronghold. They dropped to the ground, bristling with patches of brown and gray fur, sharp fangs, and fiery blank eyes.

The creatures ignored Tareah and Siya, but scurried toward the ice-encrusted Stronghold to chip their way in. They set upon the main building once more.

Between the upright pointed logs of the stockade wall, more creatures surged out. The dirt insulation between the double walls crumbled and sifted out of the holes. Several logs toppled and fell over to leave gaps in the perimeter.

The brittle casing of ice over the main building split open. The rat-creatures surged inside again, tearing holes out of the walls.

Tareah grabbed the sapphire, angry and ready to roll it. But the rat-creatures swarmed over the ground at her feet, waiting with arms outstretched. They *knew* what the Stone was now; they wanted her to roll it so they could snatch it away the instant it struck the ground.

Tareah clamped her teeth down on a frustrated scream. She couldn't even roll the Stone, and none of her minor spells would do anything. She couldn't fight, and that infuriated her even more.

Tears streaked down Siya's cheeks. Her face reddened and she panted from her effort. A strange noise came from Siya's throat as she continued to strike out at the creatures. "What do they want?"

Tareah felt the corners of the Water Stone bite into her palms as she pushed her fists together. "They're looking for the Fire Stone. Scartaris wants it back, now that he knows how powerful it is."

Siya blinked and stood with her broom upright. Her face wore an astonished expression. "But the Fire Stone isn't even here! By now, Delrael and the others should be—" She waved her hand at the crumbling walls. "By the mountains or something."

All of the rat-creatures stopped with their ears cocked. In unison, the horde turned to glare at them.

Tareah wanted to scream at Siya in anger and frustration. "You idiot! Scartaris thought Delrael was dead!"

The rat-creatures chittered among themselves—and then they all vanished into the ground, leaving no trace other than the bloodied bodies Siya had killed.

Tareah kept her voice level and cold. "You just increased the danger to Delrael and Vailret. Now Scartaris knows they're coming, and he can concentrate everything he has on stopping them."

Siya's eyes widened as big as plates when the realization sank in. She hung her head. Her shoulder blades jerked as she tried to hold the sobs in.

Tareah looked around at the ravaged Stronghold—Delrael had left *her* behind to defend it. He had counted on her abilities and her judgment. Grim anger filled her mind—but the collapsing buildings, the ruined wall brought stinging tears in front of her vision.

The fire from the broken hearths had spread into the main building, and smoke poured into the air.

INTERLUDE: OUTSIDE

David put his hands behind his head and leaned back against them. His eyes still looked red, but he smiled with satisfaction. Melanie was so angry, she wanted to punch his face, or at least dump her cold soda in his lap.

"You destroyed my Stronghold!" she said. Her voice sounded strangled, carrying more emotion than she wanted to display.

The rat-creatures, the dozens of attack rolls, the walls falling, the fire starting...She felt Tareah's helplessness, felt Siya's loss. If only the characters could have fought back more, helped *her* more.

David kept his eyes closed. "Now I think we can *officially* say that Scartaris knows Delrael isn't dead. And he also knows that the group is coming to get him."

"And this time, her characters don't *know* that Scartaris knows. Ha!" Tyrone added. "That's a switch."

"Thanks, Tyrone." Scott scowled at him.

David grinned. "That means Scartaris can now try to stop them." He shrugged. "Unless I decide to just have him blow up the map, and we can be finished with all this nonsense." He truly looked as if he was enjoying this. Melanie stood up in anger. Her chair tipped back but did not fall over.

"That wouldn't be very sporting, now would it?" Scott asked.

"Let's not let this get personal, guys," Tyrone said, waving Melanie back into her chair. "It's just for fun, remember."

Melanie and David both glared at him. Tyrone went to get another bag of chips from the top of the refrigerator, shaking his head.

"When Delrael and company get through the mountain terrain, that's when the real fun starts. The city of Tairé is my first serious line of defense." David rubbed his hands together. "We can probably end this tonight."

"What's your hurry, David?" Tyrone asked. "There's nothing on TV Sunday nights anyway."

David slapped both hands on the tabletop, startling them all with his outburst. "Because I don't want to have any more nightmares about Hexworld! I want it done and finished and *out of my head!*"

He swallowed and blinked, as if amazed at himself. Melanie felt a moment of sympathy for him. The power of Hexworld was frightening to her too, but the characters, the landscapes, the legends all gave her wondrous dreams, not nightmares. She had to save them, and the characters had to help in their own way.

"Melanie, when your characters get into Tairé, they're playing right into my hands." He avoided her gaze and looked down at the painted map. She saw that his hands were shaking.

Melanie kept her voice low. "That's exactly where I want them to be. Shut up and play."

CHAPTER 13
PEOPLE OF A DEAD CITY

By building this beautiful city in the midst of desolation, we will prove that Hexworld characters can overcome any difficulty so long as we pool our talents and work toward a common goal. We have our magic, and we have the Rules on our side. Nothing can stop us now.
—Enrod, ceremony at the founding of Tairé

They descended out of the mountains. The hard, cold ground crunched under Delrael's boots. He felt stronger now, as if he was finally opening his eyes again. Tallin was dead, but the Game went on, turn after turn—unless the Outsider David had his way.

Delrael made his facial muscles stop frowning. He remembered Rule #1. He focused on quests, treasure, action, on *getting things done*. He did not sit around and ponder everything to death. Death.

Maybe that changed too many things.

His father had sent a message stick with the aid of the Rule-woman Melanie, charging Delrael and Vailret to find some way to stop Scartaris, to keep Hexworld alive and intact. In the cold mountain air, Delrael absently clenched his fist.

The next days passed in a blur. Delrael kept his eyes fixed on the distant horizon toward the crumbled mountain terrain that marked the lair of Scartaris. After another hexagon, they crossed over grassy hills and then entered the rocky desolation, scars left from the old Sorcerer wars.

The landscape became flat and barren, like gray ash in a bleak ocean. The ground was strewn with shattered rocks and jutting boulders like broken teeth. The sun seemed hotter here, making everything look blasted and devastated. The desolation rang with silence, leaving only the crunch of their footsteps. The wind had nothing but bare rock to rustle against. No birds or insects made any noise at all.

Journeyman stumped along beside them, but the dry heat made him move more stiffly.

"Did Scartaris cause all this?" Bryl asked.

Vailret looked around, and his eyes were red. "No, that was just reopening an old wound. It's easy to destroy something that was already knocked to its knees. The final battles laid waste to a huge section of the map, right here."

He drew a deep breath. "But the Wars ended here too. The two factions of Sorcerers finally made their peace. Did I ever tell you about Stilvess Peacemaker?"

Delrael forced himself to appear interested, to be part of the group again. "Arken mentioned that name, didn't he?"

Vailret looked pleased. "By the time the Wars ended, the Sorcerers were almost worn out. Most of them had forgotten why they were fighting in the first place. How could they still be angry about the game of throwing stones at Lady Maire's wedding celebration, so many turns before?

"Then a self-appointed mediator appeared among the camps. Stilvess. He wandered from one army to the other, refusing to reveal which side he came from—but he made it clear that he wanted no more war. He was an outstanding orator."

Vailret sighed. "He brought the two sides together like a crashing wave, making them one again. He forced the factions to see they were fighting themselves into extinction.

"Finally, the son of one of the great generals was killed in a skirmish. Instead of allowing that to inflame emotions again, Stilvess used that to show the Sorcerers how much pain their battles were causing. He made the two leaders meet at the funeral pyre of the general's dead son, and he urged them to cast their ceremonial swords into the hot flames."

Vailret looked lost in his own memories. "Sardun had one of those burned swords in the museum under his Ice Palace."

"I think I remember it," Bryl said.

Delrael looked around the wasteland and imagined the furious battles—Slac regiments, human armies, characters slaughtered, old Sorcerer leaders wielding spells...

The hexagon of desolation fell away behind the black dividing line into another section of terrain that should have been lush prairie. But all the grass was brown and dry, scratching together in the breeze like a vast tinderbox. A line of brown grassy-hill terrain blocked their view of further desolation ahead.

"Enrod founded a city out here somewhere. Tairé," Vailret said. "The characters spent many turns trying to bring life back to the land, where they could be reminded of the scars left by the battles. That's why I was so shocked to hear Enrod coming to destroy us with the Fire Stone—he was always a rebuilder, not a destroyer."

Vailret bent over to snap a brittle grass blade. "Looks like the Tairans managed to reclaim these hexes, for a while. Until Scartaris sucked it all dry again. Maybe we'll find some cropland closer to the city walls."

Delrael kicked the ground, scuffing up a chunk of dead grass.

They followed the quest-path to the hills and camped at the hexline that night. When they moved on the next day, Delrael stood at the top of a ridge looking down. The hot wind whipped his hair, but they had gone far enough away from the desolation's flying dust and grit.

Among the stiff crags of the Spectre Mountains behind them, he saw a misshapen blob of black fog crawling out of the distant mountain terrain, touching the ground and wending its way down the final slope. He recognized it as the dark, shimmering cloud they had seen from the other side of the mountains. As the nebulous mass drove headlong into the grassy hills, dust churned up from its passage. He wondered if the mass was some great force summoned by Scartaris to join his armies. Or perhaps it was following *them.*

He turned and led the way down the slope, away from the cloud. They had enough problems already.

The city of Tairé lay ahead of them, large enough to cover five hexagons. It seemed gloomy, blanketed in shadows, but it was a sign of life like a bulkhead in the desolation. He wondered why anyone would remain there after Scartaris drained all life away, killed all their work.

Outside the city rose great mounds of broken rock. Apparently, the builders of Tairé had intended to make terraced gardens, but they contented themselves with arranging the shattered boulders in ornate circles. Delrael was impressed that simple characters had done all that work, picked up all those stones and stacked them there, cleared the dead hexes to make them fertile again. In vain.

By noon, they reached the black dividing line that marked the beginning of the city. The wall surrounding Tairé was made of gray stone, interlocked blocks without mortar, and marked at precise intervals by tall parapets to provide a better view of the desolation beyond.

Carved into the wall were intricate, stylized friezes depicting scenes from the Game. Vailret squinted his eyes and scanned them with apparent astonishment. His mouth opened and closed, just as it had when he confronted Arken.

Delrael did not recognize many of the scenes, but he could make out Sesteb's disputed stone throw that started the Wars, the creation of the character races as fighters, the funeral pyre in which Stilvess had the Sorcerer generals cast their swords, the surviving Sorcerers creating the four die-shaped Stones, and finally, the six Spirits rising up from the Transition.

Delrael rubbed the silent silver in his belt and thought of the Earthspirits, wishing they would somehow communicate with him. Let him know they were still alive.

The Tairan friezes were crumbling and weathered, caked with blown dust and never cleaned. The city seemed strangely silent, restless and waiting. Delrael saw windows in the towers, but they remained empty, revealing no curious faces to greet the travelers.

"And now for something completely different," Journeyman mumbled.

Tairé should have contained thousands of characters. Delrael heard no activity, none of the clanking and bustle that had marked Sitnalta from a distance. Instead, Tairé cowered in a hush, comatose from being too close to Scartaris.

The city's main gate stood tall and open, an ornate framework of wrought iron showing leaves and flowers growing up out of the ground. But the gate sagged on rusted hinges. Wind blew through the spidery ironwork, making it hum. No one greeted—or challenged—them as they entered Tairé.

"Either the Tairans aren't taking care of anything," Bryl said, "or this place is as dead as the land around it."

"Yoo hoo! Anybody home?" Journeyman called.

The Tairans had made full use of the limited resources of the desolation. The houses were constructed of broken stone blasted up in the upheavals of battle, decorated with frescoes painted into plaster made from crushed limestone. The artists had used natural pigments, ochres and reds found in the rocks, black from soot. Pieces of glistening obsidian were inlaid in game-board patterns.

Some of the flat sides of buildings showed scenes of daily life—not epic battles, but pictures of bountiful harvests, lush forest terrain, large gatherings for group games. History was depicted on the walls *outside* of Tairé; inside, they looked to the future instead.

The architecture was open, with plenty of space for meetings. Wind whispered through the buildings, weaving through open windows. Delicate metal chimes hung on corners, tinkling at random.

As they travelled deeper into the city, the neglect became more apparent. Many of the spectacular frescoes were chipped and faded, smeared with an oily soot floating in the air. Delrael saw empty troughs under the windows of some buildings, apparently intended to hold flowers.

On several larger buildings, crude doors, bars, and gates had recently been added, looking clumsy and out of place.

The noise of a dripping fountain sounded loud in the Tairan silence. Delrael put out his hand to catch the warm, rust-tinted water, but he did not drink. The sculpture above the fountain was a wrought-iron bell, ornate but silent. The fountain stood at an intersection of two streets with wide stone buildings on either side. He realized that in the middle of the desolation someone must have used magic to summon up water, but now even the fountain had ceased.

Journeyman scooped up some of the puddled water and spread it on his dry clay skin to moisten himself. He smiled in relief.

Vailret and Bryl sat down, but Delrael paced around the fountain, shading his eyes and searching for signs of life. The afternoon sunlight was bright and harsh. "I'm getting tired of this," he said.

In the shadows of one of the open buildings, he saw a figure standing between two stone columns. Delrael strode toward the building. "Come here!" He didn't know if the Tairan would hide or come to him.

To his surprise, a thin, haggard woman stepped forward. At first, she appeared ancient, but he saw that she was not old at all, despite her sunken and shadowed eyes. Dirt stained her tattered gray clothes —but she seemed unaware of all that. She took several jerky steps toward him, as if something else moved her arms and legs.

"Where is everybody?" Delrael asked her. "What's going on here? This is Tairé—what happened?"

She turned to face Delrael. Her eyes were milky white; the pupils and irises had vanished, leaving a soulless blank expression that sent a shiver up his spine. She never blinked.

Her voice sounded garbled, awkward. Her lower jaw moved up and down, clacking her teeth together, but not in time with the words she tried to form. Her tongue writhed around in her mouth, making sounds by brute force.

"Delrael. You are Delrael."

The fighter blinked, taken aback. Delrael looked behind him at the others, questioning, before turning back to the woman. "How do you know my name?"

The Tairan woman jerked backward as if her nerves had snapped like broken bowstrings. "Delrael!" She hissed and gurgled in her throat, but she stood with her arms straight at her sides. Spasming muscle tics rippled across her face.

"What's happening to you?" Delrael shook the Tairan woman by the shoulders, but he might as well have been grabbing an empty sack.

"Something is moving." Journeyman jerked his head to indicate the empty dwellings.

Delrael released the woman, and she staggered one step backward, then remained where she stood. He saw other forms inside the buildings, lining up at the entrances. A rustle crept into the air, like thousands of furtive footsteps on the cobblestones. He smelled a sharp tang that might have been his own fear-sweat. He narrowed his eyes and felt his heart pumping.

Other Tairans stepped onto the street in a strange lockstep. They moved in unison, stiff, like movable pieces in a complicated war game. All their eyes were blank.

They behaved like the ylvans in Tallin's village. Delrael winced at the cold memory.

The Tairans stepped forward from the buildings, coming through intersecting streets together. They stood close. Their hands looked torn and infected from hard work. Their faces showed no expression at all.

"They're completely mindless," Vailret said.

Journeyman spoke in a gruff voice. "A mind is a terrible thing to waste."

Delrael pulled out his sword. The silence of the city remained, doubly eerie now. The Tairans marched forward, closing in. He felt their synchronous breathing, their hearts beating together as they took one step, then another.

"We can't fight all these characters," Vailret said, but he pulled out his short sword anyway.

The golem bent his knees and banged his fists together with a smacking noise. "They've blocked off every exit. Bummer."

The blank faces of the Tairans made Delrael's skin crawl. They were unarmed. This would not be a battle—it would be a slaughter —but the Tairans would win. They outnumbered the travelers by thousands. He didn't know what to do.

Bryl took out the Fire Stone. "I can blast our way through. It'll kill a lot of them."

Delrael blinked back stinging water in his eyes. The sword felt heavy and poisonous in his hand. He thought of how all these characters had been warped by Scartaris. He saw Tallin lying dead in the catacombs of the Anteds. None of this *felt* like a simple game anymore. He couldn't just slaughter with impunity. He didn't want to. It had to be a fair fight.

"Only as a last resort," he told Bryl. "We have to think of a better way."

Delrael felt sweat dribble between his shoulder blades. He could smell the Tairans, feel them breathing, sense their body heat. The afternoon sun slanted through the streets. Ripples of warmth rose from the heated stone walls.

"If you want me to use the Fire Stone, it better be now, before they get too close." Bryl rubbed his palms on the eight-sided ruby.

Then a woman's loud voice broke the attack. Hooves rang out on the cobblestones; they heard the crack of a whip. "Hyah! What are you doing? Get away from there, all you Tairans." The whip cracked again. "Go on!"

Delrael craned his neck but could not see who had made the noise. He felt his damp grip around the hilt of his sword. His throat had gone dry.

A woman pushed her way forward on a gray horse, squeezing between the Tairans. The horse moved from side to side, nervous around the shuffling people. The woman flicked her whip back and forth, making the Tairans shrug aside. "Go on! I know you're not deaf. Get out of here!"

Reluctantly, it seemed, the Tairans moved aside. Their sluggish attack dissolved as they drifted toward the buildings. They moved backward, keeping their pupilless gaze on Delrael. He glared back at them.

Delrael drew deep breaths through his nose and let them out between his lips. He watched the woman approach on her horse. She was wiry, clad in a bright green tunic; it looked as if she had made some effort to keep herself clean. At her side hung an unsheathed sword with a rippled edge, like a tongue of flame.

Her hair was long and dark, tied out of the way in a single braid. She moved quickly, as if with an attitude that her every action counted a great deal. Her dark eyes flicked rapidly, alert and intense. A fire of anger burned in her pupils. *Pupils*—somehow this character had escaped Scartaris's touch.

"I'm Mindar," the woman said and dismounted from her horse.

She brushed at her legs and stamped her feet, looking flustered. "Did they harm you?"

Delrael glanced at his companions and answered for them. "No, I think we're all right."

"What's a nice girl like you doing in a place like this?" Journeyman asked. The others introduced themselves.

"They know who we are," Vailret said, looking shaken. He flashed an angry glare at Delrael. "They *know who we are!*"

Mindar led her horse ahead of them down the street. "Let's get farther away from this place. I never know what Scartaris is going to do."

She moved ahead with a determined step. Delrael had to hurry to keep up with her. Mindar turned, and Delrael was startled by the viciousness of the grin she flashed at them. "I don't know who you are, but I haven't seen the people so awake in a long time. Nobody's been able to arouse them since Scartaris came."

She stared at Delrael, letting the question hang in the air. Vailret shuffled his feet, but Delrael wasted no time pondering. He didn't see the point in hiding it any longer. "We're on a quest to destroy Scartaris, but he's found out about us somehow. That makes our task even riskier."

Vailret nodded. "We understand that Scartaris has the power to end the Game whenever he wants, some kind of metamorphosis. Any time he's frightened enough of us, he'll just destroy the map."

Mindar brushed aside her dark bangs and exposed a lumpy red scar on her forehead, a burning red welt in the shape of an *S*. "Scartaris will play with you as long as he can. He enjoys that. He does it to me."

Vailret squinted at her. "What happened to you?"

"Scartaris can't control me. I don't know why my mind can resist him when the other characters can't—do you think that's a blessing? Look what it did for me." She spread her hands. The spring-green tunic looked dirty, a pitiful attempt at brightness and cheer in the drab city.

Somehow Tallin had some ability to resist Scartaris too, a random trait generated by a fluke of a dice roll. Of the thousands of characters in Tairé, Delrael was not surprised that *one* had the same immunity.

"I wasn't any important person," Mindar continued. "I was just another artist, painting some of the frescoes. Two days each week, I'd go outside the city walls and help tend the fields, rebuild the irrigation channels, plant trees in the hills."

She glared at them. "All of this used to be beautiful, you know. My husband worked more than his share of time out there, so I could have extra hours for painting. We had one daughter, Cithany."

Tears glistened on Mindar's dark eyes. "The children were the first to ... to fade. We didn't know about Scartaris—but all of our crops withered and died. The grass turned brown, the trees became barren. Then our children were lost to us. Scartaris seeped into their minds and played them like puppets. We couldn't understand. We didn't know."

Mindar shook her fist in the air, facing toward the east. "Some characters were stronger, but they lost in the end. You see how they all are, mindless husks. Scartaris enjoys role-playing them, like the Outsiders Play their characters on Hexworld. I was the only one remaining. What could I do, all by myself?"

She lowered her eyes. "At least I had my anger. One afternoon, I looked around me and saw that I was no longer part of my own city, that everything else had cut itself off from me. The soul of Tairé was gone. By this time, some of us knew about Scartaris—Enrod had found out, but it was too late for him too.

"So, in my despair, I shouted into the streets. I cursed Scartaris at the top of my lungs." Her fingers rubbed the *S*-scar on her forehead. She mumbled her words. "So he cursed me back.

"The people gathered and found me. They grabbed my arms and pinned them behind me, then they carried me to one of the blacksmiths' shops. I couldn't break free because there were so many. You saw them. They held me down by an anvil in the dark. I was screaming and I could hardly breathe. I hurt myself trying to struggle.

"They took a hot iron and branded this on my forehead. Then they dunked my head in the water and left me there on the floor." She drew a deep breath and closed her eyes.

"They were people I knew! They were—" her voice hitched, "—my brother and my husband!"

She leaned against a stone wall on which had been painted an ochre sunrise shedding light over lush forest terrain and bountiful fields surrounding the reborn city of Tairé. The paint had faded, dusted with an oily smear.

"This is supposed to mark me as the lowliest character in Scartaris's domain. I am to be taunted, played with, and, worst of all, ignored. He casts aside and breaks everything I cared for—Scartaris must be laughing as he watches me try to pick up the pieces."

Mindar trembled with passion. Her hands clutched at the hilt of her rippled sword as if she wanted to damage something. She fought to bring control over herself again.

"Scartaris sent a demon watcher to make sure that I see no peace. The Cailee. It hides in the shadows, watches my thoughts to learn how it may inflict the most pain on me."

Bryl looked at the shadows of the alleys, widening his eyes. Delrael frowned. "What is the Cailee?"

Mindar straightened and began to walk down the street, leading her horse. Delrael could see nothing but the back of her head as she answered. "The Cailee becomes tangible only at night. It looks like a shadow, featureless and black, in the form of a human. But on the ends of its hands are hooked silver claws, sharp enough to rend—"

Her shoulders bunched and rippled. "The characters here are all so helpless now, so helpless."

Mindar swallowed. "The Cailee shadows me, follows me, waiting until I'm not watching—and then it slaughters!"

She whirled with such anger that her horse skittered two steps sideways. The *S*-scar on her forehead seemed to throb with a light of its own.

She dropped her voice to a quiet longing tone. "One night, the Cailee slit open my husband. And Cithany. And left them to bleed onto the floor of our home. For no other reason than that it would hurt *me*."

Delrael felt his heart pounding, thinking again of Tallin and how the Anteds had killed him. Mindar slashed at the air in her passion.

"For that, I'm going to destroy Scartaris. No matter what it takes. If you have a way, then I will join your quest." Her gaze flicked from Delrael to the others. Delrael felt the heat behind those eyes.

"We have a way," he answered.

"*I* have a way too," Journeyman said.

"We'll need all the help we can get," Delrael said. He held out his hand to her. Something inside of him felt uneasy about Mindar, but he could understand her anger and her obsession. She struck him like a true comrade, someone who had felt the same wounds. He felt close to her.

She flashed a smile, sharp and dangerous, and grasped Delrael's hand. "My friends, together we can defeat Scartaris."

Mindar stiffened and turned pale. Her eyes widened, flicking back and forth as if to see something from the corner of her eyes. "What have I done? I called you my *friends*!"

She grabbed the horse and set off down a side street. The mare's hooves made loud noises that echoed against the buildings. "You are in grave danger—follow me! It's almost sundown. The Cailee will come soon."

She didn't speak. She didn't have to. Deep shadows slanted across the street. The sky turned orange as the sun sank behind the knife-edge of the Spectre Mountains, dappling the stone walls.

Mindar brought them to a wide, squat building and opened the iron front gates. She stopped and held the horse's head in her hands. She rubbed the gray mare behind the ears.

"There now, you take care of yourself." She released the horse and clapped her hands. "Go on!" She turned it around and gave it a light kick with her boot. The mare trotted away through the streets.

"Won't the Cailee get your horse in the middle of the night?" Bryl asked.

Mindar flashed her hard smile again. "No. A horse is not like the people of Tairé—she can defend herself. And she can run. She knows where to hide. Besides, horses are much too valuable for hauling supplies to Scartaris's armies.

"This building here is one of the old storehouses." She led them inside. The windows were narrow, and the air smelled musty and empty. Dust filtered into angled shafts of light across the floor.

"Tairé couldn't raise all its own crops, of course. Sometimes we bought food from the farming villages in the mountain foothills. The half-breeds used magic to replenish our supplies of meats and grains. Mostly it's all been used up by now."

Their footsteps echoed across the floor in the empty building. Mindar led them down an open staircase to the basement, cool and dry beneath the ground. Several chambers had been hollowed out. Mindar took them to the door of one.

"I set this up for myself a while ago, when I thought someday I might have to make a stand against the people of Tairé. It's well defended and well supplied."

Inside, the room was windowless. Boxes of provisions and drinking water in sealed casks were piled against the wall. Bryl found candles in one of the boxes and took them out.

"The door is secure. It's heavy wood—and we don't have much wood here. It should keep us safe against the Cailee."

Mindar stood up straight, as if something had twisted inside her. She looked frightened and sweating, even more than before. "I forgot to lock the upstairs gate! Be ready to let me in when I come back down!"

Before they could say anything, she squeezed out through the half-shut door. Delrael heard her boots skipping up the stairs, then quick footfalls across the floor above. He looked at Vailret, who shrugged and shook his head.

And then they heard an outcry from above. "Cailee! Stay away!" They heard a clang of iron as the gates slammed, and then a loud crash of torn metal clattering to the floor. "Get out!"

A sharp sound rang out as metal struck stone. Delrael pictured Mindar swinging with her rippled sword, and then he heard frantic steps charging down the stairs.

"Get ready!" Delrael said. Vailret stood with him by the door, waiting to push it shut.

Mindar ran for them, holding the sword in one hand, her whip coiled at her hip. She leaped down the last three stairs. Her boots skittered on the floor, and her dark braid flipped back and forth.

"Close the door behind me! Close the door!"

As she ducked inside, Delrael saw an oily black silhouette creep down the stairs, moving dark and humanlike, but completely without features. A solid black mass that looked like a hole, a cut-out in the shape of a human character, gliding down the stairs, smooth and fast.

On the ends of each finger were gleaming, knifelike claws.

"Close the door!" Mindar cried.

Delrael shoved his shoulder against the door, and it thumped against the jamb. Mindar scrabbled with her hands and pulled the solid wooden crossbeam over the supports.

An instant later, they heard a howl as something massive struck the other side of the door. Delrael still had his shoulder against it and felt the wood vibrate.

With another roar, the Cailee struck the door again. Then Delrael heard sharp, splintering sounds of silver claws ripping open the wood.

CHAPTER 14
THE WOMAN CURSED BY SCARTARIS

The Outsiders put their characters through a crucible, forging us with their games, tempering us with agonies or pleasures. Some characters are destroyed by this testing. Others come through it galvanized and stronger than before.
—Stilvess Peacemaker

The Cailee attacked again.

The door thudded as the monster slammed against the wood, then screeching claws skittered up and down the jamb.

Bryl whimpered.

"That's more than just a *shadow*," Delrael said.

"Who knows what evil lurks in the hearts of men?" Journeyman said.

Mindar looked at them. The flickering candlelight washed over her face, shining with the sweat of her effort, her fear. The air felt hot and close around them. Delrael took a drink from one of the water skins, but the liquid tasted warm and flat.

Mindar turned away to stare at the door. She ran the braided end of the whip through her calloused hands.

The Cailee struck the door again.

"I've tried to hunt it down in the streets," she whispered. "I went out at night with my sword, but the Cailee always eluded me. It can vanish into any pool of darkness, hide in any corner where the light doesn't fall. I challenged the Cailee, but it chose to strike behind my back."

Her fingers clutched at the whip, as if to use it as a garrote. "I ran through the streets. Everything was dark, since no one lit lamps in their homes anymore. I found that the Cailee had torn down the door to my own home.

"I didn't try to be cautious. It wouldn't have done any good. When I pushed the torch into the shadows of my house, I could sense the Cailee. I also smelled fresh blood. When I came into the main room, I found—" Mindar choked on her words.

Delrael stiffened and wanted to go to her, comfort her. But he felt that she did not want any comfort. She might be afraid it would weaken her.

"I found my husband and my daughter. Even mindless, they still knew where home was. They lived there. They were both slaughtered by the Cailee. It had thrown their blood in all directions, like it was playing.

"They hadn't put up any struggle, of course. Scartaris killed their minds long ago. I suppose they didn't even feel any pain."

"Mindar ..." Delrael said.

"I ran outside and found the Cailee. I slashed at it with my sword and scored a blow—then the Cailee tore at me with its silver claws, laying open my side. I fell to the street with a mortal wound, bleeding for hours. But I couldn't die.

"When I woke up at dawn, I had healed completely. And I found that the Cailee had also slain my brother. The one who had helped brand my forehead."

On the other side of the door, the Cailee ran one claw down the wood in a long, slow scratching noise that made the skin crawl on Delrael's back. The Cailee seemed to be mocking them.

Bryl's face looked the color of sour milk in the dim candlelight. He kneaded his fingers around the ruby Fire Stone. "If the Cailee gets in here, I'm going to blast it."

Mindar looked at the eight-sided stone with an expression of scorn on her face. Her eyes had a dull despair to them, but suddenly, her gaze focused. "How did you get that?" Her voice carried a sharp command, and she sprang to her feet. "Where did you get Enrod's Fire Stone?"

Delrael stood up beside Bryl. Everything fell into place for him as he remembered. Vailret cleared his throat but seemed reluctant to start explaining.

"Delrael..." Mindar said, rolling the name around her mouth. "You're the ones who made the Barrier River! Enrod said you cut us off!"

Vailret coughed and turned away, as if avoiding her. "Enrod wasn't ... himself, I don't think. He tried to destroy all the hexagons west of the Barrier River. But the Deathspirits stopped him and cursed him to stay on the River until the end of the Game. They took the Fire Stone away from him and gave it to us."

He lowered his eyes. "Scartaris must have been manipulating Enrod, but the Deathspirits didn't care about any reasons, only what he was trying to do."

Mindar sat back down with slumped shoulders. She undid the braid in her hair and shook her head to loosen the strands. She closed her dark eyes.

"That doesn't surprise me. I know how upset Enrod was about your River. He had found out about Scartaris and how we'd all have to escape soon. *You* made our escape impossible. You trapped us on the same side of the map with Scartaris." She shrugged and ran her fingers through hair that hung long and dark, kinky from the tight braid.

"Enrod was strong, very strong. He resisted longer than most of the Tairans. But he became obsessed about the Barrier River. I watched him. I think Scartaris used that as a hook to trap him, to twist open a weak spot in his mind and drive in the puppet strings." She sighed. "Still, his fate doesn't seem fair."

Vailret pursed his lips. "I don't suppose the Deathspirits were much willing to compromise."

The Cailee hit the door, but its efforts seemed to be losing enthusiasm.

"In a way, I'm glad Enrod isn't here to see what's happened to his city. He loved it so much."

She took the water skin from Delrael's hands and drank a deep gulp. "Scartaris is using the characters here to make weapons, swords, and shields for his great battle." Mindar shuddered and looked at them, but seemed disappointed with their reaction. She scowled.

"You wouldn't understand how great *that* defeat is. Remember that Tairé is built on the worst scars of the ancient wars. The mechanics of game battles and personal combat are abhorrent to us. When Enrod founded this city, it was to be progressive and forward-looking. He knew the future of Hexworld lay in the hands of human characters—he wanted to make sure we succeeded without repeating the mistakes of the Sorcerers."

Vailret lit another candle to replace one of those that burned low. He spoke up. "That's where Enrod and Sardun had their differences, I think. Sardun wanted to enshrine the memory of the Sorcerers. Enrod wanted to work at keeping human characters alive and safe. Is that right?"

Mindar nodded. She kept her eyes lowered. "By using Tairé to forge swords, Scartaris struck another psychological blow—it makes his victory more fun to him. Imagine, Tairans making weapons!"

She sat brooding, thinking. They fell into silence, waiting for the night to pass. The Cailee took to scratching along the stone walls outside their room, then howling in the echoing basement.

"How many more years are we going to have to stay here like this?" Bryl asked.

"Time flies when you're having fun," Journeyman answered.

They waited.

They sat in silence, listening to the ticking, random noises of the room. Outside, they heard quiet shuffling, the unknown movements of the Cailee that were even more frightening in their stealth than the occasional violent crashes against the door.

They sat for hours with no way of knowing how much time passed. They heard nothing from the Cailee. Bryl huddled in the blue robe, running his gnarled fingers through his gray beard. Journeyman appeared dormant.

Delrael looked at Vailret and Mindar. "Do you think it's morning yet?"

Mindar stood up. "We can see if the Cailee is gone. I'll go out. You watch the door."

Delrael began to protest, but she cut him off. "No. If I find the Cailee, then I'll have what I want." She lifted her sword. "If I don't find it, then we can go to our work."

Delrael and Vailret stood close to each other by the door with their own swords drawn. He imagined the edge of the old Sorcerer blade clanging against the slash of silver claws.

Mindar popped up the sturdy crossbar, and Delrael yanked the door open. Mindar slipped through the crack and vanished into the basement. He caught a glimpse of grayish morning light before he and Vailret threw their weight against the door to close it.

They listened but heard no immediate sounds until Mindar's quiet steps went up the stairs.

"Cailee!" she cried.

Delrael tensed, ready to yank open the door and run to fight with her, but they heard no scuffle, nothing else.

She came back down the stairs and stopped by the door. "It's all right. The Cailee is gone."

They opened the door again. Mindar put her shoulders through. The anger in her eyes was rekindled.

"I saw the Cailee standing in the shadows. It was fading with the dawn light. I ran with my sword, but it was too insubstantial. Now I'll have to wait for another night."

She pushed open the door. Delrael breathed the cooler air of the basement, saw the murky light that filtered down from the narrow windows above, bright and clean after their night in the storeroom. They looked at the sturdy wooden door and stopped.

The door had been shredded. Great gouges and splinters were peeled away, torn out by hooked silver claws. The iron pins of the hinges hung loose from the wall, nearly pulled from the stone.

"That's not going to last another night," Delrael said. Bryl swayed on his feet but managed not to faint.

When they got to the open air and bright sunlight, Delrael stood blinking and breathing deeply. He liked to be out where he could *do* something, where he could fight—not trapped like a victim in a cell.

Mindar looked changed—strengthened. She had a bounce to her step, and her demeanor did not seem so hopeless. "Come. I want to show you something."

She took Delrael's elbow and led them through the streets. Nothing stirred. The Tairans seemed to be hiding.

"I painted this back when I was happy and idealistic." She pointed to one of the frescoes on a building. "It was easy to think up nice things to paint then, of our bright future and how the Game would continue forever. We were going to make ourselves strong and self-sufficient. That's what we thought the Outsiders wanted! To make lives of our own so we wouldn't be dependent on them."

She led them to the side of an old building with a flat expanse of hexagonal stone blocks. "This one I did later."

A half-finished fresco had been sketched on the blocks, but in the center of the wall, the soot-grimed plaster had been scrubbed away and overlaid with a fresh coating. Mindar had drawn a new picture showing the mountains to the east. A great featureless human figure towered over the landscape, holding his arms up in a gesture of victory. But the fresco was finished, not just a sketch. She had drawn the figure without features, but it had a mystique, a *power* to it.

"It's the Stranger Unlooked-For," she said.

Vailret looked at her, frowning as if trying to recall something he had heard. "Who was that?"

"Nobody knows. But he saved Hexworld." Mindar put her hands on her hips and walked over to the wall, inspecting her artwork. "It was just after the Transition, before Enrod established Tairé, when the rest of the Hexworld characters were fighting each other over who would rule the map."

"The Scouring," Vailret said. Mindar ignored him.

"In the middle of the desolation grew something that would have destroyed us all, something a lot like Scartaris."

Mindar stared up into the sky. "The Outsider David must have tried to end the Game once before, and failed. He failed because the Stranger Unlooked-For came and destroyed his monster. The Stranger used some kind of weapon more powerful than anything ever used in the old Sorcerer wars. Nobody knows who the Stranger was. Nobody knows how he succeeded in killing David's first monster. But we should all remember him as a hero."

She took out her rippled sword and rested its tip on the flagstones of the street. "I know one thing, though. We can't count on the Stranger to return. We've got nobody but ourselves to fight Scartaris."

Shuffling away from the painting, Mindar kept her eyes averted.

"Before we go, there's one thing I want to do. I'll need your help. I hope you'll join me."

Bryl shifted his feet uneasily.

"The journey of a thousand miles begins with a single step," Journeyman said.

Mindar took a deep breath. "Scartaris has one large smithy to fashion swords, and the tannery to make shields. I want to destroy them before we go. Strike a psychological blow back at Scartaris. That'll teach him not to use Tairé to make his weapons."

Delrael looked at the deserted streets and saw in his mind the dream that Enrod had, to raise the city out of the desolation, to turn it toward the future. And he saw how Scartaris had twisted that idea.

Yes, he liked the thought of striking a real blow, now that Scartaris knew who they were anyway. They no longer needed to keep their quest secret. It was time to stop hiding—time to start showing that they meant business.

"Yes." Delrael met Mindar's eyes. "Let's do it."

Mindar smiled, and Delrael felt a thrill, perhaps of fear, run down his spine. She looked beautiful and determined, and more deadly than any weapon he had ever seen. The angry red *S*-scar marred her forehead.

"Let me find my mare. If we get horses for you too, we can increase our travel allotment, get to Scartaris sooner."

Mindar led them through the winding streets. Delrael noticed a few Tairans shuffling along doing indecipherable tasks. They took no notice of the travelers. Mindar pointedly did not look at them.

When they reached the stables, Mindar's gray mare waited for them. Mindar patted the mare on the neck, and Delrael could see a genuine attachment between them. She left the horse outside as she motioned the others in. Only two horses remained in the stable.

"They've taken three more." Mindar shook her head in disgust. "Sometimes Scartaris sends his monsters here to get weapons. Other times, he has the Tairans use horses to haul cartloads off to his army. The horses never come back."

"There aren't enough horses for us," Bryl said, although from the tone in his voice, Delrael thought he sounded relieved. Bryl had never ridden a horse and probably wasn't thrilled at the idea.

"I don't need one," Journeyman said. "I can keep up with any pace you set."

"Bryl's light enough." Vailret stood beside the half-Sorcerer. "He can ride with me. We'll take one horse. Del, you take the other. Mindar has her own."

Mindar nodded and turned to the door. "Let's get going."

Delrael approached one of the horses skeptically, a mottled brown gelding that appeared calm enough. He ran his palm along the horse's shoulders and then, trying not to look inexperienced, he scrambled on the gelding's back. Delrael held on to the mane and swayed, finding his balance. The horse felt warm and vibrant under him, strong and alive.

"Don't worry," Mindar said. "You're a fighter character. You'll ride easily. It's natural for you. Part of your characteristics."

Vailret watched his cousin, then worked his way onto the other horse. Bryl frowned, then Journeyman picked him up bodily and set him in front of Vailret. The horses seemed anxious to leave the stables. Outside in the street again, Mindar mounted her own mare.

She stopped in the square in front of the stables to where an iron bell, embossed with flower patterns, hung over a stone foundation. Four Tairans shuffled from one building to another, keeping their heads down and slouching. Their gray clothes and sunken expressions made it impossible for Delrael to tell if they were even male or female characters.

Mindar removed the whip from around her waist and, holding on to the gray mare's mane with one hand, she lashed out and struck the bell. A *gong* echoed through the streets.

The Tairans looked up, gawked at her for a moment, then moved back inside. Mindar struck the bell again with the whip and waited. Nothing stirred in the buildings. Her expression turned dark and stormy. Tears glistened in her dark eyes. She rang the bell twice more, then hung her head. "Tairé has died," she said. "That bell should have brought all characters in the city flocking to see what the danger was." She fastened her whip then urged the mare forward.

"We'll give them some danger."

The smithy stood by itself, surrounded by smoke and noise. On three sides, the alleys were broader than usual. One wall of a nearby building had been knocked down to give greater access for raw material to be shipped in, for weapons to be carried away. The rubble lay where it had fallen; white chips and broken brick showed that the wall had been intact not long before.

Smoke curled into the bright, hot sky; feathery black stains smeared the smithy walls. A mound of pig iron lay piled near the door. From the inside came gusts of heat and banging sounds as Tairans worked on swords and shield frames.

"What are we going to do?" Vailret said, squinting his eyes as if deep in thought. "We can't burn it."

"I can still cause a lot of damage." Journeyman smacked his fists together.

"We don't need to destroy the buildings," Mindar said. "This is still my city. It won't do any good to save Tairé if we ruin it in the meantime. We'll destroy the forge and the hearth—that will ruin things so they can't be used to make swords." She stared at the smithy wall with a gaze that seemed to bore through stone. "That'll be enough for now."

Delrael climbed down off his horse and steadied himself against the gelding's back. "Vailret, you and Bryl stay out here and watch the horses. The three of us can handle this."

"You bet your life!" Journeyman said.

"Funny you should put it that way," Mindar said.

Inside, the smithy was dark, lit only by orange, smoky fires. Delrael choked on the stench of sulfur and hot iron. The clang of hammers on anvils rang out in the air.

Five Tairan men worked at the anvils, three women tended hot ingots in the forge. Another hauled pig iron from the pile outside. Their tunics had either burned away or torn off. Red welts and black scars on their skin showed where they had been seared by sparks; the untended wounds festered.

Mindar held her sword in front of her. "Stop what you're doing!" she shouted into the noise.

The Tairans turned to look in unison with blank-eyed stares, then they continued their work, banging against the anvil. She had to yell. "Stop that, I said!"

Delrael strode forward and wrenched the mallet from one of the Tairan's hands. "Drop your hammers!"

Journeyman came forward and yanked mallets out of the others' hands. The mindless men continued to raise and lower their arms for a few moments, then they stood with hands loose at their sides.

"Better move fast, before they figure out what's going on," Mindar said.

Delrael started hacking at the bellows with his sword, severing the pulley ropes. Mindar bent to her knees and used the strength in her back and arms to tip over an anvil.

Journeyman, with a huge grin of glee on his face, picked up an anvil and threw it into the stone-rimmed forge. The heavy iron smashed into the chimney bricks and punched a hole through. With another broad clay hand, he grabbed one of the stone support pillars in the center of the room and jerked it free, toppling a portion of the ceiling. The golem sputtered and brushed dust off his arms.

The Tairans stood blinking at them with murky expressions. Mindar swatted one of the workers with the flat of her blade. "Go on, get out of here! You can't do anything more."

The three of them herded the Tairans into the street. As a parting effort, Journeyman knocked down the columns in the front of the building, making the facade collapse and closing off the front of the smithy.

Several other Tairans stumbled out of buildings, watching with their unblinking gaze.

"Well, that was exhilarating!" Journeyman said.

Mindar mounted her gray mare. "We have to keep moving before they second-guess us. Scartaris enjoys watching me fail—he won't put up with this for long."

She turned the mare around and set off at a trot down the angled street. Delrael tried to figure out how to guide his gelding, but the horse followed Mindar on its own.

Tairé waited in dead silence. Delrael could sense other characters watching through the blind windows, looking at them with the pupilless eyes of Scartaris…

A chemical rotting stench told him they had reached the tannery. On an adjacent wall, Delrael saw a fresco of a dark-haired man he recognized, flowing black beard and fiery eyes—Enrod the Sentinel, wielding the Fire Stone to shine light on the desolation. The optimism in the artist's conception seemed to mock them all.

Delrael imagined a time when the streets had not been silent: horse carts taking characters to the reclaimed hexagons for work in the fields. He thought of Tairans talking, doing business, even squabbling with one another. Scartaris had taken all that away.

The tannery was one of the larger buildings in the city, now modified by adding shutters to close off the windows. A gate stood ajar on crude hinges in front of a stained leather curtain that hung over the entrance. Smoke from fires used to cure and dry the stretched leather drifted out of the window openings like fat snakes. Outside the building lay stacked rows of finished shields, varnished leather coverings over a sturdy iron frame. The bad smell forced Delrael to take short, hitching breaths.

"I don't see why we have to do this," Bryl said, mumbling his words. He covered his nose with the blue cloak. "If we've got the last horses, there's no more leather for shields *anyway*."

Mindar glanced at him with a strange look on her face. Her smile might have been wry if the expression hadn't been so bleak. "Horses are much too valuable to Scartaris. He would never use them just for leather."

She blinked her eyes at the piled shields, the pale, discolored leather glinting off the iron frames. Disgust distorted her face.

"But if it's not horsehide, then—" Bryl began.

"Shut up, Bryl!" Vailret snapped. His face turned greenish.

"We must destroy this place," Mindar whispered.

She dismounted and drew her sword. "Come on, Delrael. We'll get the people out, then Bryl can destroy it with the Fire Stone. Enrod would want that, burn it clean."

Without waiting for him, Mindar strode to the front of the tannery. Delrael took three running steps to catch up to her. She pulled open the iron gate, letting it clang against the far stone wall. She used the tip of her sword to slash across the sewn leather curtain and let it fall to pieces. Her boots stomped it flat as she entered the building.

Delrael followed her into the firelit dimness. The stench hung in the air like foul liquid pressing into his lungs. Irritated tears formed in his eyes, but he blinked them away.

"We won't fail this time, Scartaris," Mindar said at the shadows around her.

Delrael's knuckles whitened around the hilt of his sword. Other Tairans moved in the large, but somehow claustrophobic, room. As his eyes adjusted to the gloom, he staggered from the grisly sight around him.

Four Tairans grappled with a wooden frame, stretching a skin on a rack. Another woman took a flat knife and began scraping the back of the skin. Entrails, bones, and waste leather lay piled in deep stone vats, dripping in pools of clotting blood.

Against the walls sat basins filled with brine solutions, lime, and tanning chemicals, each stuffed with ragged skins. A covering of ash was scattered on the floor to soak up the blood. Brownish-red footprints left aimless trails in the gray ash.

Racks of drying treated skins hung from the stone arches, showing vague, distorted shapes of what had once been arms and legs. Piles of finished leather lay stacked in the dim corners, waiting to be mounted on shield frames.

The orange light from torches and braziers flickered with the air coming in now that the leather curtain had been torn down. Mindar let out a strangled cry at the scene, and Delrael closed his eyes with a wince, then forced himself to open them again. He was a fighter, after all. He should have been immune to the sight of gore and carnage.

A mound of human heads, useless for their leather, were piled high in the corner. Their soft jelly eyes stood open in a blank expression of terror. Some of the mouths hung open, dry and black inside.

Then Delrael noticed something that made the nausea surge up inside him. These eyes weren't the pupilless white of the other empty Tairans—they were normal, terror-stricken, brown irises and blue. Scartaris had given them back their minds an instant before death, letting them know what they had done and what was going to happen to them.

"You bastard!"

Delrael bent over, feeling his chest and stomach muscles spasm. This was foul and unfair. Scartaris did not play the same Game—no glorious combat with heroic deeds. Just slaughter, no honor or challenge or excitement. How could Scartaris enjoy this? *Always have fun* ... Such a warped character, even a monster, had to be destroyed.

The dead Tairan eyes stared up from the mound of heads. The pupils seemed dilated in the dim firelight.

He squeezed his eyelids shut and was sick on the ash-covered floor of the tannery. He wheezed and coughed.

The other Tairan workers stopped what they were doing and stood facing them. They all wore identical broad grins.

Delrael lurched back to his feet, closing his hand around the sword hilt. Stinging tears came to his eyes. Mindar gripped him by the shoulder to be sure he was all right, but he shrugged her off and lunged forward to slash at the drying skins on the racks overhead.

"Let's get the people out of here so we can bring this place down," he said. He grabbed one of the motionless Tairan workers and jerked him toward the door. The man stumbled, without cooperating or resisting. Delrael pushed him out the door. He wasted less time shoving the next person out.

Mindar went to the three other workers, but they suddenly moved and grabbed her around the shoulders. Taken by surprise, she lashed out and struggled, but they held on to her arms. The third Tairan went to the cluster of hanging skins, loosened a dangling rope, and let two intact bodies fall to the floor, one large and one small. With a thump, they sprawled on their heads, stiff arms and legs cracking into awkward positions. They lay in the blood and ash.

Delrael ran to help Mindar—but the Tairans were not trying to hurt her. One of them grabbed her head and turned it so that she had to look, had to *see*.

The two bodies were naked, but preserved by the tannery's processes—a man and a small child, a daughter. Dried blood and claw marks scored their flesh. Both faces held a fixed look of terror and eyes that were *not* milky-blank, but contained a pupil and dark iris, a mind, a soul.

"No!" With a scream, Mindar threw herself away from the Tairan workers and went wild with her sword, striking down both Tairans who held her. Her rippled blade slashed across the face of the third Tairan, obliterating the empty white eyes. Delrael drew his sword, but Mindar needed no help.

"No, Scartaris..." She hunched over the torn bodies of her husband and daughter. Her voice trembled in the silence of the tannery. She reached out to touch Cithany's stiff shoulder.

Delrael stood behind her. "We have to go." He placed his hand on her back. "Let's destroy this place."

Mindar slid shut the brittle eyelids of her daughter, brushed her fingers over the face of her husband, and then closed his eyes as well. "Now you can't see any more of what Scartaris is doing to our city."

Delrael took her arm to guide her. Mindar lurched out of the tannery and stumbled on the slippery flagstones. She fell to her knees, retching, then scrambled back to her feet. She held her sword in both hands and lashed back and forth at imaginary demons. Her eyes were clouded and gushing tears. Her lips drew away from her teeth in an angry snarl.

The others stepped back. She screamed and seemed unable to catch her breath. "Scartaris!" Mindar turned around in circles with the sword and then stopped as if grabbed by a giant hand. "You will pay for this."

She staggered toward Bryl. "Use the Fire Stone. Burn that place! Bring it down!"

"Is there anyone left inside?" Bryl asked.

"Burn it!" Mindar screamed. She reached out and grabbed his blue cloak, pushing him back toward the stone wall of another building. Bryl lost his footing and slipped, but she held on to his cloak and propped him up. "Burn it, I said!"

Her smoldering eyes seemed to cut through him. Delrael took a step forward, then hesitated, afraid to touch her, afraid that Mindar might explode or lash back at him with her rippled sword. He didn't want to hurt her, and he didn't think she wanted to hurt him either.

She wanted to hurt Scartaris. That was all for now.

"Do it, Bryl," he said.

Hands shaking, the half-Sorcerer took out the eight-sided ruby. "Move your feet. Give me some room."

Bryl stood, brushed himself off, then rolled the ruby. The Fire Stone clacked on the flagstones, showing a "6."

Mindar whirled to point at the tannery. Bryl grabbed the Fire Stone and launched fireballs with all the strength of his high roll.

Stone splinters from the tannery exploded outward as Bryl hurled crackling spheres of flame. Inside, the doors buckled. Roof shards erupted into the air; smoke belched through the window slits, reeking of burned skin, oily wood, and vats of preserving chemicals.

The tannery collapsed with a long, low rumble. The wide walls of two nearby buildings cracked with the concussion. Smoke curled around the wreckage up into the air again.

The red *S*-scar on Mindar's forehead glowed a flaming red with unnatural light. She worked her jaw convulsively and stared to the east. "I curse you, Scartaris. I will use every resource to destroy you."

Then the Tairans arrived.

Gray-clad, mindless people surged out of the buildings and moved down the streets toward them, shoulder to shoulder, a massed wall of flesh like a living, unthinking vise.

"We've got to get out of here!" Delrael cried. He grabbed his horse. Mindar stood, unable to move. Her eyes looked devastated.

"Show us the way out of here!" Delrael grabbed her by the shoulders, and she seemed to snap out of her confusion. She saw the Tairans coming.

Mindar hustled them down a narrow alley, leading the horses

and shouldering aside three Tairans who blocked their way. At the end of the alley, another group of characters moved into place to block off their escape. Mindar stopped and looked at a large pavilion to their left.

"This way. We can cut through here." Grabbing her mare's reins, Mindar ran up the steps to the pavilion and into the wide interior. Delrael and the others followed.

The stone roof overhead echoed the sounds of the horses. They passed under lattices strung with decorated clay pots from which hung curtains of dead vines. The vines must have once been lush and cool, but now the brittle strands were like dangling claws trying to scratch down.

"Quick, we can go out the other side!"

They reached the side door where polished steps spilled down onto another street. An obsidian trough that had once served as a reflection pool sat empty, caked with a ring of lime from the evaporated water.

The street in front of them looked deserted. But as they charged down the steps, Tairans moved into the area, crowding at the intersections.

"We've got to hurry," Mindar said. They turned right and ran down the only street still open to them.

"I wish I'd had a chance to study the map of Tairé," Delrael said, breathing hard. "I don't know where we're going. I don't know how to get out of this."

"I don't know *either*," Mindar said, "But we're going to find a way."

The haunted buildings around them stood tall, disorienting. The sun hung straight up in the sky, giving no indication of direction. Delrael followed Mindar, feeling that he could trust her instincts. She fought like he did.

They led the horses, running around one corner, and came

abruptly to the tall, smooth stone barrier of the Tairé city walls, blocking them off from the desolation terrain.

"Now what do we do?" Bryl said.

Vailret moved to the wall and put his fingers against the cracks of the hexagonal stone blocks. He looked up, frowning. "We can't climb this. We can't get over."

A wave of Tairans closed in from all sides, moving in a bizarre lock-step, rippling as they pushed forward. Their eyes were all empty, cold, and pupilless.

Delrael pulled out his sword. Mindar crouched with her back to the wall, holding the rippled blade in front of her. Delrael could feel her tension, flicking her dark gaze from side to side. They would fight together here, to avenge the ghosts in their pasts.

Without warning, Mindar let out a cry and lunged into the approaching crowd, swinging her sword. Some of the unresisting Tairans staggered from their wounds, but the others continued forward without heeding their injuries. They took no notice of Mindar's attack. They folded around her and kept pushing toward Delrael and the others.

She took out the whip instead, lashing out. The Tairans moved away from her but did not stop. Mindar whipped a Tairan woman in the head, leaving a bright streak of blood across her temple.

"Scartaris! I will make you notice me!"

The horses backed and reared, closed in by the stone wall behind them.

"Mindar!" Delrael called.

The Tairans moved slower, as if Scartaris wanted to relish the victory. Mindar fought her way back to the wall. Delrael used the flat of his blade to drive the people away from her. He grabbed Mindar's arm and yanked her to him.

The Tairans formed a semicircle around them.

Journeyman turned to face the wall, spreading his clay hands out against the stone. His flexible face bore an exaggerated, perplexed frown. "If we can't go over the wall—" He drew his arm back. The clay flowed, making a giant bulldozer fist. "Why can't we just go ... through it?"

With the force of a thunderclap, he smashed his arm into the wall blocks. Dust trickled down. He slammed again, and the blocks, not held together by any mortar, jumbled loose.

The Tairans let out a unanimous hiss of anger and pushed forward.

Journeyman struck one more time and, with a rumble, the blocks toppled outward. "Look out!" he said and reached out to deflect a stone block that would have struck Bryl's head.

The horses reared.

The Tairans grasped at them. Their fingers bore dirty, broken nails. Many of them gushed blood from wounds made by Mindar's sword.

The dust from the rupture in the wall stung Delrael's eyes. He coughed. "Let's get out of here!" He leaped on the back of his horse. "Come on, Mindar!"

Vailret grabbed Bryl and they both scrambled onto their horse. Journeyman, looking immensely pleased with himself, pushed around the rubble and let out a strange, primitive yell—"Yabba dabba doo!"—and crashed into the Tairans, knocking many over, cracking some ribs. He picked up bodies to fling them against each other.

"If you can't beat 'em, join 'em!" he said.

Delrael and Mindar rode side by side through the opening in the wall. Vailret led his horse over the rubble.

They galloped out into the desolation. After a moment, Journeyman leaped after them, bounding with great resilient strides and following them into the desert. "Thank you, come again!" he called back at the city.

The air was hot, and reflected sunlight rippled up from the

broken stone and caked dust. The sun had just begun to dip into afternoon.

"We have to ride—get as far away from here as we can." Mindar's voice came in gasping, clipped phrases.

Delrael looked at her and saw how torn she was inside. But a great fear seemed to underlie her anger. "I think we'll be safe now," he said, trying to be reassuring.

Mindar shook her head. "Until tonight." The dust in her hair stiffened the kinks from where she had braided it. "Out here, we'll have no protection at all from the Cailee."

CHAPTER 15
THE SITNALTAN WEAPON

Our greatest treasure is our ideas. All of the inventors in Sitnalta share them freely, and we reward any visionary with a patent of his or her own. The greatest inventors are elevated to the exalted status of Professors. The free exchange of information has made our city great—not one of us would consider changing this.
—Dirac, *Charter of the Sitnaltan Council of Patent Givers*

The cot creaked beneath him as Professor Verne sat up sharply in the middle of the night. The musty smell of the room and his folded overcoat used as a pillow signaled that he was not in his own quarters back in Sitnalta. He blinked his eyes, astonished. He felt disoriented in the darkness—too many fascinating ideas charged through his brain, clamoring to be put down on paper before he forgot them.

His heart pounded from the dream. The Outsider Scott had sent him another message.

The room was dim and cold. He noticed that the electrical heater had stopped functioning again. Outside, the wind rushed around the walls of the Slac fortress, stirring up drafts. Verne's eyes grew adjusted to the shadows, and he could see Frankenstein on the other side of the room also sitting on his cot, pulling socks on his feet. Frankenstein flung aside his blankets and began pacing the room.

Verne got up from his cot and wrapped the blankets around his shoulders. On bare feet, he hurried to the corner and flicked the electrical heater on and off, but it was no use. The device had failed again. He wished he had brought slippers along.

A sulfur match flared, and Frankenstein lit a candle. He waved the matchstick in the air until the flame went out, then he set it beside the paraphernalia on his makeshift worktable. Orange candlelight flickered in the room, disturbed by transient drafts.

"Did you dream it too?" Verne said. Looking at the wide-eyed expression on the other inventor's face, he didn't really need to ask.

"What are we going to do about it?" Frankenstein ran his fingers through his dark hair. "How are we going to implement the construction? It's so complicated."

"First we must decide even if we *should* implement it," Verne said, pondering. He pursed his lips. He picked up the matchstick and relit its end from the candle flame, sucking the flame down into the bowl of his pipe. He puffed absently and kept his voice quiet. "The idea is so awesome. I sensed it might be an incomparable weapon…but I never imagined anything so terrible."

Frankenstein snorted and ruffled through some papers on the table. He flattened a piece of parchment and picked up a scribing pencil. "Can you imagine what a buffoon like Dirac would do with such an idea?"

Verne swallowed. He had not thought of that aspect.

Frankenstein's voice became grave. "We want to do this one ourselves, Jules. And I don't think we should leave any blueprints behind. We won't even apply for a patent on this. Let's just build the weapon, make it do its task, and hope we never need to construct another one."

Verne began pacing. "This weapon is so powerful, it might be worse than letting Hexworld surrender to its own fate. What if it cracks the map open, destroys us all, and backlashes to the Outside?"

"Then it serves the Outsiders right. Nothing is ever impossible, Jules. You, of all characters, should know that. But when the power is so tremendous, I don't want to leave hints around so others can try."

Verne walked from his cot to the table. His feet were numb on the cold stone floor. "You are suggesting that we knowingly withhold scientific information from the people of Sitnalta."

Frankenstein tapped his teeth with the scribing pencil. "I am suggesting that we build this weapon ourselves, with the tools we have on hand here. Once it has destroyed Scartaris, we will never need to concern ourselves about such a weapon again. It will be an obsolete, useless invention that would serve no further purpose anyway."

Verne remained withdrawn. Frankenstein pointed to the parchment, impatient. "Come, I need your help. Is this the way you remember it from the dream?"

Within a few moments, Verne had become so caught up in the problem that he forgot about everything else.

They crept outside, careful not to wake the technicians asleep by the big fire pit in the Slac dining hall. Some of the workers had commandeered their own quarters in empty chambers, but they left the doors ajar.

The fortress was silent as Verne and Frankenstein slipped into the courtyard. Frost sparkled on the rocks, and smooth ice patches dotted the ground where standing puddles had frozen.

The ruined Outsider ship stood black and skeletal under the starlight. Verne had stuffed candles in his pockets and several sulfur matches. Frankenstein carried two electric illuminators powered by galvanic batteries. He switched them on before the two of them entered the ship's main hatch.

The illuminators shone circles of yellow light, reflecting from the polished sections of the alien alloys. They walked down the sloping central passage, under the black girders. Wind whistled through holes and cracks in the hull.

Verne saw strange light shining from behind one of the sealed portholes. After a quick inspection, he unfastened a knob holding the metal covering in place, but before he could lift the shade to look through the glass, Frankenstein grabbed his wrist.

"I wouldn't do that, Jules." He paused while the metal sections creaked around them. Frosty breath came out of his mouth when he spoke. "We have no idea what those windows look out upon. Remember what we're dealing with here."

Verne froze and backed away, apologizing for his own curiosity, his lack of control. Frankenstein was perfectly correct, of course—one glimpse of *reality* would be enough to blast them all into nonexistence. It was conceivable that he could simply push a button, energize the motive apparatus, and propel them Outside—some of the knobs and dials in the control room might still be functional. Verne wondered if perhaps he could develop some sort of protective goggles that would let them look upon *reality* and survive…

Unfortunately, they had other plans for the energy source trapped in its fragile containment below.

When they entered the excavated corridor of the ship and descended the groaning metal staircase to the control room, their electric illuminators both flickered and went out. Frankenstein tapped the lens and tried the switch several times before he set his device on the floor in disgust.

"I hate working on the technological fringe. Nothing functions the way it's supposed to."

Verne struck one of his matches against a corroded section of the hull. He lit a candle and passed it to Frankenstein before lighting one of his own. "I never imagined we would assemble a doomsday weapon by candlelight."

The control panels with their rows of dark indicator lights and color-coded buttons looked like the unblinking eyes of dead men. The air smelled dusty and metallic. Rags spotted with oils and solvents filled a container by the exterior hatch.

Outside, the girders creaked and shifted as wind whistled around the mountains. Verne knew they were alone, but he felt things watching them from the shadows. He recognized it as an irrational fear and tried to ignore it—but then he remembered the Outsiders probably *were* watching them.

"Come, Jules. We have to get started. Most of the tools we need are already here from the excavation and analysis work."

Verne blew cold air out of his nose, pondering how to put the pieces together. It all seemed so clear in his mind. "We should be able to lift enough other instrumentation from our devices at hand, especially some of the steam pumps and generator coils."

Frankenstein bent to the control-panel bulkhead. "Help me lift this cover plate off."

Working feverishly, Outsider-inspired, Professors Verne and Frankenstein hammered away at their contraption, using pieces of metal taken from the ship's hull, adapting equipment dismantled from other Sitnaltan apparatus.

They rarely spoke, but worked together, knowing what needed to be done. Verne blew on his numb fingers and searched for another instrument. All the tools felt icy in the still air of the chamber. The candles made exaggerated shadows of their movements against the curved walls.

The delicate part was encapsulating the power source in a makeshift containment vessel. Verne hoped the new rivets would hold and that their sealant goop would keep the valves and control switches in place. Verne found he was trembling, not just from the chill air but from the fear of working with such a dangerous thing.

The candles burned down, one after another, and finally, as dawn broke across the sky, Frankenstein rubbed his elbow against a bronze plate at the front of the weapon. He cracked his knuckles and sighed. When Verne looked at him, the other professor's eyes were bloodshot and weary. Verne knew he must look as haggard himself.

Frankenstein sighed. "With a device so important, I think we should make this official, even if only between ourselves." He withdrew a black grease pencil and bent over the smooth cylindrical body of the weapon. Pondering a moment with the pencil against his lips, Frankenstein scrawled a number on the silvery-white metal. "17/2."

"I think this counts as a patentable invention, don't you, Jules?" He straightened. "Even though we dare not ever tell how we created it."

Verne forced a smile, trying to lighten the mood. "I will never know how you keep track of all the numbers."

"A simple matter of concentration. Last month, we ran out of certificate numbers from the Council of Patent Givers. We forced them to create a second series, all our own. This weapon is our seventeenth invention in the second series. Such a weapon," Frankenstein said, letting his voice trail off.

He looked up at Verne with a hard light in his eyes. "It is the most powerful thing ever to come of Sitnaltan technology. But now we have to take it to Scartaris—and detonate it."

Frankenstein looked at Verne. Their eyes met in the uncertain candlelight, but neither spoke until Verne finally lowered his gaze.

"One of us will have to do it, of course."

"Yes. We must roll for it."

Verne reached deep into the folds of his woolen coat and withdrew a handheld device. In his other hand, he found two red dice with painted white numbers. "We'll use the random generator."

He placed it on a level surface of the gutted control panel, brushing dust aside. "High roll makes the journey?" He raised his eyebrows. Frankenstein nodded.

Verne inserted the two dice into the opening at the top of the device. "You roll first."

Frankenstein pushed down the spring-loaded lever on the side. The dice fell, scrambled, and bounced around inside the machine, and then tumbled out the opening in the bottom. A "5" and a "4."

Verne picked up the dice and tossed them into the top. He reset the lever, then pushed it down. He heard the dice clattering, but he felt a cold hand in his stomach. He *knew* before the dice rolled out.

Boxcars—two sixes.

Frankenstein put his hands behind his back, blinking. Verne couldn't tell if he was relieved or disappointed.

"I will help you load the weapon into one of our steam-engine cars. It will take the two of us to carry it."

Professor Verne nodded. Frankenstein hesitated a moment and then turned to extend his hand.

"Luck, Jules. Our future rides on this."

CHAPTER 16
NIGHT OF THE CAILEE

We cannot hide from anything the Outsiders sent against us. They know our fears better than we know ourselves. If we are to win this Game, we must face our greatest enemies and hope the dice roll in our favor.
—Enrod of Tairé

Gairoth did not like the Tairé city walls around him. He sniffed the air, flaring the nostrils in his potato-sized nose. He did not like the tall buildings, he did not like the feel of flagstones under his big bare feet. The buildings were too close, the alleys too narrow as he lumbered down them. The sharp spikes of his club clinked against the street. The smell of the air was dry and bland, too *human* for him.

Pictures covered the walls. He stared at them but did not understand the rituals depicted, the games, the gatherings of characters all standing side by side.

Gairoth squinted his one eye, baffled at the thought. It was repellent for ogres to work together. When he had been in Delroth's Stronghold and used the shiny rock to make illusion ogres, he could tolerate them only because he knew they weren't real. But these pictures showed human characters staying by each other because they *wanted* to.

One of the crudely drawn figures reminded him of the man Delroth. The ogre made a snarling noise and smacked the end of his club against the plaster. Great chunks of the fresco broke off and pattered onto the flagstones, exposing a jagged blot of fresh white plaster, like a wound.

"Haw!" Gairoth stomped down the zigzagging streets, satisfied. He had forgotten why he was chasing Delroth, but that didn't matter.

Everything was so quiet around him. He banged his club against the wall just to keep himself company. He wished Rognoth were there. The stupid little dragon had been a convenient companion, and now he was gone. Another dragon, a big dragon, chased him far away. Gairoth knew Delroth had something to do with that too.

When he heard the explosion and saw gouts of smoke gush into the sky from the burning tannery, he had to see what was going on. Delroth might be there.

Puffing through his dry, flabby lips, he heaved himself into motion. He got lost in several dead-ends, but with the curling smoke showing the way, he could always find his way back to the right path.

Gairoth stumbled upon the wreckage of the tannery. The foul-smelling debris reminded him of his long-lost cesspools, now drowned under the Barrier River. He drew in a deep breath. Milling Tairans stood sluggishly around the burning building, then they moved and drifted away, funneling down a side street. They didn't even react to Gairoth.

Being ignored annoyed him, and he stomped after them. The Tairans did not seem uneasy from each others' presence, from the closeness of their packed bodies. They did not get lost in the winding streets. They led Gairoth to a larger crowd, sluggish like a swarm of smoke-stunned bees. Many Tairans bled from wounds, but they didn't take care of themselves.

Gairoth elbowed the characters aside, shoving them away as he stormed forward to see the focus of their attention.

A ragged hole had been smashed in the tall Tairan wall. The ogre saw the Tairans looking out at the desolate terrain, but none of them said a word. Gairoth grabbed a man by the front of his tunic. The brownish-gray cloth ripped in the ogre's fingers, but he lifted the man high enough to stare into his eyes. The man's feet dangled in the air; his arms went limp. He didn't struggle. Gairoth shook him a bit, just to make him squirm.

The Tairan blinked and gurgled. His eyes were milky white, without pupils.

"Where is Delroth?" Gairoth demanded.

The Tairan turned his head toward the hole in the wall and the sprawling desert. Gairoth saw fresh tracks, hoof prints plowed up in the dust. His heart leaped. Delroth had been here! He was close!

Gairoth released the Tairan and let him fall. The man's arms and legs did not react quickly enough, and his knees buckled sideways. He landed on his hip on the flagstones.

The ogre bounded through the opening, bumping his head on one of the stone blocks. He ignored the pain and charged across the flat ground.

The blasted terrain flowed like magic under the horses' hooves. Vailret was amazed at how fast they approached the next hexagon of forested hills. He rode, gripping the mane in front of him because it seemed like the thing to do. He had never traveled so swiftly over land before, except in Professor Verne's balloon. At any moment, he felt as if he was going to fall off and crash on the dusty ground.

The sudden release of tension from their near death at the hands of the Tairans made him feel exhausted. Vailret's lips were dry and cracked from breathing the dusty air. When he held Bryl's frail form in front of him, he could feel the old half-Sorcerer's ribs through his blue cloak. Bryl seemed so frightened, he couldn't say anything.

At the hex-line, the forested hills rose in front of them. They had left the quest-path behind for fear of what might be on the road from Tairé to Scartaris. Now the horses picked their way among the haunted-looking slopes.

The thick trees stood black and gnarled in death. They were all relatively young, planted in neat rows in the turns that had passed since Enrod began to rebuild the land. But here, the Tairans' work had come to an end.

The horses stumbled upon a path made by the tree-planters and followed that up the slope. The dead trees scrabbled like arthritic fingers in front of their eyes. The close branches snapped and left black stains on the clothes they touched. The smell of sharp, dry death hung in the air, depressing and stifling.

Mindar rode in the lead, scowling. Her face looked full of anger and determination. The sight of each dead tree seemed like a slap in the face to her.

Vailret thought of the Tairans and their dream of rebuilding the landscape. The half-breeds had magic to renew the terrain, and the human characters used straightforward farming techniques to plant sturdy grass and stands of trees such as these. Then Scartaris came and destroyed everything again—and this time, the ancient Tairan hero, the Stranger Unlooked-For, had not reappeared to save them.

The trees thinned as they rose in the hills, letting them look back at Tairé and the surrounding devastation. Squinting, Vailret could still see fading smoke in the air from the destroyed tannery.

Mindar's face bore a stunned expression. "Delrael, what did you bring upon us?"

"It's still there!" Bryl cried, pointing.

Vailret couldn't make out details with his poor eyesight, but he could discern the boiling black mass that crept along the ground, the dark swarm they had seen following them from when they fled the Anteds. The unfocused, milling mass seemed to be skirting Tairé to the south.

Delrael scowled. "We don't know what it is."

Vailret felt his stomach tighten. He couldn't think of anything like this in the legends he had read, the accounts of wandering monsters and methods for dealing with them.

"It's making good time," Delrael said. His face was firm and emotionless. "It's either following us or it's going to join Scartaris. But we'll get there before it does."

He pushed his gelding past Mindar and rode ahead. Feeling an oppressive need to hurry, the others followed at a faster pace. Delrael spoke back to them without turning his head. "We should be to Scartaris in two days, if I remember the map right." They knew where Scartaris made his lair. Vailret saw Delrael absently brush the silver belt at his waist.

Vailret wondered if Delrael still had his complete faith in the Earthspirits. They had heard no communication to assure them that the Spirits still lived, still intended to destroy Scartaris. Vailret imagined what it would be like if they fought their way to the threshold of Scartaris, only to find they had no weapon after all...

Hexworld was fighting against the Outsiders by using the Earthspirits. But the Rulewoman Melanie had sent Journeyman. Maybe *that* would be enough.

Though Scartaris knew they were coming, he did not know what they intended to do, how they intended to fight. Since Scartaris could end the Game at any time with his deadly metamorphosis, Vailret hoped they could keep him curious until it was too late.

Mindar urged her gray mare as close beside Delrael as the trees would allow. She seemed to enjoy being by him, and Vailret smiled a little. Her spring-green tunic was marked with black and brown smears from the dead trees.

"Scartaris still has all his armies massed in front of him, ready to march out and destroy Hexworld. And before you can even get that far, he has a demon guardian waiting to stop anything that might be a threat—the Slave of the Serpent. That will be a great challenge for us."

Delrael's shoulders rippled as he gripped the horse's mane. "I'll defeat him." Then he paused and turned to look at Mindar. Their eyes met, and his expression turned more apologetic. "*We'll* defeat him."

Mindar smiled.

When they reached the crest of the hills and started down the other side, Journeyman took the lead, knocking sharp branches out of the way. The trees were thinner on the eastern slope, farther from Tairé and closer to Scartaris. The desolation terrain sprawled out in front of them; the sharp mountains of Scartaris thrust up five hexagons away.

A worn white line marked the main quest-path stretching across the wasteland, the road from Tairé to the camps of Scartaris's armies. Delrael cupped a hand over his eyes and stared. "Something's moving down the road."

Vailret couldn't make out anything so small, but Mindar agreed. "It's a troop of Slac. They're heading to Tairé, probably to take Tairan supplies to Scartaris." She frowned. "They'll start hunting us once they find out what we've done. We'll have to be careful."

Delrael's face remained expressionless. "We're always careful. It's how the Game is played."

The sun approached the Spectre Mountains behind them, casting long shadows across the dead forested hills. As they rode toward nightfall, the skeletal silence worked on Vailret's nerves. He wished he could hear birds, insects, any kind of life in the trees.

The tension kept them all from talking. Even Journeyman pushed ahead, snapping branches out of the way. "Lions and tigers and bears, oh my!" he said, seemed to wait for the others to pick up the chant, then gave up.

"I don't want to confront the Cailee in this place," Mindar said.

"I don't want to confront it anywhere!" Bryl mumbled.

Delrael pondered a moment. "I think we should get as much firewood as we can possibly haul, strap it onto the horses. Journeyman, you can carry a lot. Then we'll go as far out into the desolation as we can. We'll build a big fire—that might keep the Cailee back."

Mindar nodded. "Yes, at least it can't sneak up on us in the flatlands."

"Um, Del, won't Scartaris's armies be able to see the fire?" Vailret asked.

"Scartaris plays only one game at a time," Mindar said. "He'll send the Cailee after us tonight. I can feel it. He enjoys manipulating the fears of other characters. The Cailee will be more *fun* to him. Even Scartaris has to follow Rule #1."

They gathered firewood.

The night was black like a clenched fist around them, driven back by the orange shell of firelight. Vailret didn't know how long the wood would last, but the bright flames and the crackling sound pushed away the feeling of impending doom, leaving them in an island at the center of a black universe.

They had ridden hard, crossing another hexagon of desolation into the thick dusk until the jagged ground became too treacherous to cross in the dark.

Delrael found a spot that was clear in all directions, where they could huddle together by their fire and make a stand against the Cailee. If they had to.

They ate, speaking little. Journeyman strode around the perimeter of firelight, thrusting out his chest and swinging his fists.

The horses stayed together as a group, but Mindar found nothing to tie them to, nothing to hobble them with. She wiped her mouth on her dirty green tunic, then looked out into the darkness.

"Enrod really thought his dream for Tairé would work." Mindar seemed to be talking to herself. "After the Transition, he got most of the half-breeds to settle with him there. Enrod was brash and willing to try anything that might work. He poured himself into the effort and forced the others to do the same."

She picked up a handful of crumbly dirt and let it stream through her fingers. She cast the rest of it at the fire.

"It was a bitter and difficult life, but the half-breeds turned their magic to practical ends. They used all the spells they could to make crops grow in the desert hexagons. They summoned water up from the ground. They quelled the dust storms—I painted a picture of that once, all the half-Sorcerers standing in line, rolling dice and casting spells to drive back the winds and protect the crops. They used their powers to summon rains and dig canals."

Mindar forced a bleak smile. "How could it fail? We were united. We put our entire effort into this. But just when things were starting recover, just when the lands around Tairé began to stir—the trees died again. The crops failed. The desolation returned, and nothing any of us could do would stop it."

She stood up and stared into the fire. "To make things worse, the people didn't even care. They were all sleepwalking, getting worse every day. Scartaris was taking their minds, playing them like puppets. I watched other characters succumb, and only I could resist. I wish I knew how."

Then Mindar paused and looked at Delrael, meeting his eyes. Her brow furrowed with puzzlement. "Why are *you* protected? Do you have the same immunity that I've got?" She turned to stare at them all with a mixture of hope and challenge on her face.

Journeyman stepped back into the firelight. "*I* don't need it. The Rulewoman Melanie sent me." He returned to his guard duties.

Vailret widened his eyes. He hadn't considered the question before, but now a grin stretched across his face. He tried to communicate with Delrael through his expression. The fighter pondered, touching his belt lightly. Vailret nodded, then Delrael smiled as well.

They couldn't all have the same resistance to Scartaris that Mindar and Tallin had. The Rules of Probability made that highly unlikely. But if the Earthspirits were somehow protecting them, shielding them—that meant the Spirits must still be alive! The screeching sound they'd heard back in the forest had *not* been a death cry.

But they could say nothing of this to Mindar, especially if Scartaris watched her so closely. Vailret could think of no safe way to answer her question.

But suddenly, a sheen of sweat broke out on Mindar's forehead and around her eyes, making her face look oiled in the firelight. The horses snorted and stamped, making strange, uneasy noises. Vailret didn't know what that meant—he wasn't used to horses.

"The Cailee is here," Mindar whispered. "It's close, and it's coming."

The horses milled about in greater alarm.

Delrael stood up. "How can we hold them?"

Journeyman hurried over. The horses reared up, blowing and snorting. And then they bolted, all three of them.

"Wait! Wait!" Mindar cried.

"They're gone!" Bryl said.

Above the crackle of the fire, they heard the horses pounding off across the desert.

Mindar stood up and yanked her rippled sword away from her hip. "I'm going after them. You stay here."

"No!" Delrael said. "I'm going to help you if the Cailee's out there."

She whirled. Her jaw was rigid, and her eyes blazed with anger.

"No! You have to stay here! The Cailee wants us all to be separated, away from the fire, where it can get you one by one! The Cailee won't harm me—it wants you. *You* stay here. Together. By the fire."

Without another word, she ran off into the darkness. They heard her panting, calling for the horses, growing more distant.

Vailret waited, sitting up straight and listening to the fire burn. He looked at the stars overhead, wishing he could hear the sounds of the Stronghold village, the forest, anything. Wishing he could be by Tareah, discussing old legends. He wondered what she was doing.

Far off in the distance, they heard Mindar shout "Cailee!" Then nothing more.

"What should we do?" Bryl asked.

Delrael held his own sword, looking off into the muffling darkness. His eyes were wide and shining with worry. "We'll wait here, as Mindar said. She's right. I'm not going to let the Cailee win because it's smarter than we are."

"I'd rather have stuffing instead of potatoes," Journeyman said. He fidgeted and moved to where the horses had been.

Mindar stepped back into the firelight with such suddenness that they all whirled, startled. She looked drained, as if something had been yanked out of her. She took a drink from one of the water skins and sat down next to the warm fire.

"The horses have run off. The Cailee went after them." She took another drink and said nothing else.

Far off, they heard the oddly human screams of horses in the darkness. Vailret felt fear slice down his spine.

Mindar pulled the length of her whip between her fingers, feeling the rough braid. Her eyes were dark pools reflecting the dancing flames.

"The Cailee is there!" She lunged to her feet and pointed at the other side of the fire.

Delrael and the others turned, trying to react. Vailret saw the

Cailee silhouetted, a black human shape so dark that it made the night look dim. It moved, flowing and oily, and let out a snarl from an unseen mouth. Silver claws glinted in the firelight. Yellow pupilless pools glowed where the eyes should have been.

The Cailee danced into the light just long enough to throw something heavy and dripping into the bonfire, then it vanished again.

The head of Mindar's gray mare tumbled through the burning wood, slumping into the coals. The head smoked, and drops of blood sizzled on the embers. The mare's eyes were rolled up like tiny white plates; the tongue hung partway out of the mouth. The severed end of her neck had been torn by silver claws, the spine snapped in two and twisted off.

The fire cracked and hissed. Sparks swirled up toward the stars.

Mindar stumbled backward, gaping without words. She tripped and fell gracelessly to the dirt, never taking her eyes from the mare's smoldering head.

"I didn't even hear the Cailee come!" Journeyman said. He strode out to the edge of the light and came back again. The golem's gray-brown body absorbed the firelight and shadows. Vailret thought he looked astonished at his lapse, disappointed in himself.

Bryl held on to the Fire Stone with trembling hands. His lips were white, and his eyes glistened with fear.

Mindar's head snapped up from her grief to scan the perimeter of darkness. "Prepare yourselves!"

Vailret caught a movement out of the corner of his eye and, by some instinct driven into him from all the battle training Drodanis had forced him to endure, he knew to drop and roll. He felt the wind of something moving very fast, the sigh of silver claws whistling past his ear and grazing the back of his neck.

Journeyman leaped in to block the Cailee with a solid clay arm. The claws gouged great troughs in the golem's skin, but Journeyman slammed sideways with his other arm. He struck the shadow-thing with a soft, wet sound.

Vailret rolled onto his back and kicked his feet against the loose ground to push himself away. It was all happening so fast. Mindar and Delrael were shouting, running with their swords drawn.

An explosion of fire erupted around the perimeter to separate the golem and the Cailee. Journeyman made no sound, though the fire blackened his clay skin. The Cailee shrieked and flung itself back into the darkness.

Bryl sat with the Fire Stone cradled in his hands, biting his lip. He struck out again with the flame spell, though he saw no target. When the fire faded away, Vailret smelled smoke in the air.

He heard nothing else, no insects, no footsteps, only his own heavy breathing.

Delrael scowled and used a stick to push the mare's head out of the fire. The blackened hide smoked with the smell of roasting meat.

Journeyman paced around and remained alert. "A blast of fire and it goes away?" He used his other hand to smooth the gouges and push his clay skin back into place.

"The other Tairans never resisted it before," Vailret said. He picked himself up and brushed at his skinned elbow.

Mindar shook her head. "The Cailee is still out there. Scartaris isn't finished with us yet."

Roaring inhuman rage, the Cailee burst back into the camp, opposite from Delrael. Without an instant of hesitation, Journeyman charged at it, balling both fists.

But the Cailee knew exactly what it wanted. The shadow-thing streaked in the flickering light and reached out its silver talons for Bryl.

Mindar's whip cracked like the sound of a breaking spine. She crouched and placed herself in front of Bryl. Her gaze locked on the Cailee's pupilless yellow eyes. The moment seemed to hold for hours. Vailret could see violent emotions surging through Mindar's mind.

The Cailee laughed silently and tried to dodge sideways to reach Bryl. Bryl scurried backward, bumping into Journeyman. He cried out, but the golem held him firm.

Mindar struck out with the whip again, tearing into the lightless flesh.

A fistful of silver claws exploded forward, hooking into the leather whip, and jerked backward swift as a shadow. The claws shredded the whip into a snowflake of leather tatters, throwing Mindar's shoulder out of joint.

Though crying out in pain, Mindar was already reaching for her rippled sword with her left hand. She swung clumsily, trying to protect herself, and sank the blade into the dark void of the Cailee's body. Droplets of night sprayed onto the sand, vanishing into the shadows.

Delrael ran forward with his own sword. Bryl rolled the Fire Stone, scrambling out of the way.

With a roar of pain, the Cailee lunged at Mindar, striking in an arc of silver claws as it tore open her side, breaking through ribs to her heart.

She fell, spewing a red rain of torn flesh and spattering blood.

"Mindar!" Delrael screamed.

Bryl touched the Fire Stone again. A wall of flame erupted between the shadow-thing and Mindar, burning both. The Cailee howled, blinded by the blaze, scratching at the air with silver claws.

Delrael stabbed through the flames, probably burning his own hands, blistering his skin. Singed hair curled back away from his forehead. But the old Sorcerer sword struck something solid where the Cailee's chest should have been.

Bryl let the flames die away. Delrael staggered back, nearly tripping over Mindar on the ground. Vailret went to help him.

The Cailee made a high-pitched moan, then faded as they watched, dissolving away into the night.

Delrael stood trembling in the wake of his attack. He stared at the blade of his sword as if to see how the Cailee had stained the steel, but it seemed untainted.

Bryl whimpered in the firelight. Vailret crawled forward to join him.

Mindar made a choking sound on the ground. Delrael knelt beside her, pushing aside a sharp rock. Her spring-green tunic had been crisped brown by the fire. She shuddered, curling herself into a fetal position.

Together, Delrael and Vailret rolled Mindar on her back. Fresh, dark blood poured out of her torn side. Her face had a wet, gray appearance. Her mouth made a choking, sucking sound as she tried to breathe.

Delrael touched his fingers to her forehead. "It's gone. We killed it."

Vailret stared at his cousin, but Delrael would not look up. Mindar had no chance. Vailret was amazed she still could think or speak. He doubted even the khelebar healer Thilane, who had created a new *kennok* leg for Delrael, could have saved her.

Bryl hunkered down, wide-eyed in his fear. Journeyman appeared disappointed that he had not been able to fight again. Off in the east, behind the lair of Scartaris, dawn light seeped into the sky.

Delrael propped Mindar's head up and placed it on his knee. He brushed her singed dark hair away from the lumpy *S*-scar. It reminded Vailret of how Tallin had died in a pool of blood while Delrael held him. Delrael stiffened and seemed to realize the same thing.

"We'll destroy Scartaris, Mindar." For a moment, his face

carried enough anger to rival her own. "And I will have *fun* doing it."

The flow of blood from her wound slowed, lacking the force of a heartbeat. The last breath out of her mouth seemed to form one word.

"Luck."

But she did not die.

Mindar jerked in a convulsion that ripped through her body. She sucked a long hiss of breath through her teeth. Vailret's eyes were drawn to the livid *S*-scar on her forehead. The scar throbbed with a red light, like a twisted channel of lava.

Mindar's skin grew red, also glowing. Heat poured from her body, and Vailret had to step back. Delrael stared down. His jaw hung open in surprise; his face was ashen.

The pools of wet blood on Mindar's skin smoked, bubbled, and burned away from her form, fading even from her stained clothes. The open gash and splintered ribs clenched themselves in a staccato spasm, like a mouth smacking its lips, until the wound congealed, bound together and sealing the skin without leaving a scar.

Her eyelids jammed shut, and she wheezed a great breath into her lungs. Her chest rose and fell. She jerked.

"She said Scartaris wouldn't let her die," Vailret said. He felt as if a great weight hung on his shoulders.

Delrael grabbed Mindar's shoulder, but she was still too hot and he snatched his hand away.

Mindar twitched her muscles, then rolled over, stumbling to her knees. Tears streamed from between her closed eyelids. The *S*-scar continued to glow red. She struggled to her feet, then turned to face them.

Mindar stood straight and opened her eyes. She did not move. She made no reaction at all.

Her eyes were blank white, and pupilless. Scartaris's eyes.

INTERLUDE: OUTSIDE

Tyrone shook his head with an expression of naive astonishment.

"Man, this is getting pretty intense. How about we just, uh, take a break for a while? Watch some TV. I've got all the *Star Trek* movies on tape." He stood up and looked toward the living room, where the television sat switched off like a dull gray-green eye.

"Shut up and sit down!" David's voice had a hollow power to it, an alien sound that caused Melanie to jump.

She frowned and brought her own anger to the surface. David was doing this just to sicken her, just to flaunt his disregard for the people of Hexworld. "How can you do that to one of your own characters, David? Didn't you put Mindar through enough already?"

"She's my character. I can do what I want with her. It's *fun*." In the globe light over the dining room table, his smile looked bright and jagged. "We're playing this game for *fun*, remember?"

Melanie stared across the table at him. She felt stronger now, keyed up. It didn't matter what David did. She had her characters. They were fighting together, she and them. She had given them Journeyman and the secret weapon she had painted into the map; Hexworld had brought back the Earthspirits on its own.

"You're changing, David. What's happening to you? Are you playing Scartaris ... or is he playing *you*?"

David scowled at her but didn't seem to know how to answer. Scott cleared his throat. "It's getting kind of strange even with you, Melanie. Do you know that when you play different characters, your voice changes? You're even worse than David. Your eyes get sort of ... funny."

"Yeah," Tyrone said, not noticing the thin smear of dip on his chin, "it's like something out of *The Exorcist*."

"When you're playing your characters, it's like you're swallowed up in them. Like you don't even know what you're saying." Scott pursed his lips.

Melanie felt sweat prickle at the back of her neck. She covered it by reaching for some chips and stuffing a handful in her mouth. "That's crazy. I know exactly what was going on. I remember everything we did, like I was—" She paused and choked a little on her chips. She took a drink from her glass and swallowed before she finished her sentence. "It's like I was there myself..."

"Do you see?" David said. "Do you *see?* If we don't end this tonight, we might never be able to escape from the game! It's coming out, it's taking over. We've put too much magic in it, and now Hexworld doesn't need us to play anymore!"

"Maybe it's fighting back against you—but I'm trying to save Hexworld. I don't have nightmares. I have *nice* dreams about the world. I'm not afraid of it. You are. I'm going to fight you to the end in this battle. And I'm going to win. I'm going to save their world, and ours."

David's face looked pale and waxen. "What if you're wrong?"

Melanie shrugged. She saw the deep fear behind David's false arrogance. "If you're afraid to lose, you should never have started playing in the first place."

"I'll stop you with the Slave of the Serpent." He cracked his knuckles and looked at the wide black line on the painted map where he had marked the demon's lair. The map seemed to be cracked there, exactly along the hex-line. Puzzled, Melanie bent over to look at it, but Scott interrupted her.

"She's not the only one with plans." He drummed his fingertips on the table, then wiped his glasses on the untucked ends of his shirt. "Hurry up and finish your turn. We don't have all night."

CHAPTER 17
FIGHTERS

We must learn how to use the Rules to our advantage in any situation. That means we need to train ourselves with every weapon listed in The Book of Rules. *We must study role-playing games to enhance our experience and decision-making capabilities. Gaming doesn't come easy—it is a lot of work to have fun!*
—Drodanis, speech to trainees at the Stronghold

Tareah held the sapphire Water Stone so that it glinted in the noon light. Her eyes were tired; her body felt exhausted. But the anger and shock had given way to a clarity of thought that made her absolutely sure of what she had to do. She felt brave now.

On top of Steep Hill, in the burned and splintered ruins of the Stronghold, she turned the six-sided gem to show each of its facets to the gathered villagers. The smell of smoke still hung in the air, and the ground at her feet was muddy from the rain she had summoned to quench the flames.

"My father Sardun gave me this Stone." To her own ears, her voice sounded gruff and old. The villagers listened to her now. "He used it to build and maintain his vast Ice Palace. He used it to control the weather, and to fight against the dragon Tryos."

She narrowed her eyes and looked at the other characters, making sure she held their attention. Tareah had studied the rhetorical techniques used when the ancient Sentinel Arken tried to convince other Sorcerers to renounce the Transition.

"I am the last full-blooded Sorcerer woman on Hexworld. That's why Tryos found me so valuable and kidnapped me. You all know that story. Maybe I haven't been trained enough in fighting—" She drew

herself tall, widening her eyes. "But I have powers too. Great powers. I will have to train myself how to use them."

She sensed a *difference* within her as she stood before the villagers. Tareah could imagine herself as an old Sorcerer queen, maybe even Lady Maire herself. Her joints no longer ached, and she didn't feel out of place with the other characters. The destruction of the Stronghold had shaken her, hammered home the new turn the Game had taken.

Tareah was responsible for her actions. Her powers and her abilities would not permit her to remain passive in the coming battles.

She paced around the fallen wall where dirt trickled between toppled logs that had been sharpened on top. The Stronghold buildings were all collapsed, the sword posts knocked over, the gate and the bridge across the trench both crumbled. A crude walkway allowed the other characters to look at the result of Scartaris's attack.

Tareah ran both hands through her light brown hair. Her eyes had a distant look as she began to speak. The villagers still did not interrupt her—the destruction of the Stronghold awed them too much.

"Many turns ago, at the beginning of the Scouring, the great human general Doril founded this Stronghold. He had just lost all of his fighters as well as the Sentinel Oldahn, his friend, in a Slac fortress. Doril wanted to escape the battles of the Scouring, to live in peace away from the Game.

"He found the characters here innocent and completely unprepared to defend themselves. When he arrived, Doril strode out of the forest terrain to the fields where farmers were working. He told them of the marauding Slac armies in the nearby hexagons, and of the bloodshed in the Scouring. 'Do you comfort yourselves by thinking the Outsiders would never bring the battles here?' he asked. 'Or do you fancy you could defeat a brutal Slac regiment with your rakes and sticks?'"

As she told the story, Tareah put her hands on her hips, imitating the stance she imagined Doril had taken. "So Doril built this Stronghold. It has withstood many attacks and protected the characters in this village for all that time.

"But Scartaris sent the Slave of the Serpent here to slay Tarne. He brought the rat-creatures to destroy the Stronghold itself. Scartaris has brought the battle *here*. Like those first farmers confronted by Doril, we can no longer live our lives and ignore the rest of the Game. We must be prepared to defend ourselves in any way we know how."

She stood there watching. The forest terrain around Steep Hill seemed tranquil, filled with quiet sounds of rustling leaves, birdsong and insects. The stream gushing along the hex-line rattled over rocks. The deceptive peacefulness bothered her.

The villagers fidgeted, uneasy. "When is Delrael coming back?" Derow the blacksmith asked, mumbling the words into his full dark beard.

"Yes," Mostem the baker said, grinning. "Once Delrael destroys Scartaris, we won't have to worry anymore."

Tareah felt anger rising within her. "Delrael left *me* here! He trusted me to watch over the village and the Stronghold. Even if Delrael does destroy Scartaris, how is he going to stop a gigantic army that's waiting to charge across the map? Think about it! Scartaris has gathered ten times as many fighting monsters as ever engaged in the old Sorcerer wars. Are they just going to sit still even if Scartaris is destroyed? We have to be prepared."

Siya stood by Tareah. She appeared frightened and confused, with red-rimmed eyes that showed how tired she was. But most of all, she looked angry. "The Outsiders won't leave us alone to live our lives. If they want us to fight, then we should fight them."

Tareah went forward to the villagers. She walked among them, looking each in the eye as she talked. "None of us is trained. But we'll have to learn how. We must train ourselves."

The sun shone down on them, and Tareah felt exposed on top of Steep Hill, as if giant Outside eyes were staring down at her. She pushed the thought out of her head and turned her mind to the job before her.

She directed the villagers to sift through the wreckage of the storehouse, to pick out all the old weapons that could be used or repaired. Tareah helped them, though she grew gloomier as she waded through the splinters and broken walls. Marks from tiny teeth and claws scored every scrap of wood.

Drodanis had conducted all his private role-playing training in the darkness here, surrounded by old weapons. Vailret told her of his imaginary adventure, how real the training had been for him. Now the storehouse lay collapsed. The Stronghold was ruined. It had been her responsibility.

They separated the swords, bows, maces, spears, shields, armor all into separate piles. Tareah found herself wasting too much time staring at the inlaid designs of relics that had been gathered from various treasure hoards. Apparently, Drodanis had been as avid a collector as her father.

Tareah held one of the simple blades, a short sword, up for the blacksmith to see. "From now on, Derow, concentrate on making swords. We'll need a greater supply if we're going to gather an army. We'll send out couriers to gather all the other characters from settlements far and wide."

Derow shuffled his feet and looked at the sample blade she held up. "My craftsmanship can never match anything like this." His face turned red with shame. "The old Sorcerer swordsmiths were masters. Look at the skill in even their simplest pieces! I can't begin to—"

"You'll do fine, Derow." Tareah held up her hand. "A sword needs to *cut*. It doesn't need to be beautiful."

The blacksmith still looked at her skeptically, but he set to work gathering and studying the remaining swords.

Tareah clapped her hands and walked among the other villagers, directing some to mount the archery targets, others to erect the sword posts, using logs from the fallen wall if necessary. Others went out into the forest to find straight twigs for arrows, saplings for bows. The children made bird traps to furnish feathers for fletching the arrows.

Siya wandered around, acting busy. Tareah kept too occupied to notice what Siya was doing until the old woman picked up a sword for herself and went over to the section of the wall where they had recently buried Tarne. Siya's husband Cayon also lay there.

She stood with the sword propped in front of her, its tip stuck in the soft ground. The sun glinted off gems in the hilt. Tareah noticed a strange gleam in her eyes.

"We will train. We will be ready," Siya said. She took a step forward to stand by Tareah. The other villagers paused to look up at her.

"We will be *fighters!*"

CHAPTER 18
DELRAEL'S SECOND CHANCE

RULE #10. Combat on Hexworld follows rigid guidelines. The accompanying tables give details on how fighting is commenced according to experience, armor, available weapons, and many other factors. Combat can come in different forms, such as surprise attack, team attack, or single combat.
—The Book of Rules

Mindar's blank white eyes stared at them. She did not blink. Her skin was pale and cold.

Delrael couldn't see her breathing, but he knew she remained alive Scartaris had healed her—he wasn't finished playing with her yet.

Delrael shook her by the shoulders. "Mindar!"

Her head swayed from side to side, then righted itself and stared straight ahead. Delrael gritted his teeth and turned to glare toward the mountains in the east.

"Del—" He jumped when Vailret touched him on the arm. "With the horses gone now, we'll already be slowed down. Will we take her with us?"

"What if Scartaris is watching us through her eyes?" Bryl asked.

Delrael let go of Mindar. He hunkered down and stared into the embers of the bonfire, trying to decide. Conflicting thoughts churned through his head. He could find no clear-cut solution, and he didn't like it.

The fire burned low and crackled. The tainted wood smelled bitter and unpleasant, but the predawn air seemed clear, empty of the Cailee. They had watched the creature vanish.

He drew a deep breath. "We won't leave her behind, no matter what Scartaris wants us to do. She has as much at stake as we do. Maybe more. Look what he's done to her."

"Maybe she'll snap out of it," Vailret said, but his voice sounded weak. Delrael made no other comment.

He stood up and sheathed his sword. He picked up Mindar's tattered whip lying in the dust and dropped it into the fire, where it curled and turned black. Mindar stood stiff and unresponsive when he fastened the rippled sword at her waist.

"There, now you're ready. Whenever you want to fight, we need your help." Delrael's voice was soothing and quiet. "Journeyman, can you carry her?"

"Aye aye, Cap'n!"

He frowned. "Does that mean yes?"

"Yes."

The golem scooped up Mindar in his broad arms. Her limbs flopped and hung down. She didn't rearrange herself into a more comfortable position.

Delrael stared at her milky blank eyes and felt sick to his stomach. "Let's get moving."

∼

By noon, they had crossed an entire hexagon. The air was cool and parched, but heated up when the sun rose overhead. They spoke little as they moved. The mountains of Scartaris lay only a few hexagons distant.

But when they reached the hex-line, they stopped short. The black line separated one section of desolate terrain from the next, but instead of the narrow black boundary where hexagons butted against each other, the black line yawned five man-lengths wide. It looked to Delrael as if the Outsiders had snapped the map apart, dividing the sections with a canyon that stretched down through the thickness of the map and out the bottom of the universe itself.

Delrael stared into the deep crevasse. Warm air drifted upward, bringing odd, alien smells. In the blackness below were strange swirling images, maddening shadows of things he did not want to see. He turned away immediately, afraid he might see a deadly glimpse of *reality*.

"We can't get across." Delrael put his hands on his hips, frowning. He felt anger building. He didn't like to be delayed from his quest.

He held the silver belt at his waist, and the metal seemed to ripple beneath his fingers. He *knew* the Earthspirits were there, but they couldn't destroy Scartaris unless he took them there.

"There'll be a way, Del," Vailret said, analyzing. "If this is part of the Game, the Outsiders have to give us some way through. They can't violate their own Rules."

But as far as they could see in both directions, the chasm seemed unbroken. The wide black line extended for hexagon after hexagon, a broad crack in the map.

"We'll have to follow it until we find someplace where Scartaris *wants* us to cross."

Delrael looked up. Wheeling batlike creatures flew high above. They seemed to be staring down at the travelers, but did not come closer.

"Scartaris is watching us," Bryl said.

"Let him watch." Journeyman pushed his clay lips in a snarl. "A little bottomless chasm isn't going to stop us."

They moved along the edge, hot and exhausted. Because of the flat terrain, Delrael could see the white line of the main quest-path long before they neared it. The road to Scartaris's lair approached the zigzagging chasm, and when Delrael shaded his eyes, he could see a bridge, some kind of tunnel spanning the crack in the map.

This would be the perfect spot for Scartaris to ambush travelers, a place for a malevolent guardian to stop any enemies. He pondered and looked at Mindar's limp, blank-eyed form cradled in Journeyman's arms.

Mindar had said something about a demon guardian, the Slave of the Serpent.

Delrael took a deep breath of the dry air and blinked his eyes. His skin felt warm and sunburned, flushed. Mindar lay motionless. He had a score to settle with Scartaris. Now more than ever. He set off at a faster pace. His boots left deep, sharp prints in the dusty ground.

When they reached the wide quest-path, Delrael looked at the bridge across the chasm. A dry, unpleasant smell hung at the back of his mouth, like the taste of rusty metal.

The bridge was not just a tunnel, but the gigantic spinal column of some long-dead beast, hanging by itself. Dried strips of sinew held the vertebrae together, leaving wide gaps for the air to blow through with an eerie whistling hum. Tree-sized bones from the creature's limbs lay sprawled across the dust, a claw here, a bowed rib that had long since been cracked by smaller things that chewed away the marrow and left a hollow shell. A dust-covered mound lay off to the side of the quest-path, near where the ancient monster's skull should have been. The rest of the bones were not in sight—they had probably fallen down into the chasm.

They would have to walk through the bowed, cavelike bridge of vertebrae draped across the hex-line gap. Smells drifted out of the bridge opening, and a jungle of black shadows flickered as light flitted in and out of the gaps.

Two giant boulders stood propped against the opening. Other bones and dead things lay piled outside, though they could easily have been discarded in the black gulf.

Mindar stared up at the sky. The red *S*-scar on her forehead throbbed with the beat of her heart. She could not offer any help to them now, couldn't give them any warning about the Slave of the Serpent.

The golem set her down, straightened her legs, and made sure she had gained her balance before letting go. Mindar stood by herself but did nothing else.

"Now what do we do?" Vailret asked. "Do we just walk through?"

An ear-splitting roar burst out of the shadows of the sagging tunnel, accompanied by a sandy, grating hiss. The sound echoed in the hollow vertebrae. Something moved in the dim light of the tunnel.

"And now for a really *big* show!" Journeyman said.

A silhouette appeared, and then the Slave of the Serpent stepped into view. The monster drew in a deep breath and stood reeling, unaccustomed to the bright sunlight.

Delrael flinched. The demon was huge, more massive even than Gairoth the ogre. It was hairy and apelike but had reptilian features, a chest plate and a flat angular head set low upon its shoulders. The deep-set eyes looked pitiful and filled with immense sorrow shining out from slitted pupils.

Coiled around its body was a huge, oily green snake that raised its head high above the Slave's shoulders. The Serpent hissed at the travelers with a sound like rain pelting a fire.

The Slave took two lumbering steps forward then stopped,

planting its feet to guard the opening of the tunnel bridge. The Serpent spoke.

"So *you* are Delrael! We went to the Stronghold. We killed a human character who claimed to be Delrael. But he was old and weak. We left him smoking on the ground."

Delrael felt his heart freeze, wondering if it could be a trick. Did they mean Tarne? If the Serpent claimed to be looking for Delrael, Tarne would have tried to trick them.

The Serpent cocked its head at him. "We came to get the Fire Stone and give it back to Scartaris. Now you have brought the Stone to us—" The Serpent hissed at Bryl. The half-Sorcerer cringed.

Delrael looked back at the others. Vailret appeared weak and frightened with only his short sword; Bryl had the Fire Stone; the golem looked ready to fight.

The Slave stepped forward, and the Serpent spoke again with a note of glee in its voice. "I bind you to the protocol of single combat in Rule #10! Delrael—I challenge *you*. You must fight me alone."

Bryl let out a cry of dismay. Journeyman said, "Aww, shucks!"

Delrael stood up in shock, feeling cheated. Though the Serpent had used a loophole, the Rules still constrained all characters. The Slave of the Serpent greatly outclassed Delrael alone, but now the others could not help him. They could not break the Rules. It was unfair. Vailret, Bryl, and Journeyman appeared helpless.

Mindar stood without moving, unaware.

Delrael curled his lip and snarled at the demon. "Don't underestimate me."

The Slave made a grumbling bestial noise and tried to turn his head to glare at the Serpent. But the pupilless red eyes of the snake ignored him. The coils squeezed the Slave's chest, and he lumbered forward to meet his opponent.

"May the Force be with you," Journeyman called.

Delrael breathed in and out. He felt his heart pumping, the adrenaline flowing. He had fought a thousand mock battles, and some real ones. He had been through his father's training. He was ready. He had no choice.

Without giving any warning, he surged forward as fast as he could. He held the sword in front of him, howling at the top of his lungs, and swung.

The Slave stumbled back in surprise, leaving deep footprints on the ground. Delrael drove in, pushing his advantage of surprise for a few more moments. He swung and missed, and struck again with the blade.

The Slave grunted and roared, batting at him with a bearlike paw. Delrael turned his sword sideways and slashed the Slave's arm. The edge bit into the monster's fur but made only a minor wound.

The Serpent's fangs flashed like glistening swords. Delrael saw the snake strike an instant before it was too late. He dove for the ground, tucking the sword against him to protect it, and rolled.

The Slave bent over to give the Serpent more reach, but the fangs dug into the sand. The Serpent pulled up, hissing and spitting dust out of its mouth. Black pools of smoking slag marked where venom had squirted into the dirt.

Delrael worked his feet under him and stumbled back to a standing position. The Slave could have attacked, but it hesitated, giving Delrael time to compose himself. He wondered what was going on.

He heard Vailret and Journeyman shouting at him, urging him on. Delrael blanked that out for the moment. He needed to concentrate on the fight.

The Slave's sad eyes struck his heart. This monster didn't want to hurt him, didn't want to do what he did. The Serpent forced the Slave to do its will. He wanted no part of this. Delrael stared at the eyes. It was a trick. It had to be.

But the Slave's eyes were *not* pupilless.

Then the Serpent struck again.

This time, inexplicably, the Slave stepped sideways, deliberately throwing off the snake's aim.

In anger, the Serpent viciously nipped the bare patch at the back of the Slave's neck. The monster roared in pain and swatted with its great paws, but the snake bobbed back and forth, weaving away from the clumsy grasp. It ducked in and nipped the Slave again.

"Kill Delrael!" it said.

Wet mucus dripped from the Slave's eyes, either in pain or sorrow. With a roar, the Slave reached out his huge paws.

Delrael held his ground and lunged, trying to duck under the grasping arms. But the Slave cuffed him on the side of the head. Delrael sprawled on the ground. His vision fuzzed, and his ears rang. He heard Vailret and Journeyman shouting again. It didn't make sense. He didn't want to listen to them, but he knew he couldn't lie there.

He felt vibrations in the sand as the Slave stomped forward. Delrael half-closed his eyes, pretending to be unconscious. When he saw the Slave near him, he snapped open his eyes and grabbed the sword with both hands. He scrambled to his knees and put his chest, his shoulders, all of the muscles in his arms and back into one swing. He aimed for the Slave's thigh and felt the blade sink in, cutting into the meat of the monster's leg all the way to the bone.

Viscous yellow blood oozed out, gushing in heavy globs. The monster howled in agony.

Delrael rolled out of the way, but the monster kept staggering forward, propelled by its own momentum and forgetting its pain. Blood spattered to the ground with every step the Slave took. Delrael held the sword against him, smearing the yellow blood across his leather armor. He tried to climb to his feet but was not fast enough.

The Slave of the Serpent knocked him back to the ground, then wrapped both huge paws around Delrael's chest and jerked him into the air. The monster shook him and squeezed.

PLAY

Delrael felt the roar in his head grow louder. He couldn't breathe. He couldn't think. Loud sounds and darkness echoed at the corner of his eyes. His arm went numb. He couldn't control his fingers—they went limp, and the sword fell, embedding its point in the sand. The weight of the pommel tipped it over, spraying dirt in the air.

For a moment, he thought the Slave would cast him into the yawning black chasm where he might fall through the map and be incinerated by his first glimpse of *reality*. Then he saw the Serpent rear back. Its blank red eyes blazed fire as if Scartaris himself were looking through the reptilian skull.

The Serpent opened its mouth. The fangs oozed venom like miniature diamonds.

Mindar blinked. Her vision snapped back into focus. She stumbled, suddenly regaining her body.

In the back of her mind, she heard a mocking voice, Scartaris laughing at her, telling her to watch. Watch him die. You will lose. You will always lose.

She didn't know where she was, how she had gotten there, or what was going on. She remembered nothing beyond the Cailee and the circle of firelight. And the pain, memories sparkling with pain.

Then she saw Delrael in the grip of the Slave of the Serpent. *Watch him die.* Scartaris had toyed with her, showed his power. Now he would have fun by letting her witness Delrael's death.

The Serpent drew back to strike, and Delrael closed his eyes.

The snake's head flashed downward as Delrael heard racing

footsteps, a *swish*. It all happened too fast. He opened his eyes and saw the Serpent still descending toward him with its mouth open and fangs bared, but somehow the head had become severed from the body. Squirting blood, the snake's head continued its arc, struck Delrael in the shoulder, and bounced off. It fell on the sand, staring up with dead red eyes.

Mindar regained her balance and swung the rippled sword back through empty air, flinging droplets of the Serpent's dark blood into the air.

Apparently stunned, the Slave released his grip and let Delrael fall to the ground. His right arm was still numb, but he managed to snatch up his sword as he scrambled out of the way. He heaved in great gasps of air. His ribs ached. Sand crusted the globs of yellow blood sticking to his leather armor.

Mindar stood poised and ready to fight the Slave, wearing a snarl on her lips. Her red *S*-scar glowed. She had returned. Delrael wanted to go to her.

The Slave pivoted around. Yellow blood drooled down the matted fur of his leg. He seemed to ignore the pain of the wound. He stared at Delrael with his liquid, anguished eyes. Then he gawked in awe at the ragged dripping stump of the Serpent. His face wore an impossible, stupefied expression. When he lifted up the dead Serpent, dark blood ran down his fingers, but the poison did not harm him.

Then he raised his huge paws into the air in a gesture of triumph. "*Sadic is free!*" The monster's words were clumsy, as if the flat, plated mouth was not suited for speech. The Slave unwrapped the entwined body of the Serpent as if he were casting off a heavy chain.

Delrael continued to breathe hard. He didn't know what to think. He saw Mindar raise her eyebrows.

Moving with obvious disgust, the Slave held the snake's body away from him. Black blood drizzled from the decapitated end, leaving foul pools smoking on the ground. The Slave's fur had been worn off in pink, raw-looking patches by the Serpent's scales rubbing against his hide.

"Ring around the collar," Journeyman mumbled out of the side of his mouth.

The Slave of the Serpent stalked to the edge of the deep crevasse. He raised the Serpent's body over his head and, with a roar of exhilaration, cast it down into the void. Then he turned back to Delrael and Mindar, dragging his wounded leg behind him along a trail of thick yellow blood.

Delrael grabbed his sword, ready to fight again, though his aching ribs and numb arm protested. Mindar stood glaring at the demon. Journeyman, Vailret, and Bryl all joined them.

The Slave of the Serpent stopped and stared at them, pleading. He spread out his massive flat paws. "Sadic will not hurt you. You freed Sadic. You killed Serpent."

"Just stay away, big fella," Journeyman said.

The Slave kept his distance, trying to look harmless. He made no sudden moves. "Sadic will do no more harm."

Then Mindar turned pale and sick-looking. Her rippled sword fell to the ground. She staggered and dropped to her knees, making strange noises. She covered her face. Delrael heard her sobbing.

He put a hand on her shoulder, hesitant. She didn't flinch. Then he put both arms around her in a hug. He felt her trembling, the spasms as she tried to control herself.

Mindar choked out words. "I don't know what happened. All I remember is fighting the Cailee, and then the pain, and blackness...."

"The Cailee almost killed you," Delrael said quietly, soothing. "But Scartaris didn't let you die. He ... he controlled you. You were like the other Tairans. Your eyes ..." He let the words trail off.

"Scartaris released me only so I could watch you die. For *fun*."

She looked up, and her dark eyes were filled with a complex mix of emotions.

"I saw my daughter, I think. She was like a dream in the darkness, and it's fading. The more I try to hold on to the memory, the faster it slips away." Mindar drew a hitching breath and pulled herself to her feet, brushing her singed green tunic. Feeling awkward, Delrael took a step away.

"The first thing I saw was you fighting. And the others were just standing there, not helping you. I knew what I had to do."

Delrael saw Vailret flinch and shifted his short sword from one hand to the other. "The Serpent bound us with single combat protocol. We *couldn't* help."

Mindar let that sink in for a moment, and then a slow smile crossed her face. "Scartaris wanted to bind you with a strict interpretation of the Rules—and we turned the tables on him, hah! We can find loopholes too. Since Scartaris kept me unaware of anything that was going on, I didn't hear the challenge." Her grin broadened. "I beat Scartaris with his own trick!"

Then her expression fell again and she became serious. "I learned one other thing, though—we're already too late.

"Scartaris has informed his army that they will march tomorrow night. They will charge across the map, pillaging and laying waste to every hexagon. Even if you destroy Scartaris, there's no way you can stop the whole army."

Delrael felt betrayed. He wondered if the Earthspirits knew what Mindar had said, if they knew anything beyond Scartaris. In his belt, the Earthspirits gave no sign, no communication. If Mindar was right, then the quest, Tallin's death, the first plea in the message stick from Drodanis—everything they had done was for nothing!

"One problem at a time," Delrael said. At least they were questing and *trying* to do something. No one had thought of a better way to confront Scartaris.

The Slave made a grunting noise to attract their attention, but remained standing where he was. "Sadic will help."

Delrael scowled at the hairy, reptilian monster, feeling his aching ribs. The Slave plastered his paw against the deep sword cut in his thigh to slow the bleeding.

"Serpent made Sadic do bad things. Scartaris controlled Serpent. You freed Sadic. Sadic will help. Sadic knows you want to destroy Scartaris."

Bryl muttered, "Seems just about everyone knows that by now."

"Remember Rule #3, about taking new companions," Vailret said. "We could use all the help we can get, especially powerful help like that."

"The plot thickens," Journeyman said.

Delrael turned, still feeling weak from the combat. The wide white quest-path stretched across the desolation.

He saw the towering black cloud charging toward them, little more than a hexagon away. He heard an eerie buzzing sound, a cacophony of many noises, like a storm of voices, tormented souls. The cloud itself looked fuzzy and indistinct, rolling along the ground in thousands of frenzied pieces, large and small, looking for something to attack. Huge clouds of dust from its passage bubbled into the air.

"I want to see Scartaris destroyed," Mindar said.

"Cross tunnel," the Slave said. "Do not trust Sadic. He will cross by himself."

Mindar nodded at Delrael. "Three of us should cross, then Sadic, then the last two. Otherwise, he might push the tunnel bridge over the edge when we're all inside it."

"He looks strong enough to do it," Delrael agreed.

Sadic hunched his hairy shoulders. "Yes. Go."

They cast dice in the dust to see who would go first. Delrael, Vailret, and Bryl won the rolls and stood at the edge of the foul-smelling opening. They entered the rotting and ancient bridge of vertebrae.

Wind whistled around and through the cracks. The dried sinews stretched taut, and the giant vertebrae swayed and rattled over the gulf. Delrael took the lead and put his boot on the rough, curved surface of the inner bone wall, checking his footing.

The passage was wide and tall. Delrael strode forward. He didn't want to think about traps, didn't want to worry. Gaps and holes between the segments of vertebrae showed too plainly the depths of swirling blackness far below, the shadows of things he didn't want to see.

The sinews were dry and leathery, holding the vertebrae together. Delrael kept telling himself that armies had funneled through this, that heavy cartloads of supplies and pounding Slac regiments had gone through. The bridge would hold.

They pushed ahead and saw the other side not far away. He listened to Bryl whimper behind him. Then they hurried out of the last segment, anxious to be on solid ground again. Gasping and trembling, they emerged, each trying to cover the look of fear he wore.

Sadic came next. Delrael kept his sword drawn, uneasy. He could see the vertebrae in the tunnel sway as the massive Slave lumbered through and then emerged beside them.

"Sadic will not hurt you," he said in a low voice, trying to be reassuring.

Mindar and Journeyman rapidly followed. The shadows grew longer around them with late afternoon.

"We should hurry," Mindar said. "Within another day, we'll be near Scartaris. We have to be ready."

Delrael swallowed in a dry throat. "We will be."

They set off across the packed white quest-path.

The Serpent's head lay on the sand. Its eyes remained dead and pupilless, storm-colored jelly. Then the eyes lit up, glowing red again.

Scartaris looked through them at the questers as they set off toward his mountain lair.

CHAPTER 19
PROFESSOR VERNE'S
EXTRAORDINARY JOURNEY

I never realized the map was so huge. I never fully conceived of the parameters of Hexworld from one edge to the other. If the Outsiders can create such a world as a Game, then they must be powerful indeed.
—Professor Verne, *Les Voyages Extraordinaires*
(unpublished journal)

The steam engine car chugged along, hissing and sputtering. Professor Verne's ears rang with the racket. The steel-shod wheels rattled along over the uneven and rocky terrain. Harsh sunlight made him sweat and scratch at his gray beard. His forehead and nose stung with sunburn—he didn't usually sit unprotected in the open air for so long. His legs ached, and his buttocks felt sore from the bouncing ride hour upon hour, day upon day.

Grit and dust puffed into the air behind him, stirred up by the rolling car. Verne's warm woolen coat lay wadded in the seat beside him, but he would not put it on until the sun fell toward the horizon and the air grew cool again.

The Sitnaltan weapon was secured in the seat behind him. One monitoring gauge stuck out on an elbow of pipe. Polished bronze rivets reflected against the old metal around the chamber that contained the deadly Outside power source. The controls of the weapon consisted only of a timer knob and a detonation button. Angled red fins protruded from the sides for no reason other than that Verne had dreamed it that way.

The vehicle rolled along. The desert sprawled out gray-brown and lifeless in front of him. For a while, the sweeping emptiness of hexagon upon hexagon filled Verne with an awe at the sheer size of the Hexworld map. Then it all grew boring until he spent his time daydreaming and working out difficult ideas in his head.

In the pockets of his overcoat, Verne had tucked neatly folded sheets of paper on which he scribbled concepts and designs for other inventions. Verne's handwriting was difficult to read, and the diagrams were shaky—the vehicle jostled him too much as it bounced along. But neatness didn't count. The ideas did.

The professor also kept track of his progress so he could mathematically deduce the variation in travel allotments while journeying long distances with the steam-engine vehicle. Rule #5 specifically listed walking rates, but the supplementary tables in *The Book of Rules* made no mention of the Sitnaltan car. Verne came to the conclusion that, with the vehicle, he could proceed at about three times the pace he could go on foot.

But even as he made the calculation in his head, something made an odd *clunking* noise inside the boiler of the steam engine. The clean white exhaust belching up from the stack hiccoughed, curled black for a moment, then dissipated entirely. The machine hissed. The vehicle clattered, then slowed, coming to a stop all alone on the dusty rocks. The boiler groaned again, and the pistons locked.

Verne pursed his lips. "Hmmmm," he said, tugging at his beard. He climbed out and went around to the engine. He removed a toolkit from the sidebox and began to tinker, making sure nothing mechanical had gone wrong. But he had expected this to happen at any time ...

At dawn, three days before, Professor Frankenstein had helped him carry the Sitnaltan weapon to the back of the vehicle. Before the Sitnaltan technicians were awake, shivering but ready for another day's work excavating the Outsider's ship, Verne and Frankenstein had filled the car's main boiler and the reserve water tank from the stagnant cistern in the Slac citadel.

The boilers heated the water, raising the temperature and building up steam. Verne and Frankenstein waited, chatting, killing time and making plans. A few of the others stirred and came out into the frost-covered courtyard before the pressure-release valve in the boiler hissed, spitting out its announcement that the car was ready to travel.

Verne climbed aboard and made sure the weapon was safely secured. He waved to all of their puzzled expressions as the vehicle chugged forward, gaining momentum and traveling away from the citadel, out of the mountains.

All that day, Verne rolled on without stopping, despite difficult times on the harrowing switchbacks of the forested-hill terrain, and then going through the easier forests or, better still, the hexagons of flat grassland. Black lines marking the sections of terrain passed beneath his wheels.

Verne consulted his own map of Hexworld to make sure he was indeed taking the shortest and most efficient route. He calculated the speeds and estimated travel allowances for the best types of terrain.

He made sure to keep well away from the city of Sitnalta, just in case the weapon detonated prematurely.

The first evening, he had pulled up the vehicle and let the boiler fires run low. He found a stream and, handful by handful, he refilled the water tanks for the boiler. "Victor, why didn't you remind me to bring along a simple bucket?" He sighed. "I hate poor planning."

Verne lay down in the grass to sleep but woke up in the middle of the night, cold. He curled up next to the metal of the still-warm boiler and slept again.

The second day, he headed due east around sloping grassy hills, around a spur of the Spectre Mountains. When the mountains ended, he turned straight north across grassy hexes. At the end of the day, he entered the first section of desolation. Verne stared at the growing boundary where Scartaris's influence had drained all life dry. The long-range detectors in Sitnalta had suggested this would occur.

Verne had spent the entire day moving across barren terrain, chewing up dust and sand and rocks. He felt thirsty, but he kept most of the water in reserve for the engine. His lips were cracked, and he felt grit between his teeth. He had covered five hexagons in one day.

But now, far from the Sitnaltan technological fringe, the steam engine had died. He couldn't complain—the Rules of Probability stated that technological devices would have a smaller and smaller chance of functioning as they moved farther from the city of Sitnalta.

Verne tapped at one of the gleaming bronze piston shafts with a wrench, but it was no use. Unless he got the steam engine moving again, he could not destroy Scartaris, and Verne would be stranded out in the middle of the wasteland with a doomsday weapon powerful enough to blow a hole right through the bottom of the map.

Verne checked and rechecked the steam engine. He didn't know what else to do. He could never carry the heavy Sitnaltan weapon by himself. Nothing *mechanical* was wrong—that much was obvious. Nor was it any surprise. He muttered to himself about the vagaries of Hexworld and the rigid Rules that dictated everything. He hoped the Outsiders enjoyed making things difficult for him.

After the long day, he decided to reward himself with a precious cup of tea while waiting for the car to function again. He poured a little of the water out of his canteen into a tin cup from the car's supply case, then used his fingertips to hold the cup over the flames by the boiler. He shifted his grip from one hand to the other as the handle grew hot, but the water began to boil at last. He sprinkled tealeaves into it. They swirled with the heat currents in the water, and sank to the bottom as they let brown coloring seep into the cup. Steam rose from the hot tea.

Then Verne stood up so quickly, he sloshed some of the tea onto his pants. "Incredible!" he cried as the idea struck him. This was one of his own ideas, something clearly his own, not inspired by the Outsider Scott at all.

Here, far beyond the Sitnaltan technological fringe, water still boiled, did it not? Steam still rose, did it not?

He set his cup in a depression on the ground and went to the engine of the car. With both hands, he grabbed the pistons and pulled them out, pushed them back in. Yes, the pistons still moved, one cylinder inside the other.

The steam engine was a simple machine. He knew how it worked. Not a thing could go wrong.

It made no sense. Nothing got Verne more frustrated than things that *made no sense*. He knitted his eyebrows and pursed his lips, pacing around and around the steam-engine car. He grew angry. *There was no reason for it!* His face grew red with emotion, and he pounded his fist against the side of the boiler.

The Rules he had made a part of his life were completely arbitrary! Yes, he had always accepted that Sitnaltan technology would not function beyond the fringe—but when inspected closely, *all* technology was based upon fundamental laws of nature. Simple principles.

"It's not fair!" he shouted up, as if the Outsiders were listening. He hoped they were. He would throw their own arbitrariness back into their faces.

"I am beyond the technological fringe, yes—but what is the reason for this vehicle not working? Water still boils. Steam still rises. A piston will still move up and down. Wheels still turn.

"Everything in this vehicle *must* work, even on the other side of the fringe! I have used nothing out of the ordinary here. Just boiling water, rising steam, and turning wheels."

The sky remained silent and empty.

"You had better rethink your rules and restrictions."

Verne coughed because his throat was dry and caked with dust. In annoyance, he kicked the iron-shod wheel of the car with his heel.

The steam engine sputtered and gasped, surging back to life. Startled by the noise, Verne jumped out of the way. The vehicle lurched ahead, rumbling along the quest-path by itself.

Verne blinked and smiled. His tea sat ready on the ground, but he had no time to go get it. The vehicle moved farther away, picking up speed. He ran to catch up with it.

By noon the next day, the steam-engine car labored up a slope. The rock outcroppings had gotten larger and more jagged. Verne had to devote more attention to steering around sharp boulders and other debris that could cause serious damage to the vehicle.

He began to grow concerned. The water level was going down in the main boiler, and he had already used the auxiliary tank. But according to his calculations, based on data he'd taken from the

Sitnaltan detectors, he should be nearing Scartaris. And the doomsday weapon was still intact.

When the steam-engine car came to the crest of the hill, Verne looked down over a vast basin. A hooked line of jagged mountains bordered hexagon upon hexagon of desolation. Ah, he thought, those cliffs would be where Scartaris dwelled.

But in front of him, spread out in encampments, was the greatest horde of monsters he had ever imagined. They seemed unreal to him, all those creatures the Sitnaltans had ignored for turn after turn.

Verne pulled the car to a stop and then coaxed it into the shelter of a broken rock outcropping. The professor dismounted from the car, removed an optick tube from the sidebox, and peered down at the armies.

He saw marching angular-faced Slac covered with scales. He turned the field of view to observe monsters of all kinds, stone gargoyles, hairy brutes, a few ogres, worm-men sloughing through the broken sand in churned paths, green-skinned and pointy-eared goblins in their breeder groups.

On his scraps of paper, Verne noted the main features of each monster he saw, documenting them for future reference. With his interest in biological matters, Victor Frankenstein would probably delight in such first-hand observations.

Then Verne realized that each of these monster soldiers would stand in *his* way, block *his* passage to Scartaris. They would want to attack him, capture him, perhaps kill him. He suddenly considered what might happen if these unpleasant creatures managed to possess the powerful Sitnaltan weapon. He and Victor had not thought of that.

"This could cause a problem," he muttered to himself.

A direct road led to the mountains. He saw a wide but steep path heading directly to a great opening in the flat cliff like a lipless mouth of rock. Strange and oily colors flashed from inside the broad cavern.

As he expected, the Outsiders would make the lair of Scartaris wonderfully obvious. Reaching it, though, would be the primary problem.

He shut off the boilers in the steam engine, remembering that he had to remain hidden. The car would make plenty of noise when he restarted it. When he decided to move, he would have to make all possible speed to his goal and hope he could cover enough terrain, to get to a place where he could detonate the weapon … before the monsters got him.

Verne sat with his back against the shaded rock and took out his last clean piece of paper. He jotted down notes to himself, waiting for dark.

CHAPTER 20
SHADOW BATTLE

The Outsiders love to play at warfare with us. They can slaughter characters by the thousands without risking harm to themselves. But this is our Game too, and we must fight back.
—*General Doril*, memoirs from the Scouring

Clouds gathered over Scartaris's mountain, making the sky look like a cooling pool of molten lead. Overhead wheeled several batlike reptilian creatures. Delrael found the air thick and hard to breathe.

The Cailee had not come the night before. Mindar shook her head. "Scartaris wouldn't resurrect me without bringing back the Cailee," she said. "He's just having his fun."

"I'm not sure who our true enemy is anymore," Vailret said, "Scartaris or the Outsider David."

The Slave of the Serpent limped and dragged his leg beside them. The wound from Delrael's sword still bled slow and thick, but Sadic did not complain.

At dusk, they reached another hex-line. Only one more section of terrain separated them from the end of their quest. The ground grew more broken and jagged, as if Scartaris had tossed chunks of his mountain like giant dice in every direction.

Behind them, the monstrous black cloud rose up from the ground, near enough to hear clearly now—a constant buzzing, squawking turmoil. The cloud pushed ahead like a clawed hand scooping them toward Scartaris.

At the top of a rise, Delrael stopped, sheltered by a rock outcropping. The army of Scartaris gathered before them on the great plain. "No wonder Scartaris wasn't worried about us." He swallowed in a dry throat.

By the light of dim fires in the camps, hideous demons and reptilian things moved in organized ranks. Tall Slac generals marched about shouting orders. Delrael saw an occasional hulking stone gargoyle, like Arken. Swarms of small goblins, green-skinned and hairless, clustered together in their breeder groups. Guttural grunts and hisses carried out into the still air.

The massive enemy was preparing to march upon Hexworld. Scartaris had grown tired of waiting. The Outsider David wanted to ruin the map without further delay.

One gigantic creature strode through the army, obviously in command. He had a powerful lion's body, a wicked-looking scorpion-tail that flickered with blue lightning, and a horned head showing distorted human features. Delrael thought he had heard of such a creature in the worst old Sorcerer battles, a monster developed by gamers to be powerful enough to oppose even the great dragons.

"It's a manticore," Vailret said. His voice sounded thin with fear.

"Toto, I don't think we're in Kansas anymore," Journeyman said.

Overhead, Lady Maire's Veil reminded Delrael of green blood spilled across the sky. The mountains of Scartaris looked like a strange, warped creature made of stone, rearing its mighty head. Two symmetrical peaks curved upward from the main mountain,

PLAY

broken and pitted, similar to the horns of a giant bull. On the central rock face was a yawning grotto, a cavelike overhang that stared out of the mountain like a cyclopean eye-socket, black and pupilless.

Delrael had to take the Earthspirits into *that* cavern. It was obvious. He had gone on enough quests to identify the goal when he saw it. But the entire army of Scartaris stood ready to stop him. He felt his vision go dark and fuzzy; his breathing came short.

"The game ain't over until the fat lady sings," Journeyman said. He blinked his clay eyelids.

"Sadic will protect you," the burly Slave said and stood beside Delrael. "You freed Sadic."

Delrael felt the silver belt at his waist. All of those monsters, each one intent on destroying Hexworld, on stopping *him*—how could he ever take the Spirits the final distance? "We'd need an army of our own to get past them."

"And any time it looks as if we might succeed, Scartaris can go through his metamorphosis and end the Game anyway," Mindar sighed. "Isn't this fun?"

Bryl shuffled his feet and kept his head down. "I have an idea." He flinched when everyone looked at him at once. He ran his gnarled hands through the folds of his cloak and withdrew the Fire Stone and the Air Stone.

"Scartaris knows we have the Fire Stone, since it was Enrod's," he said, then thrust the eight-sided ruby back into his hidden pockets. "But I haven't used the Air Stone yet on this quest. Remember how Gairoth had his army of illusion ogres at the Stronghold? Gairoth has even less training than I do, and his Sorcerer blood is tainted."

He took a deep breath. "My father Qonnar was a full-blooded Sorcerer; my mother Tristane was a half-breed. I've had some training. If I use up all my spells, I can create an army for you. A good one."

267

Delrael pondered a moment as possibilities came into his head, then he grinned and clapped a hand on Bryl's shoulder.

"Whatever it takes," Journeyman said. "The Rulewoman Melanie is counting on me."

Bryl seemed small and terrified. "Just remember what I'm going to do, though. It's easy to think of one or two figures and move them around with my imagination—but I'll be keeping track of a thousand different faces, different characters, all at the same time. Each one fighting, each one moving around like a real character would."

He blinked his eyes, looking giddy. "It'll be like role-playing on a gigantic scale! It must be what the Outsiders do all the time."

Mindar held her rippled sword and stared at the army below. The expression on her face seemed explosive. "If you make it look like the monsters are being slaughtered, that'll certainly ruin their morale."

Delrael saw concern grown on Bryl's face. "Just remember, my illusions won't cause any actual damage, though the monsters will *think* they're striking something solid. At least it'll keep them busy while you slip past to Scartaris."

Bryl huddled between broken boulders in the shelter of an outcropping. "I'll need a place where I can hide and not be disturbed." He wiggled small rocks from under him, brushed his hands together, then withdrew the four-sided diamond. It glistened, even in the falling darkness.

"I'll cover myself with an illusion too. But you'd better hurry. With two Stones in my possession, I can use five spells now and another five after midnight—but I don't know how long that'll last. It depends on how I roll."

Mindar's expression hardened. "We all have to fight to our limits." She turned to Delrael; her eyes held the burning obsession he had seen there so many times before.

"But it's time for truth between us, Delrael. If we're going to fight together against Scartaris, I need to know what weapon you've got." She fidgeted, then looked up. "I want to be sure I'm gambling my life on a good chance."

Delrael frowned down at the ground. He gazed back at Mindar, her high cheekbones, her deep eyes, the tangled hair that had once been braided behind her head.

"You're right, Mindar." He turned away, for some reason not wanting to watch her face as he told his secret. "The Earthspirits want to destroy Scartaris too. I'm carrying them with me, in my belt. I have to take them there." He pointed to the jagged mountains. "They can defeat him."

Journeyman frowned. "It's not the only weapon we have."

"Are we going to end this or not?" Bryl said from his hiding place. He stroked the diamond, staring into its facets. "Let me know when you're ready to go."

Delrael nodded. "Luck."

"Luck," the others echoed.

The Slave stood beside them with shoulders squared, ready for battle. Journeyman went to Bryl and extended a clay hand in a formal gesture. "Live long and prosper."

Delrael cleared his throat. "We're ready."

Bryl took a deep breath and rolled the Air Stone.

The air shimmered with the massive illusion gelling around them. Forms appeared, snapping into sharp clarity.

On the slope overlooking Scartaris's horde, another army now stood: all human characters, clad in perfect armor, strong and proud, carrying a variety of weapons. With a start, Delrael recognized most of the faces—they were his own or Vailret's. Some bore moustaches and beards or dark hair, but Bryl had plainly used his own memory. Other soldiers looked like characters from the Stronghold village.

The fighters carried bright shields with the colors of village's hexagons distant from the Stronghold. Their boots showed scuff-marks as if they had marched across the map.

"Excellent!" Delrael whispered.

"That would impress even the old Sorcerer warlords," Vailret said.

"Now is the time for all good men to come to the aid of their country," Journeyman added.

Then a loud voice, clear as the tone from a crystal bell, rang out from Delrael's silver belt. "The Earthspirits are prepared for our final battle. We wish you luck!"

Delrael stood stunned and delighted. The others gawked at him, amazed. He didn't want to waste time thinking about it—they had to fight. Always have fun. He felt filled with confidence.

Mindar held up her rippled sword. "Let's go, before we lose our advantage of surprise." Then she ran forward with a suicidal determination on her face. Vailret and Journeyman moved side by side, and Sadic followed Delrael.

Weapons drawn, armor adjusted, the illusion army surged into motion with a muffled clanking. They kept ranks as they charged down the long slope toward the monster horde, yelling personal battle cries. They left no footprints on the sand.

Delrael let himself be hidden among the illusion soldiers. In true Game spirit, he felt he should be at the head of his fighters, leading the point of the charge like a great general in the Sorcerer wars. But calling attention to himself would defeat the entire purpose of creating the illusion army. He closed his eyes and took a deep breath.

Scartaris's army howled in confused surprise at the sudden appearance of this new force. They dropped all preparations for their charge across Hexworld. The monsters still outnumbered the illusion army—Bryl could only imagine and direct so many soldiers—but it was enough to throw the enemy ranks into turmoil. The two armies met.

Tall Slac troops stormed together, pushing their way through the other monster warriors to the front of the fighting line. Each

Slac carried an iron sword and tough shield of Tairan manufacture.

Delrael watched other illusion soldiers struck down and trampled on the battlefield. So many of them looked like *him*. It made him feel sick inside.

A tall Slac general stood in his path, cloaked in a slick black garment that hung around him, giving the reptilian arms freedom to maneuver. Platelike scales covered the Slac's head. Its eyes were emerald green, glowing and pupilless. But one of the illusion soldiers engaged the Slac, and Delrael slipped past.

The smell of smoke and blood and churned-up dust bit into his nostrils, masking the lingering stench of the close-pressed monster army.

He watched Mindar dash about, slashing with her rippled sword. Her face was drawn back in a furious expression, savoring her revenge on Scartaris. She struck one pig-snouted monster down and turned to thrash at a swarm of green-skinned goblins. The *S*-scar on her forehead glowed. The Slac ignored her and concentrated on the advancing army.

Journeyman waded in, swinging his clay fists from side to side and bowling over goblins. Swords bit into his skin, but he repaired the damage by shoving his clay back into place.

Vailret swung his short sword but didn't seem to know what to do. He kept himself sheltered and tried to remain by the golem. Since so many of the fighters looked alike, Delrael had to look twice to make sure he had really seen Vailret and not an illusion counterpart.

Near Delrael, an illusion fighter—himself, but with black hair and a beard—struck at a hunchbacked demon. The demon grunted without words and swung a jagged pike up into the human fighter's stomach. Though it was only an illusion, Delrael snarled as the fighter choked, bleeding from his mouth, and fell, still grasping the weapon stuck through him.

Delrael jumped in and chopped down on the hunchbacked monster's neck. The sword bit through the knobbed, leathery skin. The monster tried to turn, but it still *thought* its pike was stuck in the dead illusion fighter and couldn't pull it away. Delrael swung again, severing the cords in the monster's neck and watching the head fall.

Battlefield sounds roared around him. His ears were numb from the screams of monsters and human fighters, the clang of weapons, the garbled shouting of orders from Slac generals, cries of anger and confusion. He heard the booming of drums.

A mass of goblins charged into the fray, scrabbling with sharp fingers. They picked up fallen weapons and broken sticks; two carried burning brands from abandoned campfires. They made a thin jabbering as they piled on their victims, bringing them down with the force of numbers.

Delrael heard a haunting, buzzing sound with growls and cries and squawks that grew louder in an approaching storm of noise. He held his sword out to defend himself and looked behind him, up into the sky—

Poised like an axe over a chopping block, the black cloud began to fall down on the battlefield.

It dissolved before his eyes, breaking into nebulous pieces drifting down as the bottom portion, filled with dim shapes, set upon the confusion of the battleground. He could see that the cloud was not really black at all, but a garbled mass of colors blended together. Thousands of unrelated noises smothered the battlefield din.

Then a bird flashed in front of Delrael's eyes, darting forward at a hairy monster.

Dozens of biting flies flew ahead of it; beetles hummed by. A cloud of butterflies spattered themselves across the face of a demon. Tiny creatures filled the air. On the ground, larger animals attacked, moving and working together.

The clear, ringing voice of the Earthspirits spoke out from his silver belt. "Our reinforcements have arrived." The words vibrated through to his bones. "We sent out our own summons to living creatures across the map, but you did not recognize it as such. They will help as best they can."

Delrael ran forward in delight, remembering the disturbing screech his belt had made in the forest by the Barrier River. "You could have let us know ahead of time."

The Earthspirits made no reply.

A cloud of wasps and flies fell upon one of the breeder groups of goblins, stinging again and again. A gray wolf and a sharp-antlered stag charged among other demons. Beetles and spiders covered their fur, but the little creatures jumped off and set upon the monsters.

A black bear roared and threw herself on a thin, oily-skinned demon. The bear mauled the monster with spread claws while the demon defended itself with its own iron sword. The bear ripped the demon's oily flesh to spill entrails that smoked in the cool air.

Delrael continued forward, setting his jaw. He slashed at several confused goblins, but he concentrated on moving toward Scartaris. The mountain lair rose up across the battlefield, on the other side of a hex-line.

Beside him, a yellow bird took on a towering Slac, darting in and flapping at the monster's face. The Slac lunged clumsily at it, smashing the air with balled, horny fists. But the bird fluttered away, then flew in again to peck the emerald eyes.

Hundreds of tiny insects swarmed over a spine-covered creature, stinging its eyes, clogging its ears and nostrils and mouth with their dead bodies. A frenzied Slac charged in front of Delrael; its face was a black mass of crawling, biting beetles. It waved its sword wildly in the air, stumbling, until a gray wolf knocked the Slac to the ground and tore out its throat.

Explosions ripped the air, throwing up dirt and flames and chunks of clay. Delrael wondered if Scartaris's monsters used the same kind of firepowder that Tareah wanted for her Transition Day festivities. Teams of monsters used groaning catapults to lob clay pots of firepowder. The explosions only did more damage to Scartaris's horde.

Delrael stopped and realized that he had lost track of Vailret and the others. In the chaos around him, all the soldiers looked alike. The animals and the demons fought on every side of him. He couldn't shout into the din.

For an instant, he allowed himself to feel alone and frightened, then he swallowed his fear and worked his way forward. He had to get the Earthspirits to Scartaris. Characters always had to finish their quests, or die trying. It said so in *The Book of Rules*.

Vailret struggled to stay next to Journeyman. The golem charged ahead, smashing monstrous soldiers and intent on his own goal. The illusion fighters moved about, clashing, striking. Many wore an eerie reflection of Vailret's features. He watched them fall, finding it very disturbing to watch himself die.

He held his sword, but illusion soldiers engaged all monsters that came near him. He felt his mind overloading with the terror of the battle. Sharp swords, knives, clawed hands, spiked armor, terrible weapons—

Vailret looked around, frantic, but he had lost track of the *true* Delrael. He hoped that one of those slaughtered victims wasn't his cousin. "Journeyman! I can't find Del!"

The golem paused and turned. "I'm late, I'm late, for a very important date."

Journeyman knocked a Slac general out of the way, punching the reptilian creature in the stomach, then seizing the stout neck and snapping it sideways. The dead Slac stared at Journeyman with an expression of astonishment.

Vailret hurried after the golem. The mountain lair of Scartaris stood stark and clear; he could only hope Delrael would meet him and Journeyman there.

To the left, monsters lobbed pots of firepowder in bright explosions. The animals and insects massed around Vailret, swarming, but they attacked only the monsters. Animal smells mixed with the stench of the demon army's long encampment.

Ahead, the manticore stood tall over all the other monsters. With great leaps, he charged to the focus of the fighting. Indiscriminately, the manticore slashed his own soldiers out of the way. His giant paws mauled half a dozen goblins as he pushed toward the illusion human fighters. The manticore's scorpion tail flicked back and forth, striking each time with a blue flash and an explosion.

Vailret knew stories about the manticores—it was said they were so powerful that even their old Sorcerers creators could barely control them. And several Sorcerers had died trying.

Vailret caught up with Journeyman just as a stone gargoyle leaped in front of them. The ground thudded as the heavy stone creature landed and spread its feet and jagged wings, holding both cumbersome granite arms up to block their way. Demonic horns curled up from the center of its forehead, but Arken's crudely formed expression did not change. He had formed the same stone body for himself again.

"Go away, boy, you bother me." Journeyman tried to pass by.

"Shall we have a rematch, my friends?" Arken said. "Two out of three?"

Journeyman stopped and grinned broadly. "Didn't you learn your lesson the first time?"

The gargoyle heaved a rumbling sigh. "*I* learned my lesson, but apparently, Scartaris has not. Once again, he has brought me back with explicit orders to stop you. Scartaris is angry—he thinks I tricked him."

Arken seemed to smile with his craggy stone face. "And of course we did. But this time, he has given me no freedom to decide for myself. I must stop you. I can't bargain."

Journeyman stepped forward. "We'll see about that."

Vailret remembered how long and difficult their previous duel had been. He knew he couldn't defend himself for that long as the howling battle swirled around him.

Then he felt the seed of an idea in his mind and grabbed at it. He stood between Journeyman and Arken. "Wait, Arken! Scartaris gave you explicit, clear orders, correct?"

"Yes."

"All right, then. We'll make it easy for you. Journeyman—stand still." Vailret stood beside him, motionless. "There, you've stopped us. You have fulfilled your obligation to Scartaris."

Arken stood up straight, nodding his horned head in delight. "Why didn't I think of that? He told me to follow his orders exactly. Oh, this is delightful! Scartaris will be even more upset!"

"Now do what you can to help," Vailret said. "We have to get to Scartaris."

Journeyman squared his shoulders. "The Rulewoman Melanie is counting on me."

With another great bound, the huge manticore stormed toward them, striking with his explosive scorpion tail. He used his claws to tear apart illusion human soldiers four and five at a time, stomping over them without a pause. The manticore let out a howling roar, human and bestial at the same time from his distorted manlike face.

Arken turned and flashed his cavernous stone eyes at Vailret. "Here's a good opportunity. You move on, get to Scartaris. Luck!"

Turning, the gargoyle waded through the other fighting and approached the manticore from the side. Arken slammed a jagged stone fist into the wide ribs of the leonine body before the manticore had even noticed him.

With a roar and an outraged "Ooof!" of pain, the manticore turned on him, favoring cracked ribs. The great monster reared up and scored its claws against the gargoyle, leaving clean white gouges across the granite chest and raking up sparks.

The stone-winged gargoyle scrambled to his feet again and leaped up to grab the hooked bulb at the end of the scorpion tail, trying to break off the stinger. But the manticore whirled and brought the tail up. He lifted Arken off the ground and flung him forward. With another lash, the scorpion tail sparked blue lightning. It struck down with an explosive electric roar that shattered the gargoyle into lifeless stone pieces.

With a long backward glance, Vailret followed Journeyman, who pushed toward the lair of Scartaris with single-minded intent.

Delrael closed his mind to anything but moving forward. He could not find the others, but if he failed to reach Scartaris, that wouldn't matter anyway. *He* had the Earthspirits. *He* could end the Outsiders' threat.

Delrael looked ahead, paying only enough attention to keep moving. His sword arm was exhausted; he found breathing difficult —but he had reached a fever pitch of fighting, and nothing else seemed real to him.

Until one loud bellow broke through the din of the battle.

"Delroth!"

He froze and turned with stunned amazement as the one-eyed ogre plowed through the other soldiers. With a slash of his spiked club, Gairoth bowled over a mob of goblins and plodded toward Delrael.

"Haw! Now I kill you!"

Delrael couldn't believe the ogre had followed them from where they had rescued Tallin, through the Spectre Mountains where he had been swept off the ledge by the avalanche, all the way across the map to here. Somehow the ogre knew which one was the true Delrael, and which ones were just Bryl's illusions.

Delrael held his sword ready. "You're starting to bother me, Gairoth." But despite his show of false bravery, he saw how the huge ogre knocked aside other formidable demon fighters to reach him.

"Come on, then," Delrael said. He swallowed and felt his throat tighten. He got ready.

Gairoth growled and strode forward, holding his club like a baseball bat.

Then another explosive roar distracted both of them. Goblins and demons were tossed aside like dead leaves in the wind.

The Slave of the Serpent burst into view. His hairy paws dripped with blood of different colors. He grabbed two goblins and smashed their heads together into a pulpy mass. Then he tossed them aside as he strode toward Delrael.

"Sadic will protect you."

Delrael stepped back, feeling relieved. The Slave stepped beside him like a gigantic bodyguard. "You freed Sadic from Serpent."

Gairoth bellowed in annoyance as the towering Slave stepped between him and Delrael. Sadic stood a full two feet taller than the ogre and much broader across the shoulders. Globs of blood matted the Slave's fur from the monsters he had slain. The deep wound in his thigh had reopened and oozed thick yellow blood, making him limp and move stiffly.

But he stood against Gairoth. "You go," Sadic said to Delrael. "Kill Scartaris."

A V-formation of hawks swooped down and skimmed past him. They slashed out the eyes of a spine-covered monster, then struck in to tear out its throat with their long claws. Together, they flew off again.

Gairoth snorted and lunged toward Delrael, trying to duck to the side of the Slave. Sadic reached out a giant paw and caught the ogre across the tattered furs on his chest, deflecting Gairoth's charge and knocking him to the dirt.

Gairoth landed on his backside and howled. He used the club to pry himself to his feet then turned his anger toward Sadic. He swung the club with all his might, and the wicked spikes raked across where the Slave had been. Sadic leaped back but stumbled on his wounded leg, wincing in pain.

Gairoth jumped at the Slave of the Serpent; Sadic met him, grabbing the ogre around the chest. The two grappled with each other, pounding with massive fists, trying to squeeze and crack ribs. Sadic raked his long claws up the peeling skin of Gairoth's back. The ogre shifted his grip higher on the spiked club to bash at the demon's fur-covered shoulder until yellow blood oozed out. With loud bestial sounds, both opponents flung themselves away and stood panting and bleeding.

Once more, Gairoth tried to scramble around the Slave. Sadic blocked him again, but this time, the ogre leered a strange grin as if he had gotten an idea. He lashed out with one of his wide bare feet and kicked as hard as he could, smacking into the deep open wound on the Slave's leg.

In agony, Sadic buckled over, grabbing his thigh. He staggered.

Gairoth swung the spiked club up and then down, leaping into the air to put all of his weight into the swing. The club crashed down onto the demon's head, smashing through it like a soft-boiled egg.

Sadic grunted once, then collapsed to the ground.

The shock struck Delrael like a cold knife in his stomach. He had wounded the Slave with his sword, giving Gairoth his chance to play dirty. He felt responsible. Then Delrael realized how foolish he had been for not running when Sadic gave him the chance.

Now Gairoth, panting but angrier than ever, picked up his dripping club and stepped over the Slave's prone body. He advanced toward Delrael.

Sadic grabbed the ogre's ankle, driving claws deep into the thick leg and tripping him. Gairoth sprawled out on his face. With a fury greater than a sudden thunderstorm, the ogre jumped back to his feet and pounded the fallen Slave over and over with the club, sending a thick rain of yellow blood into the air.

Bleeding from his ankle now, Gairoth returned all his attention to Delrael. "Haw! Now you die, Delroth!"

Delrael held his sword in front of him. "You've said that before, Gairoth. But you keep botching it!" He felt no force behind his words. Hope drained out of him with sick dismay at seeing the death of Sadic.

Gairoth ran forward. Delrael held his ground.

Neither of them saw the shadowy, batlike forms as the reptilian flying creatures swooped down to the battlefield.

Gairoth swung.

Delrael held up his sword to block the blow, though he knew it would do nothing against the ogre's momentum.

He felt sharp pain in both of his shoulders as if two handfuls of knives had stabbed into him. His neck jerked as something snapped his body into the air. The battlefield dropped away under him, and he heard sounds like great sails rippling over his head.

The bat-creature shrieked from a pointed, fanged mouth and flew up into the sky.

Gairoth spun around when his club struck only air, and dropped to his knees, dizzy. He stared at where Delrael had been, but saw nothing. Only footprints that vanished. A single drop of scarlet blood marked the ground.

"Which way did he go? Awwww!"

Up in the sky, he saw the shadow of a flying creature carrying a man, winging toward the grotto of Scartaris.

Professor Verne stoked the steam-engine car and checked its water level. It would function for barely another hour. He took a last drink of water and poured the rest of his flask into the boiler. Every little bit would help. Verne ran the back of his hand across his lips and sighed. Then he sealed the chamber to let the steam pressure build.

The Sitnaltan weapon lay cradled in the car's seat. It was primed and waiting. Monitor lights blinked on and off.

He had pondered all day about how to get around the monster army. Though the weapon would cause immense havoc when it detonated, he still wanted to get it as close to Scartaris as possible. No sense taking chances, especially far from Sitnalta, where the world worked so differently.

Verne jotted down his last thoughts in his journal and tucked the book inside his woolen jacket. He didn't know if he would ever return to Sitnalta, or if his memoirs would ever be published, but he felt an obligation to record his thoughts and observations.

He tugged at his full beard and straightened it. He wished he had brought his pipe along—he could use a relaxing smoke right now. He blew through his lips instead. He felt queasy inside. "Great Maxwell, what have I gotten myself into?"

Steam-pressure gauges on the car's boiler rose. The vehicle was almost ready to move. Darkness had fallen.

When a great roar went up from the monster horde, Verne jumped, startled, and looked to see an army of human characters advancing down the slope a partial hexagon away. Verne blinked his eyes in amazement. He had seen no indications of an approaching army. How could all those fighters appear with no warning at all? No doubt they were that type of Hexworld character who thrived on military campaigns, went on quests. He hoped they wouldn't be too near the blast when his weapon went off.

He climbed aboard the steam-engine car and sat back in his seat. He could investigate the identity of the army later. For now, he would take advantage of the diversion. He made sure the doomsday weapon was firmly strapped in the back seat, safe from any jostling; the timer was ready to be set.

Professor Verne took a deep breath. He straightened his jacket one last time, out of habit, then released the locks on the gears. He held on to the steering levers.

The steam-engine car rattled down the slope toward the mountains of Scartaris.

Mindar slashed the air with her rippled sword. Dark blood dripped off its serrated edges. Her hair was tangled. She swept it back away from her eyes, then shouted her outrage at the monster army. "Why won't you fight me!"

She turned back and forth, but Scartaris's monsters ignored her. They would not meet her eyes. Mindar charged into a mass of goblins, but they swirled around her and moved on. They did not strike back.

"Fight me!"

Scartaris was doing this to taunt her, to have *fun*. He knew that the greatest damage he could do to Mindar was to ignore her, to refuse to acknowledge her efforts against him.

She ran at one of the towering Slac fighters and swung her sword, but the Slac lifted a Tairan-made shield and deflected her blow. Then the monster punched her with a balled scaly fist, knocking her out of the way.

She wheezed, felt the pain from her bruised ribs, and stood up. Bryl's illusion soldiers fought all around her.

Mindar stood up and glared at the jagged lair of Scartaris on the far edge of the battlefield. That was where she could strike her blow. She had lost Delrael and the others, but they were fighting, moving toward Scartaris. She belonged there too.

Mindar strode through the battle, wading into blood and fallen bodies. The other fighters did not turn to face her.

The flying creature beat its taut wings with a sound like a man gasping for breath. Delrael felt as though its claws were ripping his shoulders off.

The bat-creature rose higher. Delrael grabbed the sword in his hand, though his fingers grew cold and numb. He still ached from his battle with the Slave of the Serpent two days before, exhausted now from fighting through Scartaris's army.

Veins laced the wings of the bat-creature, visible through skin as thin as fine fabric, pulsing and rippling in the breeze. The flying thing had deep pits for eyes, blank and pupilless, and a long jagged snout in an arrow-shaped head. Its cry was so high-pitched that Delrael's ears felt ready to burst.

His feet dangled below him. He felt nothing, only air beneath his boots. The battlefield lay fifty feet below. Distinct sounds drifted up. He saw the swirling fighters, the movements of the ranks, flashes of exploding pots of firepowder. The giant manticore dominated the battle scene.

Delrael squirmed in the grip of the bat-creature. His own blood poured from gashes in his leather armor where the claws sank into him. The pain sent fire through his chest.

. . .

Scartaris's grotto lay closer than ever now. The hex-line broke the last section of desolation from the rocky, mountain terrain.

He didn't know what was happening, where the creature was taking him. But when it drifted over the sharp air currents when the terrain changed from flatland to mountains, he saw the rocks below like spears pointed up at him.

He felt the bat-creature tighten its knobby claws just for a moment—and then Delrael knew what it intended. The creature had taken him high aloft...now it was going to drop him.

Delrael ignored the daggers of pain in his shoulder. He winced but knew what he had to do. He lunged upward with his free hand, grabbing on to the bat-creature's leg just as it released its claws. He gripped hard, digging his fingernails into the rough hide. The sharp rocks seemed a long, long drop below.

The bat-creature flapped its wings in surprise and screamed a high-pitched noise. Its claws extended and retracted as it tried to grab on to something to fight back. Delrael would not let go. The bat-creature hissed and bobbed its sharp head down, but the fighter was out of its reach.

Feeling as if he were lifting a gigantic weight, Delrael heaved his sword up with one hand and thrust it through the thin membrane of a wing, ripping a gash. He had to get down. Air whistled through the cut, and the bat-creature flailed, but it could not get away.

The flying creature dropped lower. Delrael poked with the sword again. As the creature beat its immense wings, the wind and the air ripped the gash wider.

The ground rushed up at them. He had caused too much damage. They would crash and both be killed.

But then the bat-creature pumped its wings with renewed strength. It spun in a tight circle as one wing drove harder than the other, but still ascended.

Delrael grew dizzy. The ground below him spun with the crazy spiral flight. Hot tears of pain streamed down Delrael's cheeks. The strain of holding on with one hand, holding his entire weight against the long drop, drove nails into the wounds in his shoulders.

He had to get down. He wanted to scream.

Delrael reached up with the sword one more time and chopped at the other wing. The creature dropped again, hissing, but Delrael would not let go. The ground rushed up.

He tried to swing the bat-creature's body around, to direct it toward a clear spot in the foothills of the mountain terrain, but he didn't know how. The creature's fangs glistened in the starlight, and it bore a vicious expression behind the pupilless eyes. Once they struck the ground, it would attack him.

The rocks came closer—Delrael could survive now, though the fall might hurt him. He swung the sword up awkwardly. He hit the main strut of the creature's wing, chopping at its shoulder.

The rocks came up. He stabbed the creature in the abdomen and then let go, dropping the last ten feet to the ground.

The bat-creature crashed next to him. Delrael heard the dry-wood *snap* of the bones in its wings as it fell. The creature lay on the rocks, flapping and hissing, trying to get at him. It elbowed forward on the jagged splinters of its wings, but Delrael slipped in past the hissing mouth. He struck the arrow-shaped head with his sword. The creature's wings flopped and twitched, then lay still.

Blood streamed down Delrael's shoulders—his own blood—and he took ten steps away from the dead creature, up the path toward the grotto of Scartaris.

Delrael slumped down to rest on a boulder. Everything grew fuzzy. His pain, exhaustion, and hopelessness welled up. He could not find the strength to stand.

The bat-creature had carried him over most of the army. The monster hordes lay below him, fighting against Bryl's illusion soldiers. Ahead and to the right, a curved spike of rock swept up from the main mountainous mass, one of the horns bracketing Scartaris's grotto.

Delrael breathed the cool night air and saw mist rising inside the giant mouthlike opening in the mountain. Strange lights flashed, many different colors. It seemed close to him, but now he felt all alone. He didn't know where Mindar was, or Vailret or Journeyman. He had come this far.

But he couldn't make the last effort.

"You must move on," the voice of the Earthspirits said from his belt. He felt a throb of energy creep up his spine, a warmth filling his veins like molten sunshine. The pain in his shoulders lessened.

Delrael stood up, feeling vibrant. He could function now. Then an ominous thought crossed his mind. "I hope you'll still have enough energy now to defeat Scartaris."

The long pause made him feel uncomfortable even before the Earthspirits answered. "We have *never* had enough energy to defeat Scartaris."

He stumbled backward. His ears burned, and he stared at the turmoil of battle below him. All they had done, the characters who had died--Sadic, Tallin, the entire city of Tairé. "What do you mean?"

"Scartaris is too powerful. That is one of the other reasons we had you carry us across the map. Physical travel is ... *difficult* for us, now that we are only marginally connected with the map of Hexworld. We can move *you*, like a player moving a piece on a gameboard. But the hex-lines are great stumbling blocks for us. We are outside the Rules, and yet trapped by them."

The silver belt felt cold and tingling at his waist. Delrael didn't want to touch it. The Spirits continued.

"But still, according to those same Rules, when an evil adversary threatens, good characters must do their best to fight, regardless of their chances. Therefore, we will fight. Though Scartaris is much more powerful, nothing is absolute on Hexworld. We must hold on to that chance."

"You mean, you hope that Mindar's Stranger Unlooked-For shows up?" Delrael tried to keep the scorn out of his voice.

"We know nothing of that. We must fight and do our best—as *you* must, Delrael. And your sworn quest is to take us to Scartaris. Now finish your quest!"

His heart felt like a lead brick inside him, but he plodded toward the grotto. If the Earthspirits couldn't destroy Scartaris, maybe they could at least weaken him, buy time for the magic of Hexworld to find another way on its own.

Scartaris had few defenses this far behind the ranks, probably to show his overconfidence. Several minor demons wandered among the rocks where they had fled. They fought without enthusiasm, and Delrael defeated them or chased them away. He still felt new energy from the Earthspirits, along with a growing anger at the futility of it all. He stalked toward the opening and the many-colored lights inside.

Rocks crunched under his boots as he climbed up the slope. Jagged boulders stood beside the opening that led deep into the mountain. He could not see the source of the lights, but weird shadows played on the wall and spilled out onto the quest-path.

Weariness crept up on him as he approached the end of the journey. He needed only to get to Scartaris, throw down the silver belt.

Panting, he strode up to the opening and he saw a figure inside, backlit against the grotto. She stood staring, looking devastated. The *S*-scar on her forehead glowed with its own bloody light. She slumped against one of the tall rocks beside the opening.

"Mindar!" Delrael said. "You're safe."

He saw a flicker of happiness when she looked at him, but that too was swallowed by the gulf of despair behind her eyes. "Of course I survived. I had to. Scartaris won't let me die." Her misery seemed to be tearing her apart.

"What's wrong? We're almost there. We can destroy Scartaris!" The lie came out, but he had to say it for her.

She glared at him with a wasteland of expression. The rippled sword rested against her leg, stained with dark blood. Her entire body trembled. "I'm the only thing left to stop you, Delrael."

He took a step back; his thoughts churned. Her cheeks were flushed, her eyes averted. He couldn't imagine she would do anything to harm him. "What are you talking about?"

Mindar hung her head. "I lied to you."

A black shadow-form oozed out of the dark rocks beside the opening and stood silhouetted next to her. Its silver claws gleamed from the reflected light.

"I didn't know until now, but it's true," Mindar said. "*I* am the Cailee!"

CHAPTER 21
THRESHOLD OF SCARTARIS

Do you enjoy these battles, these Wars? Are they fun? Look what they have cost you!
—Stilvess Peacemaker

Delrael's heart stumbled a beat, and his breath came in ragged gasps. He wanted to reach out for Mindar, to take her arm, but he felt stunned.

"Scartaris kept the truth from me. The Cailee is my shadow, a darker part of me than I knew I had," Mindar said. A sigh hissed through her teeth.

"It splits from me each night to cause its harm. We cannot live without each other. And Scartaris won't let us die. It was part of his Game. He made me hate the Cailee, despise it—but I was only hating myself! Scartaris thinks of it as fun!"

She bit back an outcry as something forced her to take a lurching step toward the Cailee. The shadow thing moved closer to her, blotting out the flickering light from the grotto. They touched each other, overlapping.

The darkness of the Cailee flooded over Mindar's body like a blanket of tar. Long silver claws hung down from her fingers, wrapped around the hilt of her rippled sword. Shadows masked her face, but Delrael could see her features silhouetted—the high cheekbones, the angry mouth. Mindar's eyes became misty yellow and pupilless. The red *S*-scar burned through.

Delrael stood transfixed. This was too much. The Cailee took one step, powerful and deadly, blocking the way. But it was Mindar too. When the hybrid woman/shadow spoke, her voice had grown huskier.

"We know of your quest, Delrael. Scartaris is—" Mindar/Cailee tossed her head, as if fighting with herself. Something snapped inside, and she let out a strangled roar, lunging with her rippled sword.

Delrael gave a yelp of surprise and sprang backward, exhausted but still tense with battle reflexes. Mindar/Cailee slashed at him, rippled sword in one hand and silver claws in the other.

He tried to back away, unwilling to fight her, but she struck again. He stumbled on a loose rock and slid away from her blade.

"Mindar!" he said, but her eyes remained pupilless. The Cailee held her entirely now, though Delrael saw flickers of something behind her gaze.

He staggered back to his feet and swung his own sword, but it was only to deflect her. Mindar/Cailee defended herself, and Delrael ran around and pushed past into the uncertain light of Scartaris's grotto.

Mindar/Cailee bounded after him. Delrael had to stop, panting. His arms and legs ached. He could barely move. She slashed out, and Delrael brought up his blade to block the blow. The force knocked his arm aside, clanging his sword against the rock wall of the cave.

He pleaded with the woman trapped within the Cailee. "Mindar, listen to me! Can't you see Scartaris wants this?" He wheezed his words, but the angered Cailee drove at him with renewed force.

"Mindar—you've turned into the thing you hate the most! You're a creature of Scartaris!"

Delrael fought against Mindar/Cailee's growing fury. His arms felt like stone, heavy and unresponsive. He managed to fend off the blows that flashed at him, but his body trembled with exhaustion. He had used up all his adrenaline.

"Mindar, remember your daughter. Remember the tannery. Remember Taire!" His throat was raw.

Delrael gazed into the Cailee's yellow eyes. Dark pupils flickered on the verge of appearing. Mindar/ Cailee hesitated, wincing her silhouetted features and struggling with herself. "We're inseparable now," she gasped. Then the Cailee howled and slashed at the air with a fistful of silver claws. Her pupils faded again.

She struck and slashed in a storm of blows with the rippled sword. Delrael's arm seared with pain. He stumbled as he fought with the last of his strength. His sword sliced up and nicked Mindar/Cailee's arm, drawing a strange mixture of shadow-smoke and bright blood.

The Cailee howled and surged back at him with such vehemence that Delrael had no hope of defending himself. She knocked his arm aside, smashing his wrist against the rock wall. His own sword clattered to the floor.

Mindar/Cailee raised her blade to cleave Delrael's head.

"Mindar …" he whispered.

Her sword swung down, but Mindar's pupils flickered back for an instant. In her downstroke, she twisted her wrist sideways and struck him on the head with the flat of the blade.

Bright light exploded behind Delrael's eyes, then it all turned black. He slid to the floor.

Professor Verne's steam-engine car clanked down the slope toward Scartaris's mountain, skirting the edge of the battlefield. The ratcheting noise was not noticeable over the shouts of fighting monsters and human soldiers.

He stoked the fires under the boiler as high as they would go. The car picked up steam and chugged along faster than a man could run. The hex-line separated him from the rocky terrain, but he also saw the clear path leading up to the grotto.

Verne swallowed and blinked his eyes. He checked to make sure his journal was carefully secured with him. He didn't know what indignities he would have to bear on his long walk back to Sitnalta. If he survived at all.

He carried one tiny galvanic cell that powered a detector he had mounted next to the car's steering levers. It was one of the instruments he and Frankenstein had used to detect Scartaris's presence all the way from Sitnalta.

He switched the device on and saw the needle move, then fall dead, move, then fall dead. He was too far beyond the influence of Sitnaltan technology, regardless of how arbitrary he had proven the concept of the technological fringe to be. But even given the worst of situations, the Rules of Probability made the detector certain to work some of the time. The homing mechanism would need to function only at infrequent intervals to steady the course of the car along the straight path to Scartaris.

Verne knew his weapon was so powerful, he needed only to get near the grotto.

For a moment, he wondered in terror if the weapon itself might fail to work. But then he brushed that thought aside. The Sitnaltan weapon was powered by the force that had driven the Outsiders' ship. It would work anywhere on Hexworld—it had to. The Outsiders set up their own exceptions to the Rules, and they would follow them.

But this weapon combined the power of the Outsiders with the resourcefulness of Hexworld. What if he and Frankenstein had forged a destructive power greater than either world had seen before?

As the car chugged along, Verne watched the ground pass under the rattling wheels. He set his mouth in a firm line, thrusting out his beard. This was close enough for him.

He turned to the weapon and found the timer knob as the car jostled over the terrain, steering itself. Verne twisted the timer knob to a red mark on the dial and released it.

A rapid ticking came out of the weapon as the spring-driven timer began its countdown to detonation.

Verne had heard of a prophesied hero from some of the other human settlements outside the fringe, some unknown savior who would come out of nowhere and rescue them from great peril.

They called him the Unseen Stranger, or something like that. Not that Verne put much stock in prophesies, since they had no scientific basis. But after he unexpectedly used his weapon to destroy Scartaris, no doubt the storytellers would make him out to be their Stranger. He clucked his tongue in disapproval.

Suddenly, a gigantic bare-footed ogre bounded away from the battlefield toward the car, drooling down his chin. The ogre tripped twice and regained his feet to stumble after Verne. He limped from a deep wound on his ankle.

Verne had nothing with which to fight this ogre. He felt a flash of fear, but the ogre seemed more intent on the speeding car itself than on its driver. Gairoth hopped forward, clutched the side, and scrambled aboard, heaving himself over the low door. He grabbed Verne by the collar of his woolen coat.

"One moment, monsieur!" Verne stammered.

But Gairoth was not interested in him. "Haw!" he said, spraying spittle in Verne's face. With an expression of dismissal, he tossed the professor over the side.

Verne landed in a tumble, bruised and hurt. He stood up,

brushed himself off, and scowled. He watched the steam-engine car move on, homing in toward Scartaris.

Gairoth sat in the seat and bounced with delight as the car sped automatically toward the mountain.

"I don't think you want to do that," Verne muttered.

In the front of the car, the Sitnaltan weapon continued to tick.

Mindar stared at Delrael's unconscious form against the rocks. Weird lights flashed on and off in the background, bathing him in strange colors. A spot of blood blossomed on his forehead and trickled alongside his nose, into his eyes.

Mindar had forced herself to the front of her mind, but she had to grit her teeth and concentrate, not letting her thoughts lapse for a second. The Cailee gibbered in the back of her head, making her ears ring. Her anger surged, but she had to keep it directed away from the Cailee. She would gain nothing by that.

Scartaris. Scartaris was her enemy.

The Cailee was part of herself. She had to accept it, dominate it, turn it to her own advantage.

Mindar felt blackness slough away from her face and shoulders as she grew stronger. In one arm, she held her sword, and curved silver claws stuck out of her other hand—but she could see her own skin appearing in patches through the inky blackness. She was growing stronger. She knew what she could do.

Part of her felt appalled at what she had done to Delrael, but she knew he would forgive her. Mindar would never be able to forgive herself, though, not unless she finished Delrael's quest for him.

She knelt down, and with the clumsy claws on her hand, she worked the silver belt free from around his waist. She stared at it in the light, letting it dangle in front of her. The silver felt cold and slippery, tingling with power.

The Earthspirits lived in the belt. She held them, vulnerable, in her own hand—but they could destroy Scartaris. They could wipe him from the map. She cast her rippled sword on the floor. It clanged on the rock and landed near Delrael's blade.

"You won't make me cause any more harm, Scartaris!" The belt glittered in the weird light. "This is all the weapon I need to destroy you."

Heavy footfalls sounded outside the entrance to the grotto. She turned. Her black form was liquid and cast no shadow of its own.

She saw the blocky form of a huge Slac general. It dragged its feet on the rocks with scattering sounds, and the clank of a chain rattled in the silence. The monster let a needle-spiked ball dangle at its side.

"Scartaris has grown bored with you," the Slac said in its husky, grating voice. The pupilless pits of its eyes were filled with emerald fire.

Mindar/Cailee coughed out a laugh and held the silver belt as she strode recklessly toward the Slac. She held the belt between her two hands. "I'm bored with him too. Earthspirits, destroy this thing of Scartaris!"

She squeezed the belt with her shadow-stained hands and held it, waiting for some explosion of power that would whisk the Slac out of the Game entirely.

But instead, the Slac lashed down with his heavy spiked ball and smashed one of Mindar's wrists. She screamed in shock. The wrist bones snapped, and her fingers spread out as blood sprayed in the air. She backed away in agony. The silver belt fell to the floor.

The Cailee's furious presence clamored in the back of her head and tried to surge into dominance again. She pushed it away. The shadow-stain dripped from her body.

The Slac general said, "Scartaris wants you dead. You're no fun anymore."

Wincing the pain away, blind to what she was doing, Mindar/Cailee laughed again. "I can't die!"

She leaped at the reptilian creature, spreading the claws of her uninjured hand. In the back of her mind, she drove the Cailee further away with her determination and victory. The blackness faded from her arms, and she made a savage slash at the Slac's throat.

But the long silver claws snapped off and dissolved as she struck. Her hand became her own again—human and weak.

"All characters can die," the Slac said. He wrapped his spiked ball and chain around her throat, yanking it from one end to strangle her and driving the ball's spikes into the back of her head. The Slac jerked again, and Mindar's neck snapped before she felt any more pain.

The Slac let her body unravel from the chain and fall to the floor. Then the monster twirled the spiked ball in the air to clean droplets of blood from his weapon.

Delrael groaned on the floor and stirred.

The Slac general strode to him. The ball clanked at his side. Breath hissed through needle-like teeth as the Slac leaned over Delrael.

"Well, excuuuuuuse me!" Journeyman said from the opening of the grotto.

The Slac general snapped his head up and turned, hissing.

The golem looked at Vailret beside him and grinned with flexible clay lips. "He likes it! Hey Mikey!" Journeyman swaggered in, and the Slac general faced him, dangling the spiked ball.

Vailret saw Delrael's motionless form and Mindar lying dead. He stood behind and to the right of Journeyman, waiting and anxious. When he saw an opportunity, he slipped around and ran to Delrael.

"This here town ain't big enough for the both of us," Journeyman said. The Slac's green eyes blazed brighter.

Vailret cradled Delrael's head and wiped blood away from his eyes. The fighter mumbled and moaned. The bump on his head looked serious but far less severe than Vailret had feared.

He glared up at the Slac general facing Journeyman. The golem did not appear frightened at all, but Delrael lay injured, Mindar murdered. Delrael's silver belt lay beside her. Vailret did not know what had happened.

The Slac general stood tall and dark and filled with all the evil of Scartaris.

As he saw the Slac, Vailret remembered the training Drodanis had put him through back at the Strong hold, the role-playing game where Vailret was captured by Slac while his imaginary comrades were tortured and slain. An imaginary general like this one had ordered Vailret's execution, but Vailret managed to kill the Slac general before other arrows struck him down. It had felt so real to him, the terror, the helplessness, the failure. But it was only a game within the Game; this Slac battle was happening now.

He stood up as anger filled his features. He held his short sword.

The Slac general twirled his spiked ball. Journeyman waited for the monster to make the first move.

Instead, Vailret did.

In true Game spirit, he should have bellowed out a cry of challenge, but Vailret moved silently as he leaped forward. He jammed his short sword all the way up to its hilt, through the back plates of the Slac, into its kidney, and up into its pulsing heart. The tip of the sword pushed out through the reptilian chest. The Slac general gurgled in surprise and sprayed black blood out of its mouth.

"Stabbing in the back may not be fair," Vailret said, "but since when have Slac ever fought fair?"

The monster bellowed as it weakened, trying to jab backward with its elbows. But Vailret let go of his sword and stepped away. With a bestial grunt, the Slac fell to its knees. Journeyman bashed a rock-hard fist into its forehead. "Bah, humbug!"

Vailret blinked in shock. The hot Slac blood burned his hands, and he tried to wipe it on his pants and tunic, leaving dark stains there.

Delrael groaned again. Journeyman glanced from him to Vailret, then squared his shoulders. The golem stared down the tunnel to the center of the mountain. "I must go on ahead now," he said. "Take Delrael and get out of here."

Vailret looked up. "What are you going to do?"

Journeyman's lumpy clay brows twitched and knitted together. "I'm going to destroy Scartaris, as I was always meant to do. I'm glad I was created for this purpose. I'm glad I knew you. I will not be coming back."

"What do you mean? Will it destroy you?"

Journeyman didn't answer. Distressed, Vailret stood up. Delrael blinked and moved his head. He groaned.

"Wait—let Del take the Earthspirits. They'll destroy Scartaris and you can stay here. You don't need to sacrifice yourself."

The golem squared his shoulders. "It is what I am. I was made for this task. I must sacrifice myself."

"But it makes no sense!"

Journeyman stared with cavernous eyes. The clay eyelids blinked together, and he answered stiffly, "The needs of the many outweigh the needs of the few. Or the one."

Vailret pulled his short sword from the dead Slac general, but looked at it, not knowing what to do. He couldn't fight Journeyman.

The golem sighed. "Don't you know yet who I am?" He cocked his head. "My predecessor was Apprentice, many turns ago. I am Journeyman." He let the words hang in the air. The lights from deep in the grotto flashed weird patterns on the ceiling.

"I am the Stranger Unlooked-For."

Gairoth jammed his knees in the cramped seat of Professor Verne's steam-engine car. The vehicle toiled along up the hill toward Scartaris. He had seen the bat-creature take Delroth toward the mountain. The car moved faster than he could run.

Gairoth let his spiked club dangle outside the vehicle, pinging against rocks that bounced up from the ground. He saw the great cavern on the mountain face and knew that Delroth would have gone there.

"Haw!" he said. His arms were tired. His legs were tired. His feet were sore. He had traveled across the map to get Delroth. He would bash Delroth's head in for causing him so much trouble.

He shifted his knees, banging against the steering levers, and squirmed. The seat was uncomfortable, soft and human, and the space too confined for his bulky arms and legs.

The vehicle rolled up the slope, paused as if to gather its bearings, and then moved on its preset course.

Beside him, the Sitnaltan weapon continued to tick.

Gairoth bounced up and down, anxious to see any sign of Delroth. But then the steam-engine vehicle caught its wheels against the strewn boulders and stopped halfway up the side of the mountain on a blind switchback. The steam engine hissed and belched curls of gray smoke out its stack, but it could not move forward.

Gairoth fumed and tried to stand up in the cramped front of the car. He banged his knee. He roared in wordless rage and waved his club in the air. He couldn't even see the cave; one of the curved rock spires blocked his view.

He hopped out and tugged at the wheel, trying to get the vehicle to move on and find Delroth. He hollered at the useless car. When the vehicle made no response, Gairoth lashed out and kicked it with one big, bare foot.

The Sitnaltan weapon jarred on its seat, tipping over against the side of the car. The timer mechanism smashed and jammed. The ticking fell silent only seconds before its detonation was to occur.

Gairoth grumbled at the immobile vehicle and strode up the hill on foot.

∽

Journeyman marched down the low-ceilinged path, heading deep into the mountain where Scartaris controlled his armies. The golem's soft clay feet slapped on the stone floor. The temperature grew hotter around him.

His quest and his reason for existence had almost reached its end. He knew he would succeed.

"Please," Journeyman had told Vailret. "I have enjoyed knowing you. I don't want to overcome you by force. Take Delrael and head for the hills! I ... don't know exactly what I'm about to do or what will happen."

Vailret had finally agreed to take Delrael with him, leaving the golem alone to face Scartaris.

Journeyman felt a buzzing around him, power flickering unseen in the air. His body tingled when he moved ahead. Lights and echoes and frightening images floated around him, as if Scartaris was trying to frighten him away. But nothing could stop him now. He molded a determined expression on his face, squaring his shoulders.

The prospect of fulfilling his purpose brought him to a peak of ecstasy he had not known before. He felt his secret weapon growing inside, pulsing, ready to be released.

The Rulewoman Melanie would be so proud of him.

Ahead, he heard the sound of grinding rock, a restless, awesome force. The passage opened up, and Journeyman emerged onto a ledge overlooking a vast pit, the heart of the mountain.

Below him lay Scartaris.

Immense, huge beyond comprehension, bathed in colors that would have blasted human eyes from their sockets. Fluorescent orange and yellow and burning pink. Scartaris was a swelling, pulsing blob of energy, shaped like a vast brain the size of a small mountain.

The golem sensed vibrations around him. The air itself throbbed and pushed at him as he stepped to the edge. The rock tensed, as if Scartaris could collapse the mountain on a whim, but Journeyman didn't hesitate. He stood glaring down at the Outsider David's monster. He planted his balled fists on his hips.

"You know I'm here, Scartaris. But you don't know enough to be afraid," he shouted down into the roar. The colors on the blob shifted and moved. Scartaris was listening to him.

He craned his head down on his flexible clay neck. "The Outsider David created you—and the Rulewoman Melanie created me. You show off your power in extravagance. I carry mine hidden. The Rulewoman placed it in me. She knows your vulnerability."

Scartaris shifted and rose up. Disturbed rocks pattered down from the ceiling. All the air around Journeyman seemed like a bowstring ready to snap, but he continued, spilling his words like a well-rehearsed speech.

"We are only imaginary characters created by the Outsiders. We have one great weakness, something none of us can withstand. It's a simple thing, a speck of dust from Outside, a piece of another world that is so deadly to us.

"The Rulewoman Melanie brought it here, painted it into the map, inside me. It has made me see visions, made me speak of things beyond the boundaries of Hexworld.

"Now it must be released."

Journeyman ran a finger down the length of his chest, pushing a crease into the soft clay like a long zipper. He plunged his hands into his own skin and split a seam down the middle. He opened himself up where his heart would have been. Out of the cracks spewed a powerful white light, blinding bright.

"Scartaris, behold the power of something you cannot possibly withstand. Gaze upon pure reality!"

The light blasted outward as the golem spread his chest wide, folding back his body to make a great window, showing his core.

"It worked!"

"What did you do, Mel!"

"God, look at that thing!"

"David, you're sick. It's disgusting."

"It's real! I can't believe it—it's real!"

"No, we're real. And nothing there can stand it."

Journeyman did not dare look himself, but he listened to the astonished voices. One of them set him trembling, and he recognized the Rulewoman Melanie. He felt the clay dissolving from the inside out as his core of reality poured out.

Scartaris made an agonized wail that ripped through the seams of the map itself and caused all the fighters on the battlefield to stagger on their feet. He lurched back, quivering against the jagged walls of the stone chamber. Journeyman knew he could not get away.

Scartaris could not withstand even the sight of naked reality. He began to wither and shrivel as parts of the great bulk sloughed away into nothing, fading.

Delrael felt his ears ringing with a roar of blood, and he could not focus his eyes. Somehow, Vailret was beside him, pulling him to his feet, dragging him out of the grotto. His vision went dim again, then sharpened around the edges.

Vailret bent over and picked up the silver belt on the floor. The Earthspirits! Pieces fell into place in Delrael's mind.

"Del, can you hold this? Do you want to carry it?"

He grunted and nodded his head, but that made the rushing sound inside grow louder. The cold air snapped into his eyes, and after several breaths, he felt more alert.

"Mindar—" he said. His voice came out in a croak.

"She's dead," Vailret answered. "She died defending you from the Slac, I think. Is that what happened? Is that how you got injured?"

The memories came clear in his head, and Delrael stumbled on the steep path. Vailret caught him and held him up, thinking his cousin still too weak to run. Delrael hurried along—Vailret didn't know the truth about Mindar. She would have wanted it that way.

"Yes. That's what happened."

Vailret led him down a steep, narrow path on the other side of Scartaris's mountain, down to the black hex-line in front of the battlefield. They ran, and Delrael found his strength coming back. The dizziness drifted away from him. "Journeyman—?"

Vailret hesitated then tugged on his cousin's arm. They crossed the hex-line and staggered onto the soft dirt of the desolation terrain. "He's gone to Scartaris, to use the Rulewoman's weapon. He told us to run as far as we can."

The other monsters on the battlefield seemed to have lost their heart for the fight. Delrael turned and looked up at the jagged lair of Scartaris. The strange lights were flashing in wild colors.

Gairoth stood panting in the opening of the grotto as he looked back out at the massed dim soldiers far below. He had climbed half the mountain, it seemed. His feet hurt. The wound in his ankle from the Slave of the Serpent throbbed and made him angry.

He didn't know what the fighting was about, why the monsters had gathered. He only wanted to find Delroth. He suspected the fighter had something to do with it all. Delroth always made trouble.

Inside the grotto, bright lights flashed different colors from a tunnel at the far end. The sight gave him a headache. On the floor, he saw two bodies, one woman and one Slac. He curled his lip.

He squinted his one eye and stared down the tunnel, but he could not make out the source of the flashing lights, the throbbing roar that clutched at the back of his head. Gairoth didn't want to think about it. He was too tired and too angry.

The burning colors seemed to beckon him. Yes, Delroth must be down there, down in the tunnel. Gairoth stooped under the low ceiling. He would sneak up on Delroth, find him, and bash him. He made sure not to drag his club against the floor as he worked his way forward.

Gairoth thought of his lost dragon Rognoth and of his flooded cesspools. All Delroth's fault. The ogre snarled and ground his teeth together as he stomped forward, then remembering the need for stealth, tried to move quietly again.

Gairoth squeezed the end of his spiked club. He had followed Delroth across the map, and now he would get his revenge.

But when he moved past the last turn, the ceiling opened up above him into a huge vaulted cavern. He stopped and wheezed. The light danced in front of his eyes, some of it real, some of it burning reflections on his retinas.

He sensed something was wrong. Something was going on. The bright lights and the heat and the roaring power channeled into the center of the mountain seemed to be screaming, fighting back in ways that Gairoth could not understand.

Then he noticed Journeyman. The golem had his back turned and stared down into the pit, shining something out of his chest.

The clay man had been with Delroth! Back in the forest, he had smashed Gairoth on the head and helped steal the little ylvan. The ogre frowned. If he could not get Delroth right now, he would at least get this clay man.

He stepped up behind Journeyman on the ledge, raised his club to his shoulder, and belched out a loud "Haw! Now I got you!"

He drew back his club to swing, smiling, peeling his thick lips away from brown teeth.

Startled, the golem turned around, pivoting on a flexible clay waist. Gairoth saw that he had opened up his chest—but his insides seemed to be a bottomless window, an opening shining out into some other place. He gawked at the vision, and for a fraction of a second, he saw four humans crouched and staring down at him. Strange objects were scattered around the table along with food and colored dice.

"It's Gairoth!"

Someone bumped over a glass and scrambled to catch it, spilling soda.

Gairoth gaped his mouth like a dying fish and then the reality of what he was seeing struck him. Bright light washed over him and into him.

He felt a blinding wonder, and despair, as his skin seared away, disintegrating into nothingness. A long, low "Awwwww...." echoed in the air.

With nothing to hold it up, his spiked club dropped, clattering to the ledge, bounced once, and pitched over to vanish in the molten blob of Scartaris.

But in the moment that Journeyman turned away, Scartaris seized the opportunity and flexed his remaining power.

He brought the entire mountain down upon Journeyman, sealing the reality beneath uncounted tons of rubble.

The earthquake threw Delrael and Vailret to the ground. Delrael rolled onto his back to watch the mountain collapse. The horned peaks toppled aside in an enormous tremor that shook the heart of the map itself.

The black hex-line split, and sections of terrain rocked and tilted upward at the seams, as if Hexworld were falling apart hexagon by hexagon. Delrael almost lost his grip on the silver belt in his hand.

The roar continued, then slacked off as gray white dust poured up into the darkened sky.

Then, from the broken rubble of the destroyed mountain seeped a glowing brilliant light—pinks and oranges and yellows, sprawled and oozing over the debris. The immense blob crawled out of the rocks and sat pulsing, as if peering down at the gathered army.

"Is that Scartaris?" Vailret gasped beside him, but the words made little sound in the thundering echoes of the air. Every creature on the battlefield stood hushed and staring.

Scartaris moved, looking enormous and frail at the same time, damaged and retaining only enough energy to keep himself alive. He slid and rolled down the rocky slope toward the disrupted hex-line.

Delrael thought for a moment that Scartaris would reach the cracked map and spill through to where he could annihilate the Outsiders. But Scartaris stopped and throbbed, heaving himself up. At the center of the blob, Delrael could see glittering lights forming, like diamonds and stars, building up.

"It's the metamorphosis!" he heard Vailret shout behind him. "Journeyman told us about it! Scartaris is going to end the Game right now!"

"You must take us!" the Earthspirits cried in a metallic voice from inside the belt. "Take us across the last hex-line! Then we will be released."

The starbursts inside the giant blob grew brighter, fissioning with energy. Once Scartaris released his pent-up energy, he could wash the map clean of all terrain. Scartaris had lost his Game. He and the Outsider David had wanted to savor the victory, to let the vast monster army march across and lay waste to everything, but now Scartaris was forsaking that fun. He would obliterate them all and call himself the Game's winner.

"Hurry! He is greatly weakened now," the Earthspirits said. "Perhaps we can defeat him."

Delrael ran toward the gaping hex-line, but the deep crack in the map cut him off from Scartaris.

From a corner of the broken hex-line, a black wind sprang up, pouring straight into the air. Swirling, it formed into three dark hooded figures. They stood vast and awesome, cavernous hoods covered their heads, shrouding their faces.

Delrael stumbled as he ran. The figures looked familiar and yet unfamiliar. He had never actually seen them, only their white counterparts.

"The Deathspirits will not allow you to end the Game, Scartaris," the black figures said in unison.

"Play your feeble war games for terrain, but you will not destroy the map. We are bound by the Rules here too. If you destroy Hexworld, we cannot complete our own set of Rules. We are trying to escape from this existence. You may not interfere."

The Deathspirits hovered tall and black. All the monsters on the battlefield stood in a hush, appalled and uncertain.

But the starburst lights built up further within Scartaris, growing in intensity.

Delrael scrambled ahead, stumbling on the new slope from the tilted hexagon of terrain. He saw himself struggling there, an unknown human fighter from across the map. No one knew he had come, but he appeared where he was needed, bearing the weapon to save Hexworld. Delrael smirked. "Maybe they'll call me the Stranger Unlooked-For."

He crawled toward the crack in the map. When he reached its edge, the black lip of desolation sliced down into nothingness, a broad gulf apart from the adjoining mountain terrain. He could not crawl across. He could not jump the void. His body was too exhausted to do more than move.

Scartaris's internal lights grew blinding at the point of his devastating metamorphosis.

"We cannot cross the hex-line," the Earthspirits said.

Delrael held the belt. "You're not very much good, are you?" Then he threw the silver belt crafted by the old Sorcerers, a gift from his father Drodanis.

As it flew through the air across the hex-line, the silver links began to dissolve in white light. The three Earthspirits emerged just as their Deathspirit comrades swooped down upon Scartaris.

CHAPTER 22
STRANGER

Let the Game go on forever, and may your score always increase!
—Hexworld drinking toast

Three dazzling white figures rose into the air, hooded and powerful, billowing in the wind rising from the broken hex-line. They alternated with their dark counterparts.

Vailret stared at the Spirits, all that remained of the ancient race of Sorcerers. He had read so much about them, and now he saw them towering in front of his eyes. Both factions had fought each other for turn after turn in the early days of the Game. Now the six Spirits had reunited for the first time since the Transition, on the site of their worst battles.

Without a word, they fell upon Scartaris before he could complete his metamorphosis.

The titanic battle was difficult to watch. Vailret squinted, but the intangible fighters became an inferno of power and blazing lights, black and white and colors. The sounds of a storm rang on the air. Chunks of rock and dust blasted into the air in backlashes of power.

Scartaris grew dimmer and smaller in the fray. The starbursts in his body twinkled and faded.

Tension built up like a spring being wound tighter and tighter. The six Spirits combined their power into one final assault.

And Scartaris fell.

A great flare of light blasted into the air, a geyser of luminous power that sprayed outward and then faded on the winds, swirling, as if trying to find some dark corner where it could hide. One high-pitched shriek echoed around the rubble of the mountains; the astonished horror in it sliced through Vailret's bones.

The silence on the battlefield held back for a moment as the dawn itself seemed to gasp. A sudden cold wind blew by and then died away to nothing.

Professor Verne stood on the hillside, perplexed and angry. He rubbed his eyes. The flash from the battle of the Spirits and Scartaris left dancing colors on his vision, but he frowned with disappointment. The outcome of the battle didn't really matter, though the Spirits seemed to be fighting with *magic* rather than something more sophisticated.

The Sitnaltan weapon had not worked. Something had gone wrong.

"But it should have been foolproof!" He placed his hands behind his back and paced in front of a boulder. "It had to work. Did I miscalculate something? What did I forget to take into account?"

He muttered to himself, parading ideas in front of his mind. He could imagine nothing that would lead to such a failure. A burning curiosity began to grow. He stared at the crumbled mountain and squinted his eyes, wondering how difficult it would be to locate the steam-engine car in the rubble. He wanted to find the weapon and study it.

As dawn came up and lit the battlefield, Verne saw the monsters milling around, trying to organize themselves. The prime mover seemed to be the awesome manticore marching about, rallying the army of Scartaris.

Verne blew through his lips as he looked at the manticore. "What a hodgepodge," he thought. "Man's head, lion's body, scorpion tail—probably has the brain of a cactus or something." To him, it showed clearly how little the Outsiders themselves understood the basic precepts of biological sciences.

Scartaris was destroyed. Part of the map was disrupted, and he had no idea what effect such titanic forces would have on Hexworld and the Rules themselves. Perhaps it would allow technology a bit more freedom to operate. Perhaps he could fix the weapon or dismantle it. He couldn't just leave it there.

But the growing light reminded him how exposed he was on the barren terrain, with nothing but the monsters to see him. He wondered how he could possibly hide from Scartaris's entire army.

Delrael crawled back toward Vailret, trying to keep his balance on the tilted terrain. Both of them stood panting with exhaustion and the aftereffects of terror.

Around them, the stunned monsters wandered about, no longer in the grip of Scartaris. Only the manticore had a purpose, growling orders and trying to terrify the other demons into ranks again.

Delrael wondered how long the relative calm would last. The sky itself was a whirlwind of chaos, overloaded with power dissipating up and out of the map's boundaries.

Delrael could see no sign of the six Spirits, or of Scartaris.

The illusion army of human fighters shimmered and melted away as Bryl released the Air Stone. Some of the monster soldiers made angry noises, but most didn't notice in their own confusion.

Hundreds of slaughtered demon fighters lay on the ground, killed by their own weapons and the firepowder bombs. Thousands of dead animals, birds, and insects covered the sand, as if a part of the black cloud had settled to the earth. Pools of red mud dried slowly in the dim sunlight.

The surviving animals and birds gathered in a thinner, less-organized black cloud that floated up and drifted off. They struck out across the desolation back to the forest and grassland terrain.

"Scartaris is dead," Vailret whispered. He grinned and clapped a hand on Delrael's shoulder. "Scartaris is dead! We finished our quest."

Delrael looked uneasily at the gathering of monsters that stood angry and leaderless. "I still don't like this. We'd better find Bryl."

Vailret nodded, and they hurried back along the edge of the battlefield, trying to escape the notice of Scartaris's surviving fighters.

Then the air in front of them rippled. Delrael thought that heat shimmers rose up from the warming sands, but white mist swirled above them, condensing until it resolved into the transparent outlines of the three Earthspirits, flickering like a vision on the breeze.

The Spirits looked tenuous and fragile, much less substantial than when they had first appeared to Delrael in the forest. That night seemed so long ago now. That was before he had known Tallin. Before he met Mindar.

The Earthspirits spoke. "Scartaris is destroyed, and we still live. With the aid of the Deathspirits and the Stranger Unlooked-For, we did not need to sacrifice ourselves.

"But we are weak now. We must go dormant for many turns to recover our strength."

The Spirits wavered, faded for a moment, and then rose up again. The tilted hexagon of terrain settled under Delrael's feet and he stumbled. The other monsters stood uncertain and afraid of the giant hooded forms.

"By destroying Scartaris and unleashing power of such magnitude, the map has suffered severe damage. As have the Rules themselves. They are twisted and loosened.

"We have proved to the Outsiders that Hexworld is as strong as their own powers. That is a profound victory. Even now, the Deathspirits are using this to their advantage. Perhaps they will mold their own *reality*."

Delrael looked across the battlefield to see Bryl running toward them, drawn by the towering forms of the Earthspirits. Delrael waved his hands to show that he had seen him. Vailret squinted up at the Spirits with an expression of awe on his face.

"To show our gratitude, we will twist the Rules even now. The Outsider David is stunned by his defeat. We can do things the other Players will not notice, for now.

"Your quest is over. You have gained experience and won the battle. We will return you to your home. If only we were not so weak, we could do more…"

The Slac regiments had pulled themselves together again and rallied around the manticore. Several other monsters rebelled or moved too slowly, but the Slac cut them down with their own weapons.

"Hexworld is ours!" the manticore bellowed.

Then the Earthspirits swept their billowing sleeves through the air. Delrael felt a harsh wind pour into his body, his bones. The air dissolved around him. He felt dislocated and cold—

—and the terrain became the path leading up Steep Hill to the Stronghold. The morning around him was deathly quiet. He heard only the sounds from the forest.

The village seemed deserted and silent. All the people were hiding. Something had happened.

Bryl and Vailret appeared beside him. Both stumbled, suddenly finding themselves disoriented on the sloping path. "We're back home!" Bryl said. He fell to his knees. He looked exhausted

"I wonder where Tareah is." Vailret looked around him, getting his bearings. He started up the hill.

"Something's wrong," Delrael said. He strode up the hill. His body was exhausted, but he felt revitalized just by being back home.

They neared the top of Steep Hill. The forest pressed around them, thick and ready to conceal many things. They still heard no sounds. Delrael felt like a stranger outside his own home.

When he saw what remained of the Stronghold—the burned buildings, the shattered walls—he stopped and felt sick inside. "We shouldn't have left them," he whispered. "We shouldn't have left them all alone. They were defenseless!"

Suddenly, seven other characters, men and women heavily armed, leaped out of the forest terrain, pointing arrows, spears, and swords at them.

Delrael whirled and straightened, yanking free his own notched sword. Then he stared as he recognized, behind the armor and the weapons and the battle-hardened stares, Mostem the baker, young Romm the farmer, and others from the village.

"It's Delrael!" Tareah cried. "And Vailret! They're back."

Other villagers cheered as they emerged from the forest where they had been practicing and lying in ambush. They seemed terrified of an actual fight but ready to defend their homes.

Delrael stared at the wreckage of the Stronghold, at the fighting force Tareah had managed to put together. She walked up to stand next to Vailret. "I missed you." She glanced at Delrael and answered quickly, "Both of you."

Bryl shuffled his feet, scowling and looking out of place.

"I'm sorry about the Stronghold. Scartaris destroyed it. Tarne is dead." She sighed and lifted her chin, showing her new strength. "But we've sent messengers to all the other villages. We're gathering an army. We're getting ready to fight."

Delrael saw a proud, determined look in her eyes that reminded him of something he had seen in Mindar.

"The Outsiders won't ever catch us unprepared again," Tareah said.

Delrael smiled and looked up at the sky, wishing the Outsiders were watching. "If they want to fight against us, I hope they know what they're getting into."

EPILOGUE

Scott grabbed David's arm and pulled him over to the sink while the others stared in shock.

He flipped on the cold water tap and pushed David's raw hands under the running faucet. David made no sound, but his hands were burned, red and blistered, from when the map had ... exploded on them.

Scott tended David stiffly, astonished. He went through the motions of first aid as though it could keep him distracted from thinking—from thinking about what had happened at the end of the Game.

Tyrone stuck his head under the table and came back up, eyes wide. "The burn goes all the way through the wood!" he said. "Wow!" Then he paused and swallowed. "What'll I tell my mom? You're going to all have to back me up."

"And say what?" Scott asked. "That we were just playing a game, but it fought back at us? They'll say I made some explosive with my chemistry set or something." He snorted. Water from the tap splashed on the left lens of his glasses. "I haven't played with my chemistry set since eighth grade."

Melanie stared at the map. A great section of the terrain was burned black and broken. A dark, charcoaled blot had burned through the map, through Tyrone's table. He groaned and got a damp cloth to try and wipe away the dark stain. When Tyrone slid the map board sideways, a couple of hexagons fell loose from the edge like tiles in a mosaic.

But that was impossible too, because Melanie had *painted* on a smooth piece of wood. She had drawn the hex-lines with a drafting pencil. The map couldn't fall apart exactly along the lines...

But Melanie found herself feeling elated, smug. "Well, David? Are you ready to give up now? Scartaris is destroyed. You lost. That means we keep on playing."

Over by the sink, David stared at his burned hands and kept them under the water. "I still have my army of monsters. There's still Verne's weapon, on my territory now." He yanked his hands away from Scott and stood dripping on the kitchen floor. "Now your characters are going to have to fight against *me*."

David twisted his head to look at her, and Melanie jumped back. For a moment, she swore his eyes were blazing yellow and *pupilless*. He turned back to dry his hands.

Melanie swallowed, blinking her eyes until she felt confident again. "After this—" She indicated the devastated portion of the map. "—I don't think we need to be afraid of you anymore.

"Hexworld is learning how to fight back."

THANK YOU FOR READING ROLL, HEXWORLD BOOK 2

We hope you enjoyed it as much as we enjoyed bringing it to you. We just wanted to take a moment to encourage you to review the book. Follow this link: Play to be directed to the book's Amazon product page to leave your review.

Every review helps further the author's reach and, ultimately, helps them continue writing fantastic books for us all to enjoy.

Want to discuss our books with other readers and even the authors? Join our Discord server today and be a part of the Aethon community.

Facebook

Instagram

Twitter

Website

You can also join our non-spam mailing list by visiting www.subscribepage.com/AethonReadersGroup and never miss out on future releases. You'll also receive three full books completely Free as our thanks to you.

WHAT'S NEXT?

HEXWORLD

1: ROLL

2: PLAY (You just read)

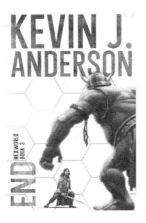

3: END

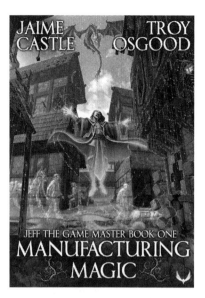

Jeff Driscoll becomes the only active Game Master for the VRMMORPG Infinite Worlds after a rogue patch turns the game into a buggy, dangerous mess. Can he fix it on his own and save the players?

GET MANUFACTURING MAGIC NOW!

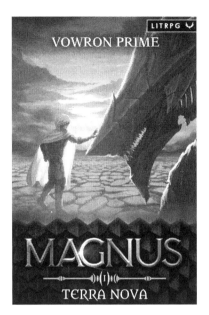

Magnus Cromwell kills for a living.

GET TERRA NOVA NOW!

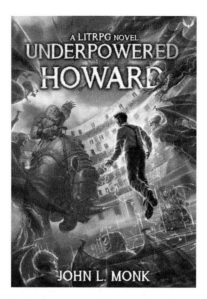

When there's no way to win, cheat, and cheat BIG. Howard, desperate to save his friends and countless innocents, hatches a plan to fix things. Using his deep knowledge of game mechanics, he'll start again as a level 0 necromancer and exploit his way to power.

GET UNDERPOWERED HOWARD NOW!

I was in my garage when the space elves addressed the whole world. Planet-wide survival reality show? Ridiculous.

GET THEY CALLED ME MAD NOW!

For all our LitRPG books, visit our website.

ABOUT THE AUTHOR

Kevin J. Anderson has published more than 170 books, 58 of which have been national or international bestsellers. He has written numerous novels in the Star Wars, X-Files, and Dune universes, as well as unique steampunk fantasy novels *Clockwork Angels* and *Clockwork Lives*, written with legendary rock drummer Neil Peart. His original works include the Saga of Seven Suns series, the Wake the Dragon and Terra Incognita fantasy trilogies, the Saga of Shadows trilogy, and his humorous horror series featuring Dan Shamble, Zombie PI. He has edited numerous anthologies, written comics and games, and the lyrics to two rock CDs. Anderson is the director of the graduate program oin Publishing at Western Colorado University. Anderson and his wife Rebecca Moesta are the publishers of WordFire Press. His most recent novels are Vengewar, Dune: The Duke of Caladan (with Brian Herbert), Stake, Kill Zone (with Doug Beason), and Spine of the Dragon.

Made in the USA
Columbia, SC
06 August 2021

43052332R00202